**Raves for the novels of Marshall Ryan Maresca:**

"[*The Way of the Shield*] is a political story, one which both demands and rewards your attention. It's a personal story, dealing with pain, loss, heartbreak and forgiveness. It's a story about morality, about sacrifice, about what people want from life. It's a fun story—there's quips, swordfights, chases through the streets. It's a compelling, convincing work of fantasy, and a worthy addition to the rich tapestry that is the works of Maradaine. Pick it up, give it a try—you won't be disappointed."
—*Sci-Fi and Fantasy Reviews*

"Veranix is Batman, if Batman were a teenager and magically talented. . . . Action, adventure, and magic in a school setting will appeal to those who love Harry Potter and Patrick Rothfuss' *The Name of the Wind*."
—*Library Journal* (starred)

"The perfect combination of urban fantasy, magic, and mystery."
—*Kings River Life Magazine*

"Maresca's debut is smart, fast, and engaging fantasy crime in the mold of Brent Weeks and Harry Harrison. Just perfect."
—Kat Richardson, national bestselling author of *Revenant*

"Maresca offers something beyond the usual high fantasy fare, with a wealth of unique and well-rounded characters, a vivid setting, and complicatedly intertwined social issues that feel especially timely."
—*Publishers Weekly*

# MARSHALL RYAN MARESCA

# SHIELD

## OF THE

# PEOPLE

A Novel of the *Maradaine Elite*

PAPL
DISCARDED

## DAW BOOKS, INC.

DONALD A. WOLLHEIM, FOUNDER

1745 Broadway, New York, NY 10019

**ELIZABETH R. WOLLHEIM**

**SHEILA E. GILBERT**

**PUBLISHERS**

www.dawbooks.com

First Printing, October 2019
1   2   3   4   5   6   7   8   9

DAW TRADEMARK REGISTERED
U.S. PAT. AND TM. OFF. AND FOREIGN COUNTRIES
—MARCA REGISTRADA
HECHO EN U.S.A.
PRINTED IN THE U.S.A.

# Acknowledgments

Several years ago I had a vision for an interconnected series of books, following four sets of characters, who each have discrete, individual stories, but a larger story brews beneath the surface, each series bringing its own pieces of the puzzle.

Back then, when it was still just ideas and outlines, I laid it all out to my dear old friend, Daniel J. Fawcett. And he said, "That's fantastic, but for it to work, for you to be able to do what you want to do, you're going to need the right editor and the right publisher."

Fortunately for me, Sheila Gilbert and DAW Books were *very much* the right editor and the right publisher. Were it not for Sheila and her astounding faith in this work and my big plan, we wouldn't be here. Everyone at DAW and Penguin—Sheila, Betsy, Katie, Josh, Leah, Alexis, Lauren—have been fantastic partners on this endeavor.

Much thanks also to another old friend, Brendan Gibbs, who helped lay the initial seeds behind Dayne, a hero who fights with his heart, who risks everything to keep people alive.

Of course, there was also my two amazing beta readers, who saw this particular manuscript through a few revisions: Kevin Jewell and Miriam Robinson Gould. They have been there to help me make each book as strong as I can make it. My agent, Mike Kabongo, has been instrumental in making this big, mad plan happen.

And finally, I could not have possibly done this without my family. My parents, Louis and Nancy Maresca, my mother-in-law Kateri Aragon, and most important my wife and son, Deidre and Nicholas. They've made all of this possible.

# CHRONOLOGICAL NOTE

*Shield of the People* takes place in the last week of the month of Erescan, in the year 1215. It is approximately five weeks after the events of *The Way of the Shield*, a few days after *Lady Henterman's Wardrobe*, and two months before the events of *The Imposters of Aventil* and *A Parliament of Bodies*.

# SHIELD
## OF THE
# PEOPLE

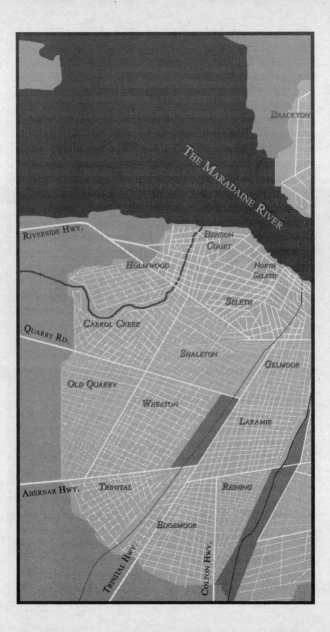

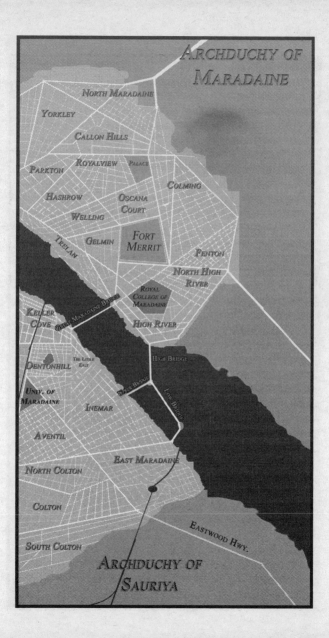

# ARCHDUCHY OF MARADAINE

NORTH MARADAINE

YORKLEY

CALLON HILLS

PARKTON

ROYALVIEW

PALACE

HASHROW

WELLING

OSCANA COURT

TRELAN

GELMIN

FORT MERRIT

COLMING

FENTON

NORTH HIGH RIVER

KELLER COVE

GREAT MARADAINE BRIDGE

ROYAL COLLEGE OF MARADAINE

HIGH RIVER

DENTONHILL

THE LITTLE EAST

HIGH BRIDGE

UNIV. OF MARADAINE

INEMAR

UPPER BRIDGE

LOW BRIDGE

AVENTIL

EAST MARADAINE

NORTH COLTON

COLTON

SOUTH COLTON

EASTWOOD HWY.

# ARCHDUCHY OF SAURIYA

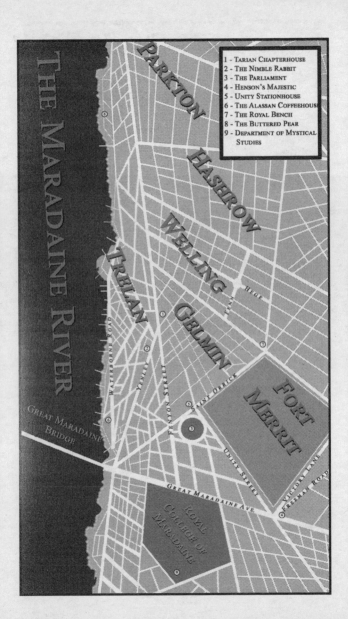

THE MARADAINE RIVER

PARKTON

HASFROW

WELLING

TRELAN

GELMIN

FORT MERRIT

GREAT MARADAINE BRIDGE

WHITBROOK ROAD

YENSEY

FENTON STREET

SAINT ORRICK

FENN HIGH

UNITA STREET

GREAT MARADAINE AVE

VICTORY LANE

FREEMAN ROAD

ROYAL COLLEGE OF MARADAINE

1 - TARIAN CHAPTERHOUSE
2 - THE NIMBLE RABBIT
3 - THE PARLIAMENT
4 - HENSON'S MAJESTIC
5 - UNITY STATIONHOUSE
6 - THE ALASSAN COFFEEHOUSE
7 - THE ROYAL BENCH
8 - THE BUTTERED PEAR
9 - DEPARTMENT OF MYSTICAL STUDIES

# PROLOGUE: The Warrior

LON ORREN, Grandmaster of the Tarian Order, had long since abandoned the idea that sleep would ever again be his friend. Too many compromises, too many deals with sinners, just to keep the Order alive and vibrant. He used to lie on his bed in restless agony, but in recent months he had embraced his penance. He had devoted his life to the Tarian Order, he would give his life for it. The cost of his conscience was a small one.

He had done what he had to, for the good of the Order. Nothing more. The Tarians would survive for a few more years, another generation, even. Maybe by then, people would understand their legacy again. Maybe by then, whoever succeeded him wouldn't have to fight to keep the lamps lit.

Maybe history would be kind to him and the legacy he left.

He wandered the chapterhouse in the hours before dawn, the only creature awake, save the cats. Quiet as the mice those cats stalked, he went from floor to floor, glancing at his fellow Tarians as they slept. The upper barracks housed the newly arrived first-year Initiates, hopefully ready and eager to begin their training.

This year there were forty-seven of them, which was an astounding number. Far more than had ever started in one year at the Maradaine Chapterhouse. It would be encouraging, except for the reasons behind that number. Most of the other chapterhouses had shuttered their Initiacy, and now the potential Tarians of tomorrow were being trained in only five cities across all of Druthal: Maradaine, Fencal, Vargox, Porvence, and Korifina.

He shook his head. In the course of his lifetime there had been chapterhouses in cities all across Druthal, and Initiates trained in every one of them. Despite his best efforts, their legacy was slipping through his fingers.

Since his best efforts had failed, he had to hope that his worst efforts would succeed.

Four members of Parliament dead, and the city terrorized, and he had to accept that he was complicit in those actions. He may not have held the sword, but he didn't raise any objection. When the other nine members of the Grand Ten said it must be done, he went along, because he needed those allies.

Promises were made, and they were people with the power to shape those promises into reality. Nobles, members of Parliament, voices of authority. He was far and away the least notable of any of the Grand Ten. But, to be a Grand Ten, they needed a Warrior, and he was the one desperate enough, weak enough, to say yes. This group—this cabal—that he had joined, fancied that they had similar goals to the original Grand Ten from centuries ago. They formed themselves in a twisted mirror of those people, taking on their iconic titles. The Parliamentarian and The Man of the People. The Lord, The Lady, The Duchess. The Priest, The Soldier, The Justice, The Mage. And him, The Warrior.

Orren knew that the Grand Ten of history had never

been a unified group fighting together, but rather key people who had stepped up and done their part for a better nation.

He knew his history, he knew about The Warrior of the original Grand Ten from two centuries ago. Oberon Micarum, the Spathian Adept who fought for Druthal's freedom and unity, and who was instrumental in shaping the nation of today. Oberon had served as Regent for young Maradaine XI in those early years of Reunification. Oberon had guided the nation to free and modern principles, encouraging the formation of the Parliament and allowing the common man to have a voice in the nation. Oberon had been a great man.

These people Orren had allied himself with were nothing like that. This was a skulking conspiracy, a plan to reinvent Druthal into the nation they wanted, with a man on the throne who suited their ends. But, as unsavory as their methods were, they were people with a vision, and that vision supposedly included the honor and tradition of the Tarian Order as a sacred part of the Druth spirit.

It was all he had to keep that tradition alive.

He stopped by the quarters of Dayne Heldrin. Dayne, that giant young man with an even larger heart, embodied that spirit more than any other person Orren had ever met. The boy was a Tarian, down to the marrow of his bones, Orren had no doubt.

So much so, the boy had almost single-handedly undermined the Grand Ten's machinations last month.

No, that wasn't fair.

If anything, Dayne had saved them from their own ploys spiraling out of control. He had stopped the madman whom they had inadvertently launched on the city. Dayne, like the true Tarian he was, risked everything to take up his shield and protect the people, the Parliament, the nation.

The poor boy was going to be punished for that. And

so much more. Orren already knew that Dayne, now starting his third year as a Candidate for the Order, would never be inducted as an Adept. After his year of Candidacy ended, he would be cashiered out, left to the winds.

Assuming he even made it through this year.

Instructions had been given by the Grand Ten, and those instructions were to put Dayne on the path they wanted. Dayne and those close to him.

If Dayne had had any idea he was being used as a pawn in this larger game, and the ends that game was working toward, he'd probably cut his own throat to prevent it.

But he wouldn't know. And he would do whatever Orren asked of him to keep alive the hope of becoming an Adept in the Tarian Order. Because he was a Tarian, true and pure, and that was the very thing Orren would be able to exploit in him.

The poor boy.

Orren sighed. Long days were ahead. Plans were underway.

# Chapter 1

DAYNE HAD NEVER SEEN as many people in one place as were in the crowd surrounding the Saint Alexis Day parade. It was a massive celebratory event, as Great Maradaine Avenue was filled with marchers, riders, dancers, and musicians from all ten archduchies, and onlookers flooded the walkways, hung on lampposts, and found every other possible place they could to gawk from.

People filled the avenue from the head of the Great Maradaine Bridge—where the parade started—to the massive street fair in Victory Plaza, where Great Maradaine Avenue intersected with Unity Street, Victory Lane, and Freeman Road. The whole plaza was overrun with food vendors, entertainers, music, dance, and merriment.

Dayne found it delightful, a glorious way to launch Victory Days, the six-day celebration of the founding of Druthal in its modern form, starting today with Saint Alexis Day, continuing through the Revels of Liberation, and culminating on the actual Reunification Day at the end of the month.

"I absolutely adore this," Lady Mirianne Henson said. "There's nothing quite like the spirit of the people, celebrating the nation, our unity, our liberation from tyrannical incursion."

Dayne noticed her sly smile. "You also like it because it suits your current enterprise."

"Of course it does, I'm not a fool," she said. "Why do you think I scheduled the Grand Opening for today?"

As much as Dayne delighted in the celebration, he felt a sense of unease. Lately, it seemed more and more people went about armed. There were quite a few folks with crossbows hanging on their hips, or swords at their belts, and that was just what he could see. No telling how many were carrying knives and knucklestuffers and handsticks. With this many people, it wouldn't take much for a misunderstanding to turn heated, to escalate into violence. Watching from a balcony three stories above the plaza, there was nothing he could do to protect the people in the street should things turn ugly.

Dayne did appreciate his view of the revelry in Victory Plaza from this vantage point, though. Lady Mirianne's private office was on the top floor of her latest venture, and many of the people in the street were incredibly excited for the opportunity to be the very first customers of Henson's Majestic, a store that promised to be an experience like none other.

At least, that's how Lady Mirianne had it promoted on the flyers she had printed and plastered all over the north side of the city.

"My lady, are we just about ready?" Mister Sefferin, her general manager, waited in the doorway of her office, wringing his hands.

She smiled and looked at Dayne, a warm twinkle in her eye. "Well, my dear, are we ready?" She certainly looked ready. She was dressed in a smart skirt suit—not dissimilar to the kind the professional women in shops and offices all over the city wore—but hers was satin and silk, impeccably tailored, with intricate embroidery and clasps of ivory and gold. She had fashioned herself as a perfect union of noblewoman and businesswoman.

"You and Mister Sefferin are far more qualified to answer that," Dayne said. "Though I would like to be close to the polling station when you open doors." He hoped she understood the responsibility, the sacred duty, she had taken on by making the store one of the polling stations in today's election. She was focused on the store itself, and how hosting the polling station would help her, and he feared she wasn't taking it seriously.

He was also anxious to cast his vote. That was his own sacred duty, as a Druth citizen, far above and beyond his duties as a Candidate of the Tarian Order.

"Yes," she said. "Mister Sefferin, you do have the polling stations arranged, with manpower at the ready to guide folks back through the displays once they vote, yes?"

"Yes, ma'am," he said. "And all the salespeople are versed in asking gentlemen to show their thumb to earn their good citizen discount."

"Excellent," Lady Mirianne said. "I think we should open the doors in—"

She held her thought for a moment, her attention returning to the street below. An announcer boomed out, "Ladies and gentlemen, the Royal First Irregulars!"

"In just a few moments," she said. "They're about to do their routine, and all eyes will be on them. But I want those doors to fly open as soon as the performance ends."

She said this all without her eyes leaving the street below.

"As you wish, my lady," Sefferin said, scurrying away.

Dayne had never heard of this group, which by its name sounded like an army unit. "What are the—"

"The First Irregulars. They're a parade and morale unit. But they are truly something."

She pointed down to the street, where ten women in uniforms were marching into the plaza. Dayne wasn't quite sure what to make of them—their uniforms were essentially Druth Army uniforms, but they had been modified to display more bare skin than any practicality demanded. Far closer to stage show apparel than military—and not the kind of stage shows Dayne would attend.

"I don't think I approve," he started.

"Hush," she said, wrapping her arm around his massive frame. "Watch."

The women fanned out, forming a circle, all the while displaying their weapons. Each one bore a different weapon, and showed appreciable skill with it. After a moment, he recognized that the weapon each wielded represented one of the ten archduchies, their "traditional" weapon. Some of those designations were based on actual history, like the pike warriors of Oblune, the chain-flail fighters of Linjar, or the axe-men of Acora. On the other hand, he was certain that there was no grand tradition of staff fighters from the Archduchy of Maradaine. If anything, it came from the Kenalian Order, one of twelve Elite Orders of Druthal, now disbanded. Of the twelve, only the Spatians and his own Tarians remained. The Kenalians disbanded some sixty years ago, and their last members were folded into the Tarians. Their techniques and skills were integrated into the Tarian discipline.

Which explained why the woman spinning her staff with deft skill and grace had a certain familiarity.

"Is that Fredelle?" he asked quietly.

"Who?" Lady Mirianne asked.

"The one with the staff," he said. "I think she was in our Initiate cohort. But she washed out during third year, never made Candidate."

"It's certainly possible. A trained Tarian would be well received in the army, especially in an exhibition unit like the Royal First."

The performance was ramping up in energy, as the women incorporated a fair degree of acrobatics into their maneuvers, spinning and flipping as they whipped their weapons around. They also showed this was not mere stagecraft or pantomime. They knew their weapons, they knew their forms. Fredelle had been trained in the staff in her time as a Tarian Initiate, and her exhibition brought her into a spar with the woman wielding the Oblunic pike. Both of them were exemplary in their skill. Even though he could see that the battle they enacted was planned performance, choreographed like a dance, it was thrilling to watch. It reminded him of the best training spars with Amaya during their Initiacy.

"I told you," Lady Mirianne said, noting his engagement.

"They're very good at what they do," Dayne said.

Their performance ended with a flourish, and they moved away as the parade continued below.

"Come," Mirianne said, turning inside. "Let's open our doors and show this city what Henson's Majestic truly is."

Dayne followed Lady Mirianne as she strode out of her office and down the hallway. Sefferin could be heard in the distance, clapping his hands and calling out instructions. Once Dayne and Lady Mirianne had reached the winding stairway, the shop staff were all standing at attention at their stations throughout the store.

And, Dayne had to admit, the store was quite a spectacle. He rarely gave much regard to clothing beyond his uniform, and things like fashion, jewelry, and haberdashery did not concern him in the least. That said, the wide array of clothing, accessories, and other wares on display was like nothing he had ever seen. The shopboys and shopgirls all looked impeccable in outfits similar to

Lady Mirianne's though far less extravagant. Dark gray suits with waistcoats and cravats, and the girls in almost identical outfits.

"Perfect," Mirianne said. "They're all perfect."

"Thank you, ma'am," Sefferin said.

She raised her voice as she floated down the stairwell to the main floor. "You all should be so proud of the work you've already done, and what you're about to do," she said. "Open the doors."

Three men went to the main doors and opened them, sunlight and crowds bursting through. If Mirianne had intended some further speech to the patrons, there was no chance for it. Within moments people were filling the aisles around the different stations of the store, examining all the bits of finery that they had for sale.

Though many of the men ignored that, instead pressing to the far side of the store where the election polls had been set up. They were clearly eager to cast their votes, a feeling Dayne shared.

"My lady," Dayne said with a gesture. "With your permission, I'm going to get in line before it gets too unwieldy."

"Of course, dear," she said. "I know you won't enjoy yourself until you take care of that. You already know who you're voting for, yes?"

"Absolutely," he said. "I would never come to the polls uninformed."

"I know you wouldn't," she said with a kiss to his cheek. "Now I should attend to the business of business."

Dayne made his way down while Mirianne went to consult with Mister Sefferin. He discovered that he couldn't quite make a straight path to the voting polls. Instead he had to navigate through several different displays, where quite a few shopboys tried to offer him new suits or hats.

"A man your size needs something custom," one

overly eager boy said. "And we've got our measuring men already right here. Just as much service as your finest gentleman's tailor."

"Not now," Dayne said, pressing through.

"Then if you'd consider, I have something else here. Not too many men come through here with a shield or sword. Rare thing, the shield, especially."

"Please," Dayne said, trying to work his way around.

"I'm saying, if you follow me, I have a fine selection of oils and polishes that would be just what you need." The shopboy placed himself right in Dayne's path. It was impressively bold, especially since he didn't even come up to Dayne's chin.

"What I need is to go vote," Dayne said. The boy didn't move. Dayne checked the badge on his waistcoat. "Eichorn?"

"That's me."

"I will tell her ladyship you were incredibly dutiful in your attempt to sell. Now move."

Eichorn seemed to take this in for a moment, and then stepped aside.

Dayne had almost approached the polling line when he was accosted by four women. They were not shopgirls, but rather primly dressed ladies, all wearing suffragette pins.

"I see you are eager to vote, young man," the lead woman said.

"I am—" Dayne started.

"As am I," she said pointedly. "And yet, I am prevented."

"I support your cause," Dayne said quickly. He did not want to deal with the whole speech right now. "I have signed petitions, and if you wish me to sign again, I gladly will."

She presented him a stylus and clipboard. "I'm glad the young men of today are so sensible."

One of the other women raised an eyebrow at him. "I wonder if he should forsake his vote in solidarity. That would be a statement."

"I can't see how, ma'am," Dayne said as he signed the petition.

"Imagine it! Thousands of men in this city not voting, to show that without our voice included, theirs will not be heard."

"Jandalyn," the lead woman said derisively. "I've told you many times how absurd that is."

"It is a statement—"

"It's handing the election to people who disagree with us."

Jandalyn huffed and walked off.

"Thank you very much for your support, Mister. . . . Heldrin," she said as she looked at the petition. "Are you from the city originally?"

"No, ma'am," he said. "I grew up in the Sharain region, near Jaconvale."

"Emma, don't you know who this is?" one of the other women asked. "He's her ladyship's beau. You know, the one who rescued the Parliament."

Dayne held up a hand in protest. "That's a bit of an exaggeration."

"No, it isn't," the woman said. "I read that pamphlet. You saved all of them from that horrible man, Tharek Pell."

"Not all of them," Dayne said quietly. Four members of Parliament had been killed. Perhaps not Dayne's fault, but Dayne felt the weight of it, regardless. The impact on the nation had been profound. Not only were there more constables patrolling the streets in this part of the city, even the sheriffs of the Archduchy of Maradaine were making their presence known. That was uncommon in the city.

It also was why this election was so important. Instead of just voting for the usual twenty members of Parliament whose terms were ending, there were the four special elections to fill the seats of the murdered members.

"Still, he's a hero!" the woman said.

"Well, then," Emma said. "Perhaps you would be willing to speak at one of our rallies? It would mean so much to have a true hero speak in favor of our cause. Especially one as young and charming as you."

Dayne hesitated. "Strictly speaking, I'm not supposed to express political opinions while publicly representing the Order," Dayne said.

"You could come out of uniform, perhaps," Emma said.

"I'll have to ask the Grandmaster," Dayne said. "But if you have a card I will get back to you."

She handed him her card, and finally let him pass. The line had already started to grow, in no small part due to an argument that had boiled up between the administrators and one of the men who had come to vote. Dayne cautiously moved in closer. He wouldn't have imposed himself into the situation, but it looked like it was growing quite heated.

"Now don't you tell me—" the man trying to vote shouted, shoving his finger just a few inches from the administrator's face.

"I told you and will tell you, shove off!"

"I got a right, and you ain't gonna—"

"You got a right to get a thumping!" The administrator pulled out a handstick, and was about to bring it down on the man's arm when Dayne jumped in. He grabbed the handstick mid-swing and wrenched it out of the man's grasp. That stung his hand, but it would have done far worse to the other man's head.

"What's going on here?" Dayne asked. They all stopped and stared at him. Towering a good head over them both probably was more than enough to claim their attention and authority. The shield and dress uniform wouldn't hurt, either.

"He won't let me vote!" the man shouted. "I got a right!"

"He can't vote," the administrator said. "Not here, and not today."

"Why the blazes not, you pussucker?"

"Gentlemen, civility," Dayne boomed out. "Why do you think he can't vote?"

The administrator shook the man's identification papers. "It says here he lives on Mastill Avenue, over in Keller Cove. That's Archduchy of Sauriya. This is Archduchy of Maradaine. He needed to vote in his own neighborhood on the twenty-second."

"Yeah, but I work over here."

"It's where you live, mate."

"And I couldn't even get to vote that night!" the man shouted. "Hooligans were causing ruckus all over the neighborhood. So I figure—"

"You figured wrong," the administrator said, shoving the man's papers back to him.

"I'm afraid he's right, friend," Dayne said. He had heard about some of the commotion on the south side of the city that night, how disruptive it had been across the neighborhoods on the riverbank. "It's a shame you missed your chance to vote, but that's how it is."

The man looked like he was going to complain more, but reconsidered it when he sized up Dayne. He shook his head and stormed off, grumbling about northsiders.

"I appreciate the help," the administrator said. "You here to vote?"

"I am," Dayne said. "But others were ahead of me, and—"

"Nonsense, you're here, and we'll get to everyone in time," the administrator said. He handed Dayne a ballot. "Get it done and that way you don't have to worry."

Dayne decided not to argue and quickly filled his ballot—Waters and Hinkle, the Functionalist candidates for the Parliament in the Archduchy of Maradaine, as well as his choices for the Archduchy Council, the representative for his district in the Council of Aldermen, and other city officials—the Commissioners of the Loyalty, as they were called. Satisfied with his selections, he pressed his thumb in the ink pad to show he had voted.

"Don't forget to show your thumb to any of the shop-folk for a fine discount," the administrator said. "And thank you for coming to Henson's Majestic!"

Dayne worked his way back through the aisleways to the sales counters—it was nearly a labyrinth—all the while being offered deals on hats and capes and perfume. He had to hand it to Mirianne—she had built something astounding and surely lucrative. As overwhelming as he found the store and this opening event, it was certainly going to be popular. People were flooding the place, and he could see some of the porters were already weighed down with towers of packages wrapped in brown paper stamped with the Henson's Majestic logo.

As he worked his way around another counter, he spotted a familiar face.

"I do like them, certainly, but with this summer heat, it will be months before I can wear them."

Jerinne Fendall, a third-year Initiate in the Tarian Order, was trying on a pair of gloves while chatting with the Waishen-haired shopgirl working at that counter. Jerinne herself looked quite at ease, even though she was hardly fashionable in her Tarian drill uniform. Dayne did notice that she was no longer wearing the brace on her foot. It must have finally fully healed after having been broken by Tharek Pell.

"Oh, you should have asked me about summer gloves," the shopgirl said.

"I've never worn gloves in the summer," Jerinne said, her full attention on the shopgirl. "Is that the fashion now?"

"It's very much the fashion," the shopgirl said, pulling out another box.

"I didn't think you'd have cause for fashion outside of dress uniform," Dayne said, coming up to Jerinne.

She looked up at him, and flashed a bright smile. "Dayne, whatever are you doing here?"

"You knew I was going to be here," he said. "Why are you here?"

"Ama—that is, Madam Tyrell ran us through our drills this morning, and then strongly suggested we rest before the formal session of third year begins tomorrow." Jerinne shrugged. "I think she wanted to be rid of us for the day."

"You'll be glad for the rest," Dayne said. "So what brought you here?"

"Well, Lady Mirianne told me she would treat me to a gift on opening day." She turned her attention to the shopgirl again. "So I was definitely interested in a pair of fashionable gloves."

Given where Jerinne's gaze was focused, Dayne was certain she was far more interested in the girl selling the gloves than the gloves themselves, but that was none of his business. Dayne nodded, glancing around. "I need to find Mirianne."

"You both . . . know her ladyship?" the shopgirl asked, her voice cracking a bit.

Jerinne leaned in conspiratorially. "He's her, you know, *intended*."

"None of that," Dayne said.

Jerinne was about to say something in response, but was interrupted by shouts and screams from outside the store. Something angry had suddenly brewed out there. Dayne didn't wait, making his way through the aisles as fast as he could without knocking people over. He was almost to the exit when he realized Jerinne was right with him, matching pace even though she still had a slight limp.

"You good to do this?" he asked.

"Don't even know what 'this' is," she said. "But I can keep up."

They reached the main entrance, but found it to be blocked. A horde of people stood in front of the doors outside, arms linked together to form a human chain. Whatever was happening outside beyond that, Dayne couldn't see.

"That's some trouble."

Dayne was surprised to find the speaker standing right next to him was Fredelle Pence, in her skirted army uniform, leaning on her quarterstaff. Even though they hadn't seen each other in nearly three years, she had a casual air toward him, as though they had been by each other's side all this time. And in many ways, she was the same as she had been—same long chestnut hair cascading down one side of her head, same weary smile. But the years had changed her—no longer the nervous Initiate who panicked each time rankings went up, she had a quiet confidence that she wore like a favorite shirt.

She tried the door, but it couldn't be budged. Dayne was still so befuddled by her sudden appearance, he said the first thing that came to his mind, even though it had nothing to do with what was going on. "Are you really a lieutenant?"

She turned to him, raising an eyebrow at him. "Good to see you, too, Dayne. How else do we get out of here?"

Whatever was happening outside involved more angry shouts. Dayne could hear someone making a speech, but he couldn't make out any details.

"There's loading docks to the alley," Dayne said. "And the restaurant on the second floor has an overlook balcony."

"I'll take the balcony, you take the loading docks," she said. She grinned at Jerinne for a moment. "Third-year, huh? You're with me, Initiate."

Dayne wanted to argue, but she was already heading toward the stairs, Jerinne following.

"I'll see you outside," he called after her, and dashed off toward the loading dock.

Jerinne chased after this bizarre army woman as she bolted through the store and up the staircase to the restaurant. People in the store were now in a state of panic, since they were being prevented from getting out. Jerinne saw the clerks and shopgirls were doing their best to calm things, lead people away from the main doors, but the unrest was growing rapidly.

When they reached the restaurant, the army woman stopped for a moment to glance around and assess her options.

"What's our plan?" Jerinne asked, while the more obvious questions like "Who are you?" and "How do you know Dayne?" stuck in her throat.

"My plan is to get out to the street and see what I can do to help," she said. "I guess we'll see what your plan is." She dashed around the tables and out to the balcony.

Jerinne followed close behind, even though her ankle flared with every step. She could ignore it, push through it. "Who are you, exactly?"

"Lieutenant Fredelle Pence," she said, tapping the braid on the cuff of her uniform jacket. "Third-year Initiate, hmm? What's with your leg?"

"It's pretty much healed," Jerinne said reflexively.

From up on the balcony, the chaos in the streets was far more clear. A large group of people had placed themselves in front of the store entrance, arms linked together. A woman was in front of the group—a cloistress in a red habit. She was shouting something to the angry people around them, but Jerinne couldn't make it out.

And the people were quite angry. They were going to get violent very shortly. It was amazing they hadn't started bashing skulls in already.

Lieutenant Pence shook her head. "Starting third year with an injury. Oh, that's rough."

"It's fine!" Jerinne argued.

Lieutenant Pence paid more attention to the crowd below. "Kelvanne!" she shouted out. "I need a box catch!"

A group of women—in uniforms that matched Pence's, which Jerinne found fetching but impractical—took note of her call and ran over.

"Why am I here?" Jerinne asked.

"Hold that," Pence said, handing her the staff. "How are your skills with the staff? Ranks come out yet?"

"Ranks, I—that's tomorrow."

Pence shook her head. "That was a rough day, let me tell you. Steel yourself, girl." With that, she jumped over the railing of the balcony. Jerinne looked over and saw that four of the army women had crossed their arms together and caught her safely. Pence hopped back on her feet and shouted up to Jerinne.

"Throw me the staff!"

Jerinne wasn't sure what else to do, so she tossed it down. "Now what?"

"Keep order inside, Initiate!"

She winked and bolted off, with the other army women behind her.

"Keep order," Jerinne muttered, wondering what Lieutenant Pence had even brought her along for. And why she had so eagerly followed. But this lieutenant was right about one thing: She had started out her third year on a bad foot, literally. Now that formal training of Initiacy was starting up, she would change the blazes out of that.

# Chapter 2

**T**HE CROWD WAS ANGRY.

When Dayne made it to the street, that was all he could see at first. Screaming, angry people, ready to riot, clustered around the main doors of the store. Were they just trying to get inside? What was stopping them? He pressed in closer, calling out for people to stand aside. His height, uniform, and commanding voice all helped him make his way to the doors and see what was happening.

A group blocked the entrance, arms locked and standing strong together. Dayne was shocked by the type of people they were, based on their dress. Somber and conservative—high-necked, light-colored suits and prim, demure dresses. The woman leading the group, front and center, was wearing the robes and coif of a Cloistress of the Red.

She paced in front of the group like a mountain lion, and her pure force of will seemed to be the only thing that kept the crowd from rushing in and beating them all senseless. No one wanted to be the one who attacked a Sister of the Church.

"How dare you?" she cried out to the crowd. The drawn vowels of her accent confirmed what Dayne had suspected from their clothing: They were from Scaloi, the southernmost archduchy of Druthal, bordering the theocratic Acseria.

Dayne pressed closer, seeing that the crowd had not fully restrained themselves. Several in the Scallic group had bleeding gashes; at least one was standing only because his compatriots were holding him up. How this cloistress had even managed to break them off was a mystery to Dayne.

"These are people of peace!" the cloistress shouted. "And you—you!" She pointed at one man in particular. "Do you have no sense of sanctity? Do you have no decency? Blood is on your hands!"

"Get them out of the rutting way!" someone shouted.

"Out of the way?" the cloistress sneered. "So you all can go inside? See all the pretty things? Spend your money?"

"We need to vote!" someone else shouted.

"Oh, vote?" she snapped back. "And who gives you that right? Who tells you that you can have a say over who commands me and mine, in our home?"

"That right is enshrined in the Rights of Man," Dayne said. Possibly louder than he intended. Many eyes turned to him, including the cloistress.

"Hey, it's Dayne!" someone shouted. "The hero of the Parliament!"

"Dayne!" another voice shouted.

"Dayne! Get them out! Clear those blighters!"

The crowd parted enough to clear a path between Dayne and the cloistress.

"So this is what it comes to?" she asked. "A giant man with a sword come to slaughter us? Pile our bodies like cordwood, so none will be inconvenienced? Greedy pockets will be filled, but all your souls will stay empty!"

"I will not draw my sword on you," Dayne said, holding his hands up away from his belt. "Nor will I use my hands on you. But you must end this disruption."

"I will tell you what is a disruption, giant," she said. "This parade, in the name of unity, in the name of Druthal, a reunified nation! But today is not Reunification Day! Today is Saint Alexis Day! And yet where is the sanctity to her? Where is the reverence?"

"No one should—" Dayne started.

"I will tell you, the only reverence is to the crowns passing between hands in there!" She pointed to the store. "And these fine folk are so excited to spend their money they are willing to beat and murder for the opportunity!"

"You can't—" Dayne tried again. The crowd was starting to rile again. Dayne turned to them all. "Everyone back up a little. Step back!"

"Just thump them!" someone shouted.

"Crack some skulls!"

"Always violence," the cloistress said.

"I'll do nothing of the sort," Dayne said. He held his hands out wide. "But I can't hold them all off."

"Is that a threat?"

That took Dayne aback. "No ma'am. I'm just saying I can only do so much. But I will do all that I can."

"Good."

"But you cannot be doing this," he stressed. "You have to let people in. You have to let people out. It isn't your place—"

"I will tell you what's my place," she said, pressing forward so she was right up on him. "Sharing the words of Saint Alexis. Do you know what she did? She stood and fought for Scaloi. When Linjari heathens came for her village, she took up her father's mace and held them back. Then she took the weapons they left behind when they fled and melted them down into her armor, which she called upon God to bless."

"I know the story, ma'am—"

"Then you know how she was betrayed, don't you?" She pointed to the crowd. "She was sent by the Scallic queen as an emissary, to answer the call of unity. She came here, to this fetid sewage pile of a city"—that drew some shocked gasps— "and it was here that the Linjari envoy, filled with treachery, assassinated her. And then rather than return her to the homeland, the so-called King of Maradaine hid her body and her blessed relics."

"What do you mean so-called?" someone from the crowd shouted.

"What do you mean Linjari heathens?" Another voice from the crowd, this one with a sultry Linjari accent.

"I mean, why should we, the good and godly people of Scaloi, be forced to kneel as one of ten archduchies, when those very Linjari heathens are treated exactly the same. These ten archduchies should not be wrapped up together like a closed fist"—she mimed this, and then spread her hands wide, splaying her fingers out— "when they should be an open hand."

The Open Hand. That's who these people were. Radicals bent on Scallic Independence from Druthal. So this was a protest specifically against the election. Against a united Druthal.

But as much as Dayne disagreed with them, they had a right to their opinion. A right to argue it.

"And you, girl," the cloistress shouted. She was pointing across the crowd, where Fredelle now stood with the rest of Royal First Irregulars at her back. But the cloistress didn't point to Fredelle. Rather, she was pointing at the woman wielding the Scallic mace. "You carry the sacred weapon of Saint Alexis, but yet you're painted and dressed like a common street doxy. How dare you—"

"I'll show you what I dare!" This didn't come from the girl with the mace, but the one next to her, wielding a chain-flail. The same one with the Linjari accent who had called out earlier.

"Oh, you have a Linjari whore standing by your side?"

The girl responded by spinning her flail so fast it became a blur, and the crowd around her cleared back. Dayne jumped up in front of the cloistress, shield up.

"Stand down, Evicka." This came from Fredelle, in the front of the Royal First with her quarterstaff. "We're not going after civilians."

"You heard what she said," Evicka said.

"Stand. Down," Fredelle said.

"We're both lieutenants," Evicka said. "You can't order me." Despite that, she stopped spinning her flail, and stepped back to the others.

"Quite a good show, Tarian," the cloistress said.

"You all need to disperse," Dayne said, turning to them. "This does not aid your cause."

"And what do you know of our cause? Why would you help?"

"I wouldn't help," Dayne said. "I completely disagree with it. But that doesn't mean you shouldn't fight for it as best you can. Properly. Legally."

"We're peacefully protesting," she said. "But we'll be treated like criminals, nonetheless. It won't be long before—"

Constabulary whistles trilled through the air.

"Here it comes," the cloistress called to her people. "Remember the rules. Remember what we were told. Do not comply, but do not resist. No one do anything violent."

The crowd opened up and a cadre of constables swept in, handsticks out. Dayne was afraid they would just start cracking skulls instead of assessing the situation. Especially since the cloistress ordered her people to stay peaceful. It should be possible to diffuse the protest peacefully.

"Officers, if we can—" Dayne started, but they came right at the cloistress and Open Hand protestors without stopping. In moments they were bringing down their handsticks on people's heads, knocking them to the ground. Two constables came at the cloistress, but Dayne stepped in, blocking their blows with his shield.

"Oy, stand down!" one of them shouted at him.

"Who do you think you are?" another yelled.

"You will not accost her," Dayne said. He stared them down, and the two of them, sizing up their ability to get past him, backed away a bit. Dayne continued, "Arrest her if you must, but there is no need for this savagery."

One of the two—the one with sergeant's stripes— glanced at his fellows, and blew his whistle. The constables all looked up, stopping their assault on the protestors.

"That's enough," he said. "Iron them up. Call Yellowshields if they need them. Take them all down to the stationhouse."

"Name our charges," the cloistress said.

The sergeant came up to her and put her wrists in irons. "You are bound by law. You will be detained and charged. The charges will include and not be limited to disrupting the public peace and blocking a public square."

In moments the doors of Henson's Majestic were clear, and people came streaming out. It didn't take long before the whole situation calmed, and traffic in the square returned to normal.

But there were still two dozen people, including the cloistress, pressed facedown on the cobblestones, ironed and waiting for the lockwagon. Dayne couldn't help but think it could have been resolved in a more peaceful manner.

Hemmit Eyairin had found the morning parades deeply uninteresting—a toothless celebration of Druth unity showing the most banal aspects of each archduchy, highlighted with the weapons display by the Royal First. That was at least well-choreographed, but fundamentally flawed. It had nothing to do with the real problems people faced, and the problems they hoped their votes would help solve. Certainly, nothing worth writing about in *The Veracity Press*.

While it was boring, it was a commotion. And a commotion meant people, people to whom *The Veracity Press* could be sold. That was the real reason he was out here today. Usually they had their cadre of newsboys selling papers, but election season had scooped up most of those boys, hired to deliver candidate flyers and pamphlets. So Hemmit had to hawk them himself.

He had gotten separated from Maresh Niol and Lin Shartien, his fellow publishers. He had already decided he should sell by himself—one publisher trying to sell their paper showed dedication. All three would look desperate. They were a ways from that. The paper still managed to cover its own costs, even with sales taking a hit right now.

But now in the crowd, he couldn't see Lin or Maresh anymore. He suspected that Lin had gone into the Majestic, and dragged Maresh along with her.

That was before the crowd turned ugly in front of the entrance to the store. Hemmit tried to approach, find out what was going on, but the crowd was far too thick and agitated to get close. More so once Dayne arrived on the scene. Hemmit should have been surprised at Dayne's sudden appearance, but he wasn't. He knew Dayne was going to be at the Majestic opening—his relationship with Lady Mirianne made that a given—and whenever there was trouble, Dayne would always step in to diffuse the situation. It was who the man was.

Dayne Heldrin was a towering example of a man. Not only was he built like a tree, but he had the heart of a champion. Dayne had stood on the Parliament floor and kept that madman Tharek Pell from killing any more members of Parliament. Even though Hemmit felt that the nation needed some kind of revolution, some change, the violent methods of Tharek and the other

Haltom's Patriots were not the way. No, it needed to be done with words, with ideas. With votes.

And a few well-chosen actions. Hemmit respected a protest, and from what he could see, these people were trying to make their point without violence. Hemmit didn't know what that point was, and he certainly didn't know if he would agree with it. But he did respect that they were trying to be heard, and not forcing their idea with the point of a sword. That was the right way to do it.

Hemmit wasn't able to get closer, not without creating trouble, so he couldn't hear the argument Dayne was having with the woman leading the commotion. He made out some salient points: The protestors were from the Open Hand, whatever that was. And they were Scallic, clearly proud of that point.

It hardly mattered, though, as the constables rushed in and started cracking protestors to the ground, ironing them up in a matter of moments. As much trouble as the protests caused—or at least inconvenience—Hemmit definitely thought the constables were going too far. Nothing they had done warranted handsticks across their heads, or pressing their faces into the cobblestone.

"Dayne!" he shouted. "Dayne, stop this!"

Dayne couldn't possibly hear him, but the big man was doing his best to keep the constables from being too violent. Hemmit pushed his way through the crowd, moving up on the constables as they finished ironing up the protesters. "You, sir! This is improper! I will have your name, as well as your supervisor's!"

"Who the blazes are you, hecker?" the constable snarled. "Maybe you should be pulled down to the stationhouse as well."

"You're already going to be written up in the press, so, certainly, make me part of the story," Hemmit said.

"Easy, Hemmit," Dayne said.

"This your friend, Tarian?" the constable asked. "Do him a favor and get him out of here."

Hemmit peered at the man's badge. "I've got you, Officer Gren Robbins. You're being written about now."

"And we see you!" the cloistress on the ground cried out. "This is how Druthal treats its people, which is why we want no part of it!"

Officer Robbins blew his whistle. "Everyone clear off!" he shouted. "Show's over, the lockwagon needs to come through."

Most people shuffled away. The women from the Royal First Irregulars came over, the one with the quarterstaff taking the lead.

"Was this supposed to be a day off?" she asked Dayne.

"We don't really have those," Dayne told her. He glanced over at Hemmit, and must have noticed the look of confusion on his face. "Hemmit, this is Fredelle Pence."

"Lieutenant Pence," she said, almost more to Dayne than to Hemmit. She took Hemmit's hand. "You're the one who wrote that pamphlet about him."

"Guilty," Hemmit said. "The truth is the truth."

She held his grip while locking with his gaze. "I was part of his Tarian Initiate cohort before being a part of this."

"Part of this," one of the other Irregulars scoffed. "Stop acting like you're above us, Frell."

"Kelvanne, if you do not shut your jaw—"

"Ladies, please," Hemmit said. "It's supposed to be a joyous day, no?"

"It certainly is." Lady Mirianne swept out the main doors of the store—her store, her grand, majestic store—with a small retinue that managed to include Lin, Maresh, and Dayne's young charge Jerinne. "And I suggest we all strive to maintain that." She came over, hooking her arm into Dayne's, and approached the First Irregulars.

"My lady," Lieutenant Pence said, bowing her head. Her other compatriots did the same. Hemmit realized on seeing the insignias on their collars that they all had the rank of lieutenant. He wondered, given their status as an honor show squadron, what that meant, exactly.

"None of that," Lady Mirianne said. "I am the biggest fan of all of you. You are truly remarkable, in your skill and the unity you represent."

"Thank you, my lady," Lieutenant Pence said. "You honor us."

"You do," said another, whose Linjari accent made Lin's seem mild. "We're very glad someone appreciates all the hard work that *we all do*."

"Of course," Lady Mirianne said. "Right now I'm about to have a luncheon in our store, and I would love all of you to be my guests. And, Dayne, you and your friends from the *Veracity*, of course."

"Thank you," Hemmit said. "We'd be honored, my lady. But I must indulge you to give me a moment first, if you don't mind."

"Of course, of course," Lady Mirianne said. "Let's come along."

They all went in, though Maresh looked absolutely terrified at the idea. Dayne hung back for a moment.

"What's wrong?" he asked.

"Wrong, besides constables pounding peaceful protestors into the cobblestone?" Hemmit shot back. "I'm serious, we must tell this out." The lockwagons had arrived, and the protestors were being roughly dragged over and thrown into the back.

"Well, there's a constable lieutenant over there," Dayne said, pointing to the wagons. "If you want to put someone in authority to the fire . . ."

Hemmit shook his hand. "I'll be along in a moment. Save me a glass of wine."

"I know you," Dayne said with a chuckle. "I'll save you two."

Hemmit went over to the lieutenant, waving him down. "Sir? Hemmit Eyairin, *Veracity Press*. A few questions?"

The lieutenant—his badge said his name was Baskins—sighed and nodded. "What do you need, inkman?"

"Your men were far too aggressive in arresting these people—using levels of violence far beyond what was necessary for the situation."

"That isn't a question."

"Do you have any concerns about that?"

"Always," Baskins said. Hemmit was surprised by that. Baskins rubbed his temple and continued. "Look, it's easy for you to watch the thing unfold and make a decision about how it ought to go down, how far is too far."

"Yes, it's easy—"

"It's different when you're in the moment. You hope you make the best decision, but at the same time, you want to shut down any trouble before it escalates to the point where people are getting hurt. The protestors weren't violent, but what was the spark that would make them violent? Or the crowd around them? Or that Tarian?"

"He would never."

Baskins shrugged. "I'm glad you know that. My men didn't. They didn't know what those protestors would do when ironed up. When you don't know everything, sometimes you just have to be quick."

"I would think you wait until you do learn everything."

"Yeah, that'd be nice," Baskins said with a heavy sigh. "You got anything else?"

"What's going to happen to these people?"

"Brought to the stationhouse, processed for arrest. Charges will be considered for them, and for those the protector deems worthy, they'll be sent to cells pending their hearing. The rest will be released with a warning." He got up on the runner of the lockwagon. "If you ask me, the protector won't touch this, and they'll all be given walking papers."

So the arrests now were just to intimidate. Get these people off the street and hush up their protest for the moment.

"So they'll be back out in a few hours."

"A bit longer," Baskins said. "The protector wouldn't be in a hurry. It's a Saint Day, after all."

"So tomorrow?"

The lieutenant nodded. "A night in the lockup will cool their heads." He gave a signal and the wagons started to roll off.

Tomorrow. More than time enough for a polite lunch, some wine, and careful questions to Dayne and the Royal Irregulars, to give him some background. Tomorrow at first light, he would camp at the Constabulary stationhouse so when the cloistress was released, he'd be ready to get her side of the story.

# Chapter 3

DAYNE HAD NOT ENJOYED the luncheon. The meal had been fine—mustard-seared lamb sandwiches with beer-cooked onions and cheese, served with duck fat-crisped potatoes and honey pickles—and Dayne definitely saw the appeal of the iced cream that Mirianne and the others had been rolling their eyes over in ecstasy. "A contribution from the great ice houses of the Earl of Carvelle," Mirianne had said. But while everyone else chatted idly, he had far too many things occupying his thoughts to relax and enjoy the moment. Seated at her large private table in the Majestic Luncheonette, Lady Mirianne was all but ignoring Dayne, her attention on the members of the Royal First Irregulars.

Dayne was concerned about the protestors—he had never seen a secessionist group in Maradaine with more than a handful of fringe folk howling on the street. Those movements were usually about as absurd and unpopular as those True Line folks, but this was an organized action, at least thirty people. That cloistress gave him the impression she was just part of a larger movement. And that was here, in Maradaine.

Was there a significant movement in Scaloi that wanted it to be an independent kingdom again, divorced from the rest of Druthal? He truly had no idea.

He watched Jerinne, who also seemed out of sorts, unusually quiet. It was possible she was intimidated by this crowd—with a lady of the peerage, these ten Irregular women, and the trio from *The Veracity Press*. Jerinne's quiet attention was on Fredelle.

Dayne could understand that. Jerinne—like anyone in the third year of their Initiacy—was probably anxiously thinking about what she might do if she wasn't promoted to Candidate next year. Fredelle provided one possible answer, and for her part, appeared to be happy in her role in the Royal First Irregulars.

Dayne found his thoughts drifting to Amaya Tyrell, even though he knew they shouldn't. That was probably because in Initiacy, Fredelle's skill with the quarterstaff was matched only by Amaya, and some of their spars were downright legendary. Now, Fredelle had been cashiered from the Tarians and was serving in this special morale unit of the Druth Army, and Amaya had, improbably, achieved the rank of Adept, an unprecedented promotion after one year of Candidacy. In the past month he and Amaya had reached a degree of accord, which mostly involved avoiding each other. It was very clear that she did not approve of his relationship with Lady Mirianne, though she had also made it clear she was not interested in revisiting their own history.

"Oh, ladies, ladies, I'm just thrilled," Lady Mirianne said. "Listen, in a few nights I am hosting a party. Not a party, but a spree. A soiree. In celebration of the Revels of Liberation. And what better way to celebrate that than with the ten of you joining me, as a very symbol of ten united archduchies?"

"What kind of soiree?" the Linjari woman with the flail asked. Dayne had heard a round of names, but all of them had left his memory. "That word means something very specific in Yoleanne."

"Something debauched," the Scallic one said.

"You need to learn what fun is, my friend," the Linjari one—Evicka, that was it—said. She then pointed to Lin. "You know what I mean, yes?"

"She's got a point, my lady," Lin said. "Are you planning a *proper* Linjari party? Something that will turn people's hair white?"

"Well," Lady Mirianne said, matching both Lin and the other woman in tone if not accent. "I definitely was not going to have your standard, staid affair of ten courses and box dances to a string quint." Dayne recognized this behavior in Lady Mirianne, and he wasn't sure how he felt about it. She often liked to put up the facade that she was far more daring and radical than she truly was. This often came out of her events—the picnic dinner with the untraditional theater performance she held in her home a few months before was an excellent example. He felt that she wanted to be seen as daring and revolutionary, but her actions rarely displayed anything beyond that hint of subversion.

Not that Dayne wanted her to be subversive, nor did he presume to dictate her actions. But he worried about the perverse thrill she seemed to get at playing at it.

And this party seemed like it was more of that same game.

"Would you like me to give a performance?" Lin asked.

"What sort of performance?" Lady Mirianne asked.

"You're not ready for it," Maresh said flatly. "What Lin does is far too provocative."

"Now I think I have to have it," Mirianne said. "Are you available?"

"For you and your soiree, my lady," Lin purred. "I will clear everything else away."

"But what do you do?" This was Evicka again.

"You know the ribbon dances?"

Evicka chuckled. "I've seen it. I would never in my life dare to do it. At least in front of people." She looked to Mirianne, and then everyone else at the table. "They might not be able to handle that."

Now Lin put on a wicked smile. Twirling her hands, she said, "Especially because my performance is enhanced." Streams of colored light curled out of her fingers, accented with sparks and flashes.

The Scallic woman's eyes went wide. "Magic!" She kissed a knuckle and put it to her chest, her head down mumbling prayer.

One of the other Irregulars wrapped her arm around the Scallic woman's shoulders. "You'll have to forgive Argenitte," she said. "She's very excitable."

Her isolated reaction to Lin's magic made Dayne wonder about how else she might differ from the rest of the Irregulars. "Argenitte," Dayne said. "You're Scallic, yes?"

She looked up at him and nodded. "Born and raised in Korifina, prettiest city in the world."

"So what do you think of the Open Hand?"

"Are you talking about those fools making a spectacle of themselves outside, may the saints bless them?"

"So you're not a fan of their movement?" Hemmit asked, coming over to her side of the table.

"Are you talking politics with her?" Miri asked. "Don't bother her with that."

"No, no, my lady, it's quite all right," she said. "It's important we engage all things with an open heart. Now, it is not my place, but the place of God and the saints who intercede in his name, to judge another man or woman for their beliefs. Especially when said woman has taken up the vestments of the church to do service in the name of God."

"You got her started, Tarian," the Oblunic pike-woman said. "Mark it, and mark well, you're going to regret getting her going."

"No, I want to understand the Scallic perspective here," Dayne said. "Those people had an agenda, after all."

"Louse up people's day," Maresh said. "Hemmit, did you vote yet? I'm sure Dayne did."

"I'll probably go down and do it after lunch," Hemmit said.

"They're amazing," Lin said. "Only three people at this table have the right to vote, and one of them doesn't even take it seriously."

"I don't see a pin on your chest," Argenitte said. "And I can see enough of it."

"I don't need a pin," Lin said. "I write about it."

"With plenty of fire, too," Lady Mirianne said.

"You read our paper, my lady?" Maresh asked.

"I certainly do," Lady Mirianne said. "Ever since your pamphlet on our dear friend here."

All eyes went to Dayne. "There's a pamphlet?" the Oblunic pikewoman asked.

"There certainly is," Fredelle said, chuckling to herself. "How he saved the Parliament and stopped Tharek Pell almost single-handedly."

"I really didn't," Dayne said, feeling the heat on his cheeks.

"He's being far too modest," Lady Mirianne said.

"We just reported what happened," Maresh said.

"I remember that," the Linjari woman said. "You're the artist who did those sketches? Ooh, those drawings of that Tharek fellow were better for me than penny-hearts." She rolled her tongue in an excited yelp.

"Please don't be obscene, Evicka," Argenitte said.

"It's poor form when you talk that way in my presence, and utterly vulgar in mixed company."

"I don't mind at all," Hemmit said.

"Cool your ink, sprat," the pikewoman said. "Evicka has a thing for boys who are trouble."

"Tharek Pell was a deranged, murderous lunatic," Jerinne said.

Evicka fanned herself. "And if those pictures were to be believed, a pretty one at that."

"Please, let's not discuss that terrible man," Lady Mirianne said. "Go back to politics."

"Absolutely, my lady," Argenitte said. Taking another spoon of her iced cream, she turned to Dayne. "Now, I don't know about the Open Hand itself, save those dear fools thinking they speak for Scaloi as a whole. But I do know that there are a fair amount of people back home who think like them. And who are those people listening to, respecting? The reverend in their neighborhood church. They don't know anything about some king sitting in a palace way up northways."

"You have a problem with the king?" Maresh asked.

"I don't have a quarrel with any man who lives a decent life, and by all accounts King Maradaine does just that, and I pray for him, hoping that no more tragedy is visited upon him, praise the saints."

"Praise," Lady Mirianne said. Dayne wasn't sure if she was joining in with Argenitte or teasing her.

"But I can understand how my fellow Scallics would think that we are too far away from him, too removed from the, I'm sorry to say, less virtuous ways of our northern neighbors—"

"Praise," Evicka and the pikewoman said together. Definitely teasing.

Argenitte glared at them but continued unabated, "That they would call themselves Scallic before calling themselves Druth. I would not do that myself, but I see it and I understand it."

Before anyone else could speak, a steward came over to Lady Mirianne. "Much forgiveness, my lady, but there is a customer who insists on a word with you."

"The managers can handle it," she said curtly. "That is their job."

The steward looked nervous for a moment. "You see, my lady, it's . . . a member of the high peerage."

That took her attention. She glanced apologetically at her guests, and then waved the steward closer. He whispered in her ear, and annoyance briefly flashed over her face. "Well, I suppose I must see to her, then."

There was a brief silence as everyone glanced awkwardly about. Then Hemmit got to his feet. "Along those lines, we have our own work to attend to. The news of today must be reported."

Mirianne smiled and gave a warm laugh. "If you must name me and can't be kind, then please be fair."

"We are always fair," Hemmit said.

Maresh and Lin got to their feet as well. "My lady, thank you so much," Lin said.

"Always, friends," she said. "And I do want that performance for my party."

"As my lady commands," Lin said with a wicked smile.

Jerinne got to her feet. "And I should probably return to the chapterhouse. We both should." She aimed that last part at Dayne.

"Of course," Lady Mirianne said, rising. "I have abused your time far too much." She kissed Dayne chastely and moved to the Irregulars to give them a proper farewell.

Fredelle came over to Dayne, giving him a quick embrace. "We didn't get much chance to talk, I guess?"

"I suppose not," he said. "Sorry, my head has been many places today. You're doing well?"

"I'm using my skills," she said with a shrug. "I presume you're going to this party?"

"I think I'm socially obligated," he said.

"Then I guess I'll see you there," she said. She glanced over to Lady Mirianne. "So you and Amaya didn't work out?"

"Oh, no," Dayne said, a bit too quickly.

Fredelle's eyes lit up. "I want to hear that story."

"There's not much story there."

"Dayne," she said. "I may not be a Tarian Candidate, but I'm not an idiot."

"I know you're not," he said. Wanting to change the subject, he asked, "Is this treating you well? You wanted to be a Tarian, and now you're—"

"Performing talent shows?" she asked ruefully. "It's not what I wanted, but . . . I've got a good squad here."

"Fred," the one named Kelvanne called. "Let's not dally further, hmm?"

"Duty calls," Fredelle said. "I'll see you at the party."

"Until then," Dayne said. He had hoped for one last word with Lady Mirianne, but she had already gone out behind the steward. Whoever had summoned her must have been someone of note to get Miri to react that way.

# INTERLUDE: The Duchess

DUCHESS ERISIA LEIGHTON, the jewel of Fencal, the High Daughter of Kesta, keeper of the Coronet of Balanside, was deeply put out.

She had been far from home for far too long, and while the affairs of the Duchy of Fencal handled themselves just fine without her, she missed her city deeply. But she was needed here in Maradaine. Someone among the High Peerage had to be present, to be a voice of reason and moderation in this deviant cesspool of a city.

She had no formal function here beyond being at court, which was a useless role for any woman of her station when the kingdom had no queen.

She had done her best when she came to Maradaine to ingratiate herself with Queen Fesia, so she could influence the young woman with her wisdom, and with that, influence the throne. But the queen had never engaged Erisia with anything more than the passing politeness that she would have given to any noblewoman. In essence, an insult.

Erisia was hardly saddened when that smug woman had bled out on the birthing table.

With no queen, the noblewoman of rank was Princess Carianna, sister to dear Prince Escaraine and second cousin to the king. Carianna kept her own counsel, and rarely involved herself in affairs of state at all. Cultivating a relationship with her was useless.

So Erisia had to use her station in other ways to gain prominence and note in this city. She had two things in abundance that most others lacked: money and taste. That led her to rescue the failing opera house and begin restoration to its former glory. When she finally opened it, it would be a triumph for her name and her status, as well as the culture at large in this fetid metropolis.

But then she became entangled with Archduke Holm Windall and the Grand Ten. Holm had plans, yes, grand plans, but while he had ambition and authority, he lacked capital. Almost all her co-conspirators lacked capital. It fell on her to finance their plans to restore Druthal and the Throne to the glory and decency they were due.

Which meant the opera house needed to stay shuttered because the restoration was now just a front to hide the funding of their quiet revolution.

No more.

She waited patiently in the private showing room of Henson's Majestic, sipping wine while a handful of shopgirls and dress models stood around her in terrified silence. It hadn't been their fault; they all behaved impeccably, but she needed to put on a good show to get their mistress's attention.

And in moments, in she came. Lady Mirianne Henson, floating into the room with all the grace and poise that breeding and education could give. The young noblewoman was a very vision of loveliness, perfect blond curls cascading down and framing her face like she had just been painted by one of the eleventh-century masters.

"Thank you, girls, you've all done very well," she said to her staff. "You are all dismissed. I will handle the duchess personally."

The shopgirls and dress models scurried away like rats.

"Your grace," Lady Mirianne said, her voice now steely. "We are not supposed to speak outside of our prescribed roles."

"Stuff your prescribed roles," Erisia said, finishing her wine. "Besides, no one would question this. Here I am, a woman of stature, attending the gala opening of this wondrous marvel in the center of the city. And as is due my station, I ask that the lady proprietress attend to me herself. No one would think anything unusual or amiss about this."

"So are you here to shop for a new dress, your grace?" Mirianne asked. "The saints all know your wardrobe could stand a bit of modernization."

"Yes, well, my funds have been tied up, haven't they?" Erisia asked. "I would appreciate you personally selecting a few pieces for me and having them delivered to my household."

"Absolutely, I'll call the seamstress in for measurements—"

"I am not finished, Miri."

Erisia did not raise her voice, nor did she move from her chair. Still, she froze Lady Mirianne in her tracks. The daughter of an earl listens when a duchess speaks.

And in their conspiracy, Erisia was *The* Duchess.

"What else can I do for you, your grace?"

"It's very simple, dear," Erisia said. "You've clearly got a sizable operation here. I can't imagine that the bookkeeping will ever be completely straight."

"Oh, I have a very talented group of—"

"Miri, you aren't listening to me. Funds need to move around, payments need to be made. For the cause."

"We are not talking about—"

"Let me make something very clear. Renovations of the opera house are almost finished."

"No, your grace, they cannot—"

"They are almost finished," Erisia said. "And I will be launching a proper opening with something spectacular in a few months. Because there is no reason why I should be made a laughingstock while you are so flush with success."

Mirianne swallowed hard. "Yes, of course."

Erisia got to her feet. "Excellent. And I can count on your patronage at the opera, of course?"

"Always," Mirianne said. "I presume you're going to focus on some classics?"

"I was thinking of opening with *Demea*," Erisia said. "I would think a doomed love story would appeal to you."

That brought some shock to her face. "Your grace—"

"Do your job," Erisia said. It was bad enough that Mirianne embraced, even courted, scandal by so publicly taking a lover of common birth. But that she would do so with that Tarian who had been such a nuisance to the Ten's plans was intolerable. "Keep that pet of yours on a tight leash. The elections are upon us, and we don't need any further surprises."

"I will serve our interests, your grace," Mirianne said. "And the interests of the kingdom, as I always have. I pray you are doing the same."

Erisia patted her on the cheek. "I look forward to seeing these new fashions you're sending me. But no need to worry your seamstress. I'll have my girl deliver measurements to you before the day is out. And may your day be filled with blessings."

She didn't stay to hear further response from Mirianne. There was no need. There was nothing that crass girl with aspirations of revolution could say that interested Erisia Leighton. She was The Duchess, and Mirianne was merely The Lady. She understood the order of things.

And if things went wrong, Erisia was already prepared for the brunt of the trouble to land at Lady Mirianne's door.

# Chapter 4

JERINNE WANTED TO GET back to the chapter-house relatively quickly, but right when they left, Dayne's attention was drawn to a bit of bad theater at the south end of Victory Square. If it had been a funny bit, she would have understood, but it was just ten people in historical clothes lined up while a narrator droned on.

"And it is due to the Grand Ten, who fought and stood strong to bring us together, whose words and deeds define our new nation, that we now celebrate a reunited Druthal. We thank Geophry Haltom, The Parliamentarian, who raised up a rebellion within the city to throw off the Black Mage's occupation. Who encouraged the newly enthroned king to form the Parliament, and wrote of the Rights of Man. We thank Jethiah Tull, The Man of the People, the farmer who diverted food and supplies from the mage's armies to the citizens of the occupied city. We thank Baron Kelton Kege, The Lord, who was imprisoned for his refusal to bow to the

Black Mage, who became a rallying point to end the terror of the Incursion."

Each person onstage stepped forward at their introduction. After a few more, Dayne shook his head and stalked off. Jerinne chased after him.

"What was that?"

"Bad history," he grumbled. "The Grand Ten is a simplified view of the people and events that formed the core of our nation today. Haltom was a writer of the Rights of Man, but he was one of eight people who worked on it. A dozen members of the peerage were imprisoned with Baron Kege. Have you read Professor Teal's *The Foundation of Modern Druthal*?"

"No. . . ."

"It's in the library at the chapterhouse. Read it."

He walked in silence for several more blocks, even as Jerinne tried on multiple occasions to engage him in conversation. Whatever was gnawing at him, it wasn't just about the play. It had started before lunch had even begun.

"So, my new gloves are lovely," she said.

"It's far too hot to wear them," Dayne said quietly. "And will be for several months."

"I suppose that's true," Jerinne said. She tried for a subject that was sure to engage Dayne: asking about the Tarians and other Elite Orders in a broad, historic context. "So, gloves are not part of our uniform, but surely there must be some sort of uniform alternatives for different seasons. The Cascians up in the mountains must have had gloves, I'm sure. But also Tarians elsewhere. They couldn't expect a Tarian Adept to be in one of the brutal winters of Acora or the northern shores, and still hold sword and shield without gloves on."

"Shield and sword," he said absently.

Jerinne had said it wrong on purpose hoping it would snap him back.

"What is wrong?" she asked.

"Nothing," he said.

"Then what was I talking about?"

"The gloves Lady Mirianne gave you at the store. I do hope your Waishen-haired shopgirl still earned her commission from those."

Jerinne didn't know how it worked if Lady Mirianne just gave her the gloves. "Well, that's an excuse to go back and give her a tip."

"I thought you were sweet on—what's her name? Raila?"

Jerinne's heart almost stopped. She had never told Dayne. "How the blazes do you know that?"

"It's pretty plain on your face whenever you see her. Even if one doesn't know your preference, it's impossible to miss."

She had never actually told Dayne anything about how she felt about Raila, or how she felt about other girls in general. She hadn't told anyone at all, except possibly Miss Jessel, Lady Mirianne's handmaid, and only after several glasses of wine and whiskey. And those memories were fuzzy at best.

She chose her next words very carefully. "And how do you feel about it?"

This actually got him to stop walking in a semi-daze. "I won't lie, I was raised to see that sort of thing as sin, and I probably held that view through most of my Initiacy."

That wasn't exactly an answer. "Most of it?"

"Then Fredelle cracked a quarterstaff on my leg and told me I was being an 'idiot of the highest order.'"

"Did she?" Jerinne asked. Her estimation of the woman went up. "Is she—"

"Maybe," Dayne said. "At the time I made a comment about two young men in the second year who were caught together. Fredelle reminded me—painfully—that it was no different from what Amaya and I were doing at the time."

"I've heard those stories."

"You have?" Dayne seemed scandalized.

Jerinne regretted saying it. "Vien mentioned it."

"Oh." He pursed his lips for a moment, then said, "Lacanja opened my eyes. It's the sort of thing that is far more . . . liberated there. If that's the right word."

"I think it's a good word," Jerinne said. Maybe she should go to Lacanja. "Maradaine is kind of a stuffy city, no?"

"It's different," Dayne said. "I hope—" He paused for a moment. "Were I to become a Tarian Adept . . ."

Were he? That sounded foolish. "Of course you are," she told him.

"Nothing is certain," he said darkly. "But were I, I would like to be assigned to a wandering post, going from city to city as needed. Really see the whole country."

"Really?"

"Those protestors came up from Scaloi. And, that's part of this nation, yet so different. And I don't know anything about it other than the stereotypes."

"Stern, religious-minded folk?" Jerinne asked. The one from the Irregulars—Argenitte? She didn't do much to counter that image.

"I'm just reminded how much of what I know of Druthal is academic." He sighed again. "I didn't enjoy living in Lacanja, but it helped me realize so many things I didn't know about the world. Not just about . . . people's romantic flexibility."

She looked at him, and he was blushing bright red. "We don't have to talk about it," she said. "But I'm glad you don't disapprove."

"Of you?" Dayne smiled. "I don't think I ever could."

They entered the chapterhouse—an old city manor house from the tenth century, repurposed for their Order's needs—to find it buzzing with activity. That made sense—tomorrow was the first official day of Initiacy, and many of the first-years were settling into their bar-racks, still getting the feel of the place. Jerinne remem-bered that from two years ago, and how glad she was to have met Raila and Enther and Iondo in those first days.

Iondo washed out in that first year, but he was a good sort.

Several of those first-years were outright running through the entrance hall, which startled Kevo, the old blind dog that rarely got up from its pile of blankets in the corner.

"Ease down," Dayne shouted to them. "You all need to respect this place."

The two first-year boys stopped in their tracks and just stared at Dayne in stunned silence.

"You two!" Madam Tyrell called from the top of the stairs. "Where have you been?"

One of the first-years found his voice. "Us two, or them two?"

"Those two," she said with annoyance. "You scatter. Calmly."

The boys did just that.

"Is something wrong, Amaya?" Dayne asked.

"I thought the day was ours," Jerinne said.

Madam Tyrell reached the bottom of the stairs. "Yes, but it would have been helpful to know where you were. Because—oh." She was staring at Jerinne's hands. He voice went cold. "You were at the opening of that store, of course."

Jerinne held up the gloved hand. "You like?"

For just a moment, she looked at the gloves apprecia-tively. "They actually are—but that doesn't matter. What matters is you've had pages waiting for you, and they've been here some time."

"I apologize," Dayne said. "They didn't just leave their messages?"

"No," she said. "They had to make sure they were delivered into your hands." Jerinne had no idea why such a thing would be necessary, but the furrowing of Dayne's brow made her think he knew exactly why.

"That shouldn't have been your problem," he said.

"Yes, well," Madam Tyrell said through her teeth. "Somehow having the lowest seniority of the Adepts means a lot of things are my problem. Anyhow, they're waiting in the dining hall."

"Wait," Jerinne said. "Pages for him, or for me?"

"Both," Madam Tyrell said. "Come on."

She led them into the dining hall, where three young boys, dressed in sharp suits, were waiting at one of the tables. An empty plate with the evidence of stray crumbs sat in the middle of them.

"Here they are," Madam Tyrell said. "Do your business and shove off."

One of the three boys hopped to his feet. "You are Dayne Heldrin?" he asked.

"Yes," Dayne said.

The boy presented a letter to Dayne. "From the office of Marshal Chief Donavan Samsell. You are requested to come to Parliament Hall and present yourself to him immediately upon receipt."

"I—what?"

"Immediately, sir," the boy said. "So let's away."

"Hold on," one of the other boys said. "I got my thing."

"Is your thing immediate, or of government import?" the parliamentary page asked. "No, so piss in your mouth."

"Saints, son," Dayne said. "There's no need for that."

"He should know his place in the order of things," the parliamentary page said.

"Ease it down," Dayne said. Looking at the other one, he asked, "What do you have?"

The boy presented his letter. "From the offices of the High City Protector, sir."

Dayne opened the letter and scanned it, his face darkening.

"What is it?" Jerinne asked.

"It's about Tharek's trial," Dayne said. "The protector wants to establish my testimony."

"I got a letter about that a week ago," Madam Tyrell said.

"They want me to go in next week for initial statements," Dayne said. He looked at the third boy. "And you're here for her?"

"Is she Jerinne Fendall?" he asked, running his finger on the empty plate, and then licking it. "And are there more pastries?"

"No," Madam Tyrell said sharply.

"Hmph."

"I'm Jerinne Fendall, yes," Jerinne said.

"Yeah," the kid said, getting to his feet. "You're requested to come to the offices of the archduke's justice advocate tomorrow afternoon." He handed her the letter.

"Justice advocate?" Dayne asked. "Why are you getting that?"

Jerinne opened the letter, just as confused. "I don't know why. It doesn't make sense unless—"

Then she saw it, written plain. The justice advocate was calling upon her to give testimony in Tharek's trial. Tharek Pell, the man who had killed four members of Parliament, countless marshals, and had snapped Jerinne's leg like a twig. And they were calling her to give testimony.

For his defense.

Parliament Square was relatively quiet this afternoon, probably because the Parliament wasn't in session. Even still, a handful of protestors with "The True Line Lives"

signs, and a few more with "Open the Chairs," congregated in front of the steps. Even these protestors didn't seem to have their hearts into it today, mostly standing listlessly, not engaging any passersby.

Dayne went up the steps to the main entrance of the Parliament without being molested by any of them. He had a strange twinge of melancholy over that. Not that he wanted to be engaged by the True Line people, but he did have some sympathy for the Open Chairs movement. It wasn't right that Druth citizens in Monitel or Corvia had no representation in Parliament, let alone the people in the island colonies.

A King's Marshal—barely any older than Jerinne—stood guard at the door. "Sir," he said, trying to hold a hand up to stop Dayne. The boy looked petrified, probably because he was imagining what he would have to do if Dayne just barreled through him.

"Yes?" Dayne asked.

"There's no public business here today, sir," the young marshal said. "I'm afraid—" He swallowed hard. "I'm afraid I'll have to ask you to turn around."

"I've been asked here," Dayne said. He quickly realized that he sounded brusque, even rude. His new job was going to involve liaising with the marshals; he might as well start here. He put on a broad smile, extended his hand. "Hi, I'm Dayne. I'm with the Tarian Order. I was asked here by Marshal Chief Samsell?"

"Oh," the boy said. Despite looking unsure, he took Dayne's hand and shook it. "Kipping. I—I wasn't briefed about anyone coming, but, well . . . I wasn't briefed on anything at all, frankly. I think that Chief Samsell is down in the lower levels, but . . ."

"But?"

"Are you cleared to go into the lower offices?"

Dayne shrugged. "I'm supposed to be a liaison between you all and the Orders. A page came and told me to come meet with him. You want to turn me away, Kipping, that's your business. But that's on you."

Kipping held up one finger and slipped inside for a moment. After a bit he came out with another marshal, this one with a first class officer chevron on his collar. "Can I help you?"

"Dayne Heldrin, of the Tarian Order. Here to see—"

"Chief Samsell, yes," the officer said. "My apologies, we're still in a bit of—" He looked at Kipping with a hint of disdain. "Disarray right now."

"I understand," Dayne said as the officer opened the door to lead him in.

The corridor circumnavigating the Parliament floor was brilliant, marble shining like Dayne had never seen. "Do you usually clean this much between Parliament convocations?"

"We don't, no," the officer said. "We're King's Marshals, not washerwomen." He sighed and looked around. "Also, it's not typical for there to be a massacre here."

Dayne winced a bit. "Yes, there—there was a lot to clean up."

"Right, you were here," the officer said, leading him to a stairwell. "The hero of the day. Do you know how many marshals died that day?"

"Quite a few," Dayne said.

"Twenty-seven," the officer said. "Including the traitor, Regine Toscan."

"Yes, I know," Dayne said.

"The point is, we've had to rebuild the security for the Parliament building from the foundations. New blood all around. Still a lot of training to do."

"I completely understand," Dayne said, though he felt this officer was driving at something he wasn't quite catching.

The officer brought him to a door, grabbing the knob in a way that was nearly an act of aggression. "I'm saying, the Parliament is our jurisdiction, Tarian. Be aware of that."

Dayne decided not to rise to this man's level. "We're all here to serve Druthal, friend." He went in before the officer could answer.

Dayne had entered a command center—the walls were lined with maps and slateboards, showing details of each of the ten archduchies, cities listed with names and dates, routes marked on the maps. A dozen marshals were working at desks, writing on the boards, sifting through reports. Most of them were so involved, they didn't even notice him—save the pale, fair-haired man in the marshal chief's uniform, who was talking to an older gentleman in an expensive suit.

"Dayne Heldrin," he said, coming over and extending his hand. "Thank you for coming on short notice."

Dayne took his hand. "Marshal Chief Samsell, I assume?"

"Please, Donavan," he said. "Welcome to our little war room, as I like to call it."

"War room?" Dayne asked, raising an eyebrow. "What war would that be?"

Samsell put on a smile. "That would be the election. Or at least, the national part of the Parliamentary election. City and archduchy results are handled elsewhere."

"I never would have thought of it as a war."

"That's because you've never had to administrate it." Samsell led him over to a desk at the far end of the room. "Forgive my manners. The honorable Wesley Benedict, Second Chair of Lacanja."

Dayne had his hand out instinctively before he registered the name. Mister Benedict looked down at the offered hand with disgust.

"I'm aware of Mister Heldrin. He's the one who gets people killed and cripples children."

"Sir, I—" Dayne sputtered out.

"No, don't even," Benedict said. "If I had my way,

you'd be nowhere near this building, and never wear that uniform again. Instead I'll settle for making sure you don't get to wear it after your Candidacy is through. And be assured, Mister Heldrin, I will be doing that."

Dayne couldn't find voice to respond to that.

"I understand you have business with Mister Heldrin, Marshal, so I'll take my leave. Please try not to have our paths cross again." He walked off at a brisk pace.

"Dayne, I am . . . I am so very sorry, I had no idea."

Dayne swallowed hard, pushing down the bile and shame rising in his throat. Because as cruel as it was, Mister Benedict was not wrong. Everything he said was true. Gritting his teeth, Dayne said, "You were telling me about the election?"

Samsell nodded. "Yes, of course. Each archduchy holds its own election on its own timeline, overseen by its election officiants. The King's Marshals coordinate oversight for the Parliamentary aspect. Our people are across the country, hoping to keep corruption to a minimum."

"Not eliminate it?"

"That would be ideal," Samsell said, sitting at the desk. "But I am a realist. Do you know what running this all entails?"

Dayne wasn't sure how to read this man. From any other marshal that question would have been a swipe, a thinly veiled attack. With any other marshal, he would suspect the scene with Benedict was a deliberate ploy to undermine him. But Marshal Chief Donavan Samsell seemed to be genuinely interested in explaining things to Dayne—genuinely interested in Dayne. He may have been the first marshal Dayne had met who hadn't re- acted to a Tarian with instant aggression.

"I presume votes are counted locally, tallied, and re- sults are sent to Maradaine."

"Roughly, yes, but more complicated than that," Samsell said. "The counting and tallying has been done on local levels, those results brought by officiants and marshals to the offices of the archdukes and their appointed governors and assemblies, who organize the official vote counts for the archduchy. Not just the winners, but tally sheets from all the precincts with the details of all the results."

"All right, that makes sense, and then that's sent to Maradaine?"

"Sealed by the archduke's office, then locked in strongboxes, and those and the officiants travel to Maradaine—under marshal protection—for formal certification."

"And you're coordinating that here?"

"Precisely," Samsell said. "I've served as chief of operations for elections for six years now. It's a great responsibility, and one I take very seriously. I've studied you, Dayne Heldrin, so I know you understand exactly what I'm talking about."

"It's a job that needs to be done with reverence," Dayne said. "It's a sac—"

"A sacred right of the Druth people, and we must honor their wishes, and through that, honor the throne and the crown." He chuckled. "Yes, I've read all of that as well."

"So what are you looking to me for?"

"Well, a few things. Right now, I'm also serving as the interim chief of Parliament sanctity. The former chief was, of course, Regine Toscan." He spit on the ground as he said that. "That's because I'm already here and working out of this office, so the bosses at the Royal Bureau feel that physical proximity is a good enough reason to give me the job."

"You need my help with that, then?"

"No, but thank you," Samsell said. "With Parliament between convocations, the duties for that role are light, and Chief Quoyell will be taking the formal position in a few days, as he's coming from Hechard. You'll meet him in due course, I'm sure."

Dayne already liked Chief Samsell, but he realized

the man was in no particular hurry to find his way to a point. "So what do you need from me?"

"You're going to be working as a liaison between us, the Orders, the Parliament, and other forms of formal authority in the city. Constabulary, archduchy sheriffs, whatever is needed."

"I hadn't been fully briefed on those duties, but I'm up for whatever is needed of me, to serve the Order and the nation."

"Good, first off is your quartering."

"Quartering?"

"I'm given to understand your appointment is through the crown and Parliament, not the Tarian Order. As such, you've been assigned a staff apartment here in the building."

That gave Dayne a bit of pause. "I was not expecting that."

Samsell shrugged. "I mean, no one is going to force you to sleep here, but you will have quarters for your use here. You might find that useful."

"Of course," Dayne said. "I didn't mean to seem ungrateful."

"Dayne," Samsell said, putting a hand on Dayne's shoulder. "This is going to be new territory for all of us. I'm not going to get offended if a few mistakes happen here and there."

"I appreciate that."

"Anyhow, you'll be on a lower level suite, number twenty-seven. It's actually one of the nicer ones here."

"Who else lives in those apartments?"

"Mostly Parliamentary staff. Not the staff and secretaries for the members, but the scribes, floor functionaries, cleaning staff. Those people."

"And the marshals on duty?"

"We have bunks down in these offices, two levels below you, but we don't formally quarter here." He shrugged. "There actually is a rule against us quartering here, if you can believe it. We're overburdened with bureaucracy. You'll probably get your share of it."

"All right," Dayne said. "I'm sensing you wanted me here for more than just telling me where my room is."

"I am." Samsell picked up a folder from his desk. "Several of the voting sites were disrupted today in the city. You were at one disruption, yes?"

"At Henson's Majestic," Dayne said. "You mean the protestors?"

"Separatists. Tried to stop people from voting." He handed the folder over. "They're called the Open Hand—"

"From Scaloi, I gathered," Dayne said. "I thought they were arrested."

"They were, but odds are against formal charges being laid. But I'm less concerned about what they did today, and more about what they might do over the next few days."

"What happens over the next few days?"

"All the election results from all ten archduchies— save Maradaine, since voting today isn't done—are on their way to the city. Here they will be validated and the official election results will be announced on Reunification Day."

This was in line with Dayne's own understanding—of course Reunification Day would be the formal announcement, it always had been.

"And you think the Open Hand might—" Dayne let it hang.

"There's credible intelligence of attempts to undermine the validity of the election process. Disrupting the voting, for one. They did it today, and several sites in South Maradaine were disrupted a few days ago on Sauriya's election day."

"By the Open Hand?"

"It's unclear who was responsible. There are several disruptive groups in the city. Some separatists, some extremists, some . . . just troublemakers. But any and all could create trouble."

"Of course," Dayne said. "Whatever you need, I'll pass on to the Grandmaster."

"Good, but there is more to do, including sharing what we know with the press, when the moment is right. That's part of what I need from you."

"Sharing with the press?"

Samsell shrugged. "For better or worse, Dayne, you're something of a golden child right now. Lauded for saving the Parliament, capturing Tharek Pell, and you have the favor of the press and the crown. We can use that right now, and that helps the government and helps your Order."

"How so?"

"By you, standing up in your uniform, shield on your arm, representing the Order as you address the people of the press. Telling them what is going on, using your honesty and credibility to get the truth out there."

"If that's what you need . . ." Dayne said, though he wasn't fully convinced.

"Excellent," Samsell said. "Now, beyond that, I think we need to deal with the Open Hand, specifically. But quietly, informally. That's an area where your status helps us greatly. I'd like you to investigate personally. Did you meet their leader today?"

"There was a woman in a cloistress habit. Is she—"

"That's one of his ringleaders. Sister Frienne Okall. She's in the file there. But the leader is this man—" Samsell opened the folder to the first page, which included a charcoal sketch of a man in a priest's cassock, with wild hair and even wilder beard. In the sketch, he looked like he was shouting at a crowd, red-faced and angry, pointing at someone whom he seemed to be damning to an eternity with the sinners.

"And this is?"

"Bishop Ret Issendel. The leader of the Open Hand,

and candidate for one of the Scallic Chairs in Parliament. He's here in the city, Dayne, and I need your help to stop him."

Jerinne had found herself in a daze after getting the letter, which lasted through dinner, her evening exercises, and meditation, which she went through like a wind-up gearbox going through its prescribed motions. There was more than one time that Raila tried to engage with her during each of those activities, and if she had responded, she didn't remember.

Instead of going to bed she walked the grounds of the chapterhouse, through the stone garden path that circled the bathhouse and the armory. The garden was lovely, well-maintained by the house staff, and in the purple haze of the late summer twilight it felt especially magical.

"You should be in bed, Initiate."

Madam Tyrell came out of the bathhouse, wrapped in a drycloth, her hair damp.

"Sorry, ma'am," Jerinne said, keeping her eyes to the ground. "I . . . I didn't know anyone was out here."

"That's why I tend to bathe now," Madam Tyrell said. "Are you ready for tomorrow?"

"Are you talking about Initiacy training, or being called to the defense of Tharek Pell?"

Madam Tyrell gave a rueful chuckle. "I meant the start of third year, but that definitely is something to consider. That's what has you distracted?"

"Among other things," Jerinne said. "I met someone from your cohort today. Fredelle Pence?"

"Really?" Madam Tyrell's tone told Jerinne she had made a mistake. "And what was Freddy doing at Henson's Majestic?"

"Well, I'm not sure," Jerinne said cautiously. "I think she was initially there for the parade."

"The parade?" Madam Tyrell shook her head. "She was in the parade, wasn't she? Part of that Royal Irregarded unit?"

"Royal Irregulars," Jerinne said quietly, even though she could tell from Madam Tyrell's face that nothing good would come from saying it.

Madam Tyrell sighed. "Third-year Initiacy, Freddy was a miracle with the quarterstaff."

"I heard you were better."

"I was better," Madam Tyrell snapped reflexively. "But I was better at everything. Freddy fumbled with her shield work, with the sword, and . . . her ranking plummeted among the third-years." Rankings came out tomorrow, and Madam Tyrell must know where Jerinne stood. "So she washed out. And now she's a show pony in a skirt."

Jerinne almost said, "She seems happy," but bit her tongue before that came out.

"Get to bed, Jerinne," Madam Tyrell said. "Tomorrow's a big day."

# Chapter 5

*A*MAYA WOKE UP an hour before dawn, as she usually did. It had become an ingrained habit, regardless of when she went to sleep. Of course, that had developed during Initiacy, specifically in third year, when she and Dayne were in constant competition for the top rank of the cohort. The other fourteen never stood a chance. Most of them didn't advance to Candidacy.

In fact, of that cohort, she was the only one who had made Adept, having achieved it after an unprecedented single year in Candidacy. She was the one who was a full Tarian.

And Dayne . . .

She pushed him out of her head. She let him live in there far too much as it was. He had made his choices, and she had to do what was best for her own well-being. And that meant keeping Dayne at a certain distance, even though he was again living just a few doors down the hallway.

Right now, Dayne would be in the practice rooms,

going through his own routines and stretches. She had yielded the room to him, her own decision to avoid unnecessary interaction. Every time they spoke, it would get heated, and if they were alone—she felt like Initiacy all over again. She couldn't have that, even if her thoughts would linger back to that moment in the baths last month.

She put that energy into discipline, exercise. Every morning, stretches and calisthenics in her quarters, and then running from the chapterhouse to the northern tip of the Trelan Docks and back. It had become a fascinating glimpse into a bit of Maradaine she hadn't seen before: the early workers on the docks, the servers and shopgirls who would ferryboat across the river from their south side homes to their jobs on the north, the constables and Yellowshields gathering up sleeping transients. In all her years in Maradaine, so much of the city had been invisible to her. She had traveled to Imachan with a diplomatic embassage, but had barely stepped foot on the other side of the river.

Had any Tarian Adept or Master? As she ran, pushing herself until her lungs burned, she wondered why the Order sometimes called themselves "The Shield of the People" when most of their energy was spent in service of nobility or members of Parliament.

*You know perfectly well why,* she told herself. *Because between the Constabulary, army, and King's Marshals, there's little place in this world for the ancient Elite Orders. Training and discipline and tradition mean nothing if no one supports us.*

By the time she returned, the sun was just peeking over the tops of the buildings to the east, shining off the high dome of the Parliament. The chapterhouse was unusually busy for this early. That was to be expected today, with formal training of Initiates beginning. The past few days had been in conference with Master Nedell and various Adepts to determine the third-year rankings. She wasn't convinced that the final decisions were fair or correct, but it wasn't an empirical process. Save intervention from the Grandmaster, it was ultimately Master Nedell who determined who was ranked where, and Amaya had to defer to that.

"Vien," she called as Vien Reston went by, coming from the dining halls. "You off to rouse the third-years?"

"I am," Vien said. "But—"

"Have them start with a run, then a double cycle of strength work, and then—"

"Well, I will, but the Grandmaster made a thing about not pushing the Initiates too hard in the early days."

"That's why just a double cycle," Amaya said, laughing it off. "We'll give them a week before the hard stuff." Even still, she had a bit of misgiving. Was the Grandmaster trying to undermine her authority with the Initiates? She was supposed to be in charge of the training regimen. Though it was possible the Grandmaster was specifically talking to Vien, who had been a bit extra zealous in her role as Initiate Prefect. But Amaya liked her energy.

Vien chuckled. "If they can all keep their breakfast down, we're being too easy on them."

"I'm all right with you pushing them harder, but you're the one who'll mop it up."

"See, that's further training and incentive for them."

Amaya sighed and rolled her eyes. The Grandmaster's admonition was clearly directed at Vien's particular enthusiasm. "Well, go rouse them, run them down five miles, then we'll do strength work in the training room."

"Five? Excellent."

"It'll do them good. Also the first rankings are up. You remember how unnerving that can be."

Vien scoffed. "Not for me. I started at first place and kept it all year."

Lucky Vien. Third-year Initiacy for Amaya had been a constant competition, she and Dayne swapping first and second place the whole time. After Third-Year Trials, Master Denbar declared them tied, both the top of the cohort as they advanced to Candidacy.

Even still, Master Denbar—family, her mother's cousin—took Dayne with him to Lacanja. Where he died.

And on his death, he had had a box sent to her, with nothing but a locket and the high trump cards of a playing deck: the Grand Ten. It was such a bizarre thing, she didn't know what to make of it. And a message that she needed to find them, stop them, and save Druthal.

It had her thinking: what was the Grand Ten? They were icons of history, heroes who worked to form the nation. What would that mean now? And why would she need to save Druthal from them? The only thing that made sense to her was that there was a conspiracy in Maradaine, powerful people who were wanted to reshape the nation to their ideals. People who chose the iconography of the Ten to give themselves the moral authority that their goals lacked. But that idea seemed patently ridiculous.

Perhaps it was a mystery she would never solve.

Vien was still waiting for a final order. Amaya keyed back into the conversation. "Get them going. I'll meet you all in the yard in an hour."

"Ma'am," Vien said, with a wicked grin. She went up to the barracks. That girl was definitely enjoying her job as Initiate Prefect. Perhaps a little too much. But Amaya wasn't going to begrudge her that. The Initiates were going to need the push. Especially Jerinne Fendall, if she was going to make it.

"The sun is up and you aren't!"

Jerinne had been half-asleep, desperate for a few

more moments before she had to wake up, but unable to rest when she knew that was about to be shouted.

That had been the wake-up call in the barracks for the third-year Initiates since they had been advanced, even though formal third-year training began today. Vien Reston—now a first-year Candidate—had taken her assigned role of Initiate Prefect with a great amount of relish. Possibly because she was the only new Candidate from her cohort who hadn't been assigned to another city. Two months ago she was Vien, an Initiate like everyone else in the barracks. Today she was Miss Reston and treated them all like sewage.

As Jerinne started to rouse from her bunk, Vien slammed a staff between her legs.

"Morning, Initiate!" Vien shouted. "Hope I didn't disturb your foot at all like that. How is your foot, Initiate? Has it healed?"

"It's fine," Jerinne said.

"Oh, good," Vien said, her tone oily with condescension. "I would hate to do anything that could break it again, forcing you to be excused from further exercises. You don't need to be excused, do you?"

"No, ma'am," Jerinne said, getting to her feet. She made a point of putting all her weight on her feet, standing tall and strong. That gave her a few inches over Vien, looking down her nose to meet her eyes. It also made her ankle twinge at her, a sharp reminder of the injury. Just about everyone in the third-year Initiacy, as well as Vien and several of the other Candidates and Adepts, had made enough of a fuss about her limping about and being excused from certain tasks that she wasn't about to give them an ounce of a reason to doubt her or her commitment. "I'm ready for anything you have for me."

"Anything?" Vien said. She turned to the room. "People, Initiate Fendall has issued us a challenge! We should all rise to the occasion. So instead of a two-mile run this morning, we will start with a five-mile one. But before you get too excited for that, on the slateboard outside are the rankings for your cohort. Starting today, those rankings will be updated daily. Learn where you stand and strive to be worthy of the name Tarian." She strode out of the barracks. "Everyone be at the main gate when I ring the bell."

All eyes were on Jerinne now, just for a moment. Then everyone ran out to the slateboard.

Raila Gendon hung back for a moment. Even fresh out of bed, Raila somehow looked luminous. "You better be ready for that run."

"I can handle it," Jerinne said.

"You better hope they all can as well." She went out into the hallway.

Jerinne followed, but as she crossed out of the threshold, something swept her leg and knocked her to the floor. Before she could react, someone else flipped her over on her back. She found herself staring at Candion and Miara, hovering right over her. Candion leaned in uncomfortably close.

"Look out there, Fendall," he said, his nose almost brushing her own. "Maybe your foot isn't quite ready yet."

"Maybe she still needs more coddling," Miara added. She almost bared her teeth at Jerinne like she was going to bite her. "I never imagined that a third-year Initiate would need coddling, but here we are."

"You would think such a person would wash out in their first or second year," Candion said.

"Especially when you look at the people who didn't make it to third year," Miara said. "You have to ask yourself how any such person would make it this far."

Jerinne had enough of that, but she kept herself from lashing out. As much as she wanted to act in anger, as much as she wanted to grab them both by their tunics and slam their heads together, she knew she couldn't.

She shouldn't. That wasn't what made a Tarian a

Tarian. And maybe Candion and Miara had forgotten that part.

"It's not yours to say," she said, sitting up, pushing her face toward them. They had already tripped her, but she wondered if they dared to take a run at her when she was ready for it. They both yielded as she sat up, standing straight and hovering over her for a moment.

"No, it ain't ours," Miara said. "But we've seen whose it is."

"Come on," Candion said. "We all have a long run this morning. Better get ready."

They went toward the bathhouses, as did the rest of the Initiates. Enther—who had been a good friend and sparring partner for two years now—went by her, not looking down as he passed. Soon everyone was gone except Raila, who stood by the slateboard with her head held low.

"Sorry," she said quietly. "They're just mad because Stancy washed out."

Jerinne got up. "Well, that's between them and him. I had nothing to do with it. I've earned my place here."

"I suppose," Raila said, looking up at the slateboard.

Sixteen third-year Initiates, their names listed up there in order. Their current rankings, which would decide their mentorships for the next months, were written plainly and boldly. Now there was no guessing who the best was, who the Masters thought had the most potential to be an Adept in the Order.

Sixteen Initiates, and Jerinne was dead last.

Dayne preferred to wake up before the sun rose, so he could do his morning stretches and routines with minimal interference. Tarians—be they Masters, Adepts, Candidates, or Initiates—tended to be early risers all around, so having the training room to himself was nearly impossible, no matter what time he got up.

Usually at this hour there were only one or two others in there. Other Candidates like Dayne, for the most part. Vien Reston, the first-year Candidate who had been assigned as the Initiate Prefect, was always up before Dayne, pushing herself through intense calisthenics that put Dayne to shame.

This morning, though, the room was almost full. Dayne had never seen it this way unless there was a scheduled training session. It seemed like every Adept and Candidate living at the Maradaine Chapterhouse had woken up in the predawn to exercise.

Dayne's confusion quickly passed. Today was the formal start day for the new year of the Tarian schedule. Why the schedule of the Elite Orders had nothing to do with the calendar or the University schedule, Dayne had never understood, and his research had never yielded a satisfying answer. He had thought someone wanted it to line up with the Victory Days, but as far as Dayne could tell, the Elite calendar predated that by centuries.

The Elite Order schedule did roughly line up with the Parliament's cycle, but that was because Oberon Micarum was a Spathian, so he used the Elite calendar as the format for the August Body. The yearly cycle ended with the End-of-Year Trials and Advancements last month in Joram, the same time the Parliament Convocation ended. The past month had been, officially, for people to travel to different cities for their new assignments. The year started now, right after elections had finished.

A handful of Adepts had come to Maradaine over the past month, and most of the Candidates had left, especially the first-years. Vien was the only first-year Candidate currently in residence, the rest heading out to cities across the country to work under the tutelage of specific masters. Much like Dayne had when he went to Lacanja with Master Denbar.

Of course, that had ended in tragedy. Denbar killed

by a lunatic, and Dayne's own career all but scuttled by the scandal.

"Morning, Heldrin," one of the Adepts said to him. Osharin, just transferred from the chapterhouse in Porvence. "Tighter in here than I expected."

"Same," Dayne said.

"Fancy a spar to loosen up?" Osharin asked.

Dayne nodded. "Happy to. Any preference as to weapons?"

"I'm partial to nothing," Osharin said with a shrug. "I don't know how it is here out west, but in Acora we always focused on going unarmed above and beyond all else."

"It was less a focus here," Dayne said, moving with him to a clear space on the floor. "But our training focused on that maxim that a Tarian might be unarmed, but never defenseless."

"Yes, exactly," Osharin said brightly. "Begin?"

Dayne nodded, and Osharin moved in with a tight and fast jab that almost cracked Dayne's nose. A quick dodge kept the blow to just a slight graze. Osharin laid into his attack: rapid, hard, focused, yet controlled and calm. Dayne responded in kind—dodging and blocking each blow with practiced ease. They fell into a rhythm for a moment, and then Osharin switched tactics, mixing punches with attempts to grapple Dayne, get ahold of his arm and pin him.

Dayne showed him that was pointless. Osharin got a grip on Dayne, but Dayne had nearly a foot over the man, and was considerably stronger. Osharin was unable to get the leverage he wanted to twist an arm behind Dayne's back.

Instead, Dayne used the man's attempt to flip him over onto the floor.

Osharin landed on his back, letting out a hard groan as he hit. Dayne wasn't sure if he had hurt him, but before he could ask, Osharin spun and landed a hard kick on Dayne's shin. That hurt hard enough to make Dayne's leg buckle, and he stumbled back to keep from falling over. Osharin popped back up on his feet.

"Not bad, Heldrin," he said. "More?"

"Please," Dayne said, and let Osharin launch another attack.

"So," Osharin said as he threw punches, talking as casually as if they were sitting down for breakfast. "You grew up in Maradaine?"

"No," Dayne said. "Grew up in Jaconvale, in the Sharain region. I came here for my Initiacy when I was fifteen."

"Jaconvale? As in the mustard?"

"Mustard and cheese are what it's known for," Dayne said. "His lordship was always proud of that."

"Oh, you're one of those," Osharin said, slipping low and sweeping at Dayne's legs. He had clearly decided that with Dayne's strength and size, his legs were his greatest vulnerability.

"Those?" Dayne asked, leaping over the sweep and diving into a roll. Show the man he was more nimble than expected.

"You know," Osharin said. "Child of service class, raised in the noble house. Singled out for talent and sent here."

"Sounds like you know the story," Dayne said.

"I know there is a story," Osharin said. "I've not read it, but I've seen the pamphlets out there with your name and likeness."

Dayne wasn't quite sure what to make of that. Osharin, despite his flurry of punches and kicks, seemed quite jovial and intrigued by the matter. Some of the other Tarians, especially the Adepts, were quite put off by the press Dayne had received after he helped capture Tharek Pell, The Parliament Killer. Master Hendron, just before he left for Lacanja to take the position left vacant when Master Denbar died—

*Killed, due to your failure,* flashed across Dayne's thoughts, almost making him miss one of his blocks. Osharin's knuckles grazed his cheek, bringing him back to the spar.

"Is it worth reading?" Osharin asked.

"Depends who you ask."

Master Hendron told Dayne that he was a stain on the name Tarian, and hoped he would never become an Adept. Of course, Master Hendron was already getting his wish, but not for the reasons he thought. Dayne's chances had already died on the same day Master Denbar did.

"I have," Osharin said. "And it sounds like a bunch of these folks are mad it wasn't them."

"I wouldn't say that," Dayne said. Osharin came in with a heavy punch, and Dayne moved to deflect the blow and use Osharin's momentum to send him flying. A simple twist-throw.

Osharin, however, flipped his legs up with that throw—like he was anticipating it—and kicked Dayne in the face. Normally, this wouldn't have achieved much, but Dayne had added his own strength to it, so the result was as if he had thrown the man at himself. That set him off balance, and Osharin pressed, wrapping his legs around Dayne's neck and head before going limp. That pulled Dayne off his feet, falling back to the floor. Somehow, faster than Dayne could register, Osharin was on top of him, one knee pressed into his neck, the other leg pinning Dayne's arm to the floor.

"Nice," Osharin said, grinning wildly while breathing just as hard. He popped up to his feet and extended his hand. "Hurt you bad?"

"Just pride," Dayne said, taking his hand and pulling himself to his feet.

"Good," Osharin said. "A guy your size, I have to use all my strength to subdue, so the line between disarm and injure, it's . . . blurry."

"I saw what you were doing," Dayne said. "I got

cocky, thinking if I didn't throw a punch, you couldn't use my strength against me."

"I had to change up my strategy, once I realized you were on the defensive."

A loud rap came from the doorway, and all eyes turned to see Grandmaster Orren standing there calmly. "Good morning, all. I'm very pleased to see you all up so bright and early, and it is an important day. In addition to it being the first day of our cycle, with Initiates beginning the new year of their training, it is also a busy time in our city. I have spoken to many of you about specific duties, and if you do not have an assignment, speak to me this morning."

"Sir, if I may—" Dayne said.

Orren's eyebrow went up. "Actually, not at the moment, Dayne. I will speak to you shortly."

Dayne held back while others approached the Grandmaster. As he waited, he took up a practice sword and shield and went through his motions. No need to waste any time, when he should maintain his skills at the highest possible level.

After a few moments of this, the Grandmaster approached, scowling. "Dayne, what are you doing?"

"Sequence Nine," Dayne said. "Is there error in my form?"

"Your form is fine, as you certainly know," Orren snapped. "I meant why are you even here?"

"I always train in the morning—"

"You were given apartments at the Parliament as part of your appointment."

"Well, yes, but—"

"There is no 'yes but,' Dayne," the Grandmaster said. "That is where you should be, not here. Don't you have duties to attend to this morning?"

"I wanted to talk to you about that. I'm supposed to address members of the press in dress uniform, according to the marshal chief. Is that appropriate?"

"Dayne," Grandmaster Orren said sharply. "You need to be able to handle this assignment without having me hold your hand. Work with the marshals. Coordinate with us as needed. But I shouldn't be seeing you here in the morning, because that tells me you are neglecting your post. Wasn't there already enough trouble with you thinking you knew better than my orders?"

"Yes, sir," Dayne said, putting the practice weapons away. "I'll dress and get over there right away."

"Do that," Orren said. "I will have your trunk sent over today, and your quarters here will be reassigned. Don't be sneaking back each night."

"No, sir," Dayne said. "As you wish."

He raced up to his quarters to get his dress uniform. As he changed, one thing seemed clear. This new assignment, this position, felt less like a way to serve the Tarian Order, and more like a place to shuffle him off to so he could serve his final year of Candidacy out of the way. A minor exile before being forced to leave the Order completely.

# Chapter 6

NORMALLY DAYNE LIKED the Tarian dress uniforms. They had a style and regality that he relished. He would have loved it if he and other members of the Order had put on their dress uniforms for the parade the other day, gleaming coats with shining buttons and bright shields on their arms, and marched through Victory Square with smiles and waves.

The Tarians were a proud part of Druth history, and that should be celebrated. The dress uniform was part of that.

But to wear it to stand on a podium and read a prepared statement for members of the press felt . . . crass.

"It's what you're here for," Samsell said. "Look good, read the statement, answer a question or two—within the bounds of what we said—and get off the dais. Are we clear?"

"I understand," Dayne said. "Let's go."

Samsell opened the door and let Dayne take the lead to a small room where a handful of press people were waiting. Dayne didn't know who any of them were, and as he looked around the room, he noticed that Hemmit and Maresh were not there. Perhaps they weren't considered important enough. Dayne would try to change that, if he could, for them and other smaller prints.

"Good morning," he said as he took his place at the podium. He noticed that Samsell stayed at the back of the room. He wasn't going to do anything but watch Dayne and make sure he followed the rules. "My name is Dayne Heldrin, and I'm with the Tarian Order."

"You're the one who caught Tharek Pell, right?" one of them asked.

"That's right, sir," Dayne said. He caught a cross glare from Samsell. "But right now I'm here to talk about the current situation with the elections. As of today, every archduchy in the nation has held its elections, and the results have been tabulated and are being securely transported to Maradaine for final verification and certification. As is custom, we will release the results on Reunification Day, at the end of the week."

A number of hands went up from the journalists.

"Please, let me finish," Dayne said, looking back to his sheet of prepared remarks. "We know there have been concerns regarding disruptions of the election. We are aware that on the day of Sauriyan elections, on the south side of the city, there were multiple incidents of unrest in western districts. While this surely made the process of voting challenging for some citizens living in those neighborhoods, it is the official opinion that none of these incidents were specifically targeting the election, and had minimal effect on its outcome."

Dayne almost choked getting that part out. He had heard about some of those incidents. Hemmit and Lin had been chasing a story in Seleth when a full-on riot broke out in the street. Lin was hit in the head with a brick. The entire neighborhood had been terrorized, and surely that had kept many people from voting.

Perhaps that wouldn't matter much in terms of the Parliamentary results, but in citywide races for the Council of Aldermen or the Commissioners of Loyalty, those few votes could make a great difference.

"Furthermore, there were multiple incidents of directed, intentional disruption yesterday for the elections for the Archduchy of Maradaine. While these demonstrations were designed to prevent good citizens from reaching the polling stations, they were dealt with quickly and judiciously."

"These were protestors, right?" one of the journalists called out. "And radicals?"

Dayne coughed and looked back at his notes. "Yes, according to reports there were at least five discrete incidents involving members of the Open Hand, the Deep Roots, the Tenfold Fire, Haltom's Patrio—" He stopped and looked to Samsell. "There are still Haltom's Patriots out there?"

"It was a small group of an isolated cell," Samsell called out from the back of the room. "It's noted there."

Dayne looked down on his sheet. "The members of the Patriots have all been arrested and charged with sedition against the crown."

"Why are you telling us this instead of him?" a reporter asked.

"Because this is his job," Samsell said. "So let him do it."

"Weren't you there for one of these disruptions? The Open Hand members at Victory Square?"

"Yes, that's right," Dayne said.

"You defended the protestors," another said. Dayne had seen him before—he didn't remember the name, but he recalled that reporter had hassled him when they had left the Parliament after subduing Tharek. "Are you sympathetic to their cause?"

"Absolutely not," Dayne struck back. "I am opposed to anyone preventing others from exercising their civic duty to vote in free elections."

"But you defended them."

"I protected them from being injured by the crowd," Dayne said. "I did not defend their position or their actions. I don't agree with their positions or their methods, but that doesn't mean they aren't human beings, and that doesn't mean they deserve to be beaten by an angry crowd."

Another hand went up, a young woman. "If you are, as you say, opposed to anyone preventing others from exercising their civil duty to vote, then are you a supporter of the Suffragist movement?"

"Mister Heldrin's personal politics are not the issue here," Samsell said quickly. "Nor should he be expressing them here under this platform, or while in his uniform."

"Marshal Chief Samsell is correct," Dayne said. "My opinion of political issues is not the matter at hand."

"But you said you disagreed with the Open Hand's position," she said. "So you have expressed some opinions."

"That was—he asked me a specific question about defending them," Dayne sputtered. "I was clarifying my actions."

"Do you feel like you have a duty to intercede in political affairs?" one reporter asked.

"What responsibility do you have?" another shot at him.

"Especially in the light of events here last month." Again, the reporter who had harassed Dayne. "You were not here under the authority of the Parliament, or the King's Marshals, or even of your own Order. You just showed up."

This riled one of the other reporters. "He showed up and saved everyone!"

"That's what we were told, but *why* did he show up?"

"Everyone!" Dayne shouted. "I understand that this

is a very . . . exciting topic. But its not the one we're here to discuss."

"No," the harassing reporter said. "But this is the first chance we've had to hear directly from you since that incident. And other than giving *The Veracity Press* an exclusive story."

"That was their own story because they were there—"

"Which is somewhat suspect!"

"All right, enough," Samsell said, coming up to the podium. "We will brief you on the state of all things involving the election—which was the only topic of discussion here today—tomorrow at the same time."

The reporters all started barking more questions, but Samsell pulled Dayne off the podium and out the door before he could respond.

"Was that terrible?" Dayne asked.

"I've seen worse," Samsell said. "For a first time, it was fine."

Dayne groaned. "And I'll have to do that all week?"

"Yes," Samsell said. "And I've got something else for you. Something a bit more . . . informal."

Dayne had a bad feeling about what that meant. "Does it involve the Open Hand? Bishop Issendel?"

"In about an hour, his people are going to be released from the stationhouse."

"No charges filed against them."

"Right," Samsell said. "Exactly why this can't be done in any official capacity. Certainly not by a constable or a King's Marshal or a member of Parliament. . . ."

He was hedging. Rarely did that mean something good. "So what do you need?"

Samsell smiled. "Go down there and gently suggest that it would be best if they recognized that their mission is finished, and they should go home to Scaloi. No threats—"

"Absolutely not!"

"Good. Just let them know that we would be very grateful if they ended their little crusade." He paused, grinding his teeth. "And less so if they don't."

"I want your faces to touch the ground when you drop!" Vien shouted. "Then when you come back up you better touch the sky!"

All sixteen third-years were out of breath, sweating through their cottons, and wishing they were dead. Jerinne felt that way, and imagined the others did as well. Even still, she followed instructions, dropping down so her nose touched the wooden floor of the training room, and then pushing herself up with her arms while pulling her legs up into a crouch, and springing up in the air as high as she could jump.

This had been going on for thirty minutes, and that was after the five-mile run, with only a brief respite for breakfast. Not that any of the third-years had been able to eat anything. At least two had thrown up after the run, and those were just the ones Jerinne had seen. Likely there were others who just hid it better.

Jerinne certainly wanted to. After the run, and then the high-intensity calisthenics, she just wanted to fall down and die. She had never been pushed—none of the Initiates had been pushed—like this in the first two years.

Madam Tyrell had pushed them through a cycle of calisthenics: salutations, crunches, jumps, pushes, crouches. As soon as Madam Tyrell was done, Master Nedell stepped in and put them through the same paces, and then when he finished, Vien came in fresh and took them through it again at double the pace.

"This is the best you have?" Vien asked. "You've got more in you, people. Just push it. Through the pain. Keep it hard, keep it strong."

Jerinne's ankle was on fire. Every ounce of her body hurt, but her ankle was the worst. But she was not going to let anyone here know that. She'd push through it all. She'd bear whatever Vien gave her.

"Come on, Enther!" Vien shouted. "Is that all you have, Initiate?"

Jerinne could see Enther from the corner of her eye. He had lost pace, lost his breath. He stumbled as he dropped into the crouch, and almost fell over. He tried to spring up for the next salutation, but Jerinne didn't think he could keep standing.

On the far side of the training room she saw Madam Tyrell go to the Incentive shelf. The Incentives—wooden balls wrapped in leather—were Madam Tyrell's favorite way to train Initiates in dodging and blocking skills. The Incentives could be thrown fast and hard, and Madam Tyrell had a strong arm and wicked aim.

In a blink Madam Tyrell scooped up three Incentives and hurled them at the third-years. The first cracked Maskier in the side, knocking him over. The second smashed Liana in her hip. And the third was coming for Enther's head.

Jerinne sprang forward, grabbing Enther and spinning him around to put herself between him and the Incentive. It hit her in the small of the back, stung like blazes. Despite herself, she cried out.

"Hold!" Vien shouted. Everyone stopped, panting, all looking like they wanted to fall over. Maskier and Liana were on the ground, and Enther was on his knees, arms clutched around Jerinne's waist.

"Initiate Fendall!" Vien shouted. "You left formation!"

"I was—I was—" She struggled just to breathe.

"You what? You thought you didn't need to continue?"

"Enther was about to be struck," Jerinne said through her wheezing breath.

"Enther wasn't keeping pace," Vien said. "Nor were Maskier or Liana. And don't you smirk, Candion, you were on the verge of dropping as well."

Enther tried to speak, but he couldn't even manage anything other than gasps, still clutching on to her.

"He needs water," Jerinne said.

"He needs to be able to dodge Incentives on his own," Vien said. "What made you think you should take the hit for him?"

Jerinne wanted to scream at Vien, pick up the Incentive and smash it on her nose. But that wouldn't help.

What would Dayne have done? What would Dayne say?

"Because I'm a Tarian," Jerinne said. "And that's what we do."

"Finally," Madam Tyrell said. "Someone gets it."

At least three of the Initiates dropped to the floor.

"All right," Madam Tyrell said. "Get some water, stretch and cool down. In twenty minutes we're on staff drills."

Jerinne let herself sink to the floor, holding Enther up. "You all right?"

"I . . . I just need a moment," he wheezed.

Raila came over with two cups of water. She handed one to Jerinne and held the other for Enther to drink. "I should have done that," she said.

"You're ranked fifth," Jerinne said. "You don't have anything to prove right now."

"We all have something to prove," Enther said. He took another gulp of water, then added, "You probably won't be last after today. Maybe now I will be."

"Nonsense," Raila said, caressing his head. "It's gonna be Maskier. We all know that."

Enther laughed, and Jerinne did despite herself.

Jerinne looked up and locked eyes with Madam Tyrell, who gave her the barest of nods.

"Come on," Jerinne said, extracting herself from Enther's body. "Let's stretch this out, or we're going to feel even worse tomorrow."

"I don't think that's possible," Raila said.

Jerinne already knew she would feel worse tomorrow. No matter where she was on the rankings, someone else in this room was going to be last, and she wouldn't wish that on any of them.

And this was going to be their life for the next year.

Hemmit had been waiting outside the stationhouse for hours. He had already gone in twice, asking when the protesters were due to be released, but they refused to give him a straight answer. The desk clerk told him enough to know that they were still there, and that no charges had actually been filed at this time. His credentials as a member of the press got her to give him that much.

He wondered how long the Constabulary could hold someone in custody in the stationhouse without specific charges being laid upon them, without being brought before a judge, and without the counsel of Justice Advocate. He did, on occasion, regret leaving the Royal College before finishing his letters, especially in his Law classes. He knew his rights—he could recite all the Rights of Man, of course—and he knew that the Constabulary would do their best to bend around those Rights as much as they could.

That was why the city needed him, needed *The Veracity Press*. The Justice Advocate's office did what it could to stem the zeal of the Constabulary and City Protector, but the power of the press was the real force for truth and justice.

Hemmit could smell injustice at work. He didn't agree with these protestors, but by Saint Illaria, they had a right, and he would support those rights with his own voice.

By midmorning, Lin and Maresh had arrived, neither of them looking too pleased. "Are we holding today's edition?" Maresh asked. "We need to start printing in an hour if we're going to get any of delivery boys working for us this afternoon."

"Where are we with the issue?" Hemmit asked.

"Well," Lin said, sounding even more vexed than Maresh. "We've spent most of the morning getting the press plates laid out, except there's a great big empty space in the center of the main page for this story that *you* said was critical."

"It is critical," Hemmit insisted. "You have my placeholder version of the story from yesterday, right?"

Maresh sighed. "It's weak."

"I know it's weak," Hemmit said. He didn't have any proper sources, or even names. Without getting to talk to the protestors, he only had his observations from yesterday's protest.

"I beefed it up a little. Did some legwork, found a pamphlet the Open Hand put out a while ago. Incorporated that into it. But even then, it's missing its heart."

"I'm aware," Hemmit said. "I managed to get some names out of the desk clerk. The ringleader—at least the one at the protest—is Sister Frienne Okall. She used her page run to contact someone at Saint Rendalyn's."

"Not to a lawyer?" Lin asked.

"Priests can also be lawyers," Maresh said. "But Rendalyn's? Isn't that the Guest House?"

Hemmit kicked himself that he didn't recognize that. Saint Rendalyn's was not a proper church, ministering to the souls of the people. Instead, it was the private retreat of the Bishop of Maradaine, a well-appointed home where he and his preferred guests in the clergy could engage in "sabbaticals."

The clergy were no different from the nobility, when it came down to it. Just as fattened, just as decadent.

"So who does she have at the Guest House who would help her?" Hemmit asked. "There's a story."

"What's a story?" Dayne had come up on them, all still standing in the square outside the stationhouse. He looked rather out of sorts, but yet still had a broad smile on his face. Even the worst of news in his life wouldn't keep him from trying to brighten someone else's day. "Have they been released?"

"Not yet," Hemmit said. "You came to check on them?"

"On the Open Hand as a whole," Dayne said. "There are . . . concerns."

"I'm sure there are," Hemmit said. "So what's your angle?"

"Talk to the cloistress, I would hope, and then maybe get a chance to talk to their leader."

"Who's the leader?"

"Bishop Ret Issendel."

"Bishop," Lin said meaningfully. She had thought the same thing that Hemmit had.

"That would explain sending word to the Guest House," Hemmit said. He started jotting down some notes, and handed them to Maresh. "Clean that up, get it in the story, and take it to press."

"Without the full story?" Maresh asked.

"That's the story we have now. We'll have more tomorrow."

"What is going on?" Dayne asked.

"You want to talk to this Bishop Issendel?" Hemmit asked. "Then stick with me, because I have a feeling he'll be coming here."

Unity Stationhouse was the largest Constabulary building in Maradaine, and second in importance to only the primary administrative center of the Commissioner's Plaza in Welling. It was an old building, a fortress dating back to at least the fifth century—though surely every stone had been repaired or replaced in all that time— when this side of the river wasn't part of Maradaine, but Anicari. The northern city wasn't absorbed into Maradaine until Haldrin IV built the new royal palace on this side of the river at the end of the sixth century.

In the years since then the building had been a garrison for royal bannermen, a meeting hall for the Duchy Council, and an executionary prison during the dark years of the Cedidore kings, and for the Inquest in the years before the Incursion of the Black Mage.

As such, it had a fair amount of holding cells, going several levels underground. It was not an actual prison, not in the same sense that Quarrygate or Fort Olesson was. Supposedly, if they had to, Unity Stationhouse could hold several hundred prisoners. Like every other stationhouse in the city, they could only use their holding cells for temporary purposes—recent arrests, people awaiting trial or transfer, or just cooling off until morning after a raucous night. But without charges filed, they were not supposed to hold anyone more than a day.

"How much longer do you think it's going to be?" Dayne asked.

"I could go ask again," Hemmit said. "But I've thoroughly annoyed the desk sergeant in there."

"Maybe I should thoroughly annoy him as well," Dayne said.

Lin came back over to them, carrying two paper sacks. "Maresh is set to print." She handed one of the sacks to Hemmit. "Crispers and tack for the both of you."

"And the other?" Dayne asked.

"Crispers and tack for me," she said. She reached into her sack and pulled out a newssheet-wrapped sandwich. "And maybe also a fish crackle."

Dayne took the sack from Hemmit. He had been at it all day and was more than a little peckish. "I had more than my share of fish crackle in Lacanja."

"That's your problem," Lin said. "So is there anything, or do I tell Maresh to go?"

"I already said he should—" Hemmit stopped speaking and looked around. "Does something seem odd to you?"

Dayne glanced around the public square in front of

Unity Stationhouse. It was a typical sort of plaza—roadways for pedalcarts and carriages along the outside, and a wide walkway that was cluttered with pedestrians and cart shops, including more than a few food vendors. As Dayne bit into a crisper, he saw it.

Most people in the square were going about their business—buying food, haggling with merchants, arguing with each other—but in motion. But there were several people, at least a dozen, who were standing still, watching the stationhouse. None of them were together, and in isolation, they didn't look odd. Saints, they wouldn't look very different from Dayne and Hemmit. But now he had noticed them, and they were standing out more and more.

"This could be trouble," Dayne said.

"They're coming out," Lin said, her mouth half-stuffed with her fish crackle.

Twenty people came down the steps from the stationhouse, with the cloistress front and center. As soon as they reached the bottom of the steps, they paused and linked arms.

Then those other people around the square moved in unison, forming more human chains around the square.

"We were locked up, treated like refuse!" the cloistress shouted. "For exercising our rights! For standing up for truth! For having the audacity to say that this country—this country which would do this to us—is not for us!"

"Shut it!" someone yelled from the crowd that was starting to form around them.

"We will not be silenced!" she shouted. "We are the Open Hand! We stand together strong! We will not be bullied into submission! We will not be kept from our mission! We will be heard, and we will be our own nation, free from this tyranny!"

"Lin," Hemmit said. "Run to Maresh. Let's hold that printing."

"I'm not moving," Lin said.

Dayne wasn't sure what to do or where to look. There were quite a lot more Open Hand members this time, enough to block the street. Pedalcarts and carriages stopped, and pedestrians were having a hard time getting around them.

"Get out of the way!" someone shouted.

"We will not!"

"That tears it!" Dayne wasn't sure who said that, but he saw the rock as it went flying toward the cloistress.

He wasn't in position to get between her and the rock. Even if he threw his shield, he could never throw it fast enough, accurate enough, to protect her.

But he didn't need to. A man—a skinny man with shaggy hair and scraggly beard—calmly stepped up next to the cloistress, catching the rock with little concern.

"Please," he said calmly. Dayne noticed the priestly collar he wore. "Let us all move forward, in the name of peace, and let our words be heard. We deserve our right of voice."

Several men in the crowd surged toward the priest and the cloistress's human chain group. Dayne tried to move closer, but the crowd was already getting thick and agitated, making it hard to force his way through without hurting someone.

"Where do you get your bones?" someone yelled.

"Who do you think you are?"

"Clear the rutting street!"

"No need to talk like that," the priest said. "We can all be people of peace."

"Who the blazes are you?"

Dayne already knew the answer.

Bishop Ret Issendel, the leader of the Open Hand.

# INTERLUDE: The Priest

**B**ISHOP TAURIAN ONELL of Abernar was grow-ing quite tired of Saint Rendalyn's. It was supposed to be a luxurious retreat in the city, but felt more like a prison every day. He had expected to be a "guest" of the Bishop of Maradaine in a very informal sense, and be allowed to pray, study, and go about his business.

Instead, Bishop Haskernell of Maradaine was con-stantly craving his company, demanding that they have breakfast and supper together daily, each meal with an extended "table talk" that lasted hours.

Blessed saints above, the Bishop of Maradaine spent most of his day at his meal table.

Bishop Onell of Abernar needed to escape from the man from time to time. In part, to slip off to his meet-ings with the members of the Grand Ten. But mostly because Bishop Haskernell was driving him quite mad.

He had hoped having a new guest at Saint Rendalyn's would give him some relief, that Haskernell would be focused on the new toy and leave him alone. There was no such fortune.

"Taurian," Bishop Haskernell called out as Onell tried to make his way out the door. "I'm about to take some tea. Come join me in the study."

Politeness forced Onell to comply, even though Haskernell did not outrank him. Only three people did: the Archbishop of Sauriya, the Cardinal of Druthal, and of course, the king. The first two weren't even in Maradaine, and the third was probably scarcely aware of his existence.

And while King Maradaine XVIII was, formally, the head of the Church of Druthal, it was not a power he actively exercised, nor would Bishop Onell respect any such exercise of power to be godly and true.

This king, this half-breed on the throne, he was not the chosen of God to rule the Druth people. Of that, Bishop Onell was certain. The nation had endured this false line as a test. God was testing the faithful, testing the pure. God had already visited tragedy upon this Untrue King, striking down his queen and child, so this sullied line of impurity would not continue.

The True Line lived, and it would be restored to the throne. Bishop Onell had joined with the Grand Ten to ensure that, to ensure a righteous, godly Druthal that was what it had been, what it ought to be. Even if he had to endure the magical abomination that was Major Altarn.

He had endured so much, including the relentless prattle of Bishop Haskernell.

"Good day," he said, entering Haskernell's study. "Didn't we just have breakfast?"

"Did we? It seems like hours ago," Haskernell said. "I've been hoping to sit with you and Bishop Issendel at the same time, but that man is quite busy."

"Aren't we all?" Onell asked.

"Well, you're here on sabbatical," Haskernell said. "He's here with his flock, on a mission."

The official excuse to be in Maradaine had proven far more trouble than it should have been. Perhaps he should have taken a page from Issendel's book. The man was here on a mission that was just as subversive and revolutionary as Onell's, but Issendel had the stones to be open about it.

Of course, that was because while Issendel's plans were subversive and revolutionary, they weren't actually treasonous. Onell could not say the same.

"Where is Issendel now?" Onell asked. "I would think he would be available now that the election is over. Wasn't that what he and his people were protesting?"

"Something about that, I didn't pay much attention," Haskernell said. "I think he is about."

"He wasn't at breakfast," Onell said. Perhaps mentioning the meals Issendel missed would keep Haskernell's attention on him.

"Yes, he received some troubling notes from a page today. He was very upset by it all. Said his appetite was quite turned by it."

"Hmm," Onell said. "Then perhaps he could use some tea. Perhaps I should go find him for you."

"Oh, no," Haskernell said, pouring a cup for Onell. "Don't be a bother to him. And nor should you trouble yourself with his problems. You are here for sabbatical, you should enjoy it."

"I really should, shouldn't I?" Onell said pointedly. Surely his tone was lost upon Haskernell.

"You should," he said. "Any day now we will hear news from Kyst, and Sauriya will be in need of a new archbishop. I think you will have many busy days in front of you then."

Many indeed. Things were proceeding according to

plan, and Onell just needed to endure it with patience. And once he was secure in his position, he would have Major Altarn arrange for Bishop Haskernell to drink down that same poison that was bringing the Archbishop of Sauriya to his slow, painful death.

Saints knew there was no shortage of opportunities to poison the man, given his constant mealtime.

So he sat down and endured. No meeting with those two from the Parliament today. They would get by. Right now, things were going as they needed to. And with some luck, Bishop Issendel and his foolery would only help their ploys even further.

# Chapter 7

JERINNE WAS NOT ABOUT to let anyone know how much she was hurting, even though she was certain everyone else in the room was hurting just as much. Except Vien. Vien seemed to be in a place of joy.

Vien was at the far end of the training room with a bow and a quiver full of blunt-tip arrows. Jerinne and the other third-years were clustered together, each with a shield on their arm. There had been a brief respite for lunch and quiet contemplation exercises, but they were back into full training by two bells.

"All right," Madam Tyrell said, taking a place against the wall. "Line up. One at a time each of you will take your place in front of me. Miss Reston will then proceed to fire several arrows at me. She will change up how many she's going to fire each time, how fast she fires, but one thing will be consistent: She will be trying to hit me."

She leveled her eyes at the Initiates. "Let us be clear on two points. One, Vien is an excellent shot. And two,

I do not wish to be hit. If I am, it's because you failed. Do not disappoint me."

Vien cracked her neck and drew an arrow. "Fendall! You'll be first!" She then fired the arrow before Jerinne had any reasonable chance to get into position. She dove forward, throwing her shield to put it in front of the arrow before it hit Madam Tyrell. It clanged off the flying shield, and both things went careening off to the far corner of the room. Vien nocked and fired two more arrows, then another. Jerinne had no chance to reclaim her shield, and nothing else to block the arrows with.

Except her body.

She jumped in front of Madam Tyrell, putting her back to Vien. Those three blunt tips smashed into her back in quick succession. It hurt far more than she was expecting or prepared for, and she cried out despite herself. She then turned around to face Vien, who had drawn another arrow. But her fingers fumbled in the moment their eyes met, and the arrow dropped to the ground.

"Effective choice," Madam Tyrell said. "Though you'd be dead under normal circumstances."

"The assignment wasn't to survive," Jerinne said, forcing the words out, despite every breath bringing pain. "It was to keep you from getting hit."

"Interesting," Madam Tyrell said, and Jerinne couldn't hear anything more in her tone.

"Begging pardon for the intrusion," someone said from the doorway. Ellist, the head of the staff. "But Miss Fendall has a visitor in the main lobby."

"A visitor?" Vien asked as she came to collect the arrows. "Isn't that special?"

"Do we know who it is, Ellist?" Madam Tyrell asked.

"Someone from the High Justice Advocate's Office."

"She should go," Madam Tyrell said, giving a small gesture to Vien to not make further comment. "Get yourself cleaned up, Jerinne. Ellist, tell our visitor she'll be with them shortly."

Jerinne left, doing her best not to show how much pain she was in until she was well out of the training room. There was no time to go to the bathhouse, though she would need that before the day was done, so she made her way to the water closet. She stripped off her pullover and splashed water on her body, hoping she washed off any blood that was on her face. She tried to inspect her side and back, assuming she was covered in bruises. What she could see was horrible, and what she felt seemed even worse. No part of her didn't hurt.

She grabbed a fresh pullover from the linens and put it on. Decent enough for guests, she went to the lobby to find a smartly dressed woman pacing back and forth.

"Miss Jerinne Fendall?" she asked as Jerinne came in.

"That's right," Jerinne said, extending her hand. "And you are?"

"Arthady Mirrendum, of the Justice Advocate. We were supposed to meet in my offices, but I was informed that you were otherwise occupied."

Jerinne had no idea who had informed her of that. "We've begun formal training for third year," Jerinne said. "It's a bit intense."

"Yes, so I can . . . perceive." She cautiously pointed to Jerinne's chin. Jerinne touched it gingerly. It was definitely bruised, though she didn't remember when that had happened.

"How can I help you, Miss Mirrendum?" Jerinne asked.

"As you are no doubt aware, the preparation for the trial of Tharek Pell is underway. You are to be called as a material witness toward the dismissal of his charges."

"The dismissal?" Jerinne asked. "I can't see how that can possibly work."

"Mister Pell believes—"

"Mister Pell killed four members of Parliament and at least fifteen King's Marshals."

"He claims those acts were necessary. And that you would testify to their necessity."

"Me?" Jerinne said a bit too loud, and her voice echoed through the hallway. "I saw him do it. He killed six in front of me."

"I understand," Miss Mirrendum said. "For today, I'm only here to establish a few particulars in the case. So you acknowledge you did witness the events in question."

"Of course I did!"

"So you can testify honest and true to what you saw?"

"Absolutely I will!"

"Excellent," Miss Mirrendum said. She extended her hand. "We will call you for initial statements on the afternoon of the twenty-ninth."

"I'm not going to say anything to clear him!"

"I only need you to tell the truth," Miss Mirrendum said, with an infuriating calm. She still had her hand out to Jerinne.

"How can you defend him? How can you want to get his charges dismissed?"

"Because it is his right, Miss Fendall," Miss Mirrendum said. "Even if he were the most depraved, maniacal murderer in the history of Druth, he would deserve that. Someone must plead the case of every single accused, so that justice remains fair and honest." She finally withdrew the offered hand. "Good day, Miss Fendall. The twenty-ninth. Four bells in the afternoon. Officers of the court will be sent for you if you do not appear."

With a final nod, she went out the door.

"Are you all right?"

Jerinne turned to see an Adept—one of the new ones. "It's nothing just—"

"Sounds like a mess," he said. "It isn't right for her to get officers of the court to drag you in to testify in his defense. That's some sewage." He was a rustic sort of man: a few days behind on shaving, a nose that had taken its share of hits, and a smile that other girls would find disarming.

"I appreciate the opinion," Jerinne said. "I don't think we've met. Jerinne."

"Osharin," he said. "Just transferred from Porvence. I'm about to head over to Fort Merrit for some sort of briefing with the army folk, whatever that means."

"Good luck with that," Jerinne said. Something about him raised the hair on the back of her neck.

He gave her a quick salute and went to the door, then turned back. "I do mean, it isn't right for her to do that. It's illegal to use the officers of the court to compel someone to testify, either against themselves or in defense of another. It's an enumerated right."

"Thanks," Jerinne said. She did know that, and didn't need Osharin to explain it to her. He left, apparently satisfied he had performed some duty.

"It does sound like a mess."

Raila was in the hallway, looking a bit sheepish.

"It is," Jerinne said. "Why are you out here?"

"We finished that exercise, and Madam Tyrell dismissed us for baths and medicinal therapy before dinner."

"Saints, I need all that," Jerinne said. "Let's go to the baths and you can tell me how bad my back is."

"All right," Raila said, a slight smile on her lips. "You promise to do the same for me?"

That was something Jerinne would gladly promise.

"Please!" Dayne called out as he approached the steps. "This isn't helping!"

"Helping what?" Bishop Issendel said as he turned his attention to Dayne. "What do you need?"

A brick came flying from the crowd, and Dayne blocked it with his shield before it hit the bishop. "They'll just get angrier."

"They will, and it's a tragedy," said Issendel.

People in the crowd were engaging with the

protestors, grabbing and shouting. No outright violence yet, but they were trying to pull the protesters apart.

"This isn't the way," Dayne said.

"What other way is there? I will stand for my cause, but I will not fight. I will not take up arms and draw blood. That is not the way."

Dayne was stunned for a moment, as he realized he agreed with the bishop.

"This Tarian engaged with us yesterday," the cloistress said. "But he was fair, and put his shield between us and the crowd's wrath."

"I respect your path, Tarian," the bishop said. "Please respect mine."

"Get out of here!" someone in the crowd yelled.

"I would love to, friend," the bishop called back. He took a few steps down the stairs. "I would love to take all my people and go home to Scaloi. That is our country, where we belong. But we don't have our own country, we are a part of yours. And so we are here, exercising our rights."

"I'll exercise a right!" one man in the crowd shouted, and bolted toward the bishop with a long knife drawn. He covered the distance before Dayne saw him coming. Dayne attempted to sprint, get to the man before he stabbed the bishop.

"Peaceful," Bishop Issendel said, holding up his hand. The word was spoken quietly but felt like a thunderclap. And the man dropped his knife on the ground. "Our ways are peaceful, son."

"We will have peace!" the cloistress shouted. "We will have freedom! We will be our own kingdom, our own country, and we will all be stronger for it. We will have the strength of an open hand!"

"We reject the closed fist," Bishop Issendel said. He touched the cheek of the man who had been going to stab him. "That is never our way."

That man burst into tears.

Despite that, the rest of the crowd was agitated, tearing at the protestors and pulling them apart.

"Bishop," Dayne said, coming closer. "I respect what you are trying to do, but these people here have no power to aid your cause. Why hassle them?"

Constabulary whistles pierced the air before the bishop could answer, and several officers came down the steps and into the square, separating the protestors and the crowd, separating the protestors from each other.

Two officers came over to the bishop, handsticks and shackles in hand. "We just cut you all loose, and this is what you do!"

"Officer!" Dayne said, putting himself between the bishop and them. "This man is a bishop in the church, a candidate for Parliament, and he was trying to calm the crowd. Leave him be."

"He started this!" one constable said.

"And we'll—" the other started, looking like he was about to make threats at Dayne, but reconsidered right away. "Look, who the blazes are you?"

"I'm Dayne, Dayne Heldrin. I'm—I'm a Tarian with the Parliament offices."

"So you think you have authority here?"

"No, I—" Dayne said, thinking. "I'm just saying, as a citizen who was here for the whole event, no crime was committed. No one should be taken into custody right now."

"What about that knife there?" the officer said, pointing to the knife on the ground. "Someone was looking to stab someone."

"But no one did," Bishop Issendel said. "I assure you, officer, should someone have been injured, I would want the malefactor arrested. No such thing has occurred."

"What is that accent?" the other officer asked.

The first said, "He's Scallic. They're all Scallic. Can't you smell the pig on them?"

"That's not necessary, officer," Dayne said. "In fact, I think you should apologize."

"I—" the officer said, and once again looked up at Dayne's face a good foot above his own. Then he turned to the bishop. "I'm sorry, your eminence. My words were thoughtless."

"Of course, son," the bishop said. He then gave a brief signal to the cloistress, and she broke her human chain, as did the others. In moments the Open Hand protestors melted into the regular pedestrians. "We have said what we need to for today."

The two Constabulary officers both nodded, and even though they looked unsatisfied with how things went, they walked away.

Dayne found Hemmit and Lin at his side. "Everything all right?" Hemmit asked.

"It seems," Dayne said, though he wasn't entirely sure.

Issendel approached the man who had tried to stab him, still standing there in almost frozen reverie. He bent down and picked up the knife. "Have more care with this in the future, son," he said, placing it in the man's hand. "A simple mistake can lead to much regret."

The man mutely wrapped his fingers around the hilt of the blade and put it back in his belt, and then nodded and walked away.

Issendel then turned to Dayne and the others. "Well, good sir. You are an interesting case."

"As are you, your eminence."

"None of that," Issendel said. "Just 'Ret' is fine, please."

"Are you the leader of the Open Hand?" Hemmit asked.

"That's very direct," Issendel said with a smile. "I appreciate that. You're with a newsprint?"

"*The Veracity Press.*"

Issendel turned to Lin. "As are you, *mesame*?"

Lin nearly snarled. "*Çe da cseseh, rezette.*"

"I do," he said with a chuckle. "And that's actually true about my father."

Lin stormed off.

"I fear I offended," the bishop said. "Have care with Linjari women, we're always told."

"So are you?" Hemmit asked.

"I speak for the interests of my people, some are here, some are home in Scaloi. I speak for what I think Scaloi should be, and hope my words can move others. Those who believe in my cause listen to me. Does that make me a leader?"

"You're running for Parliament," Dayne said.

"Accurate in premise if not agency," Issendel said. "I have been placed on the ballot; many are in favor of my candidacy. But saying I am running, implies that I am engaged in active campaigning. If elected, I will serve, but I do not seek it."

"So you aren't here to that end?" Dayne asked.

"I am here for my cause, that being an independent queendom of Scaloi, blessed and sanctioned by the church."

"Queendom?" Hemmit asked.

"As we were centuries ago," Issendel said. He reached into his robe and pulled out a pamphlet. "I have some basic literature, but that's not what you are here for, is it?"

"No," Dayne said. "Perhaps we should leave the square and talk somewhere more private."

"A capital idea, friend," Issendel said. "But I see Sister Frienne is looking at me with some urgency, as is your Linjari mage."

Hemmit started, "How did—"

"Immaterial," Issendel said. "This is not our moment, friends. Another time." He offered his hand to Dayne.

Dayne took it, but wasn't sure how to respond. "Another time, then."

"Excellent," Issendel said, shaking Hemmit's hand. "Now I must attend to other matters." He scurried over to the cloistress, and the two of them left the square.

Lin stalked back over to Dayne and Hemmit as soon as he was gone. "Scallics," she said icily.

"You all right?" Dayne asked.

"Just annoyed," she said. "And . . . you saw that? With the knife?"

"I did," Dayne said. "Magic? Is that possible?"

"I'm not sure what that was," she said. "But I can tell you it wasn't magic."

"Come on," Hemmit said. "I think we're going to be delaying our issue until tomorrow morning. But we need to get to work on it now."

# Chapter 8

DAYNE NURSED A GLASS of wine at The Nimble Rabbit, still not sure what he saw or what he thought about it. Hemmit and Maresh were hard at work at the other end of the table, writing for the issue they planned to put out in the morning. Lin had eaten several sandwiches and stalked into the kitchens, her mood foul and dark and silent.

Two things kept drumming through Dayne's mind. One, he was opposed to the Open Hand and what they stood for, which was nothing less than the dissolution of the nation. Two, despite that, he saw Ret Issendel as a man of profound peace, one who preached to his people against violence, and believed in it. That was a powerful thing, and Dayne deeply respected that.

And he could not reconcile those two things.

He didn't even want to think about the strange power Issendel exerted over the man with the knife.

Lin came back out of the restaurant and rejoined them at their courtyard table, carrying a bundle of letters and a new bottle of wine. "Post is here," she said, dropping it on the table. She sat at the table next to Dayne, refilling his glass in addition to her own.

"You receive your post here?" Dayne asked.

"Of course we do," Maresh said. "Where do you think our press is? Where do you think we live?"

"Here at The Nimble Rabbit?"

"Yes," Hemmit said, shaking his head. He pointed to the path that led behind the restaurant and kitchens. Dayne had never actually gone into the back gardens. He had barely ever eaten inside, usually sitting in the front garden tables with Maresh and Hemmit. "There's a barnhouse back there, from when this was an old Loyalty House back in the day. We rent that from the owners, and the press is in there, and we sleep in the loft."

"You as well?" he asked Lin.

"Saints above and sinners below, never," she said. "I have my own flop away from these boys, thank you very much." She snapped the server over. "Another bottle, charcuterie, bread, two orders of crisp, and the lamb shank."

"You all right, Lin?" Hemmit asked.

"It's been a day," she said. She looked at Dayne, and he was about to ask her about what they saw the bishop do. "No."

"I didn't even say anything."

"You didn't have to. I—I took a bit of higher theory and I . . ." She hesitated for a moment, and if Dayne didn't know better, he would have thought she was frightened. "Ask me in a day or two."

Dayne wasn't sure what to make of that, and he certainly wasn't sure if Bishop Issendel was a danger. "Whatever you need," seemed like the most polite, respectful response to her.

She nodded and turned back to Maresh. "What was in the post?"

"The usual," Maresh said. "Bills due, angry rants . . . oh, the mystery artist returns."

"Mystery artist?" Dayne asked.

Maresh handed over the envelope. "Someone has been sending us these sketches of various saints. It's been a whole series. Saint Julian, Saint Benton, Saint Jontlen—"

"That one was gruesome," Lin said, waving her hands over the table and crafting images of light and shadow of those same saints. Dayne recognized Benton with his bow, the cloaked woman representing Saint Jesslyn, blood-covered Saint Jontlen. "Who do we have today?"

Dayne opened the envelope to find an image of Saint Terrence, soaking wet and taking a gift out of his sack, presumably to hand to a child. "Why Saint Terrence? Terrentin is a couple months away."

Lin chuckled. "There's little reason to any of it. Though we did get the Jontlen one a couple days before Saint Jontlen Day."

"I wonder who the artist is," Maresh said. "They have talent. But there's never anything but the picture. No name, nothing to contact them."

"What do you do with the pictures?" Dayne asked.

"We've thought about running them," Maresh said. "I mean, they posted them to us, but there's no permission. No explanation. It doesn't seem right."

The work was good, there was no denying that. Simple, but something about it was inspired, and Dayne felt it came from a place of passion.

Lin finished her magical light image. "Saint Deshar of the wise eyes, and now Saint Terrence the builder. That makes six." The six figures faced outward in a circle, and she made the image rotate so Dayne saw each one in turn. "Who will we get next?"

"Do you think they'll keep going until they do them all?" Hemmit asked. "Is that twenty-six?"

"Twenty-five," Maresh said.

"It's twenty-six," Dayne said. "Sometimes people don't count Saint Bridget because she doesn't have a holiday. Because she's about humility."

The server brought Lin several plates of food, which she wasted no time getting started on. Hemmit poured himself a glass of wine. "So what's next, Dayne?"

"I don't even know," Dayne said. "I'm supposed to be coordinating between the marshals and the Parliament and the Orders, but what does that even mean? It can't just mean talking to the press."

"Which members of the press are let into that?" Hemmit asked.

"I'm not sure how it's decided. That one fellow who gave you guff last month was there."

"Harns. He's from *Throne and Chairs*. They specifically cover, well, the government and the royal family."

Dayne nodded, and had an idea that he immediately put voice to. "If I have to be the one talking to the press, being the mule to the marshals, at the very least I will decide who is in that room. And that means you and yours."

"Don't push your chin for our sake."

"No, I mean it," Dayne said, though it was, perhaps, that third glass of wine speaking. "I want them to take you all seriously as members of the press."

"No argument from me," Lin said.

"Maresh?" Hemmit asked. "You've been quiet."

Maresh was reading a letter, and he took off his spectacles and wiped the sweat off his brow. "We . . . we might have something troubling here."

"Troubling how?"

"It's from the Sons of the Six Sisters," Maresh said.

That piqued Dayne's interest, even if he didn't know what it meant. The Six Sisters were the daughters of Lady Irielle Hessen—The Lady of the Grand Ten—who hid and protected young Prince Maradaine in 1009 during the Incursion of the Black Mage. Thanks to them he was still alive when the Black Mage was defeated, able to reclaim his throne as Maradaine XI and start the

Reunification. One of those sisters even grew up to be his queen.

But Dayne had no idea who the Sons of the Six Sisters were.

"What are they threatening now?" Hemmit asked. Maresh was still engrossed in reading it.

Threatening did not sound good. "Who are they now?"

"Anti-Parliament radicals," Hemmit said. "They think that Druthal should be for the king and the throne, and the Parliament should be disbanded or destroyed to give the power back to him."

Maresh handed the letter to Hemmit. "They are fond of bold proclamations, sometimes involving violence."

"And what does it say?"

"It says they will stop the false election of unworthy leaders, by any means they must. Stop the poison before it enters the city," Maresh said. That phrase rang a bell for Dayne, as it would any history student.

"So what are they threatening?" Dayne asked.

"They intend to capture the Acoran ballot caravans with the vote results, and destroy them."

Dayne returned to the Parliament building, letter from the Sons of the Six Sisters in hand. This time, the marshals at the door gave him little trouble, waving him through as he went down to the offices below.

"Dayne," Marshall Chief Samsell said as he came in, not looking up from the papers he was consulting. "There's no press briefing in the evening. How can I help you?"

"I have some news," Dayne said, holding up the letter.

"You talked to the Open Hand and convinced them to leave the city."

"No," Dayne said. "Well, I did talk to them."

"I know you did," Samsell said. He slid a newssheet— *Throne and Chairs*—across the table. "Lovely story about you and Bishop Issendel chatting in front of Unity Stationhouse. You protected them."

"To keep things from escalating to more violence," Dayne said.

Samsell frowned, but nodded. "Fair enough. But you apparently also kept the constables from rearresting them."

"What good would that have done?" Dayne asked. "Made them martyrs? Created more unrest? If you want me to convince them to stand down, I need to reach them in dialogue. That takes trust."

Samsell looked up and put on a broad smile. "I do appreciate that you think about these things, Dayne. I'll confess when you were first sent over here I expected little more than muscle and meat carrying a shield. So what next for this trust?"

"I'm going to try to meet Issendel again tomorrow. We'll talk, and hopefully I'll get him to see reason."

"Good, good. Is that your news?"

Dayne handed him the letter. "No, this was delivered to *The Veracity Press* today."

"*Veracity Press* and twelve others, I'm sure," Samsell said, perusing the letter. "Ah, a threat against the wagons. Of course."

"I thought you should know."

"I'm aware. These things happen every year. Someone— Patriots or Deep Roots or Sons of the Six Sisters or some other group of agitators—they get themselves all fired up and write some letters and say they're coming for the ballots." He glanced at the letter. "Well, they name which one they're attacking."

"So you can stop them?" Dayne said.

"Nothing to stop," he said, handing the letter back. "Idle threats. Nothing credible."

Dayne glanced at the letter again, noting the details. "So why isn't it credible?"

"Like I said, dozens of these a year. Not worth digging too deep on. Especially since every wagon has a marshal guard, so on the off chance that they tried something, they would fail."

Dayne turned his attention toward the maps on the wall. The Acoran ballots were scheduled to come on the Old Canthen Road, through the Miniara Pass. "Read the letter again. They mention stopping the 'poison before it invades the city.'"

"What of it?"

"You've read your history, yes?" Dayne asked. "That phrase comes from the Incursion. It's from Lief Frannel's letter to Oberon when he went to ambush Tochrin's second army. In the Miniara Pass!"

"I don't get what you're driving at."

"Samsell, they know where the ballots are coming. Isn't that worth noting?"

"Not particularly," Samsell said, taking the letter back. "Probably a coincidence. Whoever wrote it is as much a history buff as you are."

"You aren't—"

"The routes are secret. At best, that's a lucky guess. And if not: guarded by marshals. I trust those men to do their jobs. You should as well."

Dayne frowned but said nothing.

"You have a briefing in the morning, Dayne. You probably should settle in. Your apartment is ready for you. I did hear you went back to the chapterhouse last night. I understand the impulse, but you probably shouldn't. Best to follow orders, right?"

"Right," Dayne said under his breath. He wasn't convinced that Samsell took this situation seriously enough, but he had done what he could. "Nine bells tomorrow?"

"That it is," Samsell said.

"Then make sure *Veracity Press* gets in," Dayne said. That was the least he could do.

"As you wish. Now, I have work to do." Samsell's attention went back to his papers.

Dayne took one more glance at the map. The Miniara Pass would be an excellent place for an ambush; it had been a favorite of highwaymen from time to time.

Samsell said it was handled, so Dayne forced himself to trust the man.

With no further excuse to stalk around the election headquarters, he went to find his new apartment.

Dayne wound his way through the hallways in the bowels of the Parliament building to the residence to find his apartments. He wanted to be happy about this new arrangement—it was an important position, helping the government and the country. He was representing the Tarian Order. It should be grand.

But walking through the cold stone hallway, it felt like exile.

The door of his apartment was open, warm, flickering candlelight spilling out into the hallway. Dayne wasn't sure who could even be there. Even he hadn't been there yet. There was likely no need for caution; it was far too likely it was someone on the staff preparing his apartment for him.

He went in, knocking on the door in polite reflex. "Hello?"

Sitting at the table, pouring wine while surrounded by candles, was Lady Mirianne. A smile leaped to his face, and the coldness that had been creeping into his heart melted away.

"I was wondering when you would come home," she said.

"Have you been waiting here for me long?" he asked.

"Oh, saints, no," she said with a trill of a laugh. "I was

told that your new assignment meant moving to the Parliament residence, and I thought I would bring some cheer to you." She approached and kissed him gently. "Was it too forward of me?"

"Not at all," Dayne said. "I'm thrilled to see you."

She gave another kiss. "And I you. I also took the liberty of bringing you some things to stock the icebox you have here."

"I have an icebox?" Dayne asked.

"You do," she said. "No proper stove here, though I'm given to understand there is a communal commissary or kitchen or something for all the residents. Do you cook?"

"Never," Dayne said. He had always lived either on her family estate or in the chapterhouses. In either place, meals were handled by staff.

"You may be frequenting the Rabbit even more now," she said with a smile. "But I do have a few things for you." She went back over to the table and produced a large basket from behind it. Dayne was impressed she was able to lift it.

"You didn't have to do that," he said.

"Nonsense," she said. "I love and adore you, and I am in a position to care for you. So I will. Sit."

Dayne did as he was instructed, and she pushed one of the glasses of wine to him. "I appreciate it."

"Now, first," she said, producing a jar out of the basket. "We have the family pride, the Jaconvale mustard. Because of course I put that in there."

"Of course," he said.

She pulled a few more things out. "A variety of cheese, mostly of the Maradinic or Patymic varieties. Though this one is a lovely Monic cheese that I find delightful."

"How will I eat all this cheese?"

"I'd be shocked if this lasted the week for you, dear," she said. "Pickled vegetables and fruit preserves—I know you like the apples."

"I do," he said, remembering more than a few incidents from their childhood where they had absconded with bread and apple preserves from the kitchens and devoured them in the stables.

"A few cured meats, and bread," she said. "So we can have a proper simple feast tonight, you and I." She produced a knife and began slicing meat and cheese and bread.

"I'm very impressed," he said.

"That I'm doing this myself?" she asked. "It's an uncommon experience for me."

"No, that . . ." He sighed. "It's been a strange day, and I'm very happy to see you."

She put the knife down and clasped his face. "And I you." She gave him a few more kisses, and then returned to preparing plates for each of them. "Especially with how busy things have been, and are. The opening, the party—you are coming, yes?"

"Of course," Dayne said, though he wasn't entirely certain what his current duties meant for evenings or social engagements.

"And make sure the *Veracity* boys and Lin come. I fear they thought I was merely being polite. I am fond of them, and I really want them there."

"I'll let them know."

"And of course, Jerinne. I would even say Amaya, though I know she is not fond of me."

"I'll make sure they all know."

"Saints, I want to be grand, and spectacular, and unique, and historical. So, frankly, anyone in a Tarian uniform is welcome. Or Spathian. Can you spread that word?"

"I'll do what I can," he said, though he wondered why he should worry at all about party logistics at this time.

"Something is weighing on your mind, though," she said, sitting down next to him.

"A threat on the election," he said. He took a piece of

the cured spiced pork and some of the Monic cheese and spread some mustard on it.

"Election is complete," she said.

"Voting is. The ballots from the other archduchies are on their way here for formal certification."

"So what's the threat?" she said.

"Someone claimed they would ambush the Acoran ballot carriages." He added some pickle to his meat and cheese, and then bit into the concoction. It was all quite delicious. As usual, Miri's tastes were exquisite.

"Goodness," she said, sipping her wine. "And what's being done?"

"I talked to the marshals in charge," he said. "But they don't take it seriously."

She mused for a moment. "And you, Dayne Heldrin, hero and Tarian, want to charge off with your shield on your arm and stop it yourself. Am I right?"

"Guilty," he said.

"And because you are expected to be here, fulfilling your duties, you cannot."

"I'm already one foot out the gate with the Order," he said. "Blazes—if you pardon—being here feels like both feet."

"I can imagine," she said. "So you feel useless, not being able to help."

"Right," he said.

"Then the answer is simple," she said. "If you cannot act, and the marshals won't, you have to tell someone who can and will."

"Who is that?" he asked.

"I can't tell you that, darling," she said, nibbling at her cheese. "Though I suspect you have someone in mind already."

She was right again. He knew exactly who he needed.

# Chapter 9

AMAYA HAD ENDED the day with her share of bruises. Several of the third-years had done quite poorly at the arrow exercise, despite the stellar example that Jerinne had set. Amaya had noted well who allowed her to get hit. Paskins, in particular, had failed spectacularly. That was a shame, because throughout the first two years of his Initiacy, he had performed quite strongly. He had been ranked fourteenth, and that must have shaken his confidence.

That, or Vien's training regimen had pushed him to exhaustion. Amaya chuckled a bit to herself over that. She had no idea where Vien had gotten that particular bit of fire, and it was far more brutal than it had been for previous third-years, certainly. But Amaya approved.

She had taken note of the reduced number of Candidates named Adept this year. She knew the Initiacy programs in the other chapterhouses had been shuttered.

She knew the Tarians were dying.

So an even higher standard might just be the best thing

for them right now. If there were going to be fewer Tarians in the world, then by every saint and sinner, they would be the best damned Tarians she could make them into.

After supper she had bathed and taken a session with the Order's muscle man, Clinan. He was an odd little man, but his hands were healing, to the point Amaya wondered if he had some form of magic. She had quietly asked him to call Jerinne in for a session, but not to let the girl know she had called for it. Jerinne needed rest and healing, but Amaya knew well enough that girl would push herself until her legs fell off.

And Amaya was almost tempted to let her.

Or at least let Vien do it.

She went up the steps to the Grandmaster's study, where he was sitting in quiet conversation with Master Nedell.

"Ah, Amaya," Grandmaster Orren said as she came in. "I trust you are well."

"Sore," she said. "It was a good first day, I think."

"A bit aggressive," Master Nedell said. "Though perhaps it's warranted."

"Vien is . . . enthusiastic," Amaya said.

"Yes, well," Grandmaster Orren said with a small cough. "Her methods were unorthodox, and I thought it worth a conversation with her. She has, apparently, taken up something of a romantic liaison in the past weeks. With a Spathian Candidate."

"Oh, she has?" Amaya asked. Not that Vien's romances were any of her business, but she was surprised to learn of this from the Grandmaster.

"She's spent a bit of that time learning their conditioning regimen, and has implemented it in her own life. And thus, brought it to the third-year Initiates."

"I'll have her tone it down," Amaya said.

"If you wish," Orren said. "I was skeptical, but I think it merits playing out for a few days. We can always learn new things from our fellow Orders, especially with only one other to learn from."

"All right," Amaya said.

"But of course, regimen for third-years is at your discretion. They have the fundamentals, and I trust you can find the best way to blossom their talents."

Master Nedell handed her a sheet of paper. "The rankings for tomorrow."

"Oh," Amaya said, surprised. She thought she would have to have given them input on the rankings. She had been the one tracking all the third-years during the day, while Master Nedell and Grandmaster Orren had been in and out. "If you've already worked it out . . ."

"Rather simple, really," Nedell said. "Nothing today showed any significant changes."

Amaya glanced over the list, and it was largely unchanged. A couple drops, and couple rises, and that all tracked with what Amaya thought. Paskins was now at fifteenth.

And Jerinne was still last at sixteenth. That didn't seem right at all.

"Are we sure about this?" she asked. "I mean, Miss Fendall pushed herself impressively today. To keep her on the bottom—"

"Miss Fendall is a unique case," Grandmaster Orren said. His lips went tight, like he was troubled by what he was saying. "While she has a strong drive and ambition, I . . ." He trailed off. Amaya wasn't sure he really believed what he was saying.

"What the Grandmaster is saying, is that Miss Fendall advanced despite an unorthodox Second-Year Trial. She was injured, and in the line of duty, and we accommodated that in our considerations for her advancements."

"She was worthy—" Amaya said.

"Undoubtedly," Master Nedell said, holding out a hand to stop Amaya before she said more. "We knew that before the trials began. But it created a circumstance where some considered her to be given special treatment. There was already resentment amongst her cohort for being assigned a protection duty when no other Initiate was."

"The point being," Grandmaster Orren said. "She needs to be pushed, and she is the type who responds best to negative pressure."

"So it's not that she's last," Amaya said. "It's that you think you'll get the best out of her by making her last."

Grandmaster Orren nodded. "Everyone responds to pressure in different ways. In your cohort, you and Dayne responded best to competing with each other for the top slot. And as a result, everyone else stepped up to try to match you. This is the same principle, but inverted."

Amaya wasn't convinced, but it wasn't her place to say otherwise. "If you say so. If there's nothing else?"

"Yes, thank you. Rest well."

Amaya folded the list and put it in the crease of her pants, nodded to the both of them, and left.

She hoped they were right about Jerinne. Maybe it was Dayne's influence on her, but the girl fundamentally understood what the Order was supposed to be, which most others missed.

Amaya went around the Initiate barracks, making sure lamps were blown out and all were asleep, or at least quiet. Then she went to Vien's room, leaving the list for her to put up on the slateboard in the morning. Despite the hour, Vien wasn't around. Perhaps she was in the bathhouse now, or perhaps meeting her Spathian lover. It didn't matter: Vien got her job done, and well.

Exhausted, Amaya went to her own room, ready to fall onto her cot. She did not expect to find anyone waiting for her there.

"Amaya," Dayne said as soon as she entered. He looked harried, desperate. "I need your help."

Amaya looked like she was ready to tear Dayne's face off. "Why the rutting blazes are you in my room?"

"I told you—" Dayne started to say, hoping Amaya wouldn't get much louder. He didn't need to draw any attention right now.

"I am not about to 'help' you, Dayne. Surely you can see your Lady Mirianne for that!"

"What?" Dayne almost started laughing, and bit his lip. "Did you think I came here for . . . no, I wouldn't do that."

Now her face got even harder. "You wouldn't?"

"Not in a sneak-in-your-room sort of way," Dayne said.

"So why are you sneaking into my room?"

"Because I'm not supposed to be here."

"Right, you're living in the Parliament now or something?" She sat down on her bunk and rubbed her feet. "How is that?"

"Odd," Dayne said. "Part of what I'm doing is dealing with the marshals who are coordinating the election. I think there's some trouble."

She perked up a bit at that. "You think the marshals are doing something fishy?"

Dayne thought on this for a moment, then shook his head. "My read on Chief Samsell is he's legitimate, but he doesn't want anyone else in his business."

"Sounds like the marshals. So what's the trouble?"

"*The Veracity Press* folk received a declaration from some revolutionary group. Sons of the Six Sisters."

"Six Sisters?" she asked. "As in the daughters of The Lady from the Grand Ten?"

That was accurate, but he was surprised that Amaya would say that. History was not a passion of hers. "Right. Lady Hessen hid young Maradaine XI with her daughters when the Black Mage took the city. So the Six Sisters have always been a symbol tied to the contiguity of the throne."

"And The Lady was part of that," Amaya said. He

wasn't quite sure where she was going with this, but she was clearly engaged. "So what about this declaration?"

"They said they intended to ambush and destroy the Acoran votes before they reached the city for certification. I told Chief Samsell, but he said threats like that happen all the time and they aren't anything to be concerned about."

"But?" she asked,

"But they were specific about attacking the train in the Miniara Pass on the Old Canthen Road, which is the very route the ballot wagons are taking."

"So you think it's real, and he's ignoring it?"

"I think it can't be ignored."

"All right, so what do you suggest? Ride up on the Miniara Pass and see?"

"I would. Except I'm stuck here talking to the press and having my time wasted."

"That's what you do?"

"That's what they have me do."

She scoffed. "It's absurd. But, fine, you're stuck. What can I do?"

"You're an Adept! Surely you have the authority or autonomy to do something."

"I have my own duties, Dayne," she said. She shook her head. "I have a responsibility to train the third-years. I can't just traipse off and— when is this supposed ambush?"

"Tomorrow night."

She screwed her face in thought. "I do have a responsibility, but I also have a fair amount of leeway of how I exercise that."

That was promising. "What do you have in mind?"

"Let's say I take the third-years on a training exercise. A fully armed and armored hike out of the city, to the Miniara Pass and back. If that threat is hollow, it's still a perfectly good training regimen for them. And if it's real, there I am with sixteen armed elite warriors. In training."

"I could kiss you."

"Don't."

Dayne reflexively took a step back. "Of course. I just meant . . ."

"It doesn't matter what you meant. We—let's just try and stay on this level. Colleagues who respect each other and want what's best for the Order."

"And Druthal."

"And Druthal," she said. "Now get the blazes out of here and let me sleep."

"Right." Dayne went to the door. "Thank you, Amaya."

"Just go."

Dayne left and slipped out the back way of the chapterhouse compound. It wasn't perfect, but now at least he could rest easy, knowing he had done what he could. And Amaya was someone he could trust to do the right thing, he was certain of that.

"The sun is up and you are not!"

Despite every part of her body still hurting, Jerinne was ready for this. She was off her cot and on her feet as soon as she heard Vien speak.

"Well, look at all of you," Vien said as she walked through the room. "You're all so very shiny and eager today. Ready for another glorious day."

"Ready and able," Candion said. "What do you have today?"

"What do we have?" Vien asked. "You're ready for another run through the city, back here for conditioning intervals, then weapons training? That what you're ready for?"

"Yes," Candion said, looking a bit annoyed. Jerinne could see it on everyone's face: Vien's attitude as Initiate

Prefect was already intolerable. Jerinne was glad she wasn't the only one. "Maybe we can stab each other today."

"You're not ready for that," Vien said. "Definitely not you, Candion, who dropped from number four to number seven. Catastrophic, Candion."

"What?" he yelped.

"New rankings?" Enther asked.

"Every day, new rankings," Vien said. "Every day, new challenges. Today we're onto something special."

"You beat us with hammers?" Candion asked.

"That's next week. No, today is a special exercise. Full dress, uniform and mail shirt, shields and your choice of weapon from the armory. Then go to breakfast and meet us in the foyer downstairs."

"No run?" Miara asked.

"Not today," Vien said. "Dressed, armed, fed, and foyer in fifteen minutes, people. Don't hold things up."

She left the barracks, and everyone scrambled to their trunks for their uniforms and armor shirts.

"What is this?" Raila asked Jerinne as she pulled her slacks on. "Something happened last night?"

"What do you mean?"

"I mean yesterday, Vien acted like today was going to be more of yesterday, and today she's changed it to something different."

"She's messing with us," Enther said.

"No," Raila said, furrowing her brow in thought. "Something did happen, but Vien doesn't really know what. She's following new orders, either from the Grandmaster or Madam Tyrell."

"You think?" Jerinne asked. Raila put on her uniform jacket, but showed a bit of her stomach in the process. Jerinne's eye went to the bare flesh, but what she noticed were the bruises. "That's from yesterday?"

Raila looked down at her stomach. "Saints, those look horrid. Though everyone here has their share."

Jerinne took a closer look, since Raila was inviting her. The bruises were a gruesome mixture of purple and yellow. Jerinne wondered if the ones on her back were the same. "We'll be keeping the infirmary busy."

"Stop dragging, you two," Enther said. He was already fully dressed. "I'm sure I'm at the bottom of the rankings now."

"Still Fendall!" someone shouted from the doorway. He rattled off the ranking, and Jerinne was indeed last. She was surprised by that, but maybe Madam Tyrell was punishing her for some imagined slight.

Jerinne ignored it and put her boots on. It didn't matter. What mattered was where they ended the year. Advancement to Candidate. Everything else was noise.

She kept repeating that to herself as she went down to the armory with the rest of the third-years.

"All right, all right, shields for everyone," droned the irritated Candidate who had pulled armory duty. "And weapons of choice. Those are the instruction."

"I'm thinking sword," Raila said. "That's traditional, no?" Raila's voice was shaking a little. She had dropped two places in the ranking, and that seemed to have rattled her.

"Sure," Jerinne said. "But I'm going to go with the quarterstaff."

"Really?" Raila asked. "Any reason?"

"Could use the practice," she said. Though she was thinking about Fredelle Pence from the Royal First, quite adept in its use. It was as much a Tarian tradition as the sword, wasn't it?

"Quarterstaff and shield," the Candidate said, handing them over to Jerinne. As soon as she had the shield, she recognized it. From the weight, the chips on the paint, she knew it was the same one she had when she went to the Parliament. When she lost to Tharek Pell.

Perhaps that was why she was dead last.

"Come on," she said to Raila. "Let's get something in our bellies before we do whatever this is."

"This is slightly unorthodox," Grandmaster Orren said, watching the staff compile the marching packs in the lobby. Amaya was rather impressed how efficiently they had put them together.

"That's true, sir," Amaya said. "But I was thinking, what's a different way we can set these Initiates off their bearings? We can train them with weapons and physical conditioning until they vomit, bruise them within an inch of their life, but that does little beyond abuse them."

"I said something to that effect last night," he said. "I'm not saying I disapprove of this plan, I simply find it odd that you came up with it so suddenly."

"Inspired in my sleep," she said. She had spent all night weighing over telling the Grandmaster the real reason she was hiking the Initiates out to the Miniara Pass. Some small instinct in her gut told her not to.

Perhaps it was because he had reacted to her and Dayne saving the Parliament with punishment. She hadn't been able to reconcile that, even if they had broken orders. And maybe the secret message from Master Denbar had put her guard up. Regardless, she definitely couldn't say she was following up on Dayne's hunch about an ambush on the ballot wagons. Even the idea of saying it out loud was ludicrous.

"I had been reading a bit of history lately, how Lief Frannel and his squad of volunteers ambushed Tochrin's reinforcements in Miniara Pass."

"And here I thought Dayne had been a negative influence on you," he said. Amaya wasn't sure how to take that.

"So I thought, training exercise of a hike in full dress,

re-create the tactics of the battle in the pass itself, spend the night under the stars and hike back."

"It has merit," he said. "Unorthodox, but merit. And the details of the third-year Initiate training are on your shoulders, so if this is how you feel the next two days are best spent, I wouldn't argue that with you."

"Thank you, sir."

"But," he said sharply, "in the future, tell me before the staff, all right?"

"Yes, sir."

He chuckled and headed up to his sanctum.

"We're all set, madam," one of the staff told her, pointing to the eighteen packs. "Food, water, camp rolls, supplies for everyone."

"I'm quite impressed," she said.

He shrugged. "The equipment is standard, and it's part of how we're trained."

"Of course," she said. She realized that for the staff here, and the whole service class in the country, there was probably just as much training, trial, and hierarchy as there was in the Elite Orders.

He nodded and led the rest of the staff off, as Vien and the third-years came into the lobby. They were all impressively decked out in their armor and tunics. If, somehow, Dayne was right and there was a fight waiting for them in the pass, they certainly looked ready.

She had no idea if any of them had been in a real fight, other than Jerinne. Maybe not even Vien.

"Good morning, all," Amaya said. "You're probably wondering what's going on today."

"Whatever it is, we're ready," Tander said. Tander, the pretty, blond-haired boy currently at the top of the ranking. And deservedly so—he had the skills, the demeanor, the drive. He was like a shorter, less annoying Dayne.

"That's good," she said. "Grab a pack, and get ready to march at double time."

"What's the mission, ma'am, if we're allowed to know?" Dade asked. A good, solid kid who probably wouldn't make Candidate, though not out of any particular failing. But in a few years he would make a fine Constabulary officer, or security chief for some minor noble.

"Who knows the history of the Battles of the Incursion?" Amaya asked. "Vien, give them the brief."

Vien stepped forward and barked out, "In 1008 the city was under siege by who?" She paused just long enough for the Initiates to think she expected an answer, and then said, "The Black Mage and his army, led by General Tochrin. The city forces were holding their own, mostly buying time for civilians to be evacuated across the river. But Tochrin had what?"

Now she paused longer, looking expectantly.

"Reinforcements from Ressinar?" Enther offered.

"Very good, Enther. Coming on Canthen Road through the Miniara Pass. Those reinforcements would have given Tochrin the edge to push into the city before the evacuation was complete. So what happened?"

Jerinne raised her hand. "Lief Frannel and his 'score of good men' led an ambush on the reinforcements in the pass, stopping them before 'their poison infected the city.'"

Amaya grinned. Jerinne had been reading, probably because of Dayne's prodding this past month. The girl had been all but bedridden for two weeks.

"Twenty-one people stopped an army there," Vien said. "And all of us make eighteen, but it'll do. We're going to go see the Miniara Pass, and learn about how the attack went."

"And how to defend against such an ambush," Amaya said. "It's twenty miles away. If we go strong, we can make it by four bells, and have several hours before sunset to look it over."

The Initiates did not look happy about that.

No matter.

"All right, let's move," she said. "Sunlight's burning." She grabbed her pack and slung it over her shoulders, marching out of the chapterhouse, hearing the boots of the Initiates behind her.

Whether Dayne was right or not, Amaya thought, this would be a good day.

# Chapter 10

DAYNE CHANGED OUT of the dress uniform and back to his normal Tarian tunic following the morning's briefing with the press. This one was nowhere near as painful, but it was still incredibly awkward. He had gotten Hemmit and Maresh into the briefing, though. If he was going to have almost no influence on what he was saying, he could at least open up who he was saying it to.

He emerged from his quarters in the Parliament to find Hemmit and Maresh waiting for him in the hallway.

"You shouldn't be down here," Dayne said.

"True," Hemmit said, "but we have something you're going to want to know about."

"They've dismissed your information on the Six Sisters. They say it's 'not a credible threat.'"

"That's sewage," Maresh said. "They aren't doing anything about it?"

"Marshal Chief Samsell says the ballots are already

under escort, and he doesn't believe there's anything else that needs to be done."

"So what are you going to do?"

"It's not like I can up and leave the city."

Hemmit smirked. "So what are you going to do?"

"Nothing," Dayne said. "But I've convinced Amaya to look into it herself. But that isn't why you came, is it?"

"No," Hemmit said. He passed a note to Dayne. "Seems you made an impression on the leader of the Open Hand. He wants to meet with you."

"With me?" Dayne opened the letter. It was from Bishop Issendel, asking for Dayne to meet him at a public house called the Buttered Pear. "Then why did he reach out to you?"

"Not sure," Hemmit said. "But shouldn't we go hear what he has to say?"

Dayne let himself smile. "So where is the Buttered Pear?"

The place in question was on the Trelan Docks, at almost the northernmost tip of the district. It was a brightly colored place—or at least it had been, but the paint had faded and chipped, now a dull shade of what it once must have been. When they entered, a white-suited proprietor rushed up to them. "Hello, gentlemen," he said in a strong Scallic accent. "Are you in need of directions?"

"Are we not welcome to have lunch here?" Hemmit asked.

"Of course, of course," the proprietor said. "It's just . . . usually when high city fellows like yourselves come in here, with a look on their face much like the one you have, well . . . usually that means they've wandered too far up the docks and don't know where they are."

"We are where we want to be," Hemmit said, his voice rising.

"This is the Buttered Pear," Dayne said, signaling Hemmit to calm down. "We came here to meet someone."

"Oh, of course," the Proprietor said. "Is it Mister Ret?"

"Mister Ret?" Dayne asked. "Isn't he a bishop?"

"He is a man of god, yes," the proprietor said. "But he is also a man of simple tastes. Come along."

He led them through the place to a porch in the back of the restaurant, overlooking the river. At the only table, Bishop Issendel sat with Sister Frienne, but they were both out of their holy vestments. Bishop Issendel wore a simple suit of pale linen, with a tied string in place of a cravat. Sister Frienne was in a matching dress, modest and simple, though it was fringed with the red of her vestments.

"Dayne," he said as he stood up. "I'm glad you could come. And you brought Hemmit and Maresh, excellent. I presume Lin declined?"

"She did," Hemmit said.

"I fully understand, and wish her no ill."

"I was surprised by the invitation, your grace," Dayne said.

"Sit, sit," the bishop said. "And none of that 'your grace' or any of that. Right now we're at a table together and I'm merely Ret, and she's Frienne, and I'm hoping we could just talk."

"Of course," Dayne said, sitting on the other side of the table from Issendel. Maresh and Hemmit flanked him as they sat down.

"Arlio, can we get some lime ricks for these boys to start?" Issendel said to the proprietor.

"I'd prefer wine," Hemmit said.

"I'm afraid there is no wine," Arlio said.

Hemmit scowled. "This is why I don't come here."

"The lime ricks are fine," Dayne said.

"And then just bring out food for all of us," Issendel said. "You decide what's best."

"Of course, Mister Ret."

As the proprietor left, Issendel turned his focus to Dayne, his bearded face bright and beaming. "Dayne, I first wanted to sincerely thank you for everything you did yesterday and the day before. I know . . . well, I can imagine, that for a man like you, the ideas we profess, what we're fighting for, well . . . I know you just don't cotton to that."

"I do not," Dayne said. "I think your goals are harmful to the nation."

"I can't deny that is true, in terms of how you define the nation."

"Which is the problem," Sister Frienne said. "Your definition is wrong."

"Now, 'wrong' is harsh," Issendel said. "Simply different."

"How am I wrong?" Dayne asked. "The nation is the ten archduchies, and you think one of them should dissolve itself from the rest."

"I think the 'unity of the ten archduchies' is a political lie we've been sold," Issendel said.

"It's obvious you do think that," Hemmit said. "That's the basis of your platform."

"Yes, it is!" He wrapped his hands together, meshing his fingers. "We are all trapped together, a tangled mess, when we could be how we were meant to be. Ten kingdoms, open and allied. Stronger through greater reach." He spread his fingers wide. "The Open Hand."

"I thought you wanted Scaloi to secede from Druthal," Maresh said.

"That would be selfish," Frienne said. "We understand the need best because we are Scallic, and we are the farthest from the rest of you. But the point is not merely a free Scaloi, though that would be a result."

"Instead of one nation, under one throne, a loose confederacy of ten countries. More, if you consider Corvia or Monitel."

"Indeed," Frienne said. "Our cause is as much for them, or the Napolic colonies, as it is for ourselves."

Dayne shook his head. He knew well enough that this was a dangerous path. "Have you no sense of history? That's the very thing that people fought and died to end. The Kingdom of Druthal shattered in the eighth century, took three hundred years to recover."

"Three hundred years of wars and horror," Hemmit added.

Issendel smiled, nodding his head in assent. "Well, that was done badly. The nation, as you said, shattered. Kingdoms declaring themselves independent from the crown, anger and acrimony the primary motives. Of course it devolved into wars."

"We still bear the scars of those wars," Frienne said. "Ruined cities along the border."

"You have a lot of anger toward the Linjari," Dayne said. He turned to Issendel. "You speak of avoiding anger and acrimony, when your second here is full of it."

"She is, and I try to heal the anger in her heart every day," he said. "Tell him your story."

"Do I—"

"Your penance," he said, and when he said it, even though he spoke softly, the words hit with a weight that shook Dayne in his bones. His voice gained depth and authority, in a way Dayne didn't understand. The same thing as the man with the knife, the power that had spooked Lin.

"Of course," Frienne said. "I grew up in a town called Elliataria, just on the Scaloi River, the border between us and Linjar. For centuries, it was, as you said, horrible war between our kingdoms. Elliataria had been a grand city, but it was decimated over and over again by the horrors of that war. It often had been the battlefield, and the fields surrounding it are deep with the dead."

"The Wall of Bones," Dayne said. "But that was long before any of us lived."

"Perhaps so," Sister Frienne said. "But those wounds are deep and long, and we still bear the scars. Elliataria is starving. We can never grow enough to feed our own people. We receive help from Iscala and the rest of the country."

"Archduchy," Hemmit said reflexively.

"On the other side of the river is a Linjari region called Henijeaut. There had been some towns there, but most of those are empty ruins now, only patches of people living there. They have nothing, no food, no help, not even a local church. My order in Elliataria, our cloister, was the closest church to them. So we gathered up some of the food we had, rafted across the river, and distributed it to the Linjari in Henijeaut."

"So that sounds like you were doing well, helping your fellows," Maresh said. "Because we are all Druth, yes?"

"That was the spirit in which it was done," she said solemnly. "But our reward was the people of Henijeaut came into our town with knives and sticks and torches, murdering us and taking whatever they could."

"And what did you do?" Issendel asked her, in a tone that showed he knew the answer.

"Our church was burned down by those . . . people," she said. "They killed several of the girls in my cloister. So I picked up a relic and brought it down on the head of one of those bastards."

"You were defending yourself," Hemmit said.

"No, sir," she said. "What I did was not so justifiable. I didn't simply fight back." Her eyes were full of tears. "In the moment I saw myself as Saint Jontlen, or Saint Terrent, doing terrible things in service of God, in service of saving others from the wicked. But I was the sinner there, for I relished their deaths. I stalked and hunted them, killing them with pain and torture. I found joy in their blood and anguish."

"And then?" Dayne asked, almost horrified.

"And then, for a year, the people of the dead moors of Henijeaut spoke in hushed voices of the Red Lady who brought death and fire with her. And I did. I have a heart filled with hate for the Linjari, and that hate has been fed with blood. But hate is never satiated." She held out her arm, showing scars—dozens of tally marks carved into her flesh. "I marked myself for every life I took."

"So what happened?" Hemmit asked.

"He found me," she said, reaching out to Issendel and putting her hand over his heart. "And with a word gave me just a taste of peace, a chance of absolution. And I knew I must serve his cause."

"Dissolution of the nation?" Dayne asked.

"Peace, Dayne!" he said. "Peace is my cause! We find peace in Druthal by not forcing everyone to live in one house, forever arguing until we tear open each other's throats. Instead we should be ten houses, good neighbors who leave each other to their business."

"And you think your methods are peaceful?" Dayne asked.

"We do not engage in violence."

"But you block people's way, chain your arms together. You prevent people from going about their business."

"An inconvenience, Dayne, but not violence," Issendel said. "Surely you can see the difference. Our message will be ignored if we do not capture the people's attention."

"Forcing a confrontation," Dayne said. "Maybe not being violent yourself, but surely instigating it. Both times a riot nearly started."

"By other people!" Sister Frienne said.

"But inspired by your actions," Dayne said.

Issendel shook his head. "We cannot be responsible for how people react to us. We will continue our work, but always through a path of peace."

"Through peace you work with a murderer?" Hemmit asked.

"Shouldn't she be in prison?" Maresh asked.

"Here, she would be. Rotting away in a cell, no chance for her soul. But the law in Scaloi is different. Through confession and absolution and penance, a malefactor can be placed in the church's hands. Instead of serving in prison, she serves God and the people."

Dayne wasn't sure if he liked that, but he acknowledged that what he had seen of prisons were unjust horrors. "And what is her penance?"

"To tell her story truly and honestly," Issendel said. "And in each telling, the anger leaves her heart, and the blight leaves her soul. Because, truly, her sins are heinous, and no simple act of absolution could possibly resolve them. She must work to be clean."

"And it's work I struggle with," she said. "But with Ret's help, I am making that journey." She reached out and took his hand. When she did, Dayne thought he saw one of the tally marks cut in her arm fade away. He blinked and looked again. There were so many tally marks, there was no way to be certain. Perhaps it was a trick of the light.

"The point is," Issendel said. "That is the Scallic way, and you would respect that we handle ours in our own way, just as we would trust you to do the same."

"But you can," Dayne said. "I mean, if your argument is let Scaloi be Scallic, your proof is here with her, isn't it? She isn't in prison, but in your hands, as per your laws."

"To some degree you're right," Issendel said.

The waiter came with trays of food, laying the plates in front of everyone. Bowls of rice, sweet-smelling meat, strong spicy odors, and every dish garnished with lime wedges and a sliced green fruit of some sort.

"Your faces tell quite a story," Issendel said. "Each of you is thinking, 'this isn't Druth food'—but it is, because all of this is quite traditional and common in Scaloi. Except Scaloi isn't what you think of when you think of Druthal."

Dayne pointed to the green slices. "Those are the eponymous butter pears, no?"

"Right," Issendel said. "The Acserians call them *avacada*, but butter pear is a good term."

"Do they taste like butters or pears?" Maresh asked.

"Neither," Issendel said, nibbling a bit of it. "It's shaped like a pear, it cuts like butter, tastes like . . . well, like itself." He took a soft flatbread and scooped some of the meat into it. He then added the sliced butter pear and spooned a concoction of a yellow fruit and green herb onto it. He wrapped the flatbread and handed it to Dayne. "Taste this, and you might fall in love with Scaloi."

Dayne took it and bit into it. Issendel was right, it was quite delicious, savory and sweet and spicy and rich all rolled together in a single bite.

His face must have told a story, as Hemmit and Maresh took their own flatbreads and prepared wraps for themselves.

"What do you think?" Issendel asked.

"Far better than Yinaran food," Dayne said.

"Ha!" Issendel said, clapping his hands together.

Dayne blushed. "I may not have the taste for the cuisines of every part of Druthal, but I respect them as part of the richer tapestry of this nation. That unity is our strength. We have a shared history, language, church . . ."

"Our iteration of the church is not yours, though," Issendel said. "We accept more precepts from the Acserian. We read their holy books and derive much insight from them, and through that, a more fulfilling practice of faith. You won't find that in the rest of Druthal."

"Perhaps not," Dayne said, "but in Acora you see Waish and Kieran traditions in their expressions of faith. Kellirac beliefs have been woven into our own."

Issendel produced a book out of his bag and passed it to Dayne. "A gift. Frienne tells me you knew a bit about Saint Alexis. She was very different from many other saints."

"Alexis is a historical figure," Dayne said, tapping on the book, a copy of *Alexis: Saint and Warrior.* "I've read this one, sir. And I appreciate the gesture. Alexis is sometimes referred to as 'the last Otajian.'"

"Otajian?" Maresh asked.

"One of the Elite Orders," Dayne said. "Mace and flail warriors from the south, its origin both Scallic and Linjari together. But the Order fell apart during their war."

"But those traditions live," Hemmit said. "We saw that with those Royal First ladies."

Frienne scoffed. "Heretics. Versed in form but not grace."

Issendel gave her a slight gesture of quiet. "Though in truth, the Otajians disbanded half a century before Alexis was born. I think the idea that she had some claim to being one of them was a bit of a romantic notion. But she wore the armor and wielded her mace, and then came here with our queen as a representative of peace for her people in the Deathly Summit."

"And died protecting others from the Black Mage and his people," Dayne said.

"And there we get the poison that infects our part in this nation, my friend," Issendel said, his voice growing more passionate with each word.

The hairs on the back of Dayne's neck went up at that phrase, the same from Lief Frannel's letter. The same from the Sons of the Six Sisters.

Issendel went on. "We were told that, in the defeat of the Black Mage and his Incursion, now we were part of Druthal again, and that the queen's idiot nephew was now the Archduke of Scaloi. We reunited with Druthal by accession, not agreement."

"This was two hundred years ago," Maresh said. "I mean, all your life, you've been Druth."

"Under duress," Frienne said.

Maresh shrugged and pushed his plate away. "It just doesn't make sense to me."

"Perhaps not, but you live here, in the center of the nation. Maybe you can't understand us and our lives." Frienne stood and walked off.

"And that is the crux of it," Issendel said. "That at our hearts, we don't understand each other."

# INTERLUDE:
## The Parliamentarian

JULIAN BARTON, 4th Chair of Maradaine, found the intercession between convocations of the Parliament to be a tediously dull time. In his seventeen years serving in the Parliament, with the exception of the years he needed to campaign for reelection—which he always won handily—he found himself falling into bad patterns. He would make a pretense of working in his office, but just read through newspapers and pence-novels by lamplight until the wee hours. Then he would sleep until midday and repeat the cycle.

Half the time he didn't even go back home. There was little cause to. His wife was dutiful enough when it came to public events, campaigning, those interminable dinners. She shone in those moments, the perfect Parliamentary wife. But beyond that, she didn't care what he did. He was reasonably certain she was having an affair with someone on their household staff, and the most surprising thing about that was how little it bothered him.

That was why he woke up on the couch in his office in the Parliament building. Woken by the sound of someone pounding on a door in the distance. Not his door. That would have been odd. There was no reason for someone to seek him out. Not even the most panicky member of the Grand Ten would seek him out to solve a problem right now. There just wasn't a real problem in the works. Their plans were moving apace, and things were underway as they needed to be. The paperwork for the promised promotions had been ratified and submitted, and the bureaucracy would grind through and do what needed to be done.

When he was actually working, when the Parliament was in session, he didn't fall into these habits. Then he had expectations upon him, and he thrived in those conditions, even when the stakes seemed to be less and less critical to him each year. That might have been the reason he joined this conspiracy when Millerson brought him in. Some sort of thrill, some sort of action.

Something to match those twenty minutes off the coast of Corvia, when he took command of the *Maradaine's Glory* upon the death of his captain and his fleet admiral. When he—as a mere Lieutenant Barton—won the Battle of Polimare Bay for his country.

A victory that ensured him his effortless election to the Parliament four times in a row.

The pounding in the hallway increased. Barton got to his feet, found his shoes, and put them on. His coat was lying on the floor, but there was no need to put it on. It was too damned hot to wear it, anyway. This was the worst summer he had felt in Maradaine.

He went out to the hallway to find the source of the knocking. A bedraggled man was pounding on the office door of Montrose, 2nd Chair of Maradaine.

"He's not there," Barton said. "He's in Hantal Cove with his family."

"How could he?" the man asked. He had wild hair

and beard, and a sallow look that made it seem like he hadn't eaten anything solid in days. Despite that, his clothing was well-appointed and tailored, a woolen waistcoat and matching cravat. This wasn't some strange transient who had wandered in here.

Not that Barton should judge. He probably looked the same.

"He's supposed to. We're supposed to return to our constituents this month, you know?"

"I know that!" the man said. Acoran accent. "But this is critical!"

Now Barton placed him—the accent and the overdramatic urgency revealed who he was. "You're Parlin's man, aren't you?"

The man approached. "Yes, sir. Mister Valclerk? I was Good Mister Parlin's chief of staff. I coordinated with your office on the museum funding."

"Right, of course."

The museum funding had been largely a ploy to put Parlin in the sights of a crossbow, a ploy that failed, thanks to that Tarian. The only reason Parlin still ended up dead was because Tharek Pell was a determined, unstoppable bastard. But this man—Valclerk—had coordinated between Barton and Parlin in their joint project of opening the museum. He was a lot more put together back then.

Parlin's death must have hit him badly.

"Why do you need Montrose?"

"Because he's the head of the party, and someone has to do something!"

The party—Montrose and Parlin were members in the inconsequential Populist Party.

"All right, slow down," Barton said. He almost called him, "son," but Valclerk was likely the same age as he. "What exactly is the problem?"

"The problem is Mister Parlin's office! I've been locked out of there, and Mister Parlin's papers and files are in boxes in the hallway!"

Barton bit back his instinct to say something crass, but truthfully, the urge was strong. Parlin was dead, and his office needed to go to the new member from Acora, once the elections had decided matters. "I'm sure it's all . . . shocking."

"It's not shocking, sir. It's appalling. That office belongs to Mister Parlin, and the trust the people of Acora have put in him to serve their interests."

"Yes, but—" Barton wasn't sure how else to put this. "The man is dead, Valclerk."

"The man is dead, but his chair—that should stand, representing the will of the people. Stand in his name until *that chair* is up for election."

"It is up for election!" Barton snapped. "Blazes, the vote boxes from Acora are on their way here now."

"No, I disagree," Valclerk said. "That chair belongs to Erick Parlin, and in his stead, a representative of his ideals for Acora and Druthal, until the proper replacement of the chair by fair election in 1218!"

This man had clearly cracked. "That . . . that isn't how it works when a member dies. It's actually clearly detailed in the Parliament charter. A staff proxy sits in his place until the next election, and as the two chairs up for normal election are won by the top two recipients of votes, the special chair goes to number three."

"That is an unjust methodology!" Valclerk shouted. "How could you stand by it?"

Barton hid his smile. He could stand for it because there were Traditionalist winds blowing in from Acora. He didn't know what was posted in those ballot boxes working their way to the capital, but rumors were that all three chairs were going to his party. Ian Callun would be reelected in a breeze, and since that fool Batts was following the custom of the Functionalist Party: He wasn't running, leaving his chair ripe for claiming. Callun had been promoting his men, Logan Theorick and Preston Willian, and if those two won Batts's and

Parlin's chairs, that would be a decisive victory for Barton's party.

They might even claim control over the Parliament, and if so, Barton was certain to be offered a High Chair, or at least a plush committee. He had been working hard for the party, for Druthal, putting his own life on the line by standing close to Parlin when the assassins came for him. He had nearly taken a bolt, so no one would suspect he had organized the whole affair with the Grand Ten.

And now the fruit was ready to taste. His fortunes grew, as did those of his associates, and that put them in place to shape the course of Druthal.

Starting with a proper king on the throne.

"How could you, sir?"

Valclerk's ranting snapped him back.

"It's how it's done, boy," he said. "We live by the rules, we don't change them. I suggest you start gathering boxes."

He went back into his office, latching the door behind him. He heard Valclerk stomp off. Good. He didn't want him lurking about there. Barton was going to have to go home soon. Get a decent meal and a change of clothes. The next few days he needed to be seen at the parties. Shaking hands and smiling. It was time to start being presentable again.

# Chapter 11

𝕬S FAR AS JERINNE was concerned the hike outside the city to the Miniara Pass was the best way to spend the day. It had been hard going, and the heat had been something to contend with, especially as they walked that last mile. Her whole body was sore, but it had been an invigorating kind of sore. She felt like she had earned it through accomplishment.

Others seemed less enthused. Many of them looked miserable, but no one actually complained. Probably no one dared, especially since Vien looked like she had every intention of walking another ten.

"All right," Madam Tyrell called out. "Let's take a breather, get some water, and assess where we are."

Jerinne unhooked her waterskin—fortunately there had been regular well stations along the road, as well as Royal Post depots, where they could stop to refill the skins—and drank greedily from it. Everyone else was doing the same, a few even sitting down on the ground and pulling off their boots.

"You all right?" she asked Enther, who was looking a bit worse for wear.

"Fine," he said. "Could have stood to have gone without the mail shirt in this heat, but fine."

"Look at Madam Tyrell," Iolana said. Iolana was someone who Jerinne had never been very close to, despite the past years in Initiacy together. She always seemed too flighty, too cloud-headed, for Jerinne's taste, and the two of them had spoken about twenty words to each other in all this time. "She's not even breaking a sweat."

"She spent a couple months in Imachan in her Candidacy," Dade said. "Watchdogging some Parli. Maybe she can take this heat."

"Yeah, well, I don't know what watchdogging a Parli really means," Iolana said, giving an almost sneering look to Jerinne.

"I'm going to look around," Jerinne said, mostly to Enther, and walked off.

The road—the Old Canthen Road, presumably—had been going on an incline for the last mile or so, and the terrain had been growing rockier. Now they were at a point where the road took a sharp decline into a narrow valley, while on either side of the road the incline continued, the escarpments looking over the road. In just a short walk, anyone on the road would be walled in by high cliffs on either side. The valley seemed to curve to the right as well, so you wouldn't see anyone here at the mouth until right before they arrived.

Indeed, a perfect ambush spot.

Madam Tyrrell paced about, looking in all directions, like she was working out the same thing.

"Paths off the road on either side," Madam Tyrell said, though it didn't seem she was saying it to anyone in particular. "So someone could easily go up over the valley from here."

"All right," Vien called out. "According to records,

the general's army was coming up the road in the valley, and Lief Frannel split his people into three groups. Archers on the right side, who rained arrows down on the army. Spears and pikes up the center, with a shield wall, to pin the army in place. And then he led the third group on the left side, where there was a steep slide-down to let him drop rocks on the army, and then make a quick descent to carve them up from behind. Now, we don't have an army coming up the road—"

While Vien was talking, Madam Tyrell was still looking around, mostly at the trailheads on the left and right. Something had captured her attention.

"Right," she said abruptly, drawing her sword. "Here's the play. Everyone, leave your packs on the ground. Vien, you go up the right path with Candion, Maskier, Paskins, and Eakin." The ones who had come with bows. "Tander, you're on the left path with Liana, Chrinten, Trandt, and Fendall. The rest, with me down the road. Shields up, weapons out. Be ready."

"Ma'am?" Vien asked. "This is an exercise, yes?"

"Shh," Madam Tyrell said, gesturing to everyone to be quiet. For a moment, Jerinne had no idea why, but then another sound could be heard over the bird calls and buzzing insects.

The distinctive clash of metal on metal.

"Go," she ordered. "Time to be Tarians."

Hemmit had left the luncheon with Bishop Issendel unsatisfied. Both in terms of the meal—Scallic food with no wine was definitely disagreeable—as well as with the discussion.

He had wanted to be able to write a new article about the Open Hand, either a fair look at their side of the issue, or a scathing tear into them and their methods. But he left with no sense of what he wanted to do. He was, at least in part, infuriated by the idea that Issendel and the Open Hand were harboring a vicious murderer as one of their key people. As much as Issendel preached a path of peace, he kept by his side a woman with so much blood on her hands.

But he didn't hide that. He made her tell her story, as a penance, and Hemmit could respect that.

Maybe he needed his own penance for his part in enabling Tharek Pell.

He had a problem with the separatist group, on principle, but he couldn't put his finger on why they bothered him so. Dayne had elucidated some of it—at his core, while he felt that Druthal and its government had many problems, he believed that its strength was in its woven tapestry of many peoples. Ten cultures, wed together, brought something unique to the world that would be diminished by one divorcing itself from the rest, or it dissolving completely.

Hemmit surprised himself that he was that much of a patriot.

Just the word crossing his mind made him shudder a bit. If there was one thing he hated, it was how the extremists had sullied a perfectly good word.

Maresh had gone to buy supplies for the next printing, and Dayne had returned to the Parliament, so Hemmit found himself walking alone back to The Nimble Rabbit.

"Hey, Hemmit," Treshtic, the main waitron of the Rabbit called to him as he approached. "Got a couple notes for you here."

"In the post?" Hemmit asked, taking the papers from him.

"Nah, one's from Lin, left it here an hour ago. The other, some guy said he knew you. When you weren't here, he wrote the note and left."

"Thanks," Hemmit said.

"You need a bottle?"

"Not right now," Hemmit said, looking at the notes. "I might need to head right back out."

The one from Lin said she was heading to the Royal College, to the Magic and Mysticism Department, and to meet her there as soon as possible. He was about to go straight there when he looked at the second note.

*Hello, Wissen—*

*Or I should say Hemmit, as that's your proper name. I wish you no ill will—reading your paper has convinced me you are a decent man who means the best for Druthal. I have information for you about a sickness that is infecting this country, one which must be cured with words and truth, not murder and blood. This is highly grave. Just as the Grand Ten brought Druthal together, a new Grand Ten seeks to undo it. Seek me at the Alassan Coffeehouse any day between four and five bells.*
*Yours, Kemmer*

Kemmer. One of the Patriots who was with Tharek Pell.

Hemmit shoved the note in his pocket. It was possible that Kemmer had some legitimate news for him. But it was more likely it was a trap. Kemmer probably wanted some form of revenge on him. He wasn't about to fall for that. Not today, certainly. Too much to do. Find Lin, and then decide what to write for tomorrow's paper.

Amaya charged down into the valley, shield high, sword raised above it. There was nothing obvious ahead, but once the road turned the curve, she didn't want to be caught unprepared.

She followed the first curve, but saw nothing ahead of her. She stopped here, letting the rest of the Initiates catch up with her. Now the sounds in front of her were clear. Around the next curve, an attack was underway. She couldn't even guess the numbers involved, but it sounded sizable.

And she was with a group of Initiates who, for the most part, had never seen real combat.

"Saint Julian, watch over them," she whispered as the Initiates rounded the corner. They looked confused, perhaps they thought this was still some sort of exercise or test. Haden had come down in his stocking feet. But they all had their shields and weapons up, perfectly executed first position.

"Wall formation, shoulder to shoulder," she said. "Move on my mark, move in time with me. Do not break formation unless I call out that order. Clear?"

"Ma'am?" Enther asked. "Is this a drill, or . . ."

"No," she said. "Whatever is happening is real, and we risk lives by waiting. But this is what your oath is, this is what you trained for. Time to put it to use. Mark!"

She charged forward—not a run, but a controlled press, so the Initiates could stay with her in formation. They held their place, pushing with her as they rounded the next curve in the highway.

Five wagons, stopped by a group of brigands in dark hats and kerchiefs covering their faces. Most of them had swords and clubs, cutting down the King's Marshals trying to guard the wagons. From the escarpment on the right, arrows were raining down from the overlook.

"Overhead!" Raila yelled, changing her shield position to cover them from above. Miara, Haden, and Dade followed suit, so their whole group was protected from the arrows, while keeping a force of shields in front of them as well.

There were only five marshals here, and each of them was outnumbered three to one on the ground, not even counting the archers overhead.

"Pair off," Amaya ordered. "One high, one forward.

Save the marshals." She tapped Raila as her partner, and charged in to the marshal who had four brigands surrounding him, as well as an arrow in the shoulder.

She crashed shield-first into the largest bruiser in that group of brigands, knocking him to the ground. Without breaking stride, she stepped on him, ribs cracking beneath her feet. With two flicks of her sword, she engaged two more brigands, pulling their attention away from the marshal.

*Thwack. Thwack. Thump.* Arrows hitting Raila's shield. From the corner of her eye, she saw Raila in her own duel with a sword-wielding brigand. Holding. He wasn't unskilled—probably a former soldier—but she had her technique and training. He didn't come close to landing a blow.

Even in the midst of the fight, Amaya couldn't turn off the teacher in her brain. Eye on Raila, noting her form, finding the small points to correct. Kicking the bruiser in the head to keep him down, she quickly assessed the others. Haden and Jollit had lost formation completely, both of them in an all-out brawl with their opponents. Miara and Dade were far more disciplined, dispatching their brigands with almost surgical talent. In an impressive bit of teamwork, Dade tossed his shield to Miara, and she held both over him and the marshal as Dade pulled the man to safety under the wagon.

Enther and Iolana were back to back, each fighting a brigand. They were having more trouble than they should for such a fight. As Amaya disarmed one of her opponents, she saw it on Enther's face.

The boy was terrified.

"I'm fine," she yelled to Raila. "Help them!"

Raila spun around and joined in with Iolana, as another rain of arrows came from above.

"Where are you, Vien?" Amaya asked herself, grabbing the marshal and pulling him to safety behind one of the wagons.

"Who are you?" the marshal asked in a hoarse rasp. "How did you—"

"Just some dumb luck," she said. "Do you know—"

"Don't worry about me," he said. "Protect the wagons and the officiants!" He pointed to the slide-down on the left side escarpment. Several mercenaries were coming down to hit the rear of the wagons. More were at the top of the cliff.

From the left side, a burst of flame rained down and hit one of wagons, igniting it. Up on the top, she saw one figure was standing in a nimbus of blue fire.

They had a mage. At least a dozen fighters and a mage. And she had sent five Initiates to that ridge, the most experienced of whom was Jerinne.

"Help us!" someone yelled from the burning wagon. "Save us and the ballots!"

*Every saint above, stand with them,* Amaya silently prayed, as she raced over to the wagon. Tander, Jerinne, and the others would need every bit of help they could get.

Tander took the lead, heading up the path on the left side of the valley, with Chrinten at his right hand. Chrinten was a tall, stout boy—probably the biggest in the cohort—and had a wicked punch that was balanced with his warm nature. If anyone in the third-years was everyone's friend, it was Chrinten. Both were moving like the wind, despite the trees and underbrush keeping them from seeing more than a dozen yards ahead.

Jerinne took a determined pace—alert, ready, saving her energy. There was an actual battle going on, and for whatever reason, Madam Tyrell had anticipated it. And that explained everything about today—the sudden change in agenda, the rapid pace of the hike, the determination to make it here before sunset. She knew what they were walking to. Or at least suspected it.

Liana was matching pace with Jerinne, but she looked like she was forcing herself to walk that fast, favoring one leg.

"You all right?" Jerinne asked.

"Rutting incentive," Liana muttered. "I'll be fine."

"This isn't going to be a drill," Jerinne said. "You get that?"

Liana looked at her, her face pale and sickened. "Yeah. But I'm here. With shield and sword."

"*Real* real?" Trandt asked from behind them. He was with them, but not hurrying at all. "Like, this is an actual fight?"

"Think so," Jerinne said. "Just have each other's backs, hear?"

Tander and Chrinten were out of sight, but shouts tore through the air. The both of them. It wasn't clear if they had let loose a battle cry, or were crying for help.

"Let's move," Jerinne said. She pushed a bit faster, and they broke from the tree line to a clearing at the top of the cliff. The view of the valley, the winding highway, and the hills of the archduchy spread out before them in a spectacular vista.

The view was marred by the twenty or so thugs with swords and clubs, half of whom were swarming on Chrinten and Tander. The boys were holding their own for a moment—they had shields and armor, while their opponents had leather coats and mismatched helmets.

Two figures were at the cliff edge, turning their attention to Jerinne, Liana, and Trandt. One of them was a woman in a fur-lined coat, armed with a pair of hatchets. The other, an older man, slim and gray haired, with a nimbus of flame surrounding him. Mage.

"Quinara," the mage said, pointing to Jerinne and the rest.

"I have them, Pria," she said. "Focus on the wagons."

She bounded forward, spinning the axes as she came at Jerinne.

The mage focusing on anything down below was a problem. Madam Tyrell was down there. Without hesitation, Jerinne pulled the shield off her arm and hurled it as hard as she could at him. It hit him square in the back, and he and the shield went over the edge. Worst threat handled.

Quinara, the axe-woman, was on them, though, with blows and kicks and flips that seemed unnaturally fast. Jerinne barely dodged a strike from one axe, but Liana took a kick to the nose, sending her down. While Jerinne centered her balance and readied her staff, Quinara laid a full assault on Trandt, hacking at his shield and dodging his feckless sword thrusts. Sparks flew as she raked the axes across his shield, blocking his sword, and sweeping in to knock his legs out from under him.

Before she could bury an axe in his head, Jerinne leaped in, staff spinning. Jerinne cracked a blow across Quinara's back, sending the woman down, but she rolled and spun around as she popped up. Back at Jerinne, axes at the ready.

"Lucky shot, sweetling," she said. "Won't get another."

"Don't count on that," Jerinne said.

Quinara launched another attack, axes moving faster than Jerinne could see. But she didn't rely on watching the axes—her eyes were on Quinara's arms, her body, her feet. Finding the dance, matching steps, parrying each blow to knock the woman off her rhythm. Let her attack, stay on the defense, wear her down. Wait for the moment.

"Jerinne!" Liana called out from the ground, her nose gushing with blood. Jerinne heard the warning and followed her instinct, ducking and pulling away.

A blast of fire whirled past her head, singeing her

hair. She pivoted to look to her left, while keeping Quinara in her field of vision.

"Well, that's not rutting fair," she muttered.

The mage—Pria—was hovering in the air above the valley, both hands ablaze and wings of blue fire sprouting out of his back.

# Chapter 12

**H**EMMIT DID NOT WANT to go back to the Royal College of Maradaine campus, a place he studiously avoided since resigning before he was drummed out. Not because he hated the school; rather, it disappointed him deeply. It should have been a haven of free thought and discussion. Instead, it was filled with closed minds and staid, conservative folks who felt nothing needed to change in the world. "Nothing but prosperity since the Island War ended! Why change that?"

A perfect demonstration of the problems in the city, and why the Populists held so few seats in the Parliament. Also why the Dishers were probably going to sweep the Parliament this election.

If he had to meet Lin at the Department of Mystical Studies, he was going with a handful of issues of *Veracity Press* as well as the *Dayne* pamphlet, handing one to every student he passed along the way. If he was going to be tarred with "subverting the student body," then by Saint Terrence, he would earn that charge in spades.

The Department of Mystical Studies was buried away

in a shady corner of the campus. The only buildings near it were the storehouses for grounds equipment and the workhouses where sheets and uniforms were laundered. You could barely even see another dormitory or class building when you stood on its steps.

Lin was skulking in the doorway, her expression sour. She was clearly as unhappy about being here as he was.

"What am I doing here?" he asked.

"Moral support," she said. "I need to talk to someone here, and I don't want to be alone."

"I thought you were done with this place when you got your Letters and your Circling."

"Same," she said. "But I need to ask some questions, and this is the best place." She opened the door and a wave of hot air that was both stale and sulfurous hit him in the face.

She led him down the dim hallway to a narrow staircase, and then up to the top level. At the top of the stairs there was a frost-glass door with ornate writing.

*Division of Integrated Mysticism*
*Prof. Samhur Jilton, Chair*

"Professor Jilton? That's who we're seeing?"

"Not if I can help it." Despite that, she opened the door and went in.

The room looked like most any other academic office on campus—several desks, cabinets, slateboards, and bookcases, papers and books everywhere. Doors to private offices against one wall. There was still some sunlight coming through the windows, but so little that the room still needed several oil lamps burning to see anything, intensifying the acrid smell of the room.

Only one other person was present, a sallow-looking fellow working at one of the slateboards, book in one hand, chalk in the other. What he was writing made no sense whatsoever to Hemmit. It seemed to be in multiple languages, multiple forms of writing, plus mathematical and scientific notations.

"Hello, Gailte," Lin said.

The person turned, and in seeing the face, Hemmit realized it was not a man, but a tall woman with short-cropped red hair. "Oh, oh!" she said. "Lin! Fancy the blazes out of seeing you in this place. What moves your feet?" She had an accent that Hemmit couldn't quite place. It definitely was from somewhere in Druthal, but no singular place came to mind.

"Hoping to find you," Lin said. "Are we alone here?"

"Oh, you mean—no, no, I think he's not about right now. Some . . . meeting with donors. Or Waisholm. Possibly both. But not around, I think."

"Good," Lin said.

Hemmit's curiosity couldn't be further contained. He approached the slateboard. "What is all this?"

"Unified Mysticism, notated," she said. "Or at least the makings of it. We're determined to publish before Salarmin's team. I'm nose deep in a Poasian text that the professor acquired last month, except I really don't know any Poasian and he doesn't want me to— Anyway, that bit's Poasian." She pointed to the figures on the board. "Tsouljan, Ancient Kieran, Bardinic *Yjaïsic* runery. It's . . . it's a lot. I should have something to eat. Maybe. Lin, do you have anything?"

Lin handed a bag to the girl. She nearly tore it open to get at what it contained: about a half-dozen small pastries.

"Caborlets!" Gailte squealed. She all but shoved one into her mouth immediately. "Oh my saints, Lin, you know how much I love these and I never can manage to drag myself off campus and across Trelan to find them." She ate another voraciously. Then she raised an eyebrow. "What do you want?"

"Am I that shallow?"

"You came here armed with pastries," Gailte said, sitting on the floor cross-legged. "So tell me the tale."

"All right," Lin said. "Unified Mysticism. The idea that there's a lot of different things besides magic in this world, and those different . . . powers?" She used that last word with uncertainty.

"I prefer to say 'forces,'" Gailte said. "We know there are five of them."

"Five different kinds of magic?" Hemmit asked. He was out of his depth here, but felt he should contribute something to the conversation.

"No," Gailte said. "I mean, sort of, from a lay perspective. It would be deeply challenging to explain without a solid foundation of Magic Theory and Advanced Integrated Mysticism, which is exactly what Lin here dropped out of before she got her Letters."

"You dropped out?"

Lin scoffed. "I dropped out of one class. I still earned my Letters."

"But you—"

"Yes, I don't understand it all. I know there are five forces, though, with 'magic' being the most prominent one, channeling *numinic* energy."

Gailte stepped in. "Channeling *numinic* energy through your own body, the vessel which serves as accumulator and lens for shaping the energy."

Hemmit took out his notebook and stylus and started jotting.

"Start at the beginning," he said. "Like you said, lay perspective."

Gailte rolled her eyes and ate another pastry. "Fine. The five forces—in as much as we understand them—are Magic, Faith, Will, Physical Focus, and Science—"

"How is Science at all like magic?" Hemmit asked.

"Why do you have to interrupt?" Gailte shot back. "I swear, Lin, most of your problems stemmed from hanging around hairy morons like this fellow."

"I think this beard is quite fetching," Hemmit said.

"Anyhow, 'Science,' in this context, represents an understanding of the true physical laws of the universe. A base standard that everything will always return to." She waved her hand, and Hemmit's stylus flew out of his hand and hovered in the air. "With magic, I can defy gravity. But if I stop—" The pencil dropped to the ground. "Gravity reasserts itself. If you can't understand how that works—understand the Science of the world—you cannot fully understand how everything else interacts. And it's that balance of the five that we're trying to fully understand."

"I remember that part," Lin said. "How Physical Focus is about the external shaping of *numinic* energy, through other objects. Like the Bardinic runes. Will is the power of Psionics, telepaths, and their ilk."

Half of what she said flew over Hemmit's head. "The who and the what?"

"Hush," Lin said. "But Faith was the one that I couldn't wrap my head around."

"Because Faith is a mystery," Gailte said. "By its very nature. We can apply the tools of science to the rest—measure *numinic* energy, register and capture Psionic imprints—oh you should see the work we've done—"

"Not now, Gailte," Lin said, almost with a snap. "But the powers—force—of Faith, you can't?"

"Strictly speaking, it's never been proven to be a real thing. At least in terms that are acceptable to the academic community. There's documentation, of course, dating back to the Pelkin Miracle, but nothing of that same level of recurrent, demonstrable proof." She raised an eyebrow. "Why are you asking? You experience something?"

"Maybe," Lin said guardedly. "I saw someone do something unnatural, and it wasn't magic."

"You mean when the bishop—" Hemmit started, but a snapped glare from Lin made him bite his tongue.

"A bishop?" Gailte popped up on her feet and grabbed a book. "I mean, despite its name, there's no direct evidence connecting 'Faith' and religion and theology. But there is correlation. And that's the attribution to what's behind the so-called 'impossible' things in so many saint stories."

"Magic can't touch people's minds or souls," Lin said, coming over to her. "I saw—I saw a man charge at someone ready to kill, and with a word, he suddenly changed. Dropped the knife, intent to kill vanished. And . . . you could feel it in your bones."

"Interesting," Gailte said. "I mean, I would hesitate to confirm that as a manifestation of Faith as a fundamental force, but . . . unofficially?" She shrugged. "Sounds like it."

Hemmit thought about the moment in the lunch, when Issendel spoke to Sister Frienne. And the scar that seemed to fade as she spoke. Was this what they meant? It didn't seem like magic, as much as Hemmit understood it.

"And if this can change someone so . . . profoundly . . . would they know? Would they still be themselves? Would they—"

Before Lin could finish, a voice called out from one of the private offices. "Gailte! I need the Third Chronicle in here."

Lin turned pale. "You said—"

Gailte snapped her fingers. "That meeting was last month," she said. "Sorry, I—"

Lin grabbed Hemmit's wrist and pulled him out of the office before Gailte could finish, and kept going until they were back outside. When she finally stopped, she leaned against a tree and closed her eyes, her breathing heavy and hard.

"Are you . . . all right?" he asked. She had never spoken about exactly what had happened in her final year at RCM, especially with the Department and Professor

Jilton. Hemmit had respected that she would talk about it when she wanted to.

"It's fine," she said. "I just—I just needed to know. I needed to be certain."

"Of what?"

She looked over at the building, her eyes filled with anger. "I'm not . . . I'm . . . ." She rubbed her temples, as if even thinking about it made her tired. "I don't want to talk about it."

Hemmit was still uncertain of what they had even learned if anything, but Lin seemed deeply troubled. So much so, he couldn't even consider burdening her with anything else, especially Kemmer's note. Instead he focused on her. "Did you get what you needed in there?"

She didn't answer that, but brushed off her skirt and walked toward the campus gates. "Come on, we've got a paper to put out."

Dayne had wandered the city for hours before coming to the Tarian Chapterhouse. The discussion with Bishop Issendel had left him more confused than ever. What was he supposed to be doing, exactly? What were his duties, and how in the name of every saint was he serving the Tarian Order this way? What was he supposed to do, return to Marshal Chief Samsell and report the meeting with Issendel? Would Samsell be interested, be angry, and what authority did he have over what Dayne did next?

There was only one person who could answer that, he decided, and he went to the chapterhouse for that. He went straight in, brushing past the servants and anyone else, heading up the stairs to the Grandmaster's sanctuary.

Grandmaster Orren was in discussion with Master Nedell. "We just don't have the—oh, Dayne. I didn't call for you, did I?"

"No, sir," Dayne said. "But I'm here anyway."

"Why ever are you?" Grandmaster Orren asked. "You have duties and an assignment, do you not? You should be attending to those."

"I have an assignment, sir," Dayne said. "I'm not so certain about duties."

The Grandmaster tightened his lips. "Master Nedell, would you be so kind to excuse us briefly. We'll return to this discussion shortly."

"Of course," Nedell said, shaking his head darkly at Dayne as he left.

The Grandmaster paced about his chamber before taking a seat on the floor, and wordlessly gestured for Dayne to join him there. Once Dayne sat down, Grandmaster Orren took a deep breath before speaking.

"What is it that's troubling you?"

"I'm not sure what I'm supposed to be doing," Dayne said. "I mean, I'm supposed to be a liaison officer between us and the Parliament, but I don't seem to be doing much liaising. Instead I'm talking to the press in the morning, and harassing priests in the rest of the day."

"Harassing priests?"

"Well, a priest. A specific one. But I—"

"Dayne," Orren said, holding up his hand. "What do you mean about the specific priest? Is this some task you've been assigned, or have you taken some initiative to solve a problem that you imagine?"

"Well, first, this problem found me—"

Orren shook his head and got back to his feet. "And you stepped in because only Dayne, hero of the Tarian Order, could possibly be trusted? Yet another story of you saving the city?"

Dayne snapped. "Sir, if people are being hurt, it is our duty, our sacred trust, to step up and be the shield between them and harm."

The Grandmaster chuckled. "I marvel at how easy it all comes for you. I'm jealous, frankly. Such . . . purity of purpose." He went to his desk and poured two cups of tea.

"Then what is my purpose? A trained clown for the press? A common thug hassling the politically inconvenient?"

That got the Grandmaster's attention. "The priest?"

"Bishop Ret Issendel," Dayne told him. "The leader of the Open Hand. They're a political dissident group that . . ."

"I've read the papers, I'm aware." He handed Dayne a cup of tea and sat back down on the floor.

"Marshal Chief Samsell wants me to 'unofficially' discourage him and the Open Hand from any further action. And, while I don't care for what the Open Hand stands for, Issendel and his people are doing nothing wrong in exercising their right to protest."

"Which is why the marshal wanted to use your informal capacity to his advantage. There is no legal recourse to stop Issendel, but through you, pressure can be applied. Sensible."

"You approve?"

"Of the logic, not the choice," Grandmaster Orren said. "So what have you done?"

"Met Issendel for lunch. We talked about his goals, his movement, and . . . well, I don't approve of the Open Hand, but I believe he is a man of peace, and that's what he preaches to his followers. I cannot, in any good conscience, stop him from performing a lawful protest in a peaceful manner."

"No, of course not," Orren said. "You said Samsell ordered you to do this?"

"He asked me, I suppose, rather than actually ordered me." Dayne sipped his tea—rich and smoky. Not quite to his taste, but he wouldn't complain to the Grandmaster about that.

"Well, yes. He's in no position to order you. He has no formal or informal authority over you, nor do any of the marshals." He shook his head. "The reason behind your role there is to provide some sort of oversight, to work with the marshals and make sure that they are operating within the bounds of legality and morality."

"What authority do I have to do that?"

"Few men have the moral authority you do, Dayne. I would think—"

"Me?" Dayne couldn't believe that. "I've failed again and again."

"Exactly, boy. You fail, you say so, and then you try again. When you're in the wrong, you're usually the first to say so. Usually."

"Am I now?"

"I really don't know. But I think you are panicking. Which is typical when starting something new and uncomfortable."

"Right," Dayne said. "So I shouldn't take orders or even 'suggestions' from Chief Samsell?"

"Well, take suggestions with your own judgment. He doesn't have authority over you, but he might have good ideas. I actually like the idea of you talking with the press on behalf of the Parliament offices, and on our behalf. I think that's a good role for you, and good visibility for us. That's important."

"If you say so, sir."

"So what else is happening? You are supposed to liaise with us, so tell me."

Dayne relaxed a little. "Well, Lady Mirianne—you know I am—"

"Yes, I'm familiar," the Grandmaster said with a bit of unease. "What about her?"

"She's hosting a party in her city home to celebrate the Revels of Liberation tomorrow night. She had extended invitations to Jerinne and Amaya, but then decided that anyone in a Tarian uniform was welcome. She asked me to spread the word."

"Hmm," Grandmaster Orren said. "I am normally

loath to accept such things—especially since we've only just started the new cycle of Initiacy and Candidacy. It would encourage a lapse in discipline. But it also is an opportunity for visibility, without putting lives at stake. I will post notice that Tarians are welcome, but I don't know how many will actually attend."

"Of course," Dayne said. "I was also concerned, with my contacts with *The Veracity Press*—"

"Another reason why you being a press contact is an excellent idea."

"Yes, through them, I learned of a possible threat to the ballot wagons. I had brought it to Marshal Chief Samsell, but he dismissed it as not credible."

"Well, that's his business. Just as you shouldn't take instruction from him—but heed advice if it's sensible—you need to give him the same trust. He knows what he needs to do as a marshal, and you know what you need to do as a Tarian."

Dayne bit his lip, deciding not to say that he had asked Amaya to help him in that regard. She hadn't told the Grandmaster, obviously, and while he wasn't sure why she didn't, he felt he needed to respect that.

"You're right, sir," he said as he stood. "I should probably go back to the Parliament and figure out what I need to be doing next."

"That isn't too different from the rest of us, you know." The Grandmaster got to his feet in a fluid motion, sipping his tea as he rose. He paused for a moment, looking at his cup. "Those are the challenges we face. But I want you to trust that the things we must do, Dayne—the things I ask of you—are always to serve the best interest of the Order. Always. I hope you know that."

"Trust and hope, in all things," Dayne said, handing over his empty teacup. "Will you be joining us for the Revels?"

"Ah, no," the Grandmaster said. "That's for those

much younger than I. But I want you to enjoy it. And I'm sure the Initiates will relish it after their adventure."

"Adventure?" That meant Amaya followed through. Dayne would have to thank her.

Assuming it wasn't a waste of time. Or a disaster.

One small grace was keeping Jerinne alive right now: Pria could fly around and throw fire at her, but he was a terrible shot. Blasts of fire scorched patches of ground all around her, while she continued her dance with Quinara and her flipping, spinning axes.

"Liana, Trandt, take him down!" she yelled out. Quinara was pummeling at her with multiple blows of her hatchets, and while Jerinne had kept up, parrying every blow, each time another chunk of her quarterstaff was chipped away. The thing was hacked to bits, and at this point, even if Jerinne landed a solid hit on the woman, the staff would more likely shatter than do anything to hurt her.

She couldn't even glance away to see what Liana or any of the others were doing. She could hear plenty of skirmishing still going on—fortunately whatever was happening kept the rest of the thugs off her back—but she had no idea how her friends were doing.

Another blow came raining down from Quinara, and when Jerinne blocked it, the staff snapped in two. Left with two battered handsticks, Jerinne swept the hatchets to the side as she danced a few steps out of the way from both Quinara's next attack and another volley of magic fire.

She pivoted toward him and hurled one stick as hard as she could at him, cracking him in the nose. He cried out, and for a moment plummeted as his wings vanished.

She turned back to see Quinara charging at her full bore.

"Jer!"

Tander tossed his shield over to her, which she caught easily and braced herself as Quinara's sprint brought her hatchets right on her. The hatchets clanged on the shield as Jerinne dropped to one knee, pushing the shield up into Quinara's gut, sending her flying.

Unfortunately, both for Quinara and Jerinne, they were far too close to the edge of the ravine. Quinara went over, falling down to the valley floor. Jerinne lost her balance and started to slip over the side as well.

A pair of hands slapped onto Jerinne's arm, pulling her up and back onto solid ground. Trandt, looking pale and ready to vomit, held on to her arm with an iron grip.

"That—you—was incred—I'm sorry—"

She pulled him into a friendly embrace. "Thank you, man."

Liana was at their side, her face gushing with blood. "Look!" she cried, pointing upward.

High in the distance Pria had reformed his wings and was carrying Quinara, flying them both away from the fight.

"Come on," Jerinne said, forcing herself to her feet. "We need to help Tander."

But Tander and Chrinten didn't need help. Several of the goons were on the ground, some with dreadful injuries, and others were running off into the forest. Perhaps seeing their leaders thrown off the cliff killed their morale.

"You all right?" she asked.

Tander spun to them, sword raised. She noticed it had quite a lot of blood on it. "What do—oh. Did. . . . Did we win?"

"We're alive," Jerinne said. "That's something. Chrinten?"

Chrinten stood dazed, and his bloody sword fell carelessly out of his hand to the dusty ground. He didn't react until Liana touched him on the arm. "I—what? I just—" He glanced about nervously, took a few steps and threw up.

Jerinne looked across the ravine, to see Vien and the others in her squad tying up archers. She whistled a signal to Vien to let her know they were clear on this side. Then she looked down to see the chaos below. Five wagons, many of them singed or charred, but fortunately none of them were actively burning. There were several injured people on the ground, mostly marshals and a handful of men dressed the same way as the people on the ridge. Madam Tyrell and the rest of the Initiates were helping a couple of marshals subdue the thugs, tend to the injured, and clear the road.

"Madam Tyrell!" Jerinne called out. "All clear?"

She looked up. "Initiate! You seemed to have dropped your shield." She pointed to the shield, lying on the valley floor.

"A tactical necessity, ma'am."

"Injured?"

"We're all on our feet. Most of our opponents fled, but a few are—"

"Dead, ma'am," Tander said, coming to the edge. "I'm afraid we had no choice."

"I understand, Initiate," she called up. "I'll be around to check on you. Plenty to be done before we can get this caravan back underway, and then make camp for the night."

"Come on, Fendall," Tander said, patting her on the shoulder. "You did damn fine out there today."

"So did you."

"Bah," he said quietly. "Gormless mooks, barely knew what to do with their weapons. And I . . . I killed them." He suddenly grabbed at her shoulders and buried his head in her neck, weeping. "I had no idea, Jerinne."

"Hey, hey," Jerinne said, putting her arms around him. "We did what we had to."

"Is this what it's always like?" Chrinten asked. "The fighting?"

"What was this even about?" Liana asked. "We almost got killed, and for what?"

"For?" Jerinne asked. "Hey, listen here. There are five wagons down there, with people in them. Those are all safe because we were here. We did what we needed to do—be the shield between them and harm. Madam Tyrell told us to be Tarians, and we were."

"You were," Trandt said. "I don't think I was."

"Come here," she said, calling the other three over. "If not for you, Trandt, I'm over that cliff, dashed on the rocks. Liana, you warned me when I needed it. We were there for each other, fighting together, and saving lives."

"Taking lives," Tander said.

"When we have to," she said. "But for the sake of protecting those who can't protect themselves. To stand and hold."

Chrinten chuckled mirthlessly. "You make it sound ... like you mean it."

"Don't we all?"

"I didn't—I do, but—" He shrugged. "I didn't really know what it meant."

"People are still alive right now because of us, innocents who needed us. Remember that."

Tander suddenly pulled away, straightening himself up and wiping the tears from his face. "Ma'am."

Jerinne turned to see Madam Tyrell standing up there, obviously having climbed up the slide-down to reach them.

"All of you, get back to our packs, gather our supplies. Fendall, hang back."

Tander and the rest went back to the path, Chrinten picking up his abandoned sword as he went.

"Ma'am?" Jerinne asked.

Amaya handed over the shield. "This was Dayne's, wasn't it? The one from his trials?"

"You recognize it?"

"It's fitting, Initiate," she said. "He . . . he told me this might be happening, but—do not tell the rest about this—he didn't have anyone else who he knew could handle it, who would help." She looked across the valley. "I swear to every saint, that man infuriates me, but his heart . . . it's the purest damn thing in the world." She clasped Jerinne on the arm. "I think he's been a good influence on you."

"If you say so, ma'am."

"I don't know all that went on up here, but . . . some of it is very clear, Initiate. Well done, Jerinne. Well done."

Jerinne let herself smile.

"Go, keep helping the others. I think they'll need you."

# Chapter 13

DAYNE LEFT THE CHAPTERHOUSE, hopeful but confused. He had faith in Amaya leading the Initiates. In the past month, he had gotten some sense of the third-years, and they were all skilled and capable. Jerinne, of course, was a credit to them. He didn't understand why she had been ranked last, and he hoped it was merely due her injuries during Second-Year Trials. He hoped, but he was far from certain.

He believed in her, though.

"You look troubled, friend."

Standing across the street was Ret Issendel, still out of his priestly vestments. He approached Dayne and offered his hand, which Dayne took in good faith.

"You came seeking me out?" Dayne asked.

"Guilty," Issendel said. "Can we walk?"

"I'm heading back to the Parliament. You're welcome to join me."

"Gladly," Issendel said. As they made their way toward the Parliament, Issendel continued. "I'll confess, something you said today laid on me, and I couldn't shake it."

"What was that?"

"You talked about our methods inspiring violence, even if we, ourselves, are not acting violently."

"You have to see that it's a problem," Dayne said.

"I do, and it tasks me. In this fight, I wonder, are we doing the right thing? Is our cause just if we perform unjust acts? And isn't blocking good citizens, at least in spirit, a form of imprisonment? To force them to hear our message?"

"I wouldn't go so far as to say imprisonment," Dayne said as they crossed the street. "But it is troubling. And, if I may, very self-involved and shortsighted."

"Really?" Issendel asked, though he didn't sound offended. If anything, intrigued.

"Well, you're presuming that your message, the hardship of your situation, is more important than whatever those people are going through. Not to mention, most of those people are powerless to help your cause."

"All good points," Issendel said. "I've been taking your words to heart, Dayne, which is why I've crafted a new plan."

"Your Grace—"

"Ret, please."

"Ret," Dayne said, even though he was a bit uncomfortable. "I do not want to be a party to your stratagem. I do not support your cause."

"We differ in our goals, my friend. But I think we are one when it comes to means. Neither of us believes that violence, that causing injury, is worthwhile or just. You are a protector of life, every life. Is this right?"

"It is," Dayne said.

"I have heard that you wept when a man you had to stop was accidentally killed."

Dayne stumbled a bit on hearing that, almost tripping and falling down in the street. He stopped walking, leaning against the storefront to brace himself. "Sorry," he said. "That's true, but I don't really talk about it."

"I understand, and I apologize. I shouldn't have pressed."

"It's all right," Dayne said.

"But this is what I wanted to talk to you about. A new plan for a demonstration. Fully peaceful, no chained arms or blocking access. No targeting powerless people."

"What do you intend?"

"Tomorrow night we will have a candlelight vigil, a march through the streets. Each of my people will walk through the streets, candle in hand. Far enough apart from each other that anyone can walk between us. No tying up traffic or blocking pedestrians."

"And you think it will help you?" Dayne asked.

"I think people will notice it," Ret said. "I hope it will make them think. What more can I ask for?"

Dayne started walking again. "It feels like you are asking my approval."

Ret caught up. "Yes! Of the methods, not the message. I understand we will not agree on that. But we can respect each other, and how we choose to act."

Dayne found himself reluctantly moved by that. "Agreed. I'll happily argue every point of your mission with you, but . . . I honor your right to pursue that mission." He stopped and grinned. "As foolish as it is."

"And here we have a miracle," Ret said, returning the wide grin. "May we have such merry arguments for days to come, my friend." He patted Dayne on the shoulder. "I'll leave you to your business, as I have much arranging of mine to do. Which will include a formal statement of intent for you to share with the press. If you choose."

"That's asking a lot," Dayne said.

"If you choose. But you will be armed with information, and one certainly wants as much of that as one can fit in one's quiver."

"Agreed," Dayne said. Ret nodded and went off down the road. Dayne returned to the Parliament and his new quarters. Hopefully, he could have a quiet evening and get some rest. Tomorrow was shaping up to be a busy day, and a busier night.

Physical injuries among the Initiates had been minimal, a point that astounded Jerinne. Mail shirts made a real difference. They kept Tander and Chrinten from being skewered even when deeply outnumbered, let them focus on putting down their opponents. Liana's busted nose had been one of the worst. Vien had taken medic duties on herself, setting Liana's nose and patching up whatever other injuries anyone had received.

"I think this will make an excellent scar," Haden said about the gash on his cheek.

Once they had escorted the wagons out of the valley and to the next post station, everyone got to work bedding down for the night, preparing supper, making camp. No one actually assigned tasks, or bossed anyone around. Everyone got to work, just doing what needed to be done. Madam Tyrell and the surviving marshals took the prisoners into the Post House, which had a small lockup cell for marshals and archduchy sheriffs to use in cases just like this.

For a moment there was no ranking, no competition, no hazing. Just Tarians working together as a unit.

There were dueling undercurrents to the evening—a nervous, excited energy from some of the Initiates, and a quiet, jagged one from the others. Jerinne understood both things—she was still intoxicated from the fight, her hands almost shaking with anticipation. But also that dread, that filled her down to her center, of what she had done and was willing to do. What almost happened to her.

She had sent both Pria and Quinara over the cliff

with intent. She had no idea that he could fly, or that he would catch her. It was a fight for her life, and she did what she had to, and she knew in the same situation she would make all the same choices.

But two people would have been dead. Killed by her.

She had been ready to kill Tharek Pell, when Dayne had already subdued him. She had wanted to. But Dayne had stopped her, talked her down.

She had never thanked him for that.

Tander, Chrinten, who knew who else—they had killed in today's fight. With those two, she could see it was the first time for them. The first real fight, the first time they had taken another life. The toll was clear on their faces. Several of the others carried some form of toll as well. Trandt walked like he was asleep. Iolana slipped off somewhere to cry.

"Hey," Enther said, coming over as she was clearing out rocks and branches to lay down bedrolls. "How'd you do out there?"

"Did what I had to," she said. "But I'm . . . I'm all right. You?"

He shook his head. "You learn . . . maneuvers and formations and . . . in the thick of that, none of it matters. All that training, everything I learned, gone. Io and I were just a mess, and she . . ."

"What happened to her?"

"I didn't see it," he said. "But she screamed, and when I looked, her sword was through some fellow's gut. And she let go, ran off into the valley. I went after her, and by the time I found her, got her back, it was all over."

"That was good," Jerinne said. "You did the right thing."

"Nothing I did was the right thing, Jer."

"No, you saw someone who needed help, who needed protection, and you went to them." She picked up another stone and threw it off in the distance. "I've been thinking—you ever talk to Dayne?"

"Once or twice."

"He's got a lot of thoughts on what being a Tarian is supposed to mean. And the big thing is, it's about life. Saving lives, helping people. The fighting, the combat skills—that's in service of that, but it's not what being a Tarian is supposed to be about. Io needed someone, and you were there."

"You seem to have it figured out," Enther said.

"Far from," she told him. "Out there today, I had a mage on one side, an axe-woman on the other—"

"A mage and an axe-woman?" Enther laughed.

"That's true," Liana called out. "Lady had moves, laid me and Trandt down in two clicks."

"Sounds like I had the wrong side of the valley," Vien said, coming over to them. "Come on, you all. Chow's on, then everyone needs to sleep. We're marching back with the caravan at first light."

"With the caravan?" Jerinne asked.

"They're supposed to be guarded, and almost all the marshals are dead. And they're supposed to reach the city by noon, so they can't wait for a Gallop Post to get back into the city, send marshals out here, and we're here. So we get the job."

"Is it safe?" Candion came over and asked. "I mean, we just did a heck of a thing, but . . . will there be another attack?"

Vien shrugged. "That's the job, Candion. Do it or walk away."

She went over to another group. As Jerinne walked over to the cooking fires, she had some small idea of what she needed to do now.

Dayne didn't know what time it was when someone came into his apartment, waking him. Whoever it was, stealth was clearly not their intention. They came straight in, not making any effort to be quiet. Dayne was still disoriented from having just woken, but he got to his feet quickly. He had no weapons or shield in his room, but if he needed to fend off an attacker, he was ready.

The bedroom door opened, revealing Marshal Chief Samsell, lamp in hand. "Evening, Dayne. Have you been sleeping well?"

"Samsell?" Dayne asked. "I was . . . is something wrong?"

"Wrong?" Samsell shook his head and went to Dayne's sitting room. "No, not at all, actually."

Dayne followed him cautiously. "So why are you here in the middle of the night?"

"Well, I've been working, Dayne. I'm not getting much sleep this week, and I've gotten used to that. Did you know I've worked on the elections in some capacity for seventeen years? And five of those as the chief of record supervising it. I do, in fact, know this job quite well."

"I'm sure you do."

"And, right around now, the certified ballots and their officiants are arriving in the city. As they do every year around this time. Seven sets arrived today. From Sauriya, Yinara, Linjar, Patyma . . . all right on schedule. Three are outstanding, as is always the way. Acora, Scaloi, and Monim."

Dayne poured himself a cup of water from the pitcher the service staff had left for him. "All right. What time is it?"

"Somewhere between three and four bells," Samsell said, sitting down at Dayne's table. "As per usual, I expect those ballots to arrive tomorrow, based on the information I have. Their routes, the reports I have from the Gallop Post, and the typical expectations of how this process works. I'm actually quite good at this job."

"I'm sure you are, Chief."

"Donavan," he said. "Please, Dayne, we should be

familiar with each other." He reached into his pocket and pulled out a note. "You see, I received this via Gallop Post just a little while ago. Confirming that the Acoran ballots are safe, bedded down at a post depot some ten miles outside the city."

"That's good news," Dayne said.

"Very good news," Samsell said. "But it almost wasn't. The wagon caravan was attacked, in the Miniara Pass, by . . . mercenaries, I presume. They were well armed, even had a mage with them. Most of the marshals assigned to escort the wagons? Dead. Only two survivors."

"I'm so sorry," Dayne said.

"In fact, it would have been a complete disaster, except for the fact that a group of Tarian Initiates happened to be on a training exercise out by the Miniara Pass, and were able to intervene. Saving the ballots, the officiants, and the last two of my men."

"That's good fortune," Dayne said.

"Oh, come off it, man," Samsell snapped at him. "You came to me and said ambush. I told you not to worry about it and then suddenly there are Tarians in Miniara Pass!"

"I don't have any authority over the Initiates," Dayne said. "I'm just a Candidate myself."

Samsell got up and went into Dayne's kitchen, grabbing one of the bottles of wine that Mirianne had left behind—the one that was only half drunk and recorked. He pulled out the cork and poured himself a glass. "Honestly, I'm not sure how I feel about it. I mean, I feel like I should be angry. I told you not to worry about it, and yet you . . . meddled. Presumably had the Grandmaster or someone below him order this 'training exercise' to check on the caravan." He drank down the wine. "You meddled, and meddling is something that I will not have, Dayne. It's not your place to put your nose in my business. In marshal business. When it comes to our work—the election, protecting the throne and the nation, protecting the Parliament—that duty is sacrosanct. We are sworn to it. Especially after the . . . debacle of Chief Toscan."

He poured himself another glass.

"But then I think, 'were it not for him.' You meddled, and for that the ballots are safe. Two of my men who would be dead are not. I . . . I should be grateful, Dayne. You'll have to forgive me that I'm not, but I don't know how to explain that."

"You don't have to," Dayne said. "Honestly, I'm wrong as often as I'm right."

"Well, keep at me," Samsell said. "And when Quoyell takes over the Parliament security, keep on him. I'll tell you I'm not going to like it. But it's probably what we need." He drank the second glass. "I should sleep. So should you."

"Yes," Dayne said.

Samsell wandered to the door, his gait making it clear those two glasses of wine had not been his first of the evening. "It's a big day tomorrow, you know. Ballots to count, results to tally. Quite a day, indeed."

He left, and Dayne latched the door behind him. He went back to his bed, but he had a suspicion that sleep was going to elude him.

The printing of the latest issue of *Veracity Press* had gone long into the night, and Hemmit had fallen asleep on the cot they kept in the printroom while Maresh finished the final run. Morning light and hard knocking brought Hemmit back into the wakeful world, after a disturbing dream where Hemmit was made of pastries, which Gailte ate while talking to Lin, both of them speaking in gibberish. The images of the dream stayed with him as he stumbled to the door.

"Hey, hey, you got a job for us?" the kid at the door

asked. Minkie—or was it Miltie?—one of the paperboss kids who handled the various clades of boys who sold newssheets on the north side. Hemmit was vaguely amused how there was, apparently, an entire system of petty kingdoms and territory wars between the paperbosses and who sold what newssheets where.

News in this city was, ultimately, controlled by the whims and squabbles of a handful of eleven-year-olds. There was something fitting about that.

"Yeah," Hemmit said. "We've got five hundred for you."

"I told you, I told you," Minkie said. "Five hundred ain't gonna move. Not for you, brother. You sell maybe two hundred. Maybe."

"I got five hundred."

"And I'm left with three that I got to sell to the fry boys to wrap crackles and crisps in. And those don't sell at rate, get?"

"You sell better, you're left with less."

"You ain't chiming, brother," the kid said. "People ain't looking to read your swill."

"You made good money on the pamphlet."

"That was a month ago, beardie," the kid said. "My boys got to fill their bellies. You're lucky I take your rag out at all. *Throne and Chairs* is looking for more boys and they actually move paper."

"It'll move if you move it." Hemmit picked up the bundle of newssheets. "Get them out there."

The kid took the bundle. "We have fifteen crowns in our pockets by the end of the day, one way or another, hear?"

"Don't make excuses not to sell."

"You're lucky I like you, beardie." Minkie tossed the bundle of newssheets into the basket of his pedalcart and went off.

Hemmit went into the back kitchen of The Nimble Rabbit, where Onnick and Hebert, the pair who ran the kitchen and everything else at the Nimble, were hard at work.

"Morning, Hemmit," Onnick said as he beat eggs. "Did the issue go out?"

"Printed and put in the paperboss's hands," Hemmit said. "The little extortionist."

"Just trying to make the rent," Hebert said. "Speaking of?"

"I will have it on the first, as always," Hemmit said, sitting at their preparation table, where a few dozen potatoes were waiting for one of them to chop them up.

"As always is a bit of a stretch," Onnick said.

"It's always around the first," Hebert said. "If you judge that on the scale of the month as a whole." He brought a cup of tea over. "You look like you need this."

"Always," Hemmit said. "Have you seen Maresh about today?"

"Not yet," Onnick said. He put a plate with hot bread and fresh butter in front of Hemmit. "And when is Lin going to let you marry her, so we don't have to take care of you?"

Hemmit burst out laughing. "Even if that's how things were with Lin and me, I don't think either of us is looking in that direction."

"Right," Hebert said, coming over next to Onnick. "I forgot you two are just such rebels against tradition or the system or whatever you're fighting against."

"You two should talk," Hemmit said.

"Hush it," Hebert said. "You should be so lucky."

"I should," Hemmit said. He took a few bites of bread. "So I have a situation. Haven't talked with Maresh or Lin about it yet."

"Oh my," Onnick said, sitting at the table with his paring knife. "What sort of situation?" He got to work peeling the potatoes.

"Treshtic had a note for me yesterday, from one of

the Patriots who was part of the whole thing in the Parliament."

"Wait," Onnick said. "I thought that fellow was locked up, awaiting trial."

"That's Tharek. But there were a couple others involved, and they didn't end up getting arrested. Probably no one else even really knows them or could point them out, except Lin and me."

"And he came here? Why?"

"He claims he has information for me," Hemmit said. "About what, I have no idea, but apparently he thinks I'd be interested. I'm not sure what to do about that."

"And why haven't you told Lin or Maresh?"

"Maresh . . . he's not saying it, but I know he's still upset about how Lin and I got involved with the Patriots and got stuck being part of their plan."

"I read that part," Hebert said, laying out lamb bones on a tray. "You were rutting stupid, boy."

"Let him be, we all do stupid things."

"But that was very stupid."

"I know," Hemmit said.

"We say this because we care," Hebert said. "Anyhow, this note came to you. Saying what?"

"That he had information for me, gravely important for the safety of the country. That he needed me to get it out in the world."

"And what do you think, hmm?" Onnick asked.

"It makes me nervous that he tracked me down!" Hemmit said.

"Well, it should," Onnick said. "It makes me nervous, because this is our place, and you've exposed us. But that's not what I'm asking. You know this man. He's asking for your trust. Given what you know, are you in danger? Or does he deserve a chance?"

# INTERLUDE:
## The Man of the People

CHESTWICK MILLERSON, 3rd Chair of Sauriya, knew how to play his part. He was a Member of Parliament, close confidant to the Duke of Maskill, and had lived most of his life sitting at the right hand of privilege. But his ability to win elections rested on appearing like someone the common man could relate to. He needed to craft the image that he was just like them, with the same concerns and troubles and petty problems. The men who came to the Parliament through military service had it easy. Simple to gain trust and support under a hero's banner. Millerson had to use different weapons. He had to use charm and charisma, of course, and a bit of the folksy accent of his cousin's family. He had to be seen out and about, having a beer in the pubs, eating a striker in the streets. He had to stop and listen, and put on the show that every person he spoke to was the center of his world.

Be The Man of the People.

Today that took the form of sitting alone in a pub in

Keller Cove on the docks, having sausages and beers while reading the papers. He sat alone, but he had his men—two good, solid mercenaries who had retired from the Army and Intelligence, respectively—in position in the corners of the room. They were subtle, but ready to move if anyone got too familiar.

This was a usual site for him to make his show, and most of the regulars ignored him. Today was no exception, and that gave him a chance to really read the newssheets. The election seemed to be going well; most of the ballots had arrived to be certified and verified in Maradaine. The official announcements of who won their elections would be coming in the next few days. But he knew some unofficial results already, at least for the Archduchy of Sauriya.

Winfell and Turncock, the 5th and 6th Chairs, were up for reelection this year. Minties both, and they were safe bets for easy wins. A shame, it would have been nice to flip those chairs to Traditionalist, but that wasn't going to happen.

But Seabrook had gotten himself killed, which put another Sauriyan chair up for election. That hadn't been part of the plan. That bastard Pell had had his own plans that involved revenge against Seabrook for some imagined slight. The loss of a Traditionalist seat stung, even if Seabrook was something of an empty suit. He was at least a useful empty suit whose vote could be counted on.

Odds were strong that his seat would be won by Golman Haberneck, who called himself a Traditionalist. From what Millerson had seen—he met the man in Kyst to endorse him at a rally two weeks ago—he was a solid sort. If Millerson had to guess, Haberneck was playing the same folksy charm game he was. He did it well. Millerson was taken in with it. Perhaps it wasn't artifice, but Millerson didn't let himself believe that.

And as long as Haberneck voted with the party, it didn't matter.

"Good Mister Millerson, I do presume," a man said, coming up to his table. "Might I have a word?" Young man, but with a degree of education and breeding. A bit out of place in the Juicy Bite Tavern.

"For a moment," Millerson said, gesturing to the empty chair. From the corner of his eye, his intelligence man took notice and straightened his back.

The young man sat down. "Kemmer. Harlston Kemmer, but you probably don't know me. You're familiar with some of the work I've done, but not my name."

"Am I?" Millerson asked.

"My previous work was . . . volatile. Not entirely by my design, of course, and I was only a minor player. But you know the names of the real movers. Chief Toscan, and Tharek Pell?"

Millerson stiffened, but the man raised a finger. "Do not engage your men, Good Mister Millerson. I'm not here to injure you, and I did not come alone. Neither of your boys would get to me."

"Then what are you here for?"

"I thought you knew, Mister Millerson. Because, let's not mince words . . . what the Patriots did last month, they did at your behest. Finding the lines of communication, the money trails between you and Toscan were not easy, but fortunately the gentlemen at the goldsmith house of Underborne and Listwell are meticulous records keepers. It took some doing, but I found my way to you."

Millerson wasn't sure how to react, but he kept his face as neutral as possible. This man, whoever he was, had learned a bit too much, and that couldn't continue. "Mister Kemmer, I'm not sure what you think you are doing . . ."

"I'm still trying to decide that, Mister Millerson," Kemmer said. "Because, the funny thing is, I still believe in the ideals behind the Patriots, even if the methods were wrongheaded. Revolution through blood and fear is merely an exchange of tyrants. But, while you funneled money and instructions to us, you never were actually interested in our cause. We were convenient agents of chaos."

"Son," Millerson said, "you're clearly confused."

"Not at all," Kemmer said. "And I did not make contact here lightly. I've decided I will not be an agent of chaos, but I will be an agent of change, and you're going to help me."

"That is patently absurd, young man. I'm not going to entertain this any further." He got to his feet.

"Archduke Holm Windall," the man said. "High Justice Feller Pin. Duchess Erisia Leighton. Do I have your attention yet?"

Millerson sat back down. This boy had a grasp on more than Millerson thought possible. He might not know the entire Grand Ten, or that they *were* a Grand Ten, but he had enough to be dangerous.

"What do you want?"

"For now . . . I think city politics. Yes, I think I'll start there, and then move up to the Parliamentary level."

"You missed the elections."

"This year, yes. But I think I'll start planning for next year. First get noticed, make speeches, challenge the system, and then get elected next year. You know, sir. Be a man of the people."

Saints, he knew.

"What do you want?"

"To start?" Kemmer gave a sly grin. "This campaign of mine will take money. Which you will provide. And we're going to meet here, weekly. We can discuss your co-conspirators, and what they're planning for this nation. Maybe I'll even agree with your plans. Maybe we can make a better nation. Wouldn't that be lovely?"

"And if I have my man there put a crossbow bolt in your neck?"

"Then all this reaches the press. Today. It's already

underway, and only if I'm alive could that be stopped. Think about that."

"How much money?" Millerson asked through gritted teeth.

"A thousand crowns is a nice round figure to start with," Kemmer said. "By six bells tonight." He got up from the table. "Oh, and enjoy the party, sir. I understand that Lady Mirianne is really planning quite the rage." He saluted to Millerson, and then to both of Millerson's men, and left the pub.

Resendrick came over. Ex-Intelligence, smart and fast. Came from Major Altarn, which meant Millerson didn't trust him, but he was good at his job.

"What was that, sir?"

"Trouble," Millerson said. "Track him, find out where he goes, who he talks to, and be ready to put a stop to him."

"As you say, sir."

Resendrick left, and Millerson, at a loss of what else he could do, went back to his lunch.

This would sort itself out. And, at worst, Millerson had plans underway to throw a lamb or two to the wolves if he needed. This Kemmer was an inconvenience, but Millerson admired the tenacity of him. And he had enough plans in place that, no matter how things unfolded, he would still be safe. At the end of the day, the people would protect him. Because he was their man.

# Chapter 14

THE INITIATES WERE UP with the sun, and with almost no prodding, packed and ready to march within minutes. Amaya was incredibly proud of them. Despite what they had gone through—some injured, some affected in their spirit—they showed steel in their hearts and bellies. Even though she was still ranking them in her head, she knew most of them would make fine Candidates now. Most.

They went with the ballot wagons and the remaining marshals, making good time as they approached the city midday.

Enther came up next to her in the march. "Madam Tyrell?"

"What is it?" she asked.

"Mentorships are based on ranking, yes?"

"What do you mean?"

"I mean, at the end of this week some of the third-years are going to get specific mentorships with Adepts and Masters, but only the top-ranked ones."

Not quite. "Why do the same rumors persist every year?" she asked him. "You'd think the truth would filter through."

"What is the truth?" he asked.

"All right, spread this around. Yes, at the end of the week, third-years get their mentorships. You're attached to an Adept or Master, and that Adept or Master takes a personal interest in your training and advancement. Our sessions under my supervision won't stop, but the structure of your training day will shift, depending on your mentor. And, yes, the Grandmaster will make Mentorship decisions based on ranking."

"So everyone gets one? And it's one on one?"

"Masters will often take on two," she said. "Dayne and I were both with Master Denbar in our third year."

"But everyone gets one?"

She sighed. This was the usual source of panic. "Strictly speaking, the Grandmaster is not obligated to assign every third-year a mentor. On paper, I believe, it's a privilege only for the top three."

"Right, those are the rules!" Enther said. He bit his lip shamefully, looking around to see if anyone noticed his exclamation.

"Technically, yes," she said. "But in practice? Everyone had one my third year. And I've always seen that be the case."

"So we shouldn't worry," he said with a sigh.

She clapped him on the shoulder. "Oh, Initiate. There are plenty of things for you to worry about. That shouldn't be one of them."

She brought up her pace before he could respond.

They arrived in the city and followed along with the caravan to the Parliament Square. Marshal Pentalin went inside and came out with a few more marshals, who brought the ballot boxes and officiants inside. A marshal chief came up to her.

"I'm given to understand we owe you a debt of thanks," he said.

"Debt isn't how I would put it," she said. "We were in the right place, and did our duty."

He extended his hand to her, which she took. "Well, your nation thanks you. You've helped keep our election sacred and safe." He then went down the line and shook the hand of each of the Initiates, as well as Vien's.

"What next, ma'am?" Tander asked.

"Now?" she said. "We go back to the chapterhouse, unpack our gear, and visit the baths and infirmary. After that, you're at liberty for the day. You've earned it."

When they reached the chapterhouse, the Initiates were more than eager to follow her instructions, half of them stripping off their blood-caked, mud-stained clothes in the foyer before running out to the baths.

"Quite a ruckus."

Grandmaster Orren was coming through the foyer with Osharin—the new Adept from Acora—at his side.

"I've put them through a bit," Amaya said.

"I have received word," Grandmaster said. "Your exercise turned into a full engagement."

"They what?" Osharin asked.

"I took the Initiates on a hike," Amaya said. "We ended up thwarting an ambush of the Acoran ballots on their way to the city."

"Great saints!" Osharin exclaimed. "That . . . so . . . are the votes safe?"

"Safely delivered at the Parliament," she said.

"Very impressive," Grandmaster Orren said, though there was an edge of judgment in his tone. "Fortune smiled on us all, that you happened to be there."

"Good fortune, indeed," Osharin said. He clapped Amaya on the shoulder. "Well done, but I shouldn't dally." He went out the door.

"I should get cleaned up as well," Vien said. Amaya had barely realized the girl was still by her side.

"Miss Reston," Grandmaster Orren said. "As Initiate Prefect, I'll charge you with making sure this mess in the foyer is attended to."

"Aye, sir," she said with a salute, and went off.

"Sorry about that," Amaya said. "The kids were . . . excited."

"And so they should be. How did they do in real combat?"

"Some quite well, some . . . had trouble." She sighed. "I'll write a full report for you tonight."

"There's no need to rush on that," he said. "I am interested in your assessment, of course, but let your thoughts center themselves for a day or two. Besides, I believe there is some . . . festivity tonight?"

"Well, it is the Revels of Liberation."

"I meant there's a specific event, in the household of Lady Mirianne Henson—"

Lady Mirianne Henson, indeed.

"She's invited all the Tarians to attend. I've told the Candidates and Adepts here they are free to go if they wish. The Initiates, at least the third-years, should be given the same liberty."

"I'll let them know," she said. They certainly did deserve a party. She'd attend as well, to chaperone them, if nothing else. But she was very curious to see this woman and Dayne together in her environment.

"I don't know how many will actually wish, but I think it will be good for morale, and our image. And Master Nedell and I will stay here on watch for the night, so no one else is troubled."

"Thank you, sir." She nodded and started to leave for the baths herself.

"Nothing else?" he asked.

"Sir?" she asked.

"Amaya," he said sharply. "You just happened to be there? Am I that old and doddering you think I wouldn't see through that?"

"No, sir," she said, feeling her cheeks flush with shame. "But, truthfully, I only had a hint that something might happen to the ballots, and felt that the hike was a valuable exercise even if nothing happened out there."

"Fortunately for you, Amaya, I agree. But next time, tell me all your thoughts before taking such actions. Yes?"

"Yes, sir."

Now she was more than ready to go to the baths, but three people came into the foyer—a prim-looking woman flanked by two armed men. She first looked at the mess of clothing and gear on the floor in disdain, and then to Amaya. "I'm here for Jerinne Fendall. She will be brought to make her initial testimony. By force, if needed."

After Dayne had delivered the day's report to the press, he was up to his neck in the sausage grind of democracy. Election results for seven archduchies needed to be certified. Officiants were put in separate rooms, with their certifications and sealed election results, while the locked boxes of collected ballots were put under guard in a vault in the marshals' offices. Each officiant had two marshals guarding them.

Then, to finalize, two members of the King's Council—the Grand High Lord, Duke Prindale of Abernar, and the High Lord of Protocol, Baron Jameson of Trentinack—oversaw a team of clerks appointed by the Parliament and certified by the Grand High Court. The team of clerks unsealed the election results, compared the results to each other, and researched possible errors or discrepancies.

And all of this was done one archduchy at a time, fully in the view of five select members of the press, from *Throne and Chairs*, *News of Throne and House*, *The Royal City Press*, the *South Maradaine Gazette*, and *The*

*Daily Maradaine.* Dayne's job in all of this was to supervise those five reporters. Which meant he watched them while they watched the clerks engage in the minutiae of bureaucracy. It was dreadfully dull, even for someone like Dayne, normally fascinated with every aspect of Druth history, governance, and tradition.

If nothing else, at least Baron Jameson was an engaging sort.

"Mister Heldrin, it really is a pleasure," he said, when they met. "I want to let you know that I have, in my limited scope, tried to be a champion for the Elite Orders. I think they are a vital part of our culture and history, and I have pressed that point with the king when I could."

"I appreciate that, my lord," Dayne said.

"And your actions last month, that gripping tale of everything you did against the Patriots and Tharek Pell, and saving our good people on the Parliament floor. I was . . . I was moved, Mister Heldrin. And I can tell you, the king was taken by it as well. I have been trying to arrange a proper event at the palace where you could be hosted as the guest of honor . . ."

"That is not necessary, my lord."

"I think it's proper, though—"

"Jameson, let it be," Duke Prindale said. "I'm sorry, Mister Heldrin. We appreciate your service, but we don't want to cause you any embarrassment."

As the day ground on, the results of the elections for each archduchy were confirmed and approved by the Grand High Lord. "Largely the incumbents," one of the reporters noted.

"Same old story," another said. "A new nobility, with lifetime appointments."

Dayne couldn't disagree with that. It was disheartening that there were few surprises. Of the fourteen regular elections they had results for, only three resulted in a new Member of Parliament. Seeing it up close gave the whole exercise a sense of futility. People were dissatisfied throughout the city, throughout the nation, but they elected almost all the same people.

When they finished, the Acoran ballots arrived, and the process began again. That, at least, had some engaging elements, as the officiants were quite excited to tell the story of being ambushed and rescued by Tarians. Some of the accounts sounded fanciful—apparently the bandits had a mage—and Dayne was going to have to get the real story from Amaya and Jerinne when he got the chance.

"Now," Marshal Samsell said to Dayne and the five reporters, "I will again make the point that *none* of the results are to be released until Reunification Day. If I see even a hint of this information being printed before then, your newssheet won't be printing bread recipes, let alone news of the government. Am I clear?"

"Does that include the story about the Acoran ballots being ambushed?" the reporter from *The Daily Maradaine* asked.

Samsell sighed, and looked to Dayne for a moment. Then he said, "That's fine, as long as there are no elements of election results."

By five bells the job was done, and he wanted little more than to go to his apartments and fall on his cot. Instead, he found a letter wedged in the door of his apartment.

*Dearest Dayne,*

*I am dreadfully sorry to have been so scarce the past few days, when I know you have been struggling with a rough transition of duties. I wanted to be the steady foundation you could rest on, a role I know you would be for me if our positions were reversed. Indeed, I was grateful to have you nearby in the past month, as we finalized the opening of the store. Now that it is up and running, I had hoped* that my direct involvement day-to-day would need to have been minimal. I had intended that my managers handle the running of the store, and I would occasionally oversee them. That has proven to have been shortsighted on my part. In retrospect, I should not have tried to launch the store and host a lavish gala for the Revels in my home all within the same week. But that cannot be helped. I must live with the commitments I have set for myself.

I am confident, as I know your heart, dear Dayne, that this is something you understand.

But to the matter at hand—the party. I would want to pick you up myself in a carriage, so we can arrive together, but even though I flout several rules of etiquette, I recognize I cannot possibly "arrive" at my own party and my own home. That would be simple absurdity.

Instead, I was quite serious about my invitation both to your fellow Tarians, and to the lovely ladies of the Royal First Irregulars. I have, then, a rather daring request of you all, and I ask that you take on a leadership role in this task, as I know that you can. Please meet with the Royal First and your fellow Tarians who are attending outside the south Acorn Lane gate of Callon Hills at eight bells. The gatesmen will be expecting you. Please, if you agree, have the Royal First lead a march—similar to the one they did at the parade—up the lane from the gate to my house, with the Tarians keeping time behind them. When you reach the house, straight through the front door and to the ballroom! It should be glorious.

I am aware this is a massive imposition, but I promise I ask only this in exchange for my hospitality.

I am deeply eager to see you tonight, my love. I hope that your duties will not force you to return to

*your dreary apartments in the Parliament straight*
*away. Of course, I will understand that if you must,*
*we all must respect your duties. But I hope that we*
*can impose upon each other a bit more time than*
*we've been able to in these past days.*

*With deep and abiding love,*
*Miri*

Miri's party.

He truly wanted to just stay in and sleep, and he was
in no mood for festivities. But at the same time, he
couldn't let her down. She had been there for him in so
many ways, and he didn't want to fail her. Sighing, he
went to the water closet to wash up. He only had a couple hours to get himself in dress uniform and be ready
to be in a parade.

All to celebrate a unity of country that he was having
a hard time feeling.

Jerinne wasn't about to be intimidated by Arthady Mirrendum, and she made that clear in how she responded
to the summons. She came to the foyer with just a drycloth wrapped around her wet body.

"Miss Fendall, you cannot come to give testimony
like that."

"True," Jerinne said. "I'm not going to."

"Then you should dress with haste—"

"No."

Miss Mirrendum raised an eyebrow. "Miss Fendall, I
made it clear you've been summoned."

"Then I'll be clear as well. No. I'm not coming."

"I have brought the officers of the court—"

"I don't care," Jerinne said. "I may not be an expert
in the law, but I know you're out of bounds, Miss Mirrendum. I am not charged with any crime so you have no
standing in attempting to force me to testify."

"In cases of the High Court, special dispensation is granted—"

"I don't care," Jerinne reiterated. She looked at the two officers of the court—almost her height, with hand-sticks at their sides, dull expressions on their faces. They looked like a couple of blokes who washed out of the Constabulary cadet program. "I mean, by Saint Julian, just try it."

"What?"

"Try to force me. With those two. Because I fought a mage and an axe maniac yesterday, so your two goons don't even make my teeth itch."

"You will be compelled by law!"

"To testify in defense of a murderer?" Jerinne snapped. "I still don't know why you would want me, and nothing I say will help his case."

"We have a different opinion, and you are honor bound to speak truthfully."

"Truthfully? How I saw him kill three King's Marshals, and then Mister Ressin, and then Mister Seabrook. Right in front of me. No doubt, no need for clarification, and certainly no mistaken identity. I will say that under oath, Miss Mirrendum, if that's what you wish."

Miss Mirrendum was quiet for a moment, then she almost whispered. "That isn't going to be the nature of your testimony."

"It's not?"

"Mister Pell wants other questions put to you."

"Like what?"

"That will be discussed under oath, in the presence of court officials."

"Not good enough."

"I will compel you—"

"Again," Jerinne said, stepping up to this woman so she could look down at her. "Try it."

Miss Mirrendum looked up at her, steely-eyed. "I am prepared to make an offer in exchange."

"What sort of offer?"

"Ten minutes with Mister Pell."

"What?"

"If you go and talk to him—safely, through bars, he will explain why he wants you to testify. If then you don't agree, the matter will be dropped. And while I am certain that you can roundly beat these two men, I do not think you will risk fines and legal charges to do so. So I offer ten minutes."

Jerinne couldn't deny that piqued her curiosity. "When?"

Miss Mirrendum gave a slight smile. "The day after tomorrow. I will come for you alone. Be . . . better prepared to join me."

With a nod, she left, her two thugs right behind her.

Jerinne let out a heavy breath, and let herself feel every inch of the disquiet the conversation had given her. She almost let herself drop to the floor, but she was already in the foyer in a drycloth, there was no need to be more unseemly.

She made her way back to the baths, hoping the water hadn't gone cold and brackish, and that maybe Raila was still there. She wasn't sure what tonight would bring, but if it was anything like the last event she went to at Lady Mirianne's, it would be quite welcome after the past two days.

# Chapter 15

DAYNE WAS AGAIN in dress uniform, buttons polished, sashes tightened. No shield or sword this time, as that was against protocol when wearing the uniform at a social event with peerage. He must have looked impressive, as many people smiled, waved, and even took his hand as he walked the streets from the Parliament to the chapterhouse.

As he approached the chapterhouse, he crossed one person who was less impressed.

"Have to say, Heldrin," Osharin said as he came out the chapterhouse gates, "I didn't think you'd be part of this frippery."

"I'm somewhat obliged," Dayne said. He noticed that Osharin was wearing his sword and shield, with his amulet displayed over the tunic and chainmail. "What are you going to?"

"I need to be useful," Osharin said. "I've spent two days talking with army folks about 'equivalence of rank' and other nonsense. You know, in my days stationed in

Porvence, I barely spent a night in the chapterhouse. Most of it was walking, through the city, and then through the forests from village to town. Just . . . looking for whoever needed my help."

Dayne sighed wistfully. "Like in so many of the chronicles."

"Yes," Osharin said. "See, I knew you understood. There's always someone else who needs our help. Always one more call to answer."

"So that's where you're off to tonight?" Dayne asked. "To answer the call?"

"At least to have my ear out for it. The rest of these folks, they seem to be ready for playing the politics game." He shook his head again. "But from the look of you, that's what's got to be done." He went off into the night.

Osharin's words stung, but Dayne pushed that aside and went into the chapterhouse lobby to find a couple dozen or so Tarians in dress uniform—mostly third-year Initiates, but a handful of Candidates and Adepts, including Amaya.

"Well, there you are," Amaya said with a friendly smile when he came in. She had applied face paint, shading her eyes and cheeks to match her uniform colors, and braided her sable locks into an intricate and elaborate tail that draped over her left shoulder. The effect was striking. "You're staring."

"Sorry," he said. "You—it's very impressive."

"Well, I don't get invited to this sort of thing very often."

"I'm still not sure what this sort of thing will be," Dayne said. "I've heard some stories of your adventure."

"Has it reached the point of stories?" she asked.

"Did you fight off a trio of mages?"

"There was one mage, and it was Jerinne who stood her ground against him." Jerinne was on the other side of the foyer, wide smile on her face as she talked to a

200 Marshall Ryan Maresca

Candidate. "Don't tell her I said so, but she was in-credible."

"Why not tell her?"

"She . . ." Amaya shook her head. "The Grandmaster thinks she needs to be given a target to strive for. You and I pushed each other because we both needed to be the best. She's different."

"You think she doesn't need to be the best?"

"Not like we did," Amaya said. "He thinks—and I suppose he's right—that too much praise will make her take it easier. She needs to feel she's low to push herself."

Dayne was skeptical. "If that's what he thinks."

She shrugged. He could tell she wasn't convinced of the idea either. "Are we all assembled here? Ready to move?"

There were general sounds of assent from those as-sembled, and Jerinne noticed Dayne. She waved and moved her way closer as the group made its way out the door to the street.

"Hey," she said, giving him a quick embrace. "Where the blazes have you been?"

"Parliament, new assignment." They started walking along toward Callon Hills.

"What, you sleep there?"

"Yes," he said.

She shook her head. "That's messed up. Did you hear what happened?"

"I heard you fought a mage."

"A mage and this crazy lady with hatchets. Hatchets, Dayne."

"How did it end?"

Her face changed, turning a bit guilty. "The whole thing was messy. A bunch—a bunch of the Initiates, I think they aren't sure what to make of it. Some of them didn't like being in an actual fight. Some . . . some real-ized they liked it too much. Maybe."

"And you?"

"I did what I needed to. Protected my people, tried to stay alive. I . . . I didn't hold back, and I nearly killed two people. I'm not sure how I feel about that."

"It's not easy," Dayne said. "I made the decision that I needed to be careful. I couldn't bear to take a life, after I made my own mistakes. But that doesn't change the fact that in an actual fight, you can't control everything. And you do what you have to."

"Like at the museum?"

He still saw that man in his nightmares, the young Patriot he pushed at the member of Parliament to save a life. The man who died because of him.

"They both lived," Jerinne said. "They got away, but . . . not from a lack of effort on my part."

"Right," Dayne said. "Of course, I've never gone in with a mage, so . . . I'm not sure what I would do. But you're all right?"

"I'm all right," she said. "And I did all right."

"Amaya said you were incredible," he said. "But she told me not to tell you."

"Incredible, really?" Jerinne said. "Half the time I'm convinced she hates me."

He shrugged. "I believed that most of the time, too, even when we—" He stopped himself. "That doesn't matter."

"Saints above, you're blushing," Jerinne said.

"Can we talk about something else?"

"Sure," she said. "Like how I'm incredible, but still dead last in ranking."

"Last?"

"Dead last. Trandt mostly froze up in the fight, and he's ranked thirteen. Iolana ran away and she's eleven. But me, incredible me—last."

"I don't understand how that works," Dayne said. "Not up to me."

"I'm worried about Mentorship."

"Oh," he said. Getting assigned a mentor was a big

part of third year, and even though in his year everyone was assigned a mentor, it was true there seemed to be fewer Masters and Adepts around to be mentors. "I'm sure it'll be fine."

"A shame you're not an Adept."

The streets were filled with revelers, most of them drinking and hollering. Some of the taverns set out great fires burning in metal barrels, as the drunken people danced around it. Dayne was certain that would end in disaster. Typically during of the Revels of Liberation, the constables, fire brigade, and Yellowshields had their hands full with the incidents and injuries brought about by drunken celebration. Dayne hoped that wouldn't extend to Miri's party.

They reached the gates of Callon Hills, where Fredelle and the other Royal Firsts were waiting. Their outfits were fascinating—as if army dress uniforms had been remade as ball gowns, each with slightly different color schemes, different cuts. Evicka, the Linjari woman, wore a dress that was slit high, showing flesh all the way to her hip, while Argenitte wore a Scallic-style dress with layers of petticoats and long white gloves past her elbows, almost no skin showing below her neck.

Dayne was reminded of his conversation with Ret, and the vast differences between Scaloi, Linjar, and the rest of Druthal.

"Amaya, love," Fredelle said as they approached. "You've got your Adept pips, I see. Well done."

"And you have lieutenant's stripes," Amaya said coolly. "You and all your . . . compatriots."

"It's sort of honorary," the Kestan one said.

"Rutting blazes it is," the Oblunic one said. "I've earned these stripes. Six generations of pikemen in the Druth Army. My great-grandfather was one of the twenty at New Fencal."

"Everyone claims—" one of the Initiates said, but stopped at a dagger-filled glare from the Oblunic woman.

"Are we going in?" Fredelle said. "Or are we just going to look fabulous and gab in the street?"

"Right," Dayne said. "Miri—er, Lady Mirianne wants us to parade march from here, up the street and right into the household. The ten of you in the lead, and then the Tarians behind."

"I hope she doesn't want a weapons show like at the parade the other day," Fredelle said. "We didn't bring ours."

"None of us are armed," Amaya said. "Who needs weapons for a party? Come on, all. We need to parade march, let's line up and get in there. The party awaits."

Hemmit had never felt quite so out of place as he did at this party.

Party was underselling the event. It seemed to be a grand ball, as several of the large rooms of the Hanson mansion were filled with people, dressed in fanciful and fantastic outfits. Some of them were even masked, which was apparently a tradition at Linjari soirees, especially when they celebrated the Revels of Liberation. Music was in each room, blaring horns and racing rhythms. Players moved from room to room, with brass and drums and even a fellow at a vertical piano that was rolled about by two muscular steves. No sign of traditional string quints or even tavern troubadours to be seen.

Once more Hemmit was aware of how little he had traveled outside the city, how little of the world he knew.

And he was here, among all these swells and nobles and saints even knew who else, in his best suit, which was especially shabby, sipping some bizarre, overly sweet cocktail.

Maresh, at least, was by his side, though he looked absolutely miserable.

"We have no place in a thing like this," Maresh said. "Literally, this is the sort of thing we mock in the paper."

"I'm aware," Hemmit said. "But at least now we can mock with authority."

"Thrilling. Where did Lin go?"

"Her ladyship spirited her away." Hemmit still couldn't believe that Lady Mirianne actually wanted Lin to perform. Not for this crowd. This party might be daring, even risqué—the servers and some of the noble guests were in Linjari style skirts and stockings, with an inch of bare skin between the bottom of one and the tops of the other. Hemmit could see that some of the older members of the noble class were already quite scandalized.

If Lin actually performed, they might go into a fit.

"She stole this from Henterman," a young man in a purple silk suit said to Hemmit. Definitely a noble of some sort. "I mean blatantly."

"Stole what?" Hemmit asked.

The purple man pointed to the sweet drink in Hemmit's hand. "That. Henterman introduced it last week at his Saint Jontlen party—real fiasco that one—and Miri is just copying it."

"First time I've tried it," Hemmit said. "I far prefer a simple Kieran red."

"A good man," the purple man said. He took the cocktail away from Hemmit. "Come this way."

Hemmit was curious enough to follow the man into the next room, which was a quieter study. A few people were gathered and chatting in low voices, but no musicians here.

"Miri is keeping the wine here," the purple man said. "Let's see if we find something to your taste, Mister— sorry I don't think I got the name."

"Hemmit. Hemmit Eyairin. And this is Maresh Niol." Maresh had stuck to him, clearly not wanting to be alone.

"Eyairin and Niol. Well met. Stephen Terrenhill. Newly minted Baron of Deering, apparently." He found a decanter of wine and poured three glasses. Handing one each to Hemmit and Maresh, he said, "Which seems to do just fine with me here and letting decent people be left alone to run it. My father, may the saints bless him in his rest, knew well enough to keep the taxes low and the appointed administrators smart, and I plan to follow his example." He picked up a glass for himself and clinked it against theirs.

"Keep taxes low?" Maresh asked. "Most nobles aren't for that."

"Because most nobles are idiots about money, Mister Niol. They expect to be supported by the populace for nothing more than the luck of crawling out of the right woman's belly. Bosh, I say to that."

"We didn't know any nobles felt that way."

"I'm an unpopular sort, though that's why Miri likes me at these things, boys. I upset the tight-cravat gaspers. And they're all a bit too happy."

"Too happy? Why?" Hemmit asked.

"Well, the election." He sipped at his wine. "I mean yes, we don't know who won what and all that, but the word is around."

"It is?" Hemmit asked. "What have you heard?"

"You want to talk about the city Council of Aldermen and the Commissioners of the Loyalty? Or you want to talk Parliament? They're all disappointments."

Local and national. Both tempting. "Let's start with Parliament."

Terrenhill poured himself more wine. "There're no surprises, and that's the shame. Most of the same old boys are back. The handful of seats that were really up for grabs, though—like the dead ones. You know about that, boys?"

"A thing or two," Maresh said flatly.

"From what I hear, every single one has gone to a Traditionalist. It might flip the coalitions. Can you imagine, if the Dishers and the Books held the Parliament? We'd be in a state, my friends."

"Hush it, Stephen," someone said from across the room.

"I will not hush anything," Terrenhill said to that person. "You all would be so happy with that, wouldn't you? Tax the sewage out of your people, give nothing back. Not my fault your grandfathers were idiots."

"Your grandfather wasn't any smarter, he just found silver mines!"

"And invested that silver smartly, fools," Terrenhill said.

"You think he's right?" Maresh whispered. "The Parliament will turn over to the Dishers?"

Before Hemmit could respond, whistles pierced the air, and then a stomping of feet demanded attention be paid elsewhere. Everyone in the study wandered out to see what the commotion was.

The commotion was ten women, in military-style ball gowns, marching into the main ballroom, followed by a horde of Tarians in dress uniform. Including Dayne, who looked a bit uncomfortable with the whole affair. As they paraded through the party, a whistle cut through the air.

"Constables already breaking this up?" Terrenhill asked.

But it was Lady Mirianne with the whistle—though hers looked like it was bejeweled and made of ivory, instead of Constabulary tin—as she stepped up on a small dais in the center of the ballroom.

"Ladies and gentlemen and all grand personages, welcome to the Revels of Liberation! Two hundred and six years ago this very night, intrepid heroes risked their lives for this country defeating the Black Mage and restoring a free and just Druthal. On this night I have the honor present to you the current saviors of Maradaine, the heroes of the hour, the very spirits of honor, without whom our very vote and voice would have been squashed. The ladies of the Royal First Irregulars, and the fine men and women of the Tarian Order! You have heard all about their exploits, I'm sure; it has been the stuff of news and of legend. Well deserved. Please, my friends, go among them, shake their hands, and thank them. Without them, we would have lost that which makes us Druth."

"Miri, darling," one woman said loud enough to command the room. "You say 'we' and 'us,' but half of us never get a vote."

"Indeed," Lady Mirianne said, with enough of a coy wink that it was clear the woman was following a script she had laid out. "This isn't just a Linjari-style party, this is a suffragette party. Look for the young ladies in the violet coats and pins on their lapels, my friends. They have petitions for you to sign."

"Ha!" Terrenhill said. "I knew Miri had some sort of scheme. That's what she does, you know."

Hemmit excused himself and pushed his way over to Dayne, though several other folk had the same idea. Dayne looked like he was trying to get away from all of them, but decorum and civility kept him from just pushing away. Most of the other Tarians were in the same position, as were the ladies from the Royal First.

It was going to be some time before any of them would get a free moment. Poor fools.

# Chapter 16

SEVERAL SWELLS AND MINOR nobles had shaken Jerinne's hand. She had been led from room to room, with little sense of where she was or who she was being introduced to. She had hoped to talk more with Dayne, tell him the whole story of the past two days, but she had lost track of him.

After each person came up to her to say a kind word of gratitude, a young woman in a violet blazer would swoop in, and speak of how Jerinne and the other Tarians had helped protect other people's votes, so wasn't it time to secure Jerinne's right to vote as well? After all, there was already a suffragette initiative on the ballot in Oblune, and wasn't Maradaine a far more progressive and cosmopolitan place? Then they shoved a petition in the person's hands and glared at him with a beaming smile until he signed.

"All right, enough of this," she heard someone say. She got pulled away from a glad-handing baron and the petitioner who had swooped in, to find herself face to face with Vien and someone in a Spathian uniform. "Don't drink too much of this in, Initiate," Vien said, though she was sipping a cocktail of some sort.

"I haven't drunk anything yet."

"I mean the accolade," Vien said. "It's dangerous."

"Makes you soft," the Spathian said.

"This is Mizarnis," Vien said.

"Candidate for the Spathian Order," Mizarnis said, offering their hand.

"Oh," Jerinne said, looking at the two of them. The rumors apparently were true. Jerinne took their hand, a grip like iron. "How did you two meet?"

"Vien spent the last few months running across the city and back each morning," Mizarnis said. "I started to run with her, and then showed her how the Spathians train their bodies."

"And hasn't it been revelatory?" Vien asked Jerinne.

"It's definitely powerful," Jerinne said. She wasn't sure how else to respond, what wrong phrase might unleash some sort of retribution during the next training with Vien.

It didn't matter, because another whistle blow took the room's attention.

"Of course, friends, this won't all be politics," Lady Mirianne said from the center of the ballroom. "That would hardly be fun, would it?"

"No!" several people in the crowd shouted.

"And we want some fun, don't we? Some truly decadent and sinful fun that would make our parents weep over what the country has come to. Don't we?"

"Yes!"

"Well, fortunately for you all, I've arranged just the thing. The very tonic we need to shock our systems. Are you ready?"

Jerinne didn't know what to make of this. She leaned over to Vien. "Last time I was here she arranged a very strange bit of theater for us. I wonder what it is now."

Lady Mirianne continued, "And so, ladies and gentlemen, for your viewing pleasure, I present a performance the likes of which you have never seen before in polite company. And possibly never will again. So turn your attention to the center of the room and Miss Lin Shartien, performing her own singular take on the Yoleanne Ribbon Dance!"

The band started to play—a deliberate beat, strong and invasive—while the strings and horns curled invitingly around the room. On the beat of the music, the doors from the far side of the ballroom flew open, and Lin stood in the doorway, the flickering candlelight playing on her face. She was wearing a simple robe, belted at the waist, hanging loosely at the top to show her bare shoulders and the Circle tattoo over her heart.

She walked into the room, each step deliberate, each step on the beat. With each step, she turned her head, her eyes finding a member of the audience. Each step, a flash of bare leg could be glimpsed from under her robe.

Lin reached the center of the room, the tempo of the music building, and her eyes found Jerinne's. For just a moment, she was staring right at Jerinne like they were the only two people in the room, and Jerinne could feel her heart racing in her chest. Jerinne had always found Lin beautiful, sensual, but in this moment she was so much more than that. She was desire personified, and Jerinne found it hard to even draw breath.

Then Lin turned away, but Jerinne still found herself deeply affected.

Lin spun quickly, the robe flaring up as she turned, and she extended her hand. Light and flame leaped from the candles and whirled down to her, spinning around her body as Lin continued to twirl on the floor, faster and faster. The music flared with a burst of horns, and bands of light encompassed her as she leapt out of the twirl, landing several feet away. Two whirling circles of blue and violet light spun around her body.

And nothing else.

The robe had been discarded on the floor. Gasps filled the room, but Jerinne couldn't even manage that. Almost every inch of Lin's breathtaking figure was on display, save the few portions hidden by the whirling ribbons of light, and Lin stood still for a moment: powerful, utterly in control.

The crowd was hers.

The music crackled with horns and strings, a symphony that screamed with a sensual rhythm that Jerinne couldn't put words to, but still felt in the center of her being.

Lin moved to that rhythm, her body a testimony of grace and perfection, the spinning light staying around her to preserve the appearance of decency. But not modesty. Lin's face shone with pride. Power. Knowledge that she owned the room. That every man in the room was focused on her to the exclusion of all else.

Jerinne found her hands trembling at the thought of it, the thought of Lin, the beauty of her body and motion.

The spinning lights intensified as the music swelled to a roaring crescendo. It reached its peak, Lin flared out her hands, and her whole body exploded with a blinding burst of light in every color.

When Jerinne could see again, Lin stood proudly in the center of the room, robe back on, bowing to thunderous applause.

Lin took her bows, as Lady Mirianne joined her in the center of the room. "Wonderful! Truly spectacular!"

"It was an honor, my lady," Lin said.

"Now, musicians!" Mirianne cried out. "Play something we all can dance to!"

Jerinne still found herself flushed, struggling to even breathe. She mumbled an excuse to whoever was near her, not sure who it was, and found her way out to a balcony into the cool night air. Gripping the railing, she tried to focus on the gardens below her, but her thoughts kept swirling back to Lin and her perfect body, to visions of Raila in the baths, the Waishen-haired shopgirl, even flitting ideas of Arthady Mirrendum, which disturbed her and excited her at the same time.

"Breathe, girl."

Jerinne looked up to see Fredelle Pence, lovely in her uniform-cut dress, holding out a glass of wine.

"You look like you need this."

Jerinne took the glass of wine and drank half in one gulp.

"Sorry," Jerinne said. "I just needed some air."

"You need to cool down, all right," Fredelle said. "I mean, what we just saw would heat up the dead, let alone your young blood."

"I'll be fine," Jerinne said.

"Probably," Fredelle said. "You know, your fellow Initiates are talking you up something fierce. I hear you were in a scuffle yesterday, acquitted yourself pretty well."

"Well enough," Jerinne said. "I'm still standing."

"And what's your ranking?"

"I don't see how that's—"

"I already know," Fredelle said. "You're at the bottom. Dead last. And your fellow Initiates—even the ones who don't like you—think that's bunk."

Jerinne shrugged. She wasn't sure if that was praise or some attempt to belittle her. "It doesn't matter, really."

"Like blazes it doesn't," Fredelle said. "Can I tell you a secret? The rankings don't really matter, not in terms of who you are and what you can do. If they've decided you're on the bottom, no power there is will convince the Grandmaster or whatever old stooge is doing the ranks to change that."

"But Madam Tyrell—"

"Amaya? She might be allowed some input, but those

old men make the decisions. And they've decided about you."

"What did they decide?"

"Same thing they did about me, dear," Fredelle said, stepping closer to her, her face just inches away. "I worked and fought, did everything I could, but still kept ranking at the bottom. And do you want to know why?"

Jerinne found her mouth dry, barely able to put out the words as her lips trembled. "Why?"

Fredelle moved closer, her lips first brushing Jerinne's, then coming in stronger. The kiss was delirious, delicious, everything Jerinne had thought it could be when she imagined someone's lips touching hers. Jerinne found herself instinctively kissing back, clutching Fredelle's hand, wanting more out of her.

Fredelle pulled away, eyes piercing at Jerinne, her hand wrapped around Jerinne's. With a slight grin, wicked and sad, she said, "That's why."

Jerinne could barely think straight.

"What do you—I—I've never—" She tried to focus herself back to what they were talking about. "Are you certain that's why?"

Fredelle shrugged. "Certain, no. But when it was me, that was my instinct. Who knows you like girls?"

"No one!" Jerinne said so loud, it was almost a shout. No one glanced at them. Anyone close to the balcony doors was paying all their mind to the dance floor.

"Really?"

"Well, Dayne figured it out . . ."

"Oh, sweet saints, child. If Dayne could tell, I'm sure many, many, many people know. You aren't exactly subtle."

"I—what?"

"It's fine," Fredelle said. "I mean, maybe not as far as the Tarians are concerned. But you'll be fine."

Fear iced into Jerinne's heart. "Are you?"

"I won't lie, it broke my heart to wash out. But I

found my path, found my place." She didn't sound that convinced. "But you shouldn't worry."

"It sounds like I should." She was thinking about every glance, every touch, every offhand comment she had made. Who had noticed? Who knew? Who hated her because of it.

"No. I've had my ears open tonight, and you know what those other Initiates and Candidates are all whispering about?" She pointed a finger at Jerinne's chest. "The girl who fought the mage. The girl who didn't flinch or blink."

"No, they're not."

"Don't do that, girl. They are going to try to grind you down at every moment. But do something for me, hmm?"

"Anything," Jerinne found herself saying all too quickly.

"When they rank you at the bottom, when they push you down, you lift your head high, and tell yourself this true, beautiful thing."

"What's that?"

"That you are rutting amazing." She leaned in and kissed Jerinne on the cheek. "Get over that crush you're nursing, and then look me up, hmm?"

"The what I'm what?"

Fredelle was already walking back into the party, though, giving a wink as she went in.

Jerinne finished the rest of the wine. "I am rutting amazing," she said to no one. "And the ranks can go to blazes."

She went into the party in search of more wine and someone to dance with.

Dayne had, after some time of handshakes and polite gratitude, retreated from the center of the party to a quiet study. There were a couple of young noblemen who looked like they were about to settle into some kissing when he came in, but they made themselves scarce when he didn't immediately step out. Normally he'd be a bit embarrassed, but this time his desire for quiet and solitude won out.

He sat down in a leather armchair—this room was probably the earl's study for when he was in Maradaine, which he almost never was—and wondered what to make of what had just occurred.

He tried to push down the feelings he was having about Mirianne. Ugly and unjust, and he didn't want to think of her that way. This party was nothing he wanted, and coming had made him feel even worse.

Used.

"You are sulking."

He looked to the doorway, where Mirianne was standing, looking lovely in her dress—blue with hints of gray. It actually was perfect, an elegant match for his dress uniform.

"I'm not good company right now," he said.

She came into the study, closing the door behind her. "And I haven't been good company," she said. "I've been very involved in all my things, and haven't been very thoughtful about you."

"That isn't it," Dayne said.

"Is this about Lin's dance?" she asked. "I know it was a bit more provocative than this crowd was ready for."

"I'm not upset about that." He changed the subject. "Can I ask why you are hosting a Linjari-themed party? We're from the Archduchy of Maradaine, as are most of the people here."

"Because the Linjari are far more interesting," she said. "They don't get hung up over propriety or tradition, which I find enlightening." She went to the desk and took a bottle out the drawer. "Jessel has been nipping at this whiskey, and she thinks I don't know."

"Don't you think that's odd?"

"No, she believes she's being—"

"Not about Jessel and the whiskey," Dayne said. He had almost snapped it at her, but clipped that back and kept his voice even. She poured two glasses and came around to him.

"Then what, my thoughts on Linjar?"

"It seems like . . . reveling in the exotic."

"Exotic?" She shrugged, handing him the glass. "I mean, in a way. But we're all Druth, and I thought that was the point of these holidays. I had considered trying to host a true Reunification party. Ten different rooms with ten different themes. Ten different outfits for me to wear . . ."

"Miri," he said.

"It was too much, of course. The menu alone would have cost a fortune. And the Scallic room would have been deadly dull."

"That . . . that's what I've been thinking about."

"How dull Scaloi is?"

"How different," he said. "I mean, a week ago, I wouldn't have given it a moment's thought, or considered the Open Hand anything but a nuisance."

"Are they anything but a nuisance?"

"I ate lunch with their leader yesterday," Dayne said. "In a Scallic pub. Their food, their thoughts. And I asked myself, is this Druthal? Should it be?"

She frowned, taking a sip of her whiskey. "All right, I tease, but yes, it is, and it should. And we are stronger for those differences."

"I would like to think so," Dayne said. "I'm sorry. Like I said, I'm not good company." He took a sip of the whiskey, which was exceptional. Smooth and velvety. She leaned in and kissed him.

When she pulled away, he continued. "But I do think Bishop Issendel has some good points."

"That's what you thought about when I kissed you?"

He took another sip. "Am I doing good things in this new position?"

"It's early in the job, dear. You still need to figure it out."

"It just seems odd, wearing my Tarian uniform and being a mouthpiece of the marshals and the Parliament."

"You look quite fetching in that uniform."

The real thing gnawing at him bubbled up. "I'm not happy about you using us as a draw toward the Suffragist petitions."

"You don't believe it's a just cause?"

"No, I do," Dayne said. "But that's me, Dayne Heldrin, citizen of Druthal. Not Dayne of the Tarian Order. Nor anyone else in the uniform. The Order must be neutral in the political process."

She frowned again. "Neutrality is a coward's way to stay complicit in injustice."

"I didn't—"

"Oh, no, I can't say anything about it," she said in a mocking tone. "I must stay above the fray."

"That isn't what I mean."

"But it is," she said. She finished her whiskey in a gulp. "My love, this country is on the precipice of change. I can feel it with every breath. You are in a position to help guide where that change will fall."

"Am I?"

"Yes, you! The Tarians have captured the love of the people again, and that is on you. You can help push this country on a path that honors its history and its legacy, while also making bold steps toward a better tomorrow for everyone."

He thought about what he had seen of the election results today. "I don't know how bold that really is going to be."

"It can be," she said. "Why do you think I'm championing the Royal First? I know the military and the royal cabinet only conceived them as some sort of show pony tour group, boosting morale of the soldiers by showing off girls in short skirts. But I see them as a sign for what the future can be. What women in this country are capable of. What I can do with my authority. What girls like Jerinne can do."

He smiled and put down his glass. "That I can get behind. I don't know that I'm in any position to do much for you, but I can get behind it."

"Good," she said, kissing him. They kissed for some time, until they were interrupted by screams and the sounds of broken glass.

Miri sighed. "That always happens to us."

# INTERLUDE: The Lord

LORD HOLM WINDALL, the Archduke of Oblune, had no peers in Maradaine. No one else of archducal rank was in the city right now, all of them being at their home estates. Windall wished he was doing the same, but right now the work was important.

There was the Royal Family, but as far as Windall was concerned, they were above him. At least, Prince Escaraine and Princess Carianna were. The mongrel Maradaine XVIII was definitely not someone Windall would consider a peer.

So he had to stoop for company. Tonight that meant the home of Lord Kell Pollock, the Duke of Maradaine. Kell was a serviceable fellow, perfectly fine person to have dinner with. Especially since, for any dinner Windall came to, he was the guest of honor.

"It's been ghastly, let me tell you," Pollock was saying as they privately adjourned to his study for pipes and whiskey. "I wish I was allowed to just appoint the

Council of Aldermen and the Commissioners of the Loyalty. But no, it has to be a vote."

"That is the way of things, friend," Windall said. He empathized, though archdukes were granted a bit more latitude. Not much, but a bit. There were elected seats for the Archduchy Convocation, but also seats he had the authority to appoint. He also appointed the civilian governor, though that person had to be elevated from the elected members of the Archduchy Convocation. And the governor had full authority to name whoever he wished to his Chairs of Commission, usually listening to Windall's advice on the subject.

The current Civilian Governor of Oblune, Elton Anderman, was a solid-headed sort who handled business with quiet competence and grace. The people liked him, and Holm Windall liked him. Oblune was running fine, even if Anderman had agreed to put the suffragette cause on the ballot. Windall overlooked little disagreements like that, because Anderman's solid work allowed him the freedom to spend most of his time in Maradaine dealing with the affairs of the capital and the throne.

And those affairs needed his help. Saints watching from above, he didn't know exactly how he had ended up on this Grand Ten, but he was glad he was a part of it. Those two members of Parliament who thought they were in charge of the venture were dunderheads who were likely to get everyone else killed.

But not Windall. Steps had been taken. He was protected.

"The alderman race, I'm told, is fine. Some troubles on the south side of the city, but that just made the north side turnout that much stronger."

"Fortunate for you that the voting in your dukedom is split into two separate days, and the more desirable franchisees are voting last."

"Even still, I worry." Pollock offered a taper for Windall to light his pipe with.

"Well, of course. But we expect no problems, yes?"

A knock came on the study door. The impetuous man who knocked didn't even wait for a response, just inviting himself in to join his betters. Windall said nothing, though, because this man was going to prove useful.

"Vice Commandant," Windall said, "we thought you might have gone home already."

"Not quite, your lordships. Not quite." He looked expectantly at the duke. Pollock, ever the gentleman, showed no disgust on his face as he selected a pipe and passed it to Vice Commandant Undenway. He happily took it and lit it off the taper. "Only a couple nights left with that title, though."

"If all goes well," Pollock said.

"And it should," Windall said. "Commissioner Enbrain is not exactly popular with the people, is he?" That was true, largely because of the extensive campaign that Windall and Pollock had funded through various firms and partnerships to discredit the current Constabulary commissioner. Undenway would be a clear favorite at the polls.

When Underway won, which he was sure to, the people would be elated by the new leadership in the Loyalty.

"Well, we're set," Undenway said, sucking on his pipe.

"My dear man," Windall said. "We have made endeavors, and all signs are that they should be successful, and in a few days' time, you will be the new commissioner of the Constabulary. But we can only do so much, and we will see the fruits of our labor soon."

"Right," Undenway said with a nod. As if what Windall had said was just an official story, and that the election was well and truly rigged.

Windall wished it was that easy.

Undenway was a horse's ass, but he was a useful one for Windall's needs. A perfectly acceptable tool, one who had vast veins of corruption and graft under his control, in the Constabulary and in the city's underworld. Normally, such a man being named commissioner of the Constabulary would be disastrous, but Windall was planning to craft some well-controlled disaster. That was what the Grand Ten needed for the next phase of things, once all the pieces were in place. The vice commandant was just such a piece.

If that meant tolerating a man like Undenway, so be it. Even though the man often smelled of fish and rank perfume.

Archduke Holm Windall would endure. It was his duty. For the throne and country. Soon he would act, the right man would be on the throne, and the great nation of Druthal would again be on the right path.

# Chapter 17

"LADIES AND GENTLEMEN, your diversions have come to an abrupt end!"

Jerinne looked up to see at least thirty men and women in fur-lined capes, crimson vests, and kerchiefs on their faces, storming into the ballroom. Only one of them wasn't covering her face—Quinara, the hatchet woman, leading the group front and center. She still had her hatchets, plus two more on her belt. The rest were armed with cudgels, handsticks, and hammers.

Jerinne had been on the dance floor with Miss Jessel—Lady Mirianne's handmaiden—and a young baroness whose name she had not kept in her memory. Fortunately, Linjari dancing was not formalized, so instead of dancing with a partner, it was common to dance in a group as the music moved your spirit. As such, several of the young women at the party were dancing in clusters together, while most of the young men hung along the sides of the room, drinks in hand. The effect meant that Jerinne could dance with Jessel and the comely baroness without questions or further damage to her surely sullied reputation.

That ended when Quinara shouted her proclamation, and her fellow subversives started smashing art and anything else in sight.

Screams of terror came out of the crowd, especially the women on the dance floor.

"Run," Jerinne told Miss Jessel, who didn't need the prompting. Most people scattered.

Two who didn't scatter were members of the Royal First. Evicka, the Linjari woman, and the Oblunic one. Jerinne had not caught her name. As Quinara and the goons charged the ballroom floor, Evicka dashed to the window, yanking down the tapestry, the chain tying it back, and the curtain rod.

"Kelly!" Evicka shouted, tossing the naked curtain rod to the Oblunic woman. She caught it, and immediately began spinning it about with blinding speed. She leaped into the fray, knocking down several of the subversives.

"Oh, it's you," Quinara said, focusing on Jerinne. "I owe you a scratch or two." She dove in with both hatchets at Jerinne.

Jerinne scrambled out the way, grabbing a fallen drinks tray off the ground. The next flurry of axe attacks were blocked with the tray, and Jerinne did her best to knock Quinara in her stupid face when she had an opportunity. Few opportunities presented themselves.

Evicka, meanwhile, had taken the chain and whipped it about with fascinating skill and lethal prowess. With simple flicks of her wrist and twists of her body, the chain sang out, wrapped around her enemies' necks and arms, and pulled them down to the ground.

Jerinne could watch Evicka and Kelly all day, if she weren't locked in her own deadly combat.

"Why are you even here?" Jerinne asked Quinara between dodges.

"You ruined my fun, thought we'd return the favor." One axe came hammering down, caving in the tray. Jerinne threw it to one side, and dashed in the other direction, sliding on the shiny, waxed ballroom floor. Quinara chased after her, but Jerinne had the chance to pick up a pair of handsticks from one of the fallen goons. Evicka and Kelly were deep in their fight, perfect dance partners as they took down the few they were dealing with. But even though they were holding a good fight here, the miscreants were running wild through the house.

Quinara jumped at her, but now armed with handsticks, Jerinne easily parried each blow, yanking the hatchets out of her grip. Quinara went for the two others on her belt, but Jerinne was faster, flipping the handsticks around to punch the short ends into the woman's face.

Jab, cross, backhand, in quick succession. Quinara backed up, shaking off the blows.

"Not bad, cub," she said, wiping the blood off her lip. "Shame about those two."

Quinara pointed out the window to the moonslit garden. Outside five men had caught Miss Jessel and the baroness, and they had the look in their eyes of men about to do unspeakable things.

Jerinne didn't have time to find another way out to the garden. She hurled a handstick, shattering the bay window, and dove outside. These fellows needed to be dealt with. Quinara could wait.

Amaya was on the balls of her feet when the screams started. She didn't know what was happening, but her instincts told her that the guests at the party needed to be protected, and fast. She was standing outside a grand dining hall, where the banquet buffet had been laid out. Five exits, but all the doors could be closed and latched. Plenty of space. A good room to keep people safe in.

"This way!" she called out in her most commanding voice. "Quickly, in here!"

People came rushing in, and Amaya saw why. Five armed people had charged into the room, clubbing and beating anyone they came across. Amaya spotted Iolana and Dade with the crowd. She grabbed them by the shoulders.

"Get in there, secure the doors."

Both of them nodded and set off. Some of the other Initiates followed into the dining hall. Others had dug into the scrum with the invaders. Raila and Enther had teamed up to keep the attention of one invader while Tander pulled injured out of the hall. A pair of the invaders had the misfortune of getting the attention of Vien and her Spathian paramour. The two of them were lightning and thunder, disarming and disabling the attackers with ruthless efficiency.

Amaya trusted them all to handle the fight, and focused on the injured and helpless, pushing them into the banquet hall. Her Initiates had secured all the doors but one, and had taken post on the open one, accepting each civilian with grace.

Amaya couldn't have been more proud of them. This was nothing they had been taught—how can you teach someone how to behave in a crisis like this—but they all took their roles with unspoken instinct, acting for the common good in unison.

Another invader came running into the room, knives high, screaming as he charged at Raila. Amaya swept in, kicking out his knee before he could reach her people. He crumpled to the floor, dropping his knives. Amaya scooped them up before he had a chance to, and then delivered a sharp kick to his head, and stomped on his shoulder to pin him down. He stopped struggling.

The civilians were in the dining hall, and all the miscreants in the immediate vicinity were incapacitated for the moment.

"You two, get in there, shut the door, and keep those people safe," she ordered Raila and Enther. To Vien and her Spathian friend, who were both heaving and flushed, she said, "Secure these idiots and then guard those doors. There're more civilians and our people in the mix out there." She could hear screams and crashes in the distance.

"But we could—" Vien started.

"Civilians," Amaya said, pointing toward the closing door. "They're your first priority, Candidate."

Vien nodded, and tossed the truncheon she had grabbed off one of the men to Amaya. Amaya caught it and belted the knives. Weapon in hand, she ran toward the chaos.

With no shield or sword, Dayne armed himself with serving tray and candelabra, slowly opening the door of the study. Sounds of chaos filled his ears: running, screaming, breaking, hitting, crying.

"Behind me," he told Lady Mirianne. "The house seems to be overrun. Your bedrooms are the safest place for you, and the easiest to reach from here."

"You expect me to be locked in my bedroom while hooligans tear my house apart?"

"I expect to keep you safe, my lady," he said. Formality to remind her their respective roles. They were not friends and lovers right now. He was a Tarian, she was nobility, and he had a duty to keep her from the harm that filled the house.

"There are at least two dozen other members of the peerage out there, Dayne," she said. "Not just me."

"One at a time, my lady," he said. "Right now you're with me, and that's my duty. When you're safe, then I'll—"

"That's hardly a—" she started.

"We're going to make for the stairs. We'll debate particulars later."

"I'm not abandoning my house, my staff, my guests to these—"

"These what?" This came from the leader of a group of five, all with knives or truncheons, standing between Dayne and the stairway. Not common hooligans. Muscular bruisers, possibly mercenaries. They certainly held their weapons with competence and confidence. There was no way to get Mirianne to safety other than to go through them.

"Gentlemen," Dayne said, taking a defensive posture with his makeshift armaments. "I've no wish to harm anyone. If any of you choose to withdraw, I'll respect that."

They responded by all charging him at once.

The two with knives were the most immediate threat. Dayne knocked one in the face with the serving tray, and used the candelabra to trap the blade of the other. That left the other three free to pummel him with their truncheons, which hurt like blazes on his arms and chest. Fortunately, none of them had the reach to hit his face.

He twisted the candelabra to yank the knife out of the one man's grasp, and then swept his arm to push one of the truncheoners into the other knife-fighter, who was moving back in. He accidentally stabbed his fellow in the gut.

Dayne took the moment to focus his attention on the other two truncheoners. They were both savage in their attacks, and were Dayne a smaller man, they would have quickly torn him down. Dayne took the blows on his arms, which were surely bruised and bloody under his uniform. He only endured this long enough to get the rhythm of their attacks, so he could strike, grabbing the wrist of the one on his right. With a hard pull, the bone cracked, and the man cried out.

The disarmed man dove to the floor for his knife. Dayne stepped on his hand, pinning him down, and with another twist of his hand, flipped the man with the broken arm on top of him.

The second knife-fighter had freed his blade from his fellow's body, and was moving in. Dayne sidestepped him, grabbing his arm and using his own momentum to throw him to the ground. Dayne made sure to throw him hard enough to knock out his breath, sending him to the floor with a resounding crack.

"You'll regret that," the one man left standing said, stepping back to regain his footing.

"You're not wrong," Dayne said. The man came back in with sharp, hard swings of his truncheon. Dayne dodged the first two, and caught the truncheon on the third swing. He wrenched it from the man's grasp, and then brought it down on his head. Looking at the five men—bleeding, gasping, insensate—he shook his head. "As I said, I had no wish to harm anyone. But I could not allow you to hurt her ladyship, either."

"Are you all right?" Lady Mirianne asked.

"Nothing that will impede me," Dayne said, scooping the serving tray back up. "Let's get you secure."

He took the lead as they hurried to the main staircase, a sweeping arc up to the hallway overlooking the main foyer, which led to the bedrooms. They ran up the stairs, and were almost at the top when a blast of fire burst in front of them.

Dayne turned to see a man hovering in the air above the foyer, wings of flame spread out from his back. "Hey, Scanlin! We found the lady!"

A man strode out of a darkened hallway—stripped to the waist, wearing only leather pants. He was obscenely muscular, and in each hand he carried a long whip.

"Excellent, Pria," he said with an oily smile. "Let's get what we came for."

Three bruisers stormed into the study, and immediately set to work beating and bashing. Hemmit didn't even know what was happening before a truncheon had already been cracked over one woman's head. She dropped like a sack, and the bruisers were invested in making everyone else in the study end up just like her.

"What in the—" was all Baron Terrenhill got out before taking a handstick to his own head. He took only a glancing blow, since Maresh had grabbed him and pulled him back from the attacker.

"Come on!" Maresh yelled, pulling the baron to his feet and dragging him to the door. Hemmit dove at the ruffian, center of the body, pushing him against the study wall. He laid several punches into the man's sides, while books from the shelves above fell on their heads. His time in the Gentlemen's Fisticuffs Club at RCM seemed to have been wasted, as they didn't even give the man pause. He slammed an elbow into the small of Hemmit's back, knocking him down. Hemmit rolled out of the way before a boot came crashing down on his head. Hemmit threw another punch at the man's knee, and then scrambled to his feet and out of the room with Maresh, who was carrying the half-limp baron.

"What were you doing?" Maresh shouted.

"Trying to—" was all Hemmit got out before someone else crashed into him. A guest, trying to run away from the attackers. One of the attackers was struck by an oil lamp, sending a spray of flaming oil at the fleeing guests. One woman's dress caught fire, and Hemmit quickly grabbed a tablecloth and tackled her, smothering the flames.

"You're all right, you're all right," he said, more for his own benefit, as she screamed and flailed. She scrambled out from under him and ran, half singed, out of that hallway into one of the water closets.

"We have to get out of here," Maresh said, grabbing Hemmit's arm.

"Yes," the baron slurred. "Most disagreeable."

"But where's Lin?" Hemmit asked. "We can't run away without her."

"He can't run anywhere," Maresh said.

"Come on," Hemmit said, pulling Maresh and the baron around a darkened corner. None of the invaders seemed to be here. Hemmit felt around until he found a doorknob—linen closet. "In here."

"We can't all fit in there," Maresh said.

"No, but you two can," Hemmit said before Maresh could argue. He shoved Baron Terrenhill and Maresh into the closet just as one of the ruffians came rushing over, cudgel in hand. Hemmit shut the door and ducked, so the bastard just smashed his cudgel into the wall. Hemmit popped up and took a good swing at the man's jaw, but once again his time in the Fisticuffs hadn't done him many favors. A solid punch, but all it did was make the fellow cross.

The cudgel swung at him again and again, and Hemmit jumped back with each swing. Unable to see where he was going, he stepped badly and lost his footing, tumbling backward into a heap on the ground. The ruffian roared and leaped on him with the cudgel.

Hemmit put up his arms defensively, but the blow didn't come. Instead, there was a great burst of light and sound. Lin was there, hands wide as daggers of color flew, striking his attacker in the face. The man screamed and stumbled away, dropping his cudgel, and he groped at his eyes and ears. Lin picked up his weapon and walloped him across the head.

"Can you walk?" she asked.

"Yes," Hemmit said, getting to his feet. "Only my pride is hurt."

"Saints, this is a mess," she said, holding the cudgel with intention. "Where's Maresh?"

"He's in that closet with Baron Terrenhill," Hemmit said. She just raised an eyebrow at that. "I would have hidden there as well, but it was small."

"Hiding, Hemmit? Really?"

"We're—" he started, but two more of those maniacs

came running into the hallway, weapons in hand. Lin spun on her heel, dazzling another blast of light at them. This wasn't effective, only giving them a moment of pause before pressing in again. Lin stumbled; she must have spent herself. Hemmit grabbed the cudgel and swung wild, clocking the first maniac across the forehead. That put him down.

The second teased her advance, twirling a pair of hatchets in her hands.

"Aren't you two some fine pieces?" she asked.

"Back off!" Hemmit said, brandishing the cudgel in his right hand while holding Lin steady with his left. The woman responded by spinning around, and in the space of a whisper, chopped the cudgel into pieces and landed a kick on Hemmit's chest.

"So," she said, her voice a purr thick with Acoran accent, "other than the very pretty beard you're sporting, is there a reason I shouldn't kill you now?"

# Chapter 18

"I WILL NOT ALLOW YOU to cause any harm," Dayne told the two. They were quite the pair: a flying mage with flaming wings, and a madman with well-oiled muscles and whips.

"Oh, I've heard of this one," Scanlin said, snapping one of his whips with a resounding crack. "He's the big hero."

"Big hero, indeed," Pria said, charging a ball of fire in his hand. "He'll burn just the same."

He threw the fireball at Dayne, who blocked it with the serving tray. The ball burst on the tray, the flames licking Dayne's fingers, forcing him to drop it. With his attention occupied, Scanlin whipped at Mirianne, wrapping her waist. With a flick of his wrist, he pulled her up the stairs past Dayne.

"No!" Dayne said, grabbing her hand. That kept Scanlin from pulling her to him, but he still had her ensnared. He cracked the other whip at Dayne's arm, leaving a harsh welt. Painful, but not enough to force Dayne to let go of Mirianne.

"Get him off!" Scanlin snarled.

"With pleasure," Pria said as he swooped around and hurled another flaming ball at Dayne. This one flew over Dayne's head and splashed fire on the wall, catching one of the tapestries.

"You will pay for that!" Mirianne shouted.

"It's you who are going to pay, sweet," Pria said. "Mark it."

Another whip snap as Scanlin yanked at Mirianne. She cried out in pain—her arm was being wrenched from Dayne's hold on her. He stepped forward to ease her pain and close the distance between him and Scanlin. If that meant a gash or two from his whips, so be it. But another fireball forced him back a step, near the upper railing.

"You want her?" Scanlin cackled, snapping at Dayne. He charged forward and shoved Mirianne at Dayne, while cracking the whip at Dayne's ankle. With a yank, he pulled Dayne off balance just as she crashed into him, and the two of them broke through the railing. Dayne fell to the floor below, landing on his hip with a resounding slam. Pain radiated through his body, but his attention was locked on Mirianne, dangling over the edge on the tips of her toes, Scanlin's whip still wrapped around her waist.

Before Dayne could get up, more fireballs rained down from above. Dayne rolled away from the foyer, slapping down the flames on his uniform jacket.

"Dayne!" Mirianne screamed as she was pulled out of view.

Dayne pulled himself up, his entire left side in pain. Pria still swooped about, hurling fire and keeping Dayne from the stairs.

"Not the big hero now, are you?" Pria taunted.

Down the hallway, Dayne spotted someone in the

fray with a couple other brigands. Fredelle, armed with a broken broomstick. She put them down with well-placed punches, and then glanced up to make eye contact with Dayne.

"Fredelle!" he called out. "Sequence Twenty-Seven!"

She came charging down the hall at him. Pushing through the pain, he forced himself to his feet and got himself under the flying mage, bracing his legs and holding his hand in position. Fredelle ran to him and leaped up, landing the ball of her foot on his hand just as he pushed up.

Fredelle flew high up to Pria and executed a perfect combination of staff blow and spinning kick as she passed him and drop punched on his head as she came back down. Pria's flaming wings were snuffed out as he plummeted to the ground. Fredelle landed in Dayne's arms.

"That was a hoot!" she said, her face a wide smile.

"Her ladyship's in trouble upstairs," Dayne said.

"On it," Fredelle said, hopping out of his arms and dashing up the stairs. Dayne couldn't move as fast as she did.

Pria pulled himself to his feet, groaning as impotent sparks came from his hands. "I do not get paid enough for this," he muttered as he wiped the blood off his nose.

Dayne grabbed him by the front of his shirt. "Who paid you? What is this about?"

"I do get paid enough not to tell you," Pria said. "But just barely." He spit a ball of fire in Dayne's face. It was too weak to do anything but startle Dayne, but that was enough for him to let Pria go. Pria dashed out the main door.

Dayne wasn't about to let him go so easily. He knew what this was about, and if he was a hired mage, he'd probably be willing to cut a deal with the constables in return for telling who hired him. He ran after the man, despite his hip joint screaming in pain with every step.

Pria stumbled and fell as he went, looking more and more terrified each time he turned back to see Dayne's relentless pace toward him. Dayne knew he was limping, left leg almost dragging as he went. That might have made him even more frightening to the man.

"You shouldn't be worried about me!" Pria shouted. "You should be worried about getting the Fire Brigade here before the house catches!"

That didn't deter Dayne, even though he knew Pria was right about that. They needed everything: constables, brigade, Yellowshields, and fast.

"Come on!" Pria shouted as he reached the gates. Dayne was briefly confused. Was he trying to taunt Dayne? Was running outside a distraction? "Come on!" Dayne pushed forward, about to grab the man.

Then it was clear. Pria was berating himself, trying to build up his magic. A pair of flaming wings—smaller and dimmer than before—sprouted from his back and he launched into the air. Dayne didn't even have anything to throw at him as he vanished into the night.

Dayne grabbed hold of the gate to steady himself. Everything hurt. But he needed to get back to the house, back to help everyone. Lady Mirianne was—

No, he had to trust Fredelle. She was excellent. She could handle an enthusiastic whip master.

He caught his breath, and looked across the street to see the one thing he really needed right now.

A whistlebox.

He stumbled over to it and checked the list of codes until he found the one he needed: one long, two short for an All-Hands Emergency.

He blasted that out several times, until he heard it repeated in the distance. Good. That meant everyone was coming: constables, brigade, and Yellowshields. The help Lady Mirianne needed.

He wanted to drop down to the ground, but he couldn't do that yet. His leg was growing stiff, and each step was harder. But it didn't matter. No matter what, he'd make it back to the house, back to Miri.

Jerinne felt a lot of satisfaction in clocking the first one of these bastards in the head with the handstick. It was in no way a weapon of choice for her, but she found the feel of the wood in her hand as it connected to his jaw and the crack his bones made as he fell to the ground very pleasing indeed.

"All of you, back away," she said as she pressed her foot on the neck of the one she knocked down. "No one is going to hurt these women tonight."

"Then we'll hurt you and then them," one of the miscreants said. "All of you."

Jerinne glanced to her left and right to see Evicka and Kelly on either side.

"You found a party," Evicka said.

"Was this a costumed soiree tonight?" one of the others said, grabbing the young noblewoman—who was wearing an elaborate mask that matched her dress—by her chin and lifting her up.

"Don't use that word," Evicka said.

"I mean," the front man of the boys said, "why else would these girls be playing at soldier, hmm?"

"We aren't playing," Kelly said, flipping her makeshift weapon into a ready position. Evicka had clearly heard enough, as in a snap she whipped the chain out, clocking him across the head and knocking him down.

Jerinne sprinted at the one holding the noblewoman, bringing her handsticks into his ribs, and pulling the woman away from him. He responded with a sharp punch, knocking Jerinne back. He hit like a horse kick, but she stayed on her feet.

"You got some fire, girl. Let's quench it."

"Not hardly," Jerinne said. Miss Jessel was on the ground, trembling. She looked too scared to move.

Jerinne wouldn't let this bruiser or anyone else lay a hand on her.

He brought a flurry of punches, strong and hard. Jerinne knew better than to block them, instead dancing and dodging. Let him keep coming like a wild carriage. At one point he grinned, possibly thinking he had her pinned against a vine-covered wall. He swung hard, but his fist only hit plants and stone as she darted down, hitting quick at his knees and slipping under his legs.

"Going to skin you, rabbit," he gasped. He was winded from that.

"Saints, man. Quench the fire, skin the rabbit," Jerinne taunted as he swung another wild punch. So wild she was able to grab his wrist and throw him to the ground. "Pick a term and stick to it." She jumped and landed on him, bringing all her weight into his sternum and tenders.

The sound he made was quite satisfying.

Evicka was thrashing one of them with her chain, and Kelly was sparring hard with one with a knife. Evicka wrapped the chain around the neck of her opponent and yanked him into Kelly's. The two of them fell onto the bruised fellow Jerinne had just dealt with.

"Saints, run, run!" one of them yelled, obviously realizing they were outmatched. The boys all scrambled away. Jerinne laughed, and Evicka, cackling, chased after them.

"We should probably catch up to her," Jerinne said, looking to Kelly.

Kelly, though, was holding her hand to her side, blood dripping through her fingers. "I think one of them got a piece of me. Stupid."

Jerinne grabbed her before she dropped to the ground. "Come on, Kelly," she said. "I got you."

"It's Kelvanne," she said weakly. "Only Evicka calls me Kelly."

"Kelvanne, sure," Jerinne said, bringing her over to a

bench. She looked to the noblewoman and Miss Jessel. "Get someone!"

The axe-wielding madwoman lurked closer. "But it is a pretty beard."

"Listen," he said, holding his arms out wide, pushing Lin behind him. He hoped this lady hadn't realized Lin was a mage, and he could keep her distracted long enough for Lin to recover. "You all, whatever you're doing, you have a cause, right?"

"Why do you think that?"

"Well, you're well-armed, skilled fighters. Not common rabble. So this means you came here with a purpose, yes?"

"Let's say yes, pretty beard. What does that mean to you?"

He slowly reached into his coat pocket. "I'm a journalist. I write for *The Veracity Press*."

"Never heard of it."

"That's all right," Hemmit said, pulling out his card. "We're a bit on the fringe of popular opinion. Which makes us perfect for someone like you. We could help get your message out in a way the big papers never would. They wouldn't listen to you. We will."

She reached in, the hatchet in her hand spinning about as she snatched the card from him. The axe blade came far too close to Hemmit's nose for his comfort. She glanced at it with the hatchet still in her right hand, while idly spinning the other hatchet in her left. "You don't even know who we are."

"I want to know who you are," Hemmit said. He lowered his voice just a little. "I want to know what you want."

"Aren't you sweet," she said. "It'd be a shame to make you bleed."

"Not today," a smooth alto voice said, and a woman in a Tarian uniform slid in next to her. With practiced, fluid moves, she disarmed the woman of one of her hatchets. The woman brought up the other, but the Tarian grabbed her wrist. The axe-woman jumped up and kicked the Tarian in the shin, and pushed into a backflip with a kick to the Tarian's chin. The Tarian stumbled back, and the axe-woman landed on her feet, running off. It all happened so fast, Hemmit didn't get a clear look at the Tarian woman until it was all over.

"You're Amaya Tyrell," Hemmit said.

"Yes, I—oh, you're the reporter. Dayne's friend."

"Is that a problem?" he asked.

She scowled for a moment. "No, it's—this place is chaos. The house is overrun. Civilians everywhere, and even with Tarians and Freddy and her friends . . . you need to get out of here."

"What about her ladyship and her guests?" Lin asked. She still appeared out of sorts, but stumbled away from Hemmit to the other side of the room, where a tray of cheeses and bread had been overturned. She gracelessly slumped to the floor and began eating whatever she found there.

"I said you need to get out of here, not me," Amaya said.

The closet door opened, and Maresh peered out. "Is it safe?"

"We have a Tarian, so reasonably," Hemmit said. Maresh came out with Baron Terrenhill, both of them looking a little rumpled.

"I'm assuming this isn't some perverse entertainment on Miri's part," Terrenhill said, holding a handkerchief to his head. "I mean, I wouldn't put it past her."

"I doubt that, sir," Amaya said. His presence changed her attitude. "Let's get you all someplace safe and secure. Have you heard any Constabulary whistles?"

"Why are these folks attacking the house?" Lin asked.

"Who even knows," Hemmit said, looking for something he could use as a weapon, if the circumstances demanded. Nothing obvious jumped out, and he had to admit to himself the best thing he could do if someone else attacked was to stand behind Lin and Amaya. "Right now in this city, we've got what? The Open Hand, the Sons of the Six Sisters, probably still some Haltom's Patriots, apparently there's a Grand Ten, and I don't even know who else . . . ."

Amaya turned to him. "What did you—"

Whatever she was about to ask was interrupted by Constabulary whistles piercing the air.

"Fantastic, rescue," the baron said. He grinned at Amaya. "No disrespect intended."

"None taken," she said. "Come on."

She led them out to the ballroom, where several of the ruffians had been laid out on the ground, battered senseless. As they came in, Lady Mirianne came in with one of the First Irregulars, both of them supporting each other. The Irregular's uniform dress was shredded in several places, but despite both looking haggard, they had enormous smiles on their faces.

"Are you all right, ma'am?" Amaya asked as they approached. "Fredelle?"

"I am as well as I can be given how close I was to abduction," Lady Mirianne said. "But this woman was a marvel."

"It was deeply satisfying to pummel that man about the head," Fredelle said. "Can you imagine, half naked and oiled up, carrying whips. Ran off as soon as those whistles started up."

"I can't imagine what he was trying to abduct me for."

"I can imagine," Baron Terrenhill said.

"Oh, hush," Lady Mirianne said to him. "Are you all right, Stephen?"

"Nothing my own bed and all the wine I own won't cure."

She chuckled. "Lieutenant, could I press upon you to escort the baron to his home once the constables secure us?"

"As you wish, my lady," Fredelle said, raising an eyebrow at Amaya.

"As for you, Miss Tyrell, I understand why Dayne speaks so highly of you."

"Thank you, my lady," Amaya said haltingly.

"So of course you won't mind making sure these fine people of *The Veracity Press* get home safely." She went over to Hemmit. "I hope you can find some form of kindness to write about these events for tomorrow."

"I should check on my Initiates. I have many of them guarding your guests in the banquet hall."

"Splendid," Lady Mirianne said. As she said it several constables and Yellowshields came running in. She turned to them, opening up her arms. "Gentlemen! Thank you for rescuing us from this nightmare!"

Hemmit wasn't sure what to make of that, beyond Lady Mirianne's intense flair for the dramatic. As a Yellowshield came over to check Hemmit out, he noticed that Amaya Tyrell's attention was on him. She definitely had the bearing of a woman with questions that she wanted him to answer, but wouldn't ask in present company. Whatever those questions were, he wanted to know.

"Evicka really just ran off, huh?" Kelvanne asked as she looked up at the sky. "She's a wild one."

Miss Jessel had regained her composure and came over to the bench with them, opening up the soldier's uniform coat. The injury was a glancing cut on her side, hard to tell how serious it was. But there was a fair amount of blood.

"Just hold on," Jerinne said. Whistles were now piercing the air. "Yellowshields are coming."

"Just keep breathing," Miss Jessel said. "You're going to be fine."

"Still hurts like blazes," Kelvanne said.

More whistles. Shouts and calls in the distance. And

someone running out of the house. A woman with two hatchets.

Quinara.

Jerinne looked back to Kelvanne, whose eyes were watching the same thing. She pressed her curtain rod weapon into Jerinne's hand.

"Go."

Jerinne moved like the wind was with her, running as hard as her legs would let her. For the first time in as long as she could remember, there wasn't any pain at all. Despite the blows she had taken in the scrum this night, despite her ankle, despite the abuse of training, in this moment it was all gone. There was just purity of purpose.

Releasing a savage cry as she closed the distance, she smashed the curtain rod across Quinara's body, which broke into three pieces as it sent her to the ground.

"You are not getting away from here," Jerinne snarled.

"You're going to stop me, bobcat?" Quinara shot back, snapping to her feet as she took out her hatchets. "I've had more than enough of you."

"I don't need to stop you," Jerinne said, blocking the first blow of the hatchets with the remnant of the curtain rod. "I just have to keep you here until the constables arrest you."

"Well, I can't have that," Quinara said. "Big plans are afoot." Spinning swipes with the hatchets in tight circles, as Jerinne ducked and dodged. Just a few moments more. She could see some people running up the lawn, the first of the constables. Most were heading to the house, but at least one was coming their way.

"You ruined my plans for tonight. It seems only fair to do the same. Constable!"

Quinara turned her head, which gave Jerinne the opportunity to land a punch. The constable had his crossbow up.

"You are bound by law! Stand and be—"

That was all he said before a hatchet was buried in his

chest. Quinara winked and sent a back fist into Jerinne's face. Jerinne was startled and dazed for a moment, and when she shook off the blow, Quinara was out of sight.

But the constable was on the ground, coughing and spurting blood.

"No, no, no," Jerinne said, dropping on her knees next to him. "You're, you're—you're going to be all right." She grabbed the handle of the hatchet, not sure if she should pull it out of his chest, or if that would just make things worse. "I'm sorry, I'm sorry, I don't know what I should . . ." She looked up, hoping to see a Yellowshield or anyone else coming to help. Three figures were charging at her.

"Hey, we—"

Before she could say anything else, the three tackled her, twisting her arms behind her.

"You are bound by law and your crimes will be charged upon you!"

"But I—"

That earned her a punch across the jaw from one of them, as the other two slapped their irons around her wrists. The one who punched her dragged her to her feet. "Go secure the back of the house. I'll put this garbage in the lockwagon."

"I'm not—"

Another punch, to her gut. That knocked the air out of her. As she gasped, unable to draw breath or say anything else, he whispered in her ear, "You're lucky you're making it to the wagon after what you did to Tenzy."

Jerinne tried to protest, but she couldn't get any words into her mouth as she was dragged back down the lawn and tossed into the back of the lockwagon.

"Are there more coming?" he asked the wagon driver.

"Saints, yeah. There's two more pulling up the road!"

"Good, then let's get this minx to the station right away. A stick-killer gets to ride all by herself."

# Chapter 19

DAYNE'S LONG, slow walk back up to the house was filled with constables, Fire Brigade, and Yellowshields all passing him as they raced up the drive. Surely the smoke coming from the house marked it as a higher priority, and Dayne was more than happy to stay out of their way as they went to work. He was halfway there when one Yellowshield stopped mid-run to tend to him.

"You all right, man?" he asked.

"Decidedly not," Dayne said. "But I will make it back to the house."

"Hold up," the Yellowshield said. "You hit your head."

"Actually, no," Dayne said. "Landed on my hip from a fall. Some whiplashes, some burns."

The Yellowshield let out a low whistle. "Sounds like quite the party here."

"It wasn't—"

"I don't judge. After a month working as a yellow in

the dark, you see stuff you never forget. Especially here." He knelt down and groped Dayne's leg and hip. "Your muscles are like rocks. Tender here?"

"Yes."

"Yeah. But you're standing and walking, so I got to think you're basically all right." He dug into his satchel and pulled out a flask and tin cup, pouring a bit of liquid out. "For the pain."

"Is that *doph*?" Dayne wasn't sure if he should take such a thing, risk clouding his mind at all.

"For the pain," the man insisted. "This is what it's for."

Dayne was in no mood to argue, so he took the cup and drank the bitter fluid down.

"Good," the man said. "I'm going to see what's needed inside, but get those burns checked out by one of us, hear?" He dashed off.

Dayne limped the rest of the way, past the foyer where brigadiers had beaten the flames into an ashy smolder, until he reached the ballroom. Many people were sitting on the floor, being checked by Yellowshields, questioned by constables. Dayne worked his way over to the one he was most concerned about: Lady Mirianne, who was with Hemmit, Maresh, and Lin, as well as Amaya and Fredelle.

"Dayne!" Mirianne said as he approached. She wrapped her arms around his neck and kissed him. "I didn't know what happened to you."

"I . . . I was trying to stop that mage and—"

"Mage?" Amaya asked.

"Real odd one," Fredelle said. "Fiery wings."

"What?" Amaya said. "He was at the attack on the votes yesterday."

"That can't be right," Hemmit said.

"He was—saints, so was that woman with the hatchets."

"Wait," Dayne said, his head now reeling a bit from the *doph*. "This attack was by the same people who attacked the votes. The Sons of the Six Sisters?"

"The who?" Mirianne asked.

"A group of radical subversives, my lady," Hemmit said.

"But why would they—saints, I don't even want to think about it." She looked to Dayne with despair in her eyes. "Can we speed this along, get everyone out? I . . . I just want to go to bed."

Amaya coughed and stepped forward. "I've already had other Adepts and Candidates start escorting your guests home safely."

"Thank you, Miss Tyrell."

Amaya gave a sharp whistle, and Vien Reston came over with a Spathian Candidate by her side. "Ma'am?"

"Get the Initiates home now," Amaya said.

"There's three unaccounted for," Vien said. "Jerinne, Miara, and Candion."

"Get the ones you've got home. I'll round up the rest." Muttering she added, "Miara and Candion probably holed up in a spare bedroom together."

"Oh, please, no," Mirianne said.

"If I've found that to be the case, they will be severely disciplined, my lady."

One of the other First Irregulars came over, holding her hand to her side. "One of yours is missing? The one at the lunch, brown hair and a nose that looks like it's been broke?" Her face looked like she had bad news to share with them.

"That's Jerinne," Dayne said. "Is she all right?"

"I saw some sticks grab her and put her in a lock-wagon. I was in no shape to stop them, sorry. That lady with the axes—"

Amaya, Hemmit, and Lin all groaned at that.

"She killed a stick, but then they grabbed your girl instead. So—"

"Oh, saints," Amaya said.

Dayne was already moving, limping over to one of the constables. "Officer! What's your stationhouse?"

"Pardon?"

"Anyone arrested, where were they brought?"

"Unity, most likely."

He went back over to Amaya and the others. "I'll go."

"She's my charge," Amaya said.

"As are the other two who are missing," Dayne said. "You find them, I'll get to Jerinne."

"Do you need anything?" Hemmit asked. "If they think she's a stick-killer, they won't release her on your say so."

"Jessel!" Lady Mirianne called out to her lady-in-waiting, being led into the house by a Yellowshield. "Are you all right?"

"Nothing but my nerves, my lady. Thanks to Miss Fendall. But apparently she—"

"I've heard. Are you well enough to run to my attorney's home? I need her to meet Dayne at Unity Station-house immediately."

"For Jerinne?" Jessel asked. "I'll run all night, ma'am." She went off as if she'd been renewed.

"And, you, Dayne, take Kaysen and my carriage. I insist."

"Thank you," Dayne said.

"Thank you, my lady," Amaya said. "I can't thank you enough."

"Thank me when she's at liberty," Mirianne said. "I'm very fond of that girl, and the last thing I would want is for her to be incarcerated for saving my people and guests."

"I'll get her," Dayne said to Amaya. Then to Mirianne he said, "I'm sorry for the night, and that I failed you—"

"You did nothing of the sort," she said. She kissed him again. "Go, save your friend. I'll be fine."

Jerinne was dragged to the work floor of the Constabulary stationhouse, still in irons, and nearly thrown in front of one of the desk clerks. The whole floor was full of constables working like madmen, and dozens of people nearly piled up on each other on the benches in the large lock cage in the center of the room.

"What are you doing?" the desk clerk asked the officer who had arrested Jerinne. "You need to wait your turn!"

"My turn? What are you on about?"

The clerk waved at the people on benches. "Do you know how many arrests we've had tonight? It's the revels, it's always madness!"

"Drunken vomiters. That's not important! This girl killed Tenzy!"

"I did not!" Jerinne shouted.

"I saw you! You had the axe in his chest!"

"I was fighting the woman with the axe!"

"Saints, Jondel, she's a Tarian! You think she killed a constable?"

"I know what I saw."

"He's wrong!"

The clerk shook her head. "Tell it to your justice advocate. But you also still have to wait to be processed before even going to a proper cell, and then . . . we'll see."

"But we have to—" Jondel started.

"No. Put her in the cage until it's her turn," the clerk said. "I have a damned system tonight, and you're not going to ruin it."

Jondel grumbled and grabbed Jerinne's arm, dragging her over to the lock cage. It was just a great box of metal bars in the middle of the work floor, with all those arrested and not processed milling about within. Jondel opened the door and started to shove Jerinne inside.

"Take the irons off her," the clerk said, standing up.

"I won't!"

"You will."

Jondel fumed, and then said, "Fine." He unlocked the irons on her wrist and shoved her in the cage.

The collection of prisoners was quite the motley

crew. Several looked like drunken university boys, the social house types. Others were sailors and dockworkers, also clearly drunk.

Jerinne found a bench by herself and sat down.

"Saints, girl, you're covered in blood. You kill your man?"

A woman who looked like she had had far too many unkind years approached, sitting down without invitation. She looked like she expected an answer.

"I didn't kill anyone," Jerinne said. "I was protecting people."

"They said she's a stick-killer," one of the dock steves said.

"You killed a stick?"

"No," Jerinne said pointedly.

"She's too young for that," the steve said.

"I was younger when I first killed a man," the older woman said. She leaned in to Jerinne, as if speaking in confidence. "He thought he could walk away without paying. I showed him he was wrong. That what happened?"

"Not at all!" Jerinne slid a bit down the bench. But then she looked at the eyes of this woman—haunted, hurt. "Five men were trying to hurt two women. Friends."

"So you killed them?"

"I stopped them." Jerinne smiled, realizing the core of what Dayne had been trying to tell her a month ago in the Parliament. "Those men wanted to hurt someone, so I stepped in to stop them. You never need to kill if you can just stop them."

"Saints," the woman said. "Five men?"

"I only had to deal with two of them."

"World would be a better place if you killed them."

"Not for me," Jerinne said. It hit her how grateful she was that Dayne hadn't let her kill Tharek Pell when she wanted to. She didn't know how it would have affected her, but now that she saw Tander and others so troubled by the lives they took, she was happy not to have that on her conscience.

Now Tharek Pell wanted to talk to her. At first Jerinne had thought this was some strange ploy on his part, but now she was very curious about what he had to say to her. But she also wanted to look him in the eye. She wanted him to know she wasn't afraid of him.

The cage doors opened again, and constables were shoving in several men—arrested from the party. "Look who it is," one of them said as he locked eyes with Jerinne. "The Tarian bird."

Jerinne got to her feet, instinctively putting herself in front of the older woman. "You'd all do yourself some good staying on the other side of this cage."

One of them had a massive bruise across his face. He stepped forward. "Or what's going to happen, girl? There's maybe ten of us, one of you. It'll take a while for those sticks to come in and stop us. We'll take you down."

"Yeah, you probably will," Jerinne said, holding her chin up. "By the time the three or four of you move in, it'll be impossible to hold you off. But the one who comes first, he's getting his neck snapped. So go ahead."

All of them looked to each other, waiting for one of them to take the lead, but none of them did.

"Fine. I'm at your disposal." She sat back down next to the older woman.

"Saints," the woman whispered. "You've got some brass."

A few minutes later Dayne came storming into the stationhouse. "You are going to let that girl out right now!"

"Who the blazes are you?" one of the constables asked.

"Dayne Heldrin, of the Tarian Order, and liaison to the Parliament and King's Marshals. And I can tell you that any accusations made against her are false and misleading."

"That sounds terribly fancy," the clerk said, getting up from her desk. "But I can't just take that on your say so."

Dayne came across the floor like he had every bit of authority to do so. He approached the cage. "Her lawyer is on the way, but she should not be sitting in that cage."

"I can't—"

"I told you—"

"Mister Heldrin," the clerk said sharply. "I understand your feelings, but you do not have authority here. You say she has a lawyer coming?"

"I have a lawyer coming?" Jerinne asked.

"Lady Mirianne is sending one."

"Oh, my, Lady Mirianne," the old woman said. "You are a fancy one."

The clerk sighed. "When your lawyer arrives, we'll see what we can arrange. A serious charge has been laid upon her."

"They think I murdered a constable, but it was the woman with the hatchets."

Dayne looked over at the other invaders from the household in the cage. "She cannot be left in there with them."

"I've handled it, Dayne."

He gave her a slight smile. "I'm sure you did. But it isn't right."

The clerk touched Dayne's arm. "You can wait over there. Let me know when her lawyer arrives."

Dayne, however, was not deterred. Instead he moved to the other side of the cage. "You. Who hired you? What were you trying to do?"

"Leave me alone, man. I'm already ironed up."

"Why were you trying to steal the Acoran votes and then abduct Lady Mirianne?"

One of the ruffians slammed on the gate. "You'll learn, man! We are never free as long as elections are a sham pretense that keep the elite in power!"

"What do the Sons of the Six Sisters want?"

"Truth and freedom!" the ruffian shouted. "Truth and freedom!" The rest started chanting with him.

"Stop riling them up!" one of the constables shouted, grabbing Dayne and pulling him away.

"We've got more trouble!" A group of constables were hauling a large number of people in, these looking quite different from any of the other people in the cage. These people were prim and modest-looking. A couple were even in religious vestments. And they all were singing.

*"For the light of God*
*And the blessed Queen*
*The fruits of Scaloi*
*Are ever green—"*

"Shut them up!" a constable shouted, clocking one— the priest—with a handstick.

"That is enough!" Dayne said, racing over.

"Who is this guy?" a constable asked.

"Dayne, what are you—" the priest started.

The ruffians were still chanting. Over and over. "Truth and freedom! Truth and freedom!"

Another swipe of the handstick knocked the man down. Dayne grabbed it out of the constable's hand. "I will have charges laid against you, man."

"Who the blazes do you think you are?"

"Get them in the cage, now!" the clerk shouted. "And shut all their mouths!"

One constable grabbed the woman in the cloistress habit and dragged her over to the cage, but when he opened the gate, all the ruffians stormed him. In a moment they were out of the cage and others rushed to join them. Jerinne instinctively put a hand on the old woman next to her.

"Don't. You'll get hurt."

The ruffians and other prisoners broke into a full-out

brawl with both the constables on the work floor and the new prisoners they were bringing in. The cloistress, despite being ironed, responded to the men attacking her with matching ferocity. Dayne scooped the priest up from the floor and pulled him away from the uproar.

"No, no—" the priest said. "No, we cannot, we must not—"

Jerinne dashed forward and closed the gate. Best way to protect the people still inside.

"Truth and freedom!" one yelled as he grabbed a handstick from a constable and brought it cracking down on the cloistress. Blood gushed from her head, but she was not deterred as she grabbed him by the throat.

"No, this . . . we cannot—" the priest said, looking pale and distraught.

Dayne tried to hold him up. "Come on, we'll get you safe—"

"No," the priest said again, his voice a low growl of thunder. "No!" The ground shook as he shouted, *"Be still!"*

The two words echoed through the room, and cut through Jerinne's spine like a knife. As if ice filled her veins all the way to her heart, stopping it and everything else in her body. It wasn't just that she couldn't move, it was as if any desire to move had been torn out, written over her soul.

She wasn't alone. Every brawling person was stopped in place. The stationhouse was completely silent, save for the tears of the priest.

Dayne had never before felt so helpless, even when he had failed Master Denbar. He couldn't move at all, not even to breathe.

It was as if Ret had commanded them with the voice of God itself.

Ret stepped away from him, walking through the

tableau of mannequins. "This was not how it was supposed to be. This was never what we wanted." He was crying openly, as he knelt next to Sister Frienne. "You were supposed to be on a path of peace, child."

He touched her head, and she started weeping. Then she looked up at him, her face changing from sorrow to anguish. She reached out to him, and the scars on her arms had changed to angry, red welts.

Ret then reached through the bars of the cage, touching Jerinne, who was still frozen at the gate. "Look at this girl, Sister. Risking herself to protect people. This is how you find a path to redemption. You look to her."

He brushed her away, and for a moment she stared at Jerinne as her cries turned to screams. Tearing at her cloistress robes, she ran out of the stationhouse. Once she was gone, Ret slumped down to the floor.

In an instant, whatever the hold was over Dayne released. He nearly fell over, as many people did. He felt as weak as a kitten.

More constables rushed in, looking utterly bewildered. They quickly grabbed just about everyone who wasn't a constable and corralled them back in the cage, locking it shut. Ret went inside mutely, sitting on the floor in a collapsed heap. When the constables were finishing cleaning up the mess of the work floor, a Waishen-haired woman came in with an air of authority.

"Who is in charge right now, and why are they charging a Tarian Initiate with murder when she was defending people from violent interlopers?"

A clerk with sergeant's chevrons came over, looking dazed by whatever happened. "Miss Wade. You're the girl's lawyer?"

"I am representing her. What has she been spuriously charged with?"

"Officer Jondel accused her of killing another officer."

"Hmm," Miss Wade said. She centered in on Dayne.

"You must be Mister Heldrin. Jelia Wade, Master of Law. We will deal with this. Where is Officer Jondel?"

The sergeant pointed across the room, where Officer Jondel was sitting on a desk. Miss Wade strode over and grabbed him by the chin. "This man is drunk."

"No, no, I'm—" he said.

"Officer, when you responded to the whistle call, where were you?"

"With Uskly and Tenzy at the Lantern—"

"Hmm. So Miss Fendall is being held on charges based on the witness of a drunk man, when I can produce several other witnesses who will attest that she was attempting to subdue the true murderer, including Miss Jessel Mandelin and Baroness Yesenia Rinnar of Upper Tissen, both of whom are women of exceptional character." She turned to the sergeant, stalking toward him like a cat. "Given that, any further imposition on Miss Fendall is criminal negligence on the part of the house, and I will make sure you, Officer Jondel, the lieutenant of the watch, and the captain of this stationhouse are all brought up on multiple charges!"

There was a stunned silence, broken by the old woman standing next to Jerinne in the cage. "Can she be my lawyer, too?"

The sergeant whistled to an officer to let Jerinne out of the cage, which he did with incredible speed.

"Thank you," Jerinne said. "Both of you."

"Glad to do it," Miss Wade said. "I prefer not to have to come out at this hour, but it's better that I did, and you didn't have to spend the night here, or have them actually process an arrest. They didn't process you yet, did they?"

"No, they seem rather backed up," Jerinne said. "Can we go?"

"Yes, let's," Dayne said. They only made it three steps before Donavan Samsell and a cadre of King's Marshals strode into the stationhouse.

"Excuse me," Samsell announced. "We will be taking custody of Bishop Ret Issendel and any members of the Open Hand." He stopped cold upon seeing Dayne. "The blazes are you doing here?"

"Getting Miss Fendall released, but—"

"Well, it's good you are. I'll want you on this. Sergeant, let's get about this quickly."

"Sorry, chief," the sergeant said. "We're rather overwhelmed here. Who is it you need?"

Samsell went to the cage. "That man, and those other dozen people."

The sergeant threw his hands up. "If you want people still in the cage, you're welcome to them. One less problem for us."

"Chief," Dayne said, leaving Jerinne and Miss Wade by the door. "What's going on? Why are you taking Ret?"

"Ret?" Samsell raised an eyebrow at that. "Well, Dayne, it seems Ret and his friends have been busy. Today they stole the ballots and abducted the authenticators for the Scallic election."

# Chapter 20

DAYNE COULDN'T BELIEVE what he was hearing. After everything he did, the election was still subverted. "By who? Where?"

"I'm certain the bishop here will be able to tell us," Samsell said. "Won't you, your grace? You'll let us know where your friends are."

"My . . . friends?" Ret looked almost in a daze. "Almost all my people are here."

"Except the ones who took the votes."

"Took what votes?"

"The votes from Scaloi!" Samsell smacked the bars of the cage.

"How would I—"

"Who else would subvert the Scallic election, your grace?" Samsell snarled.

"Chief, that's enough," Dayne said, putting a hand on the marshal's shoulder as the cage was opened up.

"You're going to tell us."

"I would never," Ret said, coming out of the cage. "As much as I will fight for Scallic independence, I would never, not ever, subvert the will of the people. That is sacred. Dayne, please!"

"Don't you—" Samsell said, bringing up his fist. Dayne grabbed his arm before he could strike.

"No," Dayne said sharply. "You're not going to do this. Not this way."

"Don't you tell me, Dayne—"

"I will," Dayne said. "Lest you forget, my job is oversight of you. I've been politely yielding to your expertise, but not about this. Beating suspects for information they may not even have? That isn't who we are."

"We?" Samsell asked. "Are you a marshal now?"

"Marshals were once the Hanalian Order," Dayne said. "We are all still the Elite. We all still stand by a code. And I will hold you to that."

"What?" Samsell asked, his voice rising.

Dayne turned to the other marshals as the constables pulled out the rest of the prisoners and handed them over. "I'm going to be supervising your interrogation of these people, Donavan Samsell. To confirm that it is being conducted in a fair and humane manner."

"Don't you interfere, Dayne," Samsell hissed. "This is about the election!"

"All the more reason," Dayne said. "Jerinne, go report this to the Grandmaster. And the Justice Advocate Office."

She gave a slight smile to him. "And the press?"

"Absolutely," he said. "And we'll be keeping them updated at a conference in the morning."

"I swear, Heldrin," Samsell growled.

"Swear all you want," Dayne said. As the constables put irons on Ret, Dayne took him by the arm, making his intentions as clear as he could to Samsell. "But we're doing this the right way. Because that's what Druthal is."

The eerie light of high summer dawn filled the eastern skyline when Jerinne made it back to the chapterhouse.

The streets were a mess, largely devoid of people, but filled with trash, glass, and smoldering remnants of fires. The Revels were often a raucous holiday, but this one seemed worse than most.

"Hello!" she called as she got into the lobby of the chapterhouse.

The Grandmaster came down the stairs in a rush with Master Nedell right behind him, carrying a lamp. "Miss Fendall," he said. "Are you hurt?"

She looked down at her uniform—it really was a fright. "No, sir. I got caught in quite a bit of business, but this isn't my blood."

"One of ours?"

"No, sir," she said.

"Good." He shook his head. "I mean, of course it isn't good, but . . ."

"I understood, sir." She looked about. "The party was attacked, and I'm afraid in the chaos there was a misunderstanding with the constables . . ."

"I've heard some of it from the Initiates who have returned already. Are you still in legal trouble?"

"I don't think so," Jerinne said. "But sir, Dayne wanted me to—"

He closed his eyes and took a deep breath, as if the mention of Dayne had been enough to push his temper, and he needed to center himself again just to continue. "Of course you were with Mister Heldrin."

"We shouldn't be surprised at all that he's at the center of this," Master Nedell said. "Or that she—"

"Dayne is the one who came for me," Jerinne said sharply over Master Nedell. "He's the one who got me—"

The Grandmaster raised a hand, silencing her. "What is the situation?"

"The Scallic ballots were stolen, and the marshals arrested some bishop and his people, and Dayne went with them but . . ."

"My," the Grandmaster said, "it seems Dayne has

once again found himself in the center of serious events."

Jerinne wasn't sure how to take that. "He said to tell you—"

"Yes, I understand what is going on. I will gather some Adepts and attend to what needs attending. Master Nedell, I would like you to rouse two or three Candidates and make your way to Callon Hills to seek out the last of our missing people and bring them home."

"But—" Jerinne said.

"As for you, Initiate, I suggest washing yourself and getting some small amount of sleep. Despite these events, training for Initiates will not be interrupted. Attend to that, as you certainly need to devote your attention to your training."

"Especially with your ranking," Master Nedell added.

The bile filled Jerinne's throat at that, but she bit back the words that she wanted to scream at him. Instead she said, swallowing down the anger, "I'm aware of my ranking."

"Then be aware of orders, Miss Fendall," Grandmaster Orren said sharply. He snapped a finger, and one of the servants brought him a sword and shield, which he strapped on. "Bring our people home, Master Nedell." With that, he went out into the dawn.

"Wash up, Miss Fendall," Master Nedell said with a sneer. "Not that it can get you clean."

That was the limit. She was not about to let that slide. "If you doubt my skill, old man, you can try me any time you want."

Master Nedell released a flurry of punches and kicks, all while maintaining a calm, confident air, as if knocking her down would be effortless.

That was clearly what he was expecting, but Jerinne slipped and dodged out of the way of every blow, never letting him score even a glance on her. Her rage was fueling her, but she turned it inward, not letting it come out in an attack. Instead, it drove her focus, eyes on his body, watching the flex of his shoulders, the step of his foot. Every punch that came, she dodged or blocked adroitly.

His moves were flawless, truly spectacular, but they were to the sequence, which made him easy to predict. She expected, anticipated, the moment where he would change that up, lull her into complacency and use that to baffle her defense. But that moment never came. His attacks followed sequence in order, each meticulous step in the combat training cycles. Not an ounce of imagination.

Her thoughts went to Evicka and Kelvanne, improvising weapons and styles in the midst of a fight. That was real. Impressive. Inspirational.

As she anticipated exactly where he was about to step, her hand went to her belt buckle. In one swift motion, she whipped the belt off and shot it around his leg just as he was stepping into the end part of Unarmed Attack Sequence Nine. She gave a hard yank before he was able to plant his leg, and that was enough to send him to the ground.

She dropped the belt as he lay there, winded, saying, "Bottom ranked, my foot."

That was all she needed to prove to herself, and she went to the baths. Master Nedell would make her life torture, surely, if not have her cashiered out, but it didn't matter.

She knew who she was, and he couldn't define her.

She approached the bathhouses, hearing low voices inside, which was very odd for this hour. Unless a couple people were taking advantage of the hour, confident they'd have the place to themselves.

Jerinne gave the bathhouse door a knock before opening it. "All right, I'm coming in, so be a little decent."

She opened the door, not prepared for what she saw.

Two people were in the bathhouse, a man and a woman. The man was a Tarian—that new one from up north, Osharin—and he was attending to the injuries on the woman.

Not just any woman.

Quinara.

Jerinne narrowed her eyes and leaped in.

Hemmit wanted to sleep for a week. The revels had calmed, or at least there was no one left reveling in the dawn-touched streets. Despite that, he kept close step with Amaya Tyrell, who was Dayne's equal in intensity and bearing. He was glad to have her company as they made their way back to The Nimble Rabbit. They had stayed behind with her to find the two missing Initiates. With a bit of investigation on his part, it was determined that those two had left the party together before the invasion. That having been settled, Amaya insisted on escorting him home, though she seemed to have something else on her mind. But she didn't address it as they walked with Lin and Maresh shuffling a few steps behind them, both of them looking exhausted.

"I hate when I'm still up at this hour," Maresh said.

"I'm usually getting up at this hour," Amaya said.

"I'm sleeping on your cot, Hemmit," Lin called out to him. "I'm too tired to make it to my flop."

"Is this typical for you all?" Amaya asked.

"It is our second street riot in as many weeks," Hemmit said.

"There was a riot last week?" Amaya asked.

"In North Seleth," Lin said. Amaya glanced back at her, and Lin pulled back her hair from her forehead and released her magical glamour, revealing the yellowing bruise there. "I got hit with a brick."

"Why haven't I heard about this?" Amaya asked.

"You wouldn't see anything much about it in any

newssheets but ours. I think the *Maradaine Standard* covered it with an article about how the entire southwest part of the city is full of animals."

"I swear, we're . . ." Amaya shook her head as they continued walked. "We're supposed to be there for the people, but we just lock ourselves away in our chapterhouse. We service the Parliament and the nobility and . . . to what end?"

"You're starting to sound like Dayne," Hemmit said.

"He's just—" She stopped herself. "I don't want to talk out of turn about him."

Hemmit waved her off. "He's got his own secrets, and that's fine. We know he went through something in Lacanja, and he's suffering because of that. He'll tell us when he's ready."

Amaya nodded. "Look, I . . . you said something earlier about a Grand Ten."

"I did?" Hemmit asked. He vaguely recalled mentioning it earlier. "I mean, we get a lot of letters from people on the fringe. Sometimes it pays off—"

"Like the attack on the ballot carriages."

"Right," he said.

They had reached The Nimble Rabbit. Maresh and Lin stumbled off to the barn, and Hemmit recognized Amaya had the bearing of a person needing confession. She looked about hesitantly. "I know—I don't know what I know, but . . . maybe we should talk about this seriously. I need to talk to someone."

He nodded and led Amaya to the back kitchen. Hebert and Onnick were already at work kneading dough and preparing vegetables.

"Oh, saints almighty, what happened?" Onnick asked.

"There was an attack on the party," Hemmit said. "This is Amaya Tyrell."

"Another Tarian friend?" Hebert asked, pulling out a chair for her and clearing bowls of diced vegetables from the table. "I already like her better than the tall one."

"He's a doll," Onnick said. "I take it you both need tea. And eggs. Perhaps bacon and bread."

"Just the tea is fine," Amaya said. She looked about nervously. "We . . . we can talk here?"

"We're fine," Hebert said. "Unless you actually have a royal secret or something, but we never see anyone besides the boys, each other, and our wait staff, who don't care about anything."

"Trust them as much as you trust me," Hemmit said. "Which is . . . as much as you do."

Onnick put down two cups of tea, followed by bread and preserves. Hemmit tucked in, and Amaya hesitated for a moment, and did the same.

"All right, but . . . for right now, it's important not to talk to Dayne about this."

"You don't trust Dayne?"

"I'm not ready to get into this with Dayne. Our history is complicated and . . ."

"You have secrets," Hemmit said. "I get it."

She pulled a pendant out from under her tunic. "This was my mother's, but I only recently got it from my uncle. My uncle, Master Denbar of the Tarian Order."

"Wasn't that who Dayne—"

"Went to Lacanja with? Yes. He was our trainer in our Initiacy, and he chose to take Dayne with him when he was reassigned. Because no one—and I mean no one, not even the Grandmaster—knew we were family. We knew I would not be treated seriously in the Order if they knew."

Hemmit nodded, and gave a slight glance to Onnick and Hebert. Hebert put a plate of egg tartlets in front of them, saying, "Come on, let's check on the herb garden."

"Right," Onnick said. They grabbed a basket and went out the back.

"All right, so then, this starts with Master Denbar?"

"He died a couple months ago in Lacanja, but he arranged to send me a message with this pendant. A coded message, with the cards of the Grand Ten."

That was fascinating. "What was the message?"

"Lacanja is an exile. Be wary. Find them. Stop them. Save Druthal."

Hemmit no longer needed tea to wake up. His heart was racing. "And he says it was a Grand Ten?"

"That was implied," she said. "What do you know?"

"Not a lot," Hemmit said. "I was contacted by . . . well, one of the Patriots."

"The ones who were with Lannic and Tharek?"

"Exactly. But one of the less . . . excitable ones. From what I gathered of this fellow, he was far more comfortable with pamphlets and rallies than threats and assassinations."

"Hmm."

"I didn't go meet with him. I wrote the whole thing off as bait. But now I'm thinking there might be something to it."

"So how do you find him?"

"I'll go where he said to meet," Hemmit said. Something didn't sit right. "Why are you wanting to keep quiet about it?"

"Because . . . if there's a group calling themselves a Grand Ten, wouldn't they be like the original? I keep thinking about it, that the titles of each of the Ten matter."

"Iconic figures, like in the cards." Hemmit understood. The icons, the symbols, they had a kind of power, imprinting themselves on people's hearts.

"Right." She took a sip of her tea, and then slugged it all down. "I think the Warrior is a Tarian."

Hemmit let out a low whistle. "You . . . you don't think it's Dayne?"

"Oh, saints, no. Dayne . . . he gives me a headache,

but he's a straight arrow if you ever saw one. He would never be part of a dark conspiracy, but . . . he might trust the person who is."

Hemmit nodded. "We'll tread carefully. I'll keep this quiet for now, and look into my contact. I'll let you know what I find."

"Thank you," she said. She picked up one of the egg tarts and bit into it. "I can see why Dayne is fond of this place."

"Everything is delicious. These two know their stuff," Hemmit said.

Maresh came bursting into the kitchen with a copy of *Throne and Chairs*. "We need to get to work."

"I need to sleep," Hemmit said.

"Sleep later." Maresh threw the newssheet on the table. The big headline popped out: SCALLIC BAL-LOTS STOLEN! OPEN HAND SUSPECTED!

"Sweet Saint Marian," Amaya said. "I should get back to the chapterhouse. I'll—I'll be in touch!" She dashed out the door.

Hemmit cursed. Getting up from the table, he said, "Get our landlords working on a fresh pot of tea. I'm going to close my eyes for twenty clicks. Come wake me then."

"I'll throw a bucket of water on you if I have to," Maresh said. "We've got—"

"We've got a lot," Hemmit said. "But I need to clear my head. Give me twenty clicks, and then let's go to work."

"Let me make something clear about the role I want for you, Heldrin," Samsell said as they descended to the holding cells in the marshals' offices beneath the Parliament. "You are going to observe, nothing more. You don't touch the prisoners, you don't talk to them, you don't interfere with my people."

"I will if I deem it fit," Dayne said. "And I won't accept you telling me otherwise."

"Where do you—" Samsell's finger was in Dayne's chest. Dayne took him by the wrist—no force, no pain, just holding it. But strong enough that Samsell couldn't pull his hand free.

"Let me make something clear. I finally understand what my job is. My job is to repair the damage caused by Regine Toscan. And you are going to let me do that, Mister Samsell, because you're who I'm protecting."

Ret had been led into the cells. The same cell block where Dayne had been locked up a month ago, where Tharek brutally murdered Regine Toscan.

"Check him for weapons," Samsell said.

"He doesn't have any," Dayne countered. They all glared at him. "Fine, check."

Two marshals stripped off Ret's cassock, leaving him in just his skivs. His chest was covered in simple black ink tattoos, each a figure in silhouette.

"Icons of the saints?" Samsell asked. It was hard to read his tone—somewhere in a gray area between derogatory and respectful.

"Five so far," Ret said, looking at his chest. "Starting with Saint Alexis, and the rest as they've revealed themselves to me over my life. I needed to mark myself, embrace the pain and truth."

Samsell peered closer at them. "I like the Benton. My birth saint is Benton."

"He stood on the bridge and let none cross, so the rest of his village could escape," Ret said. "Arrows so fast—"

"'Arrows so fast his fingers bled, and he shaped more from his blood.'" Samsell shook his head. "I can quote the books as well. What's going to go there?" He tapped at the blank part of Ret's chest over his heart.

"That hasn't been revealed to me. In time, I'm sure."

"I don't know how much time you have," Samsell said.

"Why, Marshal Chief?" Ret asked. "Are you threatening me?"

"I'm saying, the Scallic votes were stolen—"

"Not by me!"

"Well, of course not by you, your grace," Samsell said. "You're right here. So where would your people go?"

"My people are also here!"

"They did something. Or saw something. We will find out what they know. No matter what it takes."

"Chief," Dayne said sharply.

Samsell spun on him. "In nearly two hundred years we have never had a ballot wagon robbed. Never had an officiant kidnapped. But this year? Nearly with the Acoran, and actually with the Scallic? Under my watch? No, I will not have it!"

"Who went after the Acoran?" Ret asked.

"You keep your mouth shut!"

"I thought you wanted me to talk?" Ret raised an eyebrow. "Think clearly, Chief. If two ballot trains were targeted, it was likely the same perpetrators."

Samsell's fist swung out, knocking Ret in the jaw, sending him to the floor. Dayne jumped on the marshal, locking his arms and pulling him out of the room.

"You take your damn hands off me, Heldrin! I will have your medallion! You will wish you were cashiered from the Tarians when I'm done!"

"Calm the blazes down!" Dayne said. "If I have to I'll drag you to an icehouse and throw you in the coolers."

"That blasted priest—"

"Is certainly right!"

"He's blinded you, Dayne!"

Dayne pushed Samsell away, keeping himself between the man and the doors to the cells. "Maybe. Maybe he's polished this whole pacifist performance, and I've bought into it. Maybe I'm the heel who's been tricked by the huckster. But then it's quite the act, because the man I've met, he wouldn't do this."

Samsell fumed around the room, and then punched the wall, cracking the plaster. Shaking it off his hand, he turned back to Dayne. "You saw his file, yes?"

"Does it say something about him being a master of deception?"

"No," Samsell said.

"Is everything all right?"

Dayne looked to see Grandmaster Orren approaching them both.

"Sir," Dayne said. "I'm glad you're here. This is Chief Samsell."

"Donavan," Samsell said, offering his hand to the Grandmaster. "I'm honored to have you here, sir, but we've got a situation."

"A serious one," Orren said. "Precisely why you should seek all the help you can muster. I am here, and I have several of my Adepts and Candidates at work in the streets. The Spathian Grandmaster is on his way here as well."

"That seems . . . excessive," Samsell said.

"The circumstances call for excess," Grandmaster Orren said.

One of the marshals came out of the cells. "Hey, he says they have a headquarters, out on the west docks."

"Near the Buttered Pear?" Dayne asked.

The marshal shrugged. "I don't know where that is. But he says that if you go there, search it, you'll find everything about their plans."

"Doesn't prove anything," Samsell said.

"Dayne," Ret called out. Dayne came back into the cells. "It's offices on the second floor of the building across the street from the Pear. You'll find everything; we have nothing to hide. Maybe you'll find Sister Frienne there."

"I will?" Dayne asked. He was still disturbed by the

sight of her scars, the memory of her screaming as she fled the stationhouse.

"She'll do whatever you ask of her, if you tell her it is part of her penance. Say that from me. I have to do right by her."

"I will," Dayne said.

The Grandmaster touched Dayne's shoulder. "I would say you should stay, but you seem familiar with the particulars here. Are you well enough?"

"I'm fine, sir," Dayne said. "But I am worried the marshals might be . . . overzealous in their questioning of these prisoners. Samsell was quite upset."

"I will stay and prevent such things," the Grandmaster said. "Go look into this. But if it's nothing, go to the chapterhouse, get yourself attended to. I can tell you're in pain."

"I'll manage, sir," Dayne said. "I can rest when the ballots are secure." He left before the Grandmaster could say anything else.

# INTERLUDE: The Soldier

COLONEL ESTIN NEILLS LAY awake as the sun wormed its way into the window, the bustle and flurry of the usual morning activity at Fort Merrit filling his ears.

This was not his bed, not today. But it would be tonight, since these were the quarters for the base commander. By midday that position would be his.

"You all right?" Danverth asked. Danverth—Colonel Danverth Martindale—was watching him from the other side of the bed. His bed.

"How long have you been awake?" Estin asked.

"Only a few minutes," Danverth said. "But you seemed lost in thought, and I liked to watch that."

"I was thinking about the formality of ceremony," Estin said. "We'll have a whole event on the lawn where you stand down from command and say I'm ready to stand, and we shake hands like . . ."

"Cordial colleagues?" Danverth asked.

"It does seem like a strange bit of theater,

considering," Estin said. He got up from the bed and crossed to the water closet.

"Are you having regrets?" Danverth called out to him. "I mean, you've been angling for my job since you arrived here."

"You never had a problem with that," Estin said as he came back out. Danverth was up from the bed, standing powerful, strong, beautiful.

"I think you're the best man for the job. I've been lucky, having such a dependable soldier, friend, confidante, and partner as my second here." He wrapped his arms around Estin's shoulders.

"I just wish getting it didn't mean you leaving Maradaine," Estin said.

"Your friends did a very good job arranging an attractive position," Danverth said. "I would thank them, but they probably shouldn't know I'm aware of them."

"They're not my friends. Except Silla. They're just people I share mutual goals with." He had told Danverth everything about the Grand Ten, of course, no secrets between them. Foolish, probably, but Estin's capacity for deception had its limits, and the Grand Ten already pushed it. Some of them wanted to oust Danverth with scandal so they could get Estin promoted to base commander. Estin would not hear of it. But he knew they needed him in charge here, so he would be in a position to launch the training and programs Silla and the others needed. It would be on his shoulders to shape the Druth Army, and with a proper king, make Druthal stronger than ever.

Bells rang out from across the lawn.

"We should get dressed and look presentable before my adjunct comes in," Danverth said with a melancholic smile. "Never enough time."

Estin kissed him, one to sustain him for the months to come. It would have to.

Five minutes later they were both in uniform and sitting at Danverth's table when the adjunct came in.

"Good morning, Colonel," he said as he came in. "Or, colonels, rather." He looked at Estin with awkward embarrassment.

"Morning, Endly," Danverth said as the young man laid a tea tray on the table. "I thought Neills should be here for my morning brief, since by midday this will be his command."

"Of course, sir," Endly said. "I only brought tea for you, though."

"I'm fine," Estin said.

"What's on the night report?"

"One of the ladies from the Royal First was injured last night."

"Injured?" Estin asked. "But they were guests at a party."

"Apparently it was attacked by radicals." Estin did not like that, though he did hope Lady Mirianne's household wasn't too badly damaged. She had agreed to make herself a target for subversives to aim at, but he didn't think decent people like the ladies of the Royal First would have gotten hurt.

"How badly?" Danverth asked.

"Not too badly. They'll have to delay the start of their tour a few days, but she's expected to recover."

"Glad to hear it," Danverth said. He sipped at his tea. "What say you, Neills? One last inspection of the cadets with me before you ship me off?"

"If one last inspection is all we have time for," Estin said, forcing his heart down from his throat. He was sacrificing the only thing that mattered to him, for the good of the country, for the good of the throne. That was what a soldier did, after all.

He just hoped the Grand Ten were right.

# Chapter 21

JERINNE WAS ONLY HALFWAY through the swing of her punch when Osharin wrenched her arm behind her and dunked her head into one of the baths. She struggled to get free of Osharin's grip, but he was too strong and she had no leverage. She hadn't had the chance to take a breath before she went under. Unable to pull herself up, she thrashed with her legs, hoping to kick him hard enough to release his grip, so she could get a gulp of air.

Her senses went gray, a calm washing over her despite her need to breathe. Before everything went black, she was pulled out and dropped to the ground.

"Begging your pardon, sir, but abusing the Initiates is my job."

Jerinne panted to catch her breath, but even in her dazed, dizzy state, she could see Vien Reston near her in a defensive crouch.

"She attacked me," Osharin said. "She went wild and—"

"And you decided to drown her?" Vien asked.

"Unbecoming." Someone else. Mizarnis, Vien's paramour. "You were at the party. Uninvited."

"Also the raid," Jerinne croaked out.

Vien glanced down at her, and in that moment Osharin struck, knocking Vien in the head, and then grabbed her to use her body as a shield against Mizarnis's attack. Mizarnis had launched a whirlwind of punches, which all struck Vien as Osharin kept her between himself and Mizarnis's fists. Osharin matched the Spathian's speed, throwing a combination of punches, sending Mizarnis reeling.

Jerinne struggled to get to her feet, which felt like jelly, but Quinara leaped over the baths and got behind her, hooking both her hatchets around Jerinne's neck.

"All right, hold it!" Quinara shouted. She drew Jerinne up by her chin with the hatchets. "You all step back, and we're walking out of here, or the little girl will bleed all over the floor!"

Jerinne wanted to strike back, but she could feel the sharp points of the hatchets on her flesh. It would take only a flick of Quinara's wrists to tear her throat out.

Osharin tossed Vien's battered body on Mizarnis and stepped over to Quinara. While she stayed perfectly still, he slipped off his belt and bound Jerinne's hands behind her. Jerinne didn't dare struggle. She didn't have the strength, and she didn't have a position to gain an advantage.

"Vien," she whispered. "You all right?"

"Fine," Vien croaked, blood gushing from her nose. She looked up at Osharin, who was picking up his sword. "You will not walk out of here."

"We will," Quinara said. "Or she's dead."

Osharin opened the bathhouse doors, and grabbed Jerinne's arm to pull her out while Quinara kept pace, hatchets still at her throat.

He guided them halfway across the courtyard, where

a small group of Initiates in their sleeping clothes had gathered, as well as Master Nedell.

"Osharin," Nedell said. "What in the name of every saint are you doing?"

"We're walking out of here," he said. He pointed to an Initiate—Enther. "You, go summon a cab, now."

"But—" Enther said.

"We will kill her," Osharin said. "And then more of you. Have no doubt."

"You will do nothing of the sort," Master Nedell said, taking a step closer.

"We'll do it!"

"He doesn't care," Jerinne said, hoping to goad them into a mistake. "He doesn't even like me."

Master Nedell sprung, pushing Jerinne in the center of her chest, knocking her back. For a moment the blades weren't pressed into her skin. He grabbed for the hatchets with one hand while drawing his sword with the other, but Quinara was faster. She slashed, and he screamed, blood gushing from his hand.

Osharin was on him, grabbing Nedell's sword arm and disarming him in a fluid motion. He hammered Nedell over the head with the flat of his own sword, and the old man crumpled to the ground. Jerinne's head was spinning too hard to take advantage of the opportunity he gave her, and Quinara had her back in a grip with the hatchets at her neck.

"No one else test me!" Osharin shouted. "Get me that cab!" Vien and Mizarnis stumbled out of the bathhouse, joining the crowd of Initiates who were watching in horror.

Jerinne looked over the small crowd. One Candidate besides Vien. Vien battered. Mizarnis dazed. Master Nedell on the ground, bleeding. The rest, Initiates. Second- and third-years. Iolana and Enther looking terrified, Trandt's hands trembling. Even Kevo, the old half-blind dog, was out there, growling at Osharin.

All of them unarmed, while Osharin and Quinara had swords and hatchets.

She couldn't let them fight, let them risk themselves, not for her. She couldn't let any of them get hurt.

*You're a Tarian. Protect them.*

"Do what he says," she said. She locked eyes with Enther. He, of all of them, should understand her. "It's all right."

Enther ran out of the courtyard, and Jerinne let herself be dragged along after him.

"Where do you think you're going to go?" Vien shouted out.

"Don't follow us," Osharin called out. "Or she dies!"

Enther came running back. "It's there. Just let her go."

"We'll let her go when we do," Quinara said. "If we do."

Jerinne was dragged past him, and only had the chance to say two quick words to Enther before being pulled into the cab. She made those words count.

"Get Dayne."

She saw Enther nod as she was pulled up on the cab seat, tips of the hatchets still poised on her throat. Osharin jumped up to the driver's seat and pushed the cabbie onto the cobblestone. He snapped the reins, and the cab sped off.

"You think someone's going to save you, dear?" Quinara whispered. "I'm going to enjoy making you bleed."

"Not yet," Osharin snapped at her. "For now, we might need her."

Jerinne didn't say anything. She focused on her breathing, finding a calm center. Just like the nightly exercises in meditation. Let her head clear, wait for her moment. When the opportunity came, she would move.

The sun was up by the time Dayne made his way up to the north end of the Trelan Docks, and the streets were crowded with morning activity, including workers of all stripes repairing the damage from the revelry last night. But Dayne found it heartening how many people were just going about their day, not letting the ugly incidents deter their lives one bit. That spoke well of the character of the people of the city.

"Tea and cresh! Who needs a tea and cresh!" one woman called out from a shop stand. Despite the urgency, Dayne's stomach growled at him, and his eyes were far too heavy. He hadn't slept at all, and the *doph* was wearing off. The dull ache in his hip was creeping its way back into pain.

The Grandmaster had said to take care of himself.

"Three cresh rolls and tea with cream," he said to the woman at the shop window. "As quick as you can."

"Quick is what we do," she said. She pointed to a bench on the side of the shop. "Sit there, twelve ticks."

Dayne handed her a coin and took his place on the bench. In moments, she put out a cup of tea and a plate of cresh rolls—sausage and potato and egg wrapped in piping hotcakes. Dayne blew on them before taking a bite.

While he started on his breakfast, people sat on the bench on either side of him.

"Mister Heldrin," one said quietly. "You've come with a purpose."

He turned to the man. "Right now my purpose is breakfast, and you've got me at a disadvantage."

"You didn't charge out to the western docks just to get some cresh rolls," the woman on the other side of him said. "I imagine you are here to investigate the headquarters of the Open Hand."

"What do you two know of it?" he asked.

"Not that much, Mister Heldrin," the man said. "But we do know the marshals arrested most of the Open Hand over the stolen Scallic votes. And that is very interesting."

Dayne put down his cresh roll and turned sharply on the man.

"What are you getting at?"

"Let's not make a scene, Mister Heldrin," the woman said. "We're just three people sitting for breakfast. No need for agitation."

"I'm quite agitated," Dayne said.

"But we're confident you won't do anything rash or violent," the man said. "We're well aware of who you are. That isn't what you do."

Dayne took a moment to breathe and find his calm. "So you've been following me?"

"We've kept our eye on you this past month," the man said. "We're aware of the missing Scallic votes, which is apparently getting blamed on the Open Hand. That is very interesting to us, especially in light of events earlier this week."

The woman continued, "Namely, the thwarted attempt on the Acoran votes, which was blamed on the Sons of the Six Sisters."

Dayne turned to the woman and raised an eyebrow at that. "That wasn't made public. What are you, Intelligence?"

"No, Mister Heldrin," she said firmly, looking into his eyes. "We're with the Sons of the Six Sisters."

Dayne started to jump off his stool, but the pain in his hip screamed at the sudden movement. "Then what are you—"

"We had nothing to do with either ballot robbery," she said.

"And we never would," the man said. "That would go against everything we believe in."

"And what is that?" Dayne asked. "I thought you wished to destroy the Parliament."

"Nothing of the sort. King Maradaine XI established the Parliament, and we are dedicated to what he built."

"But the attack on the Acoran votes was blamed—"

"Yes, it was," the man said.

"But it wasn't us," the woman said.

"Six sisters hid and protected young Maradaine XI. We would never dishonor their memory by subverting the will of the Druth people."

They both stood up, tossing coins on the counter. "We don't know who stole those ballots, Mister Heldrin," the woman said. "But they are an enemy to the people, and we wish you luck in finding them."

"Wait a moment," Dayne said, getting up.

"Don't waste time following us," the man said. "Think about who would want to sabotage the Acoran election."

"The Scallic votes were taken."

"After failing to capture the Acoran ones," the woman said. She pointed to a building up the street. "There's the Open Hand headquarters. I doubt you'll find what you need there."

"When you're ready to talk to us," the man said. "There's a bookstore on Candolyn Way, in Fenton. We welcome your voice, Mister Heldrin."

They both nodded and walked away, and Dayne wasn't sure if he should chase after them, or continue with his original plan. His head was still far too clouded with fatigue to even make a meaningful decision. He swallowed down the rest of his tea, and picked up his cresh rolls, eating them as he walked to the headquarters. The time on the stool had started to make the joints in his hip and leg stiff. They howled at him as he started to walk.

The headquarters was exactly what he expected—a small office above a storefront, with a handful of desks, walls covered in maps of the city, papers and letters in disarray. A quick scan of the letters and documents confirmed Dayne's instincts: These people did not plan any attacks on either the Scallic or the Acoran ballots. Every piece of paper showed him the character of the Open Hand. There were pamphlets and manifestos that matched Ret's message: a desire for an independent

Scallic nation, a restoration of the royal line of the Scallic queen, and the elevation of the Archbishop of Scaloi to Cardinal of the Scallic Church.

And one point was made over and over: it must be done through peaceful means.

These people were not the criminals the marshals wanted to make them into.

This was the wrong place to be. Those votes needed to be found, whoever took them needed to be stopped, and he was wasting his time here. He had to get back.

Each step brought more pain, but he forced his way down to the street, and then the slow walk east. It didn't matter how much it hurt. Everything counted on him.

The chapterhouse was far too quiet this late in the morning. Amaya didn't like it one bit. There should have been sounds of Initiates training, if nothing else, but when she came in the foyer was empty and no one was in the training room.

"Hello?" she called out. "What's going on?"

Someone came running over in a rush. Iolana. Her eyes red, tears down her cheeks. "Madam Tyrell! You're here! Thank the saints you are!"

"What's going on?" Amaya asked. The girl was in a state. "Where is everyone?"

"Most of us are in the dining hall, those that are all right. Come on." Iolana grabbed her hand and pulled her along.

"Those that are all right?"

"Master Nedell is in the infirmary, as is Miss Reston . . ."

"The infirmary?"

They reached the dining hall, where most of the Initiates, as well as the service staff, were sitting around with a sense of morose expectation. What was happening?

"Where's the Grandmaster?" she asked, looking to

Ellist. The head of the service staff looked like the closest thing to a responsible adult here.

"We're not sure, miss," Ellist said. "He left at first light with a few of the Adepts, and hasn't returned yet."

"But what is this about Master Nedell, and Vien?"

"There was an altercation in the bathhouse and the adjoining gardens," Ellist said.

"Rutting Osharin!" Enther shouted. In three years Amaya had never seen him even approach anger. Now he was red-faced and fuming. "He was a rutting traitor!"

"Osharin?" The new Adept from Porvence. "Wait, what did he do?"

"He was in league with that lady with the axes," Tander said. "I don't know all of what's what, but Jerinne and some others caught him. Next thing, he's laid out Vien, her Spathian friend, and Master Nedell, and he and that lady abducted Jerinne with an axe at her throat. And then they're off in a carriage."

"Where's Dayne?" Enther said. "Jerinne said to find Dayne."

"Wait, wait," Amaya said. "Are you saying Osharin is working with them—the ones who attacked the ballots and the party?"

"Yes!" Miara said.

"It would seem to be the case," Ellist said.

"And Jerinne?"

"Taken." Amaya turned to see Vien in just her cottons, with Clinan from the infirmary right behind her. She was limping, her face blue and yellow with bruises, and fresh blood seeping from the bandages around her abdomen. "That bastard took her from us, and we need to get her back."

"You need to get back to bed," Clinan said. "You're in no shape to—"

"Shut it!" Vien said. "Let's track them all down."

"Hold up!" Amaya said. "Where are the rest of the Adepts, or even the Candidates?"

"Some haven't come in yet," Ellist said. "Others went off in search of Mister Osharin."

"Leaving only the Initiates here."

"But we're ready, Madam Tyrell," Tander said. "You give the order, and we'll arm up and go where you lead."

"No," Amaya said. "Saints, you kids—you've already been in two fights with these people, I'm not leading you into another. You all will stay here. Half of you haven't even—I mean, blazes, Vien, look at yourself."

"I'm not going to let him—"

"You can barely stand. To bed. That's an order."

Vien scowled and limped off.

"As for the rest of you, focus your energy on something productive now. Tander, Raila, take all three Initiate Cohorts and run drills and intervals with them. All of you. Go."

There was a brief moment of stunned silence, until Raila spoke up. "All right, we have our orders. Let's head to the training room and start with some calisthenics. Come on, people."

They filed out of the dining hall, Raila stopping briefly to nod at Amaya. Amaya gave her the same back. She needed Raila right now, she needed Raila to know she trusted her. Right now, someone with a cool head had to be in front of the Initiates.

That person was not Amaya. She was ready to take a sword and cut heads off until she had Jerinne Fendall safe and back home. But she didn't know where to go, and that was tearing her apart. It was all she could do to keep these kids from flying apart; she couldn't let them see her do the same.

"Ellist, until the Grandmaster comes back, just . . . just make sure meals and household and—"

"I will attend to all the things, Madam Tyrell," he said. "You do what you have to."

She went to the armory first, selecting her favorite shield and sword, and then made her way to her quarters to change into her mail shirt and regular uniform, passing through the foyer.

Dayne was there, leaning against the doorframe, looking pale and clammy. "Amaya."

"Saints, what are you—"

"I need to get to the Parliament," he said, taking a halting step in. "I hurt my leg last night, and I just need a moment."

He looked like he was upright on sheer willpower. "Have you even slept?"

"Have you?"

"No, I—look, something's happened."

"I know," Dayne said. "We need to find where those ballots were taken and—"

"Ballots?" She swore. "No, Dayne, I'm not talking about the ballots. Something much worse has happened."

# Chapter 22

JERINNE MUST HAVE FALLEN asleep in the back of the cab, Quinara's blade still on her neck. She wasn't sure if she should be comforted or disturbed that she was able to sleep in those circumstances, but it didn't matter. She needed any bit of rest that she could manage at this point, and her situation wasn't any worse than it was before.

Except she was now tied up with sturdy bonds in a dark, musty room.

No, not musty. The scent was rich, but not unpleasant. She couldn't quite identify it, but it felt almost comforting.

Which didn't change the fact that she was a prisoner.

The room wasn't small, which was more than a little surprising. As her eyes adjusted to the dimness, she could see she was in a wide hall, filled with long tables. Not unlike the mess at the chapterhouse. She was tied to one of those tables, seated on the wooden slat floor.

"Why didn't you just kill her?"

Voices outside the nearby door. Sunlight shining under that door, interrupted by the shadows of passing feet.

"Thought about it." Quinara. "We needed her to get away."

"Yes, but why bring her here?" Not a voice she recognized. Man. Strong accent. Acoran, but educated.

"If you let me explain." Osharin. Also that Acoran accent, but more provincial.

"Please."

"We have leverage right now, but nothing we can use for initial exchange."

"So she's, what?"

"A sacrificial lamb, if we need one. No need to kill her now, when we can kill her later to demonstrate how serious we are."

"Ah," the unidentified man said. "All right, I can respect that. It's a risk, but I trust your judgment."

"Good."

"Despite the two of you getting caught in the chapterhouse and destroying your value."

"My fault," Osharin said. "She came to me, injured, and I was careless."

"So what's next?" Quinara asked.

"You're right on one point. We have something of value now, but it doesn't help us get what we want. We need to make demands, and for that we need a messenger. Maybe this girl can serve that purpose."

"No," Quinara said. "I've got a better idea. But I'll need some people to go back to the city."

Back to the city. Which meant they weren't in it right now. Where was she?

"We're running low on good people. You can't get Pria back?"

"Not unless you want to spend three hundred crowns a day on him," Quinara said. "He and the other Firewings say it costs more to fight Tarians."

"Rutting mages. Greedy bastards."

"You're safe to go back alone?" Osharin asked.

"Yeah," Quinara said. "I know exactly what we need, and it won't be a fight. We'll do it quiet, be back in an hour or two."

Not too far away from the city. She couldn't have slept long.

"No more than two," Osharin said. "We can't risk anything else."

"Let's get some breakfast and figure out the details," the unnamed man said. Footsteps and voices faded.

That room must have been an office. Near this large dining hall. Outside the city. Maybe some abandoned workhouse or highway camp.

Jerinne twisted at her bonds. Well-tied ropes. Nothing she'd get out of easily.

But she'd keep trying, regardless. She couldn't count on rescue, so she'd have to do that herself. Get out, find out where she was, get back to the chapterhouse, and then bring the wrath of the Tarian Order upon these people.

Dayne couldn't believe what Amaya was telling him. It was far too much.

"Osharin?" he finally said. He started to go to the armory. He would need his shield; he would need to be ready for Osharin and the rest of his subversives. "We have to stop them." He took two steps, grinding his teeth as the fire shot up from his leg.

"Dayne, you can barely walk."

"I can—"

"Dayne," she said firmly. She took his face in her hands and locked eyes with him. "I know what you want to do. I want to do the same thing, and I want to do it together. All right?"

"I can't let Jerinne—"

"She is my charge. And technically, so are you."

"But—"

"This is what you are going to do. We're going to get you up to that infirmary and let Clinan tend to that leg. No argument. I'm going to search Osharin's quarters, see what I can find. You get yourself right, and when we know where we're going, you can count on every saint that you and I will ride there together. We will get her back. Am I clear?"

Dayne nodded. She was right. He'd be no good to Jerinne if he couldn't stand against her abductors. And Clinan's ministrations were exactly what he needed.

"Help me get there," he said.

She put herself under his shoulder and bore his weight. "Always."

Clinan was a strange sort, a wiry old man with leathery skin and powerful forearms. He was a fixture in the infirmary, but not a proper doctor. He had never gone to university, but he seemed to have an innate understanding of bodies, muscles, and pain.

"Hey there, Dayne," he said as Amaya helped him into the infirmary. "Looks like you've twisted something up."

"Rather. Fell off a balcony onto my side. I don't think anything's broken."

"Yeah, but there's a lot more to pain than broken. Strip to your cottons and get on the floor. You're a little too big for my table. We'll work out what's going on with that leg of yours."

Amaya helped him get his dress uniform off and lie down on the floor. "I won't go running off without you."

"Don't worry about my feelings," he said. "If you can save Jerinne, get on it."

She smiled warmly. "Get him up and running again, Clinan."

"We do what we can here," Clinan said. She left, and he knelt down next to Dayne, massaging the leg with his strong, powerful hands. The pain of it was intense, but Dayne was familiar with Clinan's methodology. Work through the pain to get to the other side of it.

"Yeah, that's a banger, all right," Clinan said. "You just shut your eyes, and focus on your breath. Let's get this back together."

The Alassan Coffeehouse had a reputation, especially amongst the students at the Royal College, so all but the most daring or degenerate were terrified to step foot in the place. Hemmit had tried it once, entering entirely because of its reputation, but found Imach coffee was not to his taste at all. The usual customers were the type who would sit around talking revolution, talking about it as an end in itself. Hemmit wondered why Kemmer wanted to meet here of all places.

"But why do we want to find Kemmer?" Lin asked as she followed behind Hemmit and Maresh. Her nose was crinkled in disgust. "This place smells awful."

"Hey, hey," the man behind the counter—an Imach man with a thick mustache and thicker accent—said, snapping at them. "What you want?"

"Three coffees," Maresh said, putting a couple coins on the counter.

"You want the cream? You want the *sukkar*?"

Maresh looked at Hemmit for guidance, but Hemmit had none to give him. "Yes, of course."

"Three! With the cream and *sukkar*!" The man behind him went to work filling mugs.

"We really aren't here for the coffee," Lin said. "In fact, I've heard—"

"We can't be impolite," Maresh interrupted.

"Come on," Lin said. She looked at the man behind the counter. "We're looking for a fellow named Kemmer. Is he here?"

The man just snarled something in Imach and looked away.

"Is that a no?"

The other man, the one putting their mugs of coffee on the counter, shook his head. "He is old country." His accent was not as pronounced. "Does not want to talk to women who are not his wives."

"Wives?" Lin asked.

"The man you want is in the back." He pushed the three mugs forward. "Enjoy."

Hemmit picked up a mug, and went to the back room, Lin and Maresh following him. And there was the man himself—Kemmer, looking rather smart and well-groomed. That was the biggest surprise of all. On seeing Hemmit, he waved to the chairs at his table.

"Hemmit," he said. "Good to see you—the actual you, without the disguise. And I presume your name isn't Jala."

"Lin Shartien," she said.

"Well," he said. "I wasn't expecting you to be Linjari. I must congratulate you on your excellent deceptions. And you must be Maresh."

"I must be," Maresh said, sitting at the table.

"So what can you tell us?" Hemmit said, taking his seat. He sipped at the coffee, which was somehow bitter and sweet, rich and light, intense and mild all at the same time. Perhaps the last time his mistake was not taking it with the cream and *sukkar*.

"Right to business," Kemmer said. "I presume you weren't followed or such."

"No," Hemmit said. "Nor did we bring authorities."

"I'm not that worried about constables or marshals right now. And, frankly, none of them are looking for me. At least not in regard to last month's unpleasantness."

"That's what you call four members of Parliament murdered, not to mention—"

"Tharek Pell's doing, not mine. From reading your pamphlet, and what I've pieced together, he had his own agenda. In fact, many people did, and none of it to help Druthal or its people."

"But you're not like that," Lin said with condescension.

"I was an idiot. Probably still am. But I'm an idiot who's got a hold of something real."

"A Grand Ten?" Hemmit asked. "Some high conspiracy against the crown and country?"

"I can't say I know what they want. But I can say they were the impetus behind the initial attacks from the Patriots."

"I thought Chief Toscan—"

"Was pulling the strings? Yes. But they were pulling his."

"Who are they?" Maresh asked.

"Still working on that," Kemmer said after a brief pause. "I don't know who they all are, but one of them—"

Before he could say, the woman with the hatchets came right up behind him and clocked him across the head. Kemmer fell like a sack of potatoes.

"I don't care what he was saying," she said. "You are coming with me." She had a pair of musclebound guys behind her to back up the assertion.

"All of us?" Maresh asked.

"Not her," she said, pointing an axe at Lin. "I don't need to deal with a magic girl."

Lin grabbed Hemmit's wrist. "Where are you taking them?" Hemmit noticed a spark of shock at her touch.

The axe-woman looked at Hemmit. "You said you could tell our story, pretty beard. So it's time to hear it."

"Well, I—"

"Let me make something clear," she said, spinning the hatchet in her hand and then bringing it to Maresh's face. "You and Spectacles are going to come with me, or he gets a very close shave."

Lin stood up sharp, and the woman brought another axe up. "Don't even try it, lady. I know a thing or two about mages." She moved behind Maresh, kissing his forehead as she slid the axe blade up his cheek. "In fact, you drink those three cups right now."

"You want me to what?"

"Drink the coffee. All three."

"Lin," Maresh said in a terrified whisper.

She picked up her cup, her hand trembling, and drank its contents down.

"Go on."

With a hard sneer, she picked up Maresh's and drank it down as well. Then she picked up Hemmit's and did it again. "Are you happy?"

"Quite."

Lin was about to say something, but crackles and sparks began to snap and pop from her fingers. Then a large crack of lightning jumped from her hands to her feet, making her knees buckle.

"What—" she said, and another series of crackles ran up and down her body.

"What did you do?" Hemmit asked.

"Coffee doesn't agree with mages," the woman said. "Get him."

Her goons grabbed him and started to drag him out. Lin, writhing on the floor while sparks and flashes danced all over her, reached out to him. Despite the fact she was obviously suffering, she mouthed something out to him.

"Go. I've got you."

That was all he saw before he was dragged out of the Alassan. It was notable how no one else in the place tried to stop them, or even reacted. As if abductions were so common, it wasn't worthy of notice.

"Come along," she said as they reached the street. There was a carriage waiting outside, which they shoved him and Maresh into. The rest of the goons all got in, crowding their bodies into the two of them.

"Where are we going?" Hemmit asked.

"You don't need to know that," the axe-woman said as she hopped into the driver's seat. As if in response to that, one of the goons threw a sack over Hemmit's head, leaving him in the dark as the carriage surged forward.

# Chapter 23

DAYNE'S HIP MADE a very satisfying pop as Clinan pulled and stretched his leg out wide.

"Yeah, that's what we wanted," Clinan said. "Let's see if you can get on your feet." He took Dayne's hand and helped him off the ground. It was something of a marvel how strong this wiry man was. Dayne tested putting weight on his leg, and while it was still sore, he could bear it. He took a few tentative steps, and it was miles better than when he had arrived.

"Another miracle," Dayne said.

"I don't know about that. Just doing what I do, so you can do what you do."

Amaya came in, carrying two sets of shield and sword. "You able?"

"Absolutely," he said. "What do we know?"

"Not a lot. Looks like Osharin was part of something called the Deep Roots, and he had some letters from his cousin, a woman named Quinara Essaryn, but nothing that gave me a sense of where we might find them."

"Deep Roots?" Dayne asked. "Chief Samsell mentioned them, in the same context as the Patriots, the Open Hand, Sons of the Six Sisters."

"Some other radical group bent on tearing down Druthal?"

"Sounds like you two should get out to the marshals," Clinan said.

"Shall we move?" Dayne asked. She handed him the shield and sword. As he put the sword to his belt and his hand through the shield's straps, the words came to his mouth like instinct, a whisper in volume but shouted from his heart.

*"With shield on arm and sword in hand*
*I will not yield, but hold and stand.*
*As I draw breath, I'll allow no harm,*
*And hold back death with shield on arm."*

Amaya said it with him, the smile on her face growing as she did. "Come on. Let's ride."

"Ride?"

Amaya had two horses saddled and ready outside the chapterhouse, and Dayne happily mounted the larger one. Amaya got on hers, a stallion with a brilliant rich brown coat, and spurred it to a canter. She was riding, perhaps too recklessly for the city, but Dayne matched her speed as they pounded down the streets to the Parliament building. They tied off the horses and went up the steps to the Parliament.

"Did you have the authority to requisition horses for us right now?" Dayne asked as they approached the doors.

"I would have to clear it with the ranking member at the chapterhouse, which was me. So I'm saying it was fine. Where is the Grandmaster?"

The question was answered for them as they entered the marshals' offices in the Parliament. The Grandmaster was waiting in Donavan Samsell's "war room" with two senior Adepts, and a man Dayne recognized as the Spathian Grandmaster, as well as a Constabulary officer and an archduchy sheriff.

"There's the man," Samsell said when Dayne entered. "That took you some time, so you must have learned something."

"A few things," Dayne said. He noticed all eyes were on him. "Grandmaster, we have a situation."

The Grandmaster gave him a dismissive wave. "I'm well aware of that, Dayne. What have you learned, and why did you bring Miss Tyrell with you? Surely she should be focused on the training regiments with Master Nedell."

"Master Nedell is in the infirmary, sir," Amaya said.

"How is that?"

"Osharin," she said. "He's apparently in league with some group called the Deep Roots, who were responsible for the attack on the Acoran ballots."

"The Acoran ballots were attacked by the Sons of the Six Sisters," Samsell said. "That's what you told me, Dayne."

"I believed that at the time, but now I'm not sure. Members of the Sons of the Six Sisters reached out to me."

"They did what?"

"They approached me and said they were not responsible for the attack on the Acoran ballots, or taking the Scallic ones."

"Well, we know that," the constable lieutenant said. "It was those Open Hand people."

"I don't think so," Dayne said. "I went through the papers in their headquarters, and there was nothing that indicated their involvement."

Samsell scoffed. "Please, Dayne, don't be naive. Of course they did."

"Sir," Dayne said, looking to the Grandmaster. "There were detailed plans and letters for each of their campaigns—disrupting voters, the demonstration at Unity Stationhouse, their silent vigil last night. But nothing about stealing ballots."

The Spathian Grandmaster stepped forward, his dark eyes boring into Dayne. "So who do you suspect?"

"Right now, these Deep Roots folks."

"Whatever they want," Amaya said.

Samsell dug through his files and threw one on the table. "The Deep Roots are Acoran revolutionaries who want to dismantle the entire nobility system and be run entirely as a democratic republic."

"A return of the Nation of Acoria," Dayne said. "So therefore—"

"Therefore they could not care less about Scallic ballots, Dayne," Samsell said.

Grandmaster Orren looked at both Dayne and Amaya with focused interest. "This is not why you came."

"Osharin fled from the chapterhouse," Amaya said, "injuring Master Nedell and Vien Reston, and abducting Jerinne Fendall. He has her, somewhere."

"That is quite distressing," the Grandmaster said. "I didn't know much about the man, but Master Escanline in Porvence spoke well of him. We are certain of all this?"

"We're certain he's with the people who attacked the Acoran wagons and the party," Amaya said. "And he had Jerinne."

"Even if they had nothing to do with the Scallic votes, we need to find them and save her," Dayne urged.

Samsell came over, clapping Dayne on the shoulder. "I understand your concerns, but there are larger ones at play right now. If anything in that folder can be of help, you are welcome to it."

Amaya took that cue and starting thumbing through it.

"In the meantime, Dayne," the Grandmaster said,

"while I am troubled by this development, right now we must be focused on the good of the nation. Shortly we anticipate having the intelligence we need, and then we will go to action. Together."

"What intelligence?"

"Done." A Spathian Adept strode into the room, with a woman in a gray Druth Intelligence uniform. Her smile was demure, subtle, but the Spathian had a grin as wide as the sky. "We know where the ballots are."

Jerinne made no progress on the ropes, beyond rubbing her wrists raw. Escaping from bonds seemed like it was something Tarian Initiates should learn, but it was not part of the training curriculum. Jerinne certainly would have found such lessons useful now.

The door opened and Osharin came in purposefully. He knelt down in front of her and put a cup to her lips. She twisted her head away, not that she'd be able to resist for long.

He sighed, and took a drink from the cup. "It's water."

She was absurdly parched, and this room was dry and dusty. "Fine." He put the cup to her lips and let her drink it all down. It helped, but it was hardly enough to slake her thirst.

"Sorry to get you mixed up in all this," he said. "I overreacted when you came across Quinara and me."

"You tried to drown me," Jerinne said.

"I overreacted. And I apologize." He said this like it was impolite of her to not accept his apology. "And I've kept Quinara and the others from killing you. That's not something I want. Please understand that."

"Thank you so much," Jerinne said, letting the condescension drip from her voice.

"You're angry, of course you are. You have every right to be."

Jerinne couldn't believe this fellow. He actually thought he was giving her permission to feel angry. "What do you want?"

"I want the future," Osharin said, as if that was response enough. Jerinne didn't give him the satisfaction of asking for clarification, and he frowned at her for a short while before going on. "Look, this country is in shambles, thanks to puffed-up nobles shutting down the voice of the people. That's what we're supposed to be supporting. That's what this uniform is supposed to mean."

"How is stealing ballots or attacking a party supporting the voice of the people?"

"That's just it! The voice of the people has been suppressed. The election is a joke! Pretense all around like it gives a voice to the people, when all it does is create a puppetry for the nobility to control."

"So you want to, what, get rid of the Parliament?"

"No, you silly child," he said, standing up and pacing off. "I mean, yes, but only because this Parliament is a sham, and we should not give it honor or credence. What we need is a true congress of the people, like Acoria had before it was destroyed."

"Saints, more of this," Jerinne muttered. "So why attack the party?"

"Because all of you Tarians in Maradaine were far more interested in sucking up to those swells instead of respecting this!" He beat his chest and grabbed his uniform. "All of you in dress uniform, rubbing elbows with the nobles and fancy folk, instead of being on the street, shield high!"

"So you brought the fight to us?"

"I reminded you who you are! We aren't supposed to get accolades from those people! The Tarian Order was always supposed to protect the common man *from* those people. I thought if anyone would understand that, it was Heldrin."

"Dayne knows what it means to be a Tarian."

"But he's being poisoned by that . . . woman. I hoped that if we got rid of her, he'd be free. He'd see what we needed to be."

"All right, you've lost me," Jerinne said. "Is all this about freeing Druthal or freeing Dayne?"

He shook his head in disgust. "I should have known better than to explain this to a stupid girl like you. The two are one and the same. The cause is the same, be it for the nation or just one man."

"Dayne will never side with you on this," Jerinne said. "Though, he'd be the one who'd defend your right to say it."

"No, Dayne is going to understand. You all will."

Jerinne strained at her bonds to lean forward. "There's nothing to understand besides your mania."

He jumped at her and grabbed her by the chin. "Maybe next time I won't argue so hard to spare your life. Remember that, Initiate. Remember your place."

"My place is standing with a shield between you and the people of Druthal. And Dayne will be right by my side."

He cracked her jaw with the back of his fist and stormed off. Jerinne spit out blood, but getting under his skin was worth it. Now alone, she started again on the ropes binding her. Even if she rubbed her wrists raw to the bone, she would get out of here, and do whatever she needed to stop Osharin, Quinara, and the rest of these bastards.

"Come on, Saint Julian," she whispered. She rarely prayed to any of the saints in any seriousness, but in this moment it made sense to call on the shielded pilgrim. "I could use a bit of blessing right now."

Hands touched hers from behind. "We all could, child." A cold blade touched her skin, and then it cut through the rope. Free from her binds, she got to her feet and turned to her rescuer.

A Cloistress of the Red—a woman of middle years and haunted face. Not just any cloistress.

"You were at the stationhouse," Jerinne said. "You're with that Scallic group."

"Sister Frienne," she said, sheathing the knife at her belt. Her hands were shaking as she touched Jerinne's face. "I needed to look to you, and I found you. Now we need to get out of here before they notice you're gone. Come."

"What did you do?" Dayne asked, looking to the Spathian and back to Samsell. "You didn't torture Ret or his people, did you?"

"Saints, Dayne, you're far too excitable about these things," Samsell said. "But, no, we didn't hurt them. Did we?"

"It's amazing what some people will do when they believe you will hurt them, though," the Spathian said. "All I did was get in the cell with one of them, and start unloading a bag of tools. In thirty seconds he started talking."

"It's true," the Intelligence colonel said. She handed a paper over to Samsell. "A series of warehouses in North Druthal. I find the information credible, and therefore actionable."

"Who is she?" Amaya asked.

"Colonel Silla Altarn," Samsell said. "The marshals and Druth Intelligence openly cooperate in situations like this."

"So you'll be heading out with your men?" she asked. "Or perhaps a joint operation with our Elite Order friends would be good fodder for the newssheets."

The Grandmaster sighed. "That wouldn't be why I would suggest it, but I would be honored to assist the marshals here. And the Spathians?"

"Yes," their Grandmaster said tersely.

"But, sir—" Dayne started.

"Dayne," the Grandmaster said, taking his arm and pulling him aside, almost snarling in anger. "I recognize that you are feeling left out of these decisions, and that your position here—"

"I don't care about the position!" Dayne snapped. "Jerinne is in danger."

The Grandmaster's face fell a bit. "Of course. That seems to be independent of these other matters. We will handle the troubles of the nation, rescue the ballots and their escorts. If you wish to be excluded, you can focus on rescuing the Initiate from whatever trouble she's found herself in."

"I do," Dayne said. Something else burst forth from his gut. "And we were supposed to keep them from torturing the prisoners, sir."

"And no torture occurred," the Grandmaster said. "Untoward and unorthodox, but Colonel Altarn assured me . . ." He stopped and pursed his lips, and when he spoke, all the harshness in his voice had gone. "I recognize the discomfort here. But trust that what I am doing is what's best for the country. And the Order."

"And for Jerinne?" Dayne asked.

"For that, I count on you to handle it as best you can," he said. "I'm sorry I—that's how it has to be today."

Dayne nodded and walked away. He didn't even want to look at the Grandmaster right now. That he would be so dismissive about the life of one of his charges was appalling.

He was out of the war room and down the hall before he realized that Amaya was right by his side.

"I don't even recognize him right now," she growled.

"So we're alone in this," Dayne said. "You have the file?"

"I do, for all the good it will do us. Some names, some information on properties and money and suspected supporters. We're going to have to do real legwork for this to pay off."

"Then let's not waste time."

They emerged from the Parliament to the bright daylight, and Lin Shartien on the steps, half-crawling her way up. Her hands were trembling as lights and sparks popped off of her.

"Lin!" he shouted, running to her. "Are you all right?"

"H-h-had to f-f-find you," she stuttered out. "F-f-for Hemmit and Mar . . . mar . . . Maresh." Now that he was close, he saw she also had several bruises and scrapes on her face.

"She needs food," Amaya said, and she dashed over to a street cart.

Dayne scooped Lin up and carried her over. Amaya had bought a couple of lamb sausage sandwiches, which Lin scarfed down with no decorum.

"More?" Amaya asked.

"Please," Lin said. Amaya went for another pair of sandwiches.

"What happened?" Dayne asked.

"That woman with the axes, she took Hemmit and Maresh."

"Them too?" Amaya asked, bringing more food.

"Too?"

"She already kidnapped Jerinne. What are they about?"

"And what happened to you?"

"Imach coffee," Lin said between bites, now eating in a bit more civilized manner. "It and magic do not play together well. Which that woman knew. But it doesn't matter . . ."

"Imach coffee did that to your face?"

She touched at the bruises. "That . . . the patrons of the coffee shop were not well disposed to me once I started bursting with magic. But none of that matters."

"Now we need to find all three of them," Dayne said. "We can't waste any more time."

Amaya started thumbing through the folder. "Maybe there's a property they might have gone to. Did you see which way they went?"

"I don't need to see it," Lin said. "Just listen, you fools. Before they took Hemmit, I was able to tether myself to him. And even with the magic going haywire from the coffee, and the beating, I held on to that. Despite the fire and pain it all put me through, I held it. I wasn't about to lose him."

She turned her hand over, showing a faint spiderweb of light spun from her fingers, forming a taut line heading to the east. She let it fade, almost invisible, as she took the last bite of her fourth sandwich.

"Let's stop wasting time, all right? We've got people to rescue."

# Chapter 24

**S**ISTER FRIENNE LED HER through one of the doors to a darkened corridor.

"Where are we?" Jerinne asked.

"Sawmill and log camp, about three miles east of the city. It's empty or abandoned for some reason."

"And how did you get here? When you ran from the Constabulary station you were—"

"I was wild when I ran from there. Mad with pain, punishment from God. But in that pain, God showed me the path to you. I felt a call in my soul that brought me to you. And . . . these people . . . these people had . . . and I wanted to—" Her voice had darkened with rage, but then she stopped and dropped to her knees. "I will abide, God, I will hold my sacred oath and harm no one else. I will be strong for you."

"Sister," Jerinne said. This was probably not the moment for prayer, especially prayer directly to God, as opposed to asking a saint to intercede on one's behalf. Even with minimal religious instruction in her past, Jerinne had always understood it was prideful to presume to speak directly to God. But perhaps in Scaloi, perhaps for their clergy and holy orders, the rules were different.

"I will stay true and not harm another soul. I will not raise my hand in violence. I will stay true and not harm another soul."

The woman was in a reverie. Jerinne needed to break her out of it, grabbing her shoulder. The cloistress's hand went for the knife at her belt as if it was an instinct, and Jerinne let go. She noticed that the woman had dried blood on her knuckles, and her arms were covered in tally mark scars, angry and red.

Perhaps the sister needed to pray right now. Perhaps she needed to convince herself to hold this oath of hers.

"How do we get out of here?" Jerinne asked cautiously.

"This leads out to the barracks, and then from there we can cross the field to the backhouses and make our way to the river. There might be rowboats or rafts there and we can get downstream back to the city. As long as they have no guards there."

"So there are guards," Jerinne said.

"They have quite a few people here. I couldn't count them all. At least twenty."

That was quite a lot for the two of them, especially if Sister Frienne was swearing to do no violence. That was not a helpful oath in this situation.

"And that's not even counting the ones they're holding captive."

"Captive?"

Frienne nodded. "The Scallic ballots. Several people in the warehouse, as well as carriages, horses."

"They took the ballots from Scaloi? Why?" Though

perhaps it made perfect sense. These people tried to take the Acoran ballots. In failing that, they captured another set.

"We can do nothing for them. But I can get you out. I had to save you. My charge, my penance."

Jerinne wasn't sure what that meant. That priest who had touched her when he was yelling at the sister had said something about looking to her. Perhaps Sister Frienne had taken it too literally. But perhaps she was right as well. If they could get back to the city, she could bring Dayne, Madam Tyrell, marshals, everyone. Going for help was the best thing.

"Come on," Jerinne said. "Let's move now."

They made their way to a door that led outside, with a short stone path to a set of barracks. Beyond that building, there was an open clearing, on the other side of which Jerinne could see backhouses and glimpses of water past the tree line. If any guards were out here, they'd have to just run and hope for the best.

Sister Frienne glanced about, and dashed from the door to the barracks, hiding on the far side of it. She waved for Jerinne to follow.

Jerinne was about to move when she heard the sound of horses and carriage in the other direction. She saw it coming down the drive path, with Quinara at the reins. She stayed crouched in the doorframe, watching as the carriage came to a stop. Quinara hopped down and opened the carriage, where two goons pulled out a couple of men with sacks over their heads. Even with the sacks, Jerinne recognized those two men.

Hemmit and Maresh.

She looked to Sister Frienne, who was desperately waving to her to run.

She shook her head. It was one thing to escape to get more help, but there was no chance she would abandon Hemmit and Maresh to these people. She was a Tarian, and she knew what her duty was.

After a carriage ride where Hemmit had lost all sense of direction and time, they came to a stop and were pulled out. Hemmit was certain they were out of the city. Dirt under his feet, the sound of singing insects, and they definitely were in the carriage long enough.

The woman barked out a few orders, and rough hands grabbed him and took him inside somewhere.

"Maresh!" he yelled. "You all right?"

"Right here," Maresh said.

"Shut it," someone told them. He was forced into a chair, and his hands bound behind him. Once he was secure, the sack was pulled off his head.

His eyes adjusted to the light—sun still streaming in the windows—he saw he was in a large warehouse work floor. The far end of the room had tarps covering large devices and huge wooden planks stacked against the wall. In the center of the floor, five carriages sat without horses, and a series of lockboxes were lined up in front of the carriages. Ten people—bound, gagged, stripped to skivs, and blindfolded—were kneeling on the concrete floor, as a dozen armed men paced around them. It didn't take long for Hemmit to realize these were the stolen ballots.

Some of their captors stood out. There was the woman with her hatchets, wearing a fur-lined coat that seemed unseasonably warm for this hot summer. There was a man stripped to the waist sitting off to one side, rubbing oil on a leather whip. And oddest of all, a man in a Tarian uniform. Hemmit didn't recognize him, but given his relaxed ease in this situation, Hemmit quickly decided he was someone he didn't want to know.

"So these are the journalists," a voice said behind them. The speaker walked in front of them, an older man whose bedraggled, exhausted appearance and unkempt beard and hair were in sharp contrast to his fine tailored clothes, with matching waistcoat and cravat. His accent was Acoran and educated. "What newssheet are they from, Quinara?"

The axe-woman shrugged and pointed at Hemmit. "Answer him."

"*The Veracity Press*," Hemmit said.

The older man shrugged. "Serviceable enough, I suppose. So I'm told you two will tell our story to the city. That's just what we need."

Hemmit glanced over to Maresh, who gave an expression of curiosity. "All right," Hemmit said. "Who are you and what is this about? I assume you absconded with the Scallic ballots for a reason."

"We did," the man said, coming in closer. His breath was heavy with the stench of rotten beer. "Admittedly, it is not in service of our goals, not directly. Which is why we need you to tell our story."

"And you are?" Maresh asked.

"My name is Mister Valclerk. Until recently, I was the chief of staff for the Honorable Member of Parliament, Erick Parlin. I served in his offices for seventeen years, since he first was elected, and I have been deeply proud of the work we did together. I was . . . we all were . . . deeply troubled by his death. Not only for our own, personal connection, but what it meant for Acora."

"I'm sure he was a good man," Hemmit said. In truth, he had found Parlin to be something of a feckless twit— often talking a good game for the Salties, but then being just as much of a pampered dandy as many of the other members of Parliament.

"We lost the true voice of the people. They voted for him, and he was taken from them."

"All right," Maresh said. "So how does that connect to the Scallic votes?"

"We were thwarted," Quinara said. "We just wanted to get the Acoran votes, but those children kept us from them."

That brought more questions to Hemmit's mind. "So, why are you so concerned with the Acoran votes?"

"Because they're illegitimate," Valclerk said. "I reject the premise that they can elect someone new—most likely a Traditionalist—to take Erick Parlin's chair, which is his for three more years!"

"But he's dead," Hemmit said.

"But what he represented is not! That chair should speak for his views, vote as he would have. And if we had gotten the Acoran votes, we would have been able to stop that before the ballots were tallied and certified. But we failed."

"So the ballots from Scaloi were our only option," the Tarian said.

"Wait a minute," Hemmit said. "You're Acorans, yes? How does this fit the goals of the Sons of the Six Sisters?"

"The who?" Valclerk asked.

Maresh posed the obvious questions. "Aren't you the Sons of the Six Sisters?"

"No, we're not," Valclerk said. "Why would you think that?"

"We're the Deep Roots," the Tarian said.

"They're Deep Roots," the man with the whips said. "I just thought the job sounded fun."

"Then why did the Sons of the Six Sisters warn us that they were attacking the Acoran ballots?"

That silenced the room for a bit.

"What are you talking about?"

"We got a letter from the Sons of the Six Sisters, telling us that they planned to attack the Acoran ballot wagons. We told Dayne, he told the other Tarians, and off they went to stop it."

That got a reaction. The Tarian screamed, and then stalked off and punched the wall.

"Someone rutting warned them?" Valclerk snarled. "Who the blazes did that?"

"I didn't do it," Quinara said.

"None of us did that!"

"Did that rat Pria do it? Never trust a mage for hire, I'm telling you!"

"I don't know who did it, but—"

"It doesn't matter!" Valclerk shouted. "It's done, over. All we can do now is keep moving with our plan. And here's what's going to happen." He walked over to Hemmit and poked him in the chest. "You, young man, are going back to the city, and there you are going to put out our statement. Get it in the hands of your friends in the Tarians and the marshals and whoever else. This one is going to stay here as leverage."

Hemmit swallowed hard. These people were unhinged, and any wrong word could get him or Maresh hurt. "What's your statement?"

"We have the Scallic ballots and the authenticators. We will trade them in exchange for the official results of the Acoran election, to not accept whatever pretender has laid claim to Erick Parlin's seat, and instead name a proper proxy to hold his seat and vote in his name until his chair is properly up for election."

"And who would this 'proper proxy' be? You?"

"If asked I will serve. But I will accept any Acoran who represents the interest of the people and the party."

"And what happens if they refuse?" Maresh asked.

"At midnight," Valclerk said, pointing to the ten captives. "They will all be executed, and the ballots burned. We already have them all doused with lamp oil, so it'll only take a spark to light them up."

That set off cries and whimpers amongst the captives, who were otherwise unable to articulate their fear.

"Now," Valclerk said. "It's already three bells, so we only have nine hours to get you back and—what is that?"

"What?" the Tarian asked, coming over to Hemmit.

"It looks like a . . . thread of light coming out of him,"

Valclerk said. He went behind Hemmit. "It is! Very faint, out of his wrist!"

"Magic!" the Tarian shouted.

"That magic-spinning bint!" Quinara shouted. "She must have connected herself to him. She's tracking him!"

"What do we do?" Valclerk asked.

"I know what to do," Quinara said, and the sack went back over Hemmit's head.

"I lost it!"

Lin had clutched Amaya's waist so strongly when she shouted that, she almost made her throw up, which was not something she needed when driving her horse at a full gallop down the eastern highway. She pulled the reins and stopped.

"What happened?"

"I don't know, but the tether is gone," Lin said. She flailed her hand fruitlessly. "Nothing."

"How could that happen?" Amaya didn't mean to make that sound like an accusation, but it surely did. She couldn't help the anxiety in her voice. Jerinne had been taken hours ago, and the best lead to find her just vanished. The girl was her charge, her responsibility, and she wasn't there for her.

"If they spotted it?" Lin said. "Maybe they could have done something to sever it."

Dayne had gotten his horse turned back around and reached them. "What's the problem?"

"I've lost the connection to Hemmit. I can't track my way to him anymore."

"How could they sever it?" Amaya asked.

Lin was in tears. "I tried to make it as faint as I could, but my skills are all about light . . ."

"They had a mage at the party," Dayne said. "Perhaps he could have done it."

Lin nodded. "Possible. There might also be mundane ways. The tether was connected to his wrist, so just—oh dear saints." She started to gag.

"What?"

"If they cut off his arm!" she said.

"Let's hope they're not complete savages," Amaya said. Dayne got his horse close so he could take Lin's hand.

"What else?"

"Cover it in iron or some other metal, submerge it in water, maybe something else. I was not a good theory student!"

"All right, all right," Dayne said. "How close were we to him? Could you feel that? Before you lost it?"

She thought about it for a moment. "Close. Half, quarter of a mile."

"All right, what's up this way?" Dayne asked, looking to Amaya. "Some farms, a fishing village, the house of the baron of that village, a sawmill camp, a hunting lodge, a weather post, and then you reach Dondiren . . ."

Amaya thought for a moment and dug into the saddlebag, pulling out the marshal's file on the Deep Roots. "Maybe we've got something here that will help."

"Hunting lodge?" Lin asked. "I mean, that'd be off the highway a ways, out of sight."

"Wait, wait," Amaya said as she thumbed through the marshals' notes. One name jumped out. "Is that sawmill camp part of the Faltor Wood and Lumber Company?"

"I don't really know," Dayne said. "It's possible."

She scanned over the page. "The marshals think Curtis Faltor has sympathies with the Deep Roots. They suspect he helps fund them."

Dayne looked down the road. "Then maybe camp is a safe haven for them."

"It's as good a guess as any," Amaya said. "I think it's the best chance."

Dayne nodded. "You're right."

"Then let's ride," Amaya said. She closed the file and put it back in her saddle bag. There was one other thing that caught her eye before she had put it away. There was a note written on the file—different ink, different handwriting—underlining Curtis Faltor's name, and then the words "Ask SA about the list."

Amaya kicked her horse to a gallop, and Dayne did the same with his. Right now, it only mattered to find Jerinne and get her safe. She could worry about Faltor and whoever "SA" was another time.

# INTERLUDE: The Mage

SILLA ALTARN RARELY had cause to wear her gray and green Intelligence uniform. It was the sort of thing one only put on for official or ceremonial functions—not daily operations. But today she wore it as a victory banner, with new colonel's stripes on her collar as proof of her domination. She strode through the halls of the Central Office. After months of organization, of moving pieces around, of favors and promises and agreements, she had won.

She was now the highest ranking mage in Druth Intelligence, and now she had a seat at the Colonel's Table, the commanding body of Druth Intelligence. She was probably the most powerful woman in the country not to have noble blood in her veins, too.

An impressive feat for a skinny orphan from the impoverished bowels of Marikar, until her innate magical talent plucked her away from a future in gutters, slums, or back alley brothels. Every day she pushed herself throughout her education, mastering her craft and skill in magic. She embraced the debt owed to the Red Wolf Circle, taking thankless assignments in Intelligence and humbly accepting the praise and promotion she was given.

She had embedded herself in all the dark corners of power she could find. The Hierarch of the Brotherhood of the Nine had given her connections and influence like she had never dreamed. Intelligence was foolish enough to give her access to disgraced agents and rogue telepaths, crafting a spiderweb of power centered on her. She heard whispers that the fools calling themselves the Grand Ten needed a Mage, and she provided herself.

Clandestine power, secrets, and collaboration had opened the doors. Legitimate power was now handed to her. The keys to the kingdom, and the purses to match.

"What do you mean reassigned?" she heard shouted from one of the offices as she walked to her new one. "I have evidence that Liora Rand is alive and operating in Maradaine. I have agents in the field. I was barely able to untangle the local election corruption with what I have, stopping those fake ballots for Undenway! And you take my teams away from me?"

Altarn chuckled wryly to herself. Major Grieson was going to be a problem. For a while she had seen him as beautifully corrupt, maybe even a kindred soul. He had made his bones in the Central Office nearly fifteen years ago with the Innetic Project, his operation to keep the Waish throne away from clans opposed to Druth interests. That had made him the golden boy for some time, and he had coasted on that prestige. She had thought he had a certain darkness, a corruption in his spirit she could exploit. But it had become clear that Grieson was actually an idealist at heart, almost as pure as Lady Mirianne's Tarian lover. So she took a certain childish glee in the fact that her final moves to endgame in the past week had castrated him in here.

Plus she did not need him finding Liora. Her tasks

were far too critical to the Brotherhood and the Hierarch. Liora had finished her job with Lord Henterman, like she had with Alderman Strephen, and once she was fully recovered she would move on to the next name on the list. The last thing she needed was Grieson sticking his perfect chin into that business.

As Altarn reached her office, Ebbermin, the young lieutenant assigned as her admin, handed her a file. "Morning, ma'am. For your final approval."

"Thank you, Ebbermin. Tea with cream and honey, and three pastries, please."

"Yes, ma'am," he said.

She sat down at her desk and looked over the folder. This was it, the fruit of her labors. The budget, the approvals, the operatives and authority—all of it.

Now she was free to shape Druthal into the magical superpower it was destined to be. Now she could set the pieces for the next game: Ithaniel Senek would be able to finish his twisted experiments, the High Dragon Crenaxin would have his zealots, and Lord Sirath would be made whole again. Soon the Brotherhood would have the knowledge and power they needed.

All of that would come, as her plans entered the second phase. Starting with the Altarn Initiatives.

# Chapter 25

THE ROAD TO the logging camp led off toward the river, with enough trees and underbrush to keep the camp hidden from sight from the highway. A good location for a secret base of subversives. Halfway down the road Dayne got all the proof he needed that they were in the right place—two guards with crossbows.

"Hey, you—" one of them said when they approached, but that was all he got out before Amaya charged her horse at him and hammered her shield into his face. The second brought up his weapon and fired at Dayne, but it clanged uselessly off his shield. Amaya threw her shield at him, knocking the man senseless.

"That was a bit aggressive," Dayne said as she dismounted.

"Can't have them alerting the camp," she said, dragging the two men over to the edge of the road. "Do you have a better solution?"

Dayne shook his head, but he didn't want to do this by smashing in with weapons and maiming people.

Dismounting, he said, "We should leave the horses here and scout on foot. Get a feel for what we're looking at."

"Probably looking at more than the two of you can handle," Lin said. "No offense. This is clearly the place."

"Just the two of us?" Dayne asked. "You can—"

"I'm no good in a fight, Dayne." Lin started to breathe faster and heavier, holding a hand to her chest.

"She's right," Amaya said. "We can't put her at further risk."

They were right, and Dayne was ashamed he had even thought to ask Lin to put herself in further danger. She had been through enough today.

"Can you ride?" Amaya asked her.

"I can muddle along."

"Get back to the highway. There should be a sheriff post about a mile or so farther east. We're likely going to need backup."

"Wouldn't it make more sense to go back to the city?" Lin asked.

"The city is at least three miles away, and these horses are already tired. The mile to the sheriff post is about all either will have in them."

"I'll get back here as soon as I can," she said, and turned her horse around to trot back up to the highway.

Dayne tied his horse to a tree while Amaya secured the two guards, binding and gagging them with their own shirts and vests.

"Resourceful," Dayne said.

"I have a few tricks," she said, collecting her shield and getting it back on her arm. "Let's stick to the tree line, try to stay out of sight."

The actual camp was on the river, consisting of three main buildings, a wide field with a series of wagon houses and stables on the east side, and docks down the slope. The biggest building had large bay windows and loading doors, likely the work floor and warehouse. From their vantage point at the edge of the trees before the open field, they could see some people moving about in that building.

"No one patrolling the outside here," Amaya said. "But there's no way to get to the buildings without just walking in the open. We'll be spotted."

"And we don't know where Jerinne and the others are. If Jerinne is even here."

"We should try to find her first," Amaya said. "Maybe scout those other two buildings. One looks like barracks."

"For all we know, those are filled with their people," Dayne said. "We're not going to fight our way through this, regardless. Even the two of us."

"What do you have in mind?"

He unbelted his sword and handed it to her. "I'm going to walk right up to the front door."

"Are you crazy?"

"Possibly. But maybe I can talk them into a peaceful resolution. And while all attention is on me, you can move faster and quieter on your own through the brush and get to those other buildings."

"They could kill you, Dayne." Her voice broke a little when she said it. "I—I can't—"

"Hey," he said, taking her hand. "I'm going to be fine. Because if something goes wrong, you're here. You've got me."

She squeezed his hand. "Yeah, I do. Now go do your stupid plan."

"You find our people," Dayne said. "I'm counting on you."

She nodded and slipped into the underbrush. Dayne came back out to the road and walked into the open, arms raised high. When he was halfway to the large building, one of the bay doors flew open, and a dozen people armed with crossbows and bludgeons swarmed out, as well Osharin and that Scanlin fellow.

"Easy, Heldrin," Osharin said, sword drawn. "The blazes are you doing here?"

"I'm just here to talk," Dayne said.

"Drop the shield," Osharin said. "I know what you can do with that."

Dayne complied, dropping it to the ground. "I don't want to have a fight at all."

Scanlin snapped a whip at him. "You're going to get one."

"No, no," Osharin said, waving Scanlin off. "We can talk, we can be civilized." He glanced around. "You didn't bring a cadre of marshals with you, hmm? Because we're prepared to incinerate the ballots and the authenticators if that happens."

Dayne kept his face calm. The Scallic ballots were here. The ballots, Hemmit and Maresh, and hopefully Jerinne—if she was still alive—all here. But he couldn't give Osharin any sense of surprise on his part, and used the truth to his advantage. "No marshals. To be honest, they were certain the Open Hand was behind the ballot abduction, and are chasing a lead on the north side of the city."

"Well, that's fascinating," Osharin said with a wry smile. He looked to his people. "Sweep the perimeter. And tell Quinara to get back here when you see her."

Scanlin snapped a whip again, knocking Dayne's shield a few feet farther away. "Let's go, big guy."

They brought him inside, where he immediately spotted the ten people—clearly the Scallic authenticators—stripped, bound, and gagged in the middle of the work floor, as well as the strong scent of lamp oil. Maresh tied up in a chair. No sign of Jerinne or Hemmit.

Right now the ballots were his priority, so he hoped Amaya was able to help Jerinne and Hemmit, wherever they were.

"Maresh, are you all right?" Dayne asked.

"Typical day at the office," Maresh said. "They took Hemmit—"

"Hush," an old man with a wild beard and fancy suit said. He was standing behind Maresh, one hand casually on the artist's shoulder. "Who is this titan of a man?"

"His name is Dayne Heldrin," Osharin said. "Surely you've heard of him, Valclerk."

"Ah, yes," the old man said. "You failed to save Parlin's life."

"Parlin?" Dayne asked. He let that sink in. The man had a certain fire in his eyes that told Dayne that Parlin's death was something personal to him. "I should have done better that day. I'm sorry."

The man stepped away from Maresh. "I appreciate you saying that, son. It doesn't change the mess we're all in right now, but it does mean a lot that you've said it."

Dayne looked over at the hostages, ten terrified men and women lined up on their knees, each surely hoping he would save them. "You're saying this is about Parlin?"

"It's all about him," Valclerk said.

Osharin came over to him. "That's where it starts, Dayne. Our enfranchisement in Acora has been taken from us. We had to do something to take it back."

The pieces fit together. "Parlin's chair, going to someone else. That's what you mean."

"It shouldn't." Valclerk went over to the ballot boxes, looking at them with burning contempt. "And they have no right to take it away from the people."

"All right," Dayne said. The old man, despite his refined accent and expensive suit, had a sense of madness and danger about him. Dayne quickly assessed the rest of the room. Scanlin was bristling with nervous energy, anxious for a fight at any moment. The other dozen men and women, they looked organized and competent. The way they held their weapons, held their bodies, told Dayne he wasn't dealing with amateurs. And they were spaced out around the hostages in such a way that there was no easy way to subdue all of them before the situation turned deadly.

It would only take a spark to send the whole thing up

in flames. Any of the four lamps currently burning in the room could provide it.

Osharin was the calm center. Even though this old man was obviously the leader, Osharin was who the rest looked to. Dayne had to hope that the man was still Tarian enough that he could be reasoned with.

"Let's assume I accept that," Dayne said. "Aren't you doing the same to the people of Scaloi?"

"We don't mean them harm," Osharin said. "It's tragic, I know, but it's just what needs to be done."

That was almost enough to snap Dayne's temper. "You have them bound and terrified, man! How are you—"

He stepped forward, and in that action Scanlin and all the mercenaries snapped into movement. Muscles tensed, crossbows up. Dayne eased down.

"How are you holding to your oath as a Tarian by being the harm?"

"I'm sorry, Dayne," Osharin said. "But you have to see that sometimes you need to do a little harm to protect the people. Like amputating an infected limb to save the body."

"I don't accept that," Dayne said. "It's not too late to clean these people off, turn yourselves in, and end this."

"End this?" Valclerk said. "This is just the beginning. Not just saving Parlin's chair for the people, but cutting the puppet strings the noble class uses to yank the Parliament around. What right do those people have to determine the fate of free men of Druthal? Because they came from the right woman's belly?"

"Dayne," Osharin said, pleading. "Can't you see this is about more than a few votes cast by people a thousand miles away, and a few petty officials?"

"A few votes?" Dayne asked. "Those people, the officials, the voters, they are us, Osharin! Every one of them matters." He pointed at Osharin for emphasis, and that gesture was a step too far. With two resounding cracks, both of Scanlin's whips ensnared Dayne's arms.

"Enough of that, big fella," Scanlin said.

Dayne instinctively flexed, about to yank himself free, but he knew that would trigger a full fight, if not inspire one of these people to start the fire. He couldn't have that. He relaxed his arms, letting Scanlin think he was subdued.

"We're wasting time," the old man said. "Where's Quinara with that reporter? It's time to send him back to the city with our demands." He gave a signal, and two of the mercenaries went outside. Still ten in here. Too many.

So Hemmit was alive, and part of their plans. That was good. And if they were going to send demands back to the city, that gave Dayne the time he needed to find a way to save these people and get them safe. That was the most important thing. And Jerinne.

Hemmit couldn't see anything, but he could smell, and what he smelled was the most vile stench of sewage and rot he had ever encountered in his life. He had been dragged outside by Quinara and two of her goons, and taken into another building, where he was dropped into a pit, landing in a pool of olfactory horror, deep enough that with his hands still bound, he could barely keep his mouth and nose above the water line. In as much as this was water.

It was all he could do not to vomit into the sack that covered his head.

"How long he got to stay down there?" one of the goons asked from above him.

"That should be enough to sever the magical connection," Quinara said. "Really, as soon as he was submerged in the septic slop, it probably snapped. But let's let him marinate a bit down there."

"How do you know about how magic works?" the goon asked.

"Took a couple theory classes at the Acorian

Conservatory. There was the one girl in my dormitory. Mage. Pain in the ass, always giving me the business. So I took theory classes to learn how to wreck her day up. And I gave her some business, let me tell you."

"Nice."

"Useful stuff to know when I was hunting mage bounties."

"Should have gone to school," the goon said.

"You wanna come up now, pretty beard?" she called out.

"Yes," Hemmit managed to say without releasing the contents of his stomach.

"Fish him out," Quinara ordered.

The goons grumbled, but in a few moments he was hooked under his arms and pulled out. As soon as he was on his feet on solid ground, he couldn't hold back any longer, and threw up in his sack. Quinara pulled it off his head.

"Not very pretty now," she said. She exhaled sharply and stepped away. "Take him down to the river and rinse him off. He can't be completely disgusting when he delivers our message."

Hemmit was too weak to respond as the goons grabbed him, or even to lift his head. He stared at the ground as they carried him by his arms out of the backhouse. They stopped after just a few steps out.

"You're going to let him go."

Hemmit looked up to one of the most glorious sights he had ever seen.

Jerinne Fendall, still in her dress uniform from the night before, which was torn and stained with blood and dirt, stood in front of him armed with a boat oar. Her face told an entire story, one of anger and determination, an expression that made it clear she had walked to the blazes and back and was not going to brook any more nonsense.

Her knuckles turned white as she gripped the oar tighter. "Or do we have to make this hard?"

# Chapter 26

JERINNE TOOK THE LACK of immediate surrender as a sign, and whipped the oar around to knock down both goons at once before they called out.

"Hard it is," she said as they dropped, Hemmit collapsing on the ground with them.

"You want it hard?" Quinara came out of the backhouse twirling her hatchets about. "I'm more than happy to give that to you, girl."

She swung one hatchet down to crack open Hemmit's skull, but Jerinne whirled her oar into position to block it. "I owe you all sorts of hard."

"Then let's give each other what we owe," Quinara said, and with a wink, spun into action.

In their previous fights, Quinara had been nimble and vicious, but now she was an absolute whirlwind of limbs and axes. Quinara's every move, every jump, kick, flip, and swipe was precise, and each blow would be a killing one. They would have been, had Jerinne not been on her game, ready eye on every attack, dodging and parrying. With each strike, every block, she heard Madam Tyrell in her head.

"You need to move, Initiate! If you don't move, if you stop for a second, you are dead! Push harder, strike quicker!"

She took the blows, letting Quinara hack the oar up with each swing of her hatchets. With each one of those, Jerinne dodged away, remembering her footwork, minding each step down the hill to the river. She was giving Quinara the higher ground, and the woman was using it, but the most important thing was that she drew her away from Hemmit.

Quinara hammered both hatchets down from high, and Jerinne brought up the oar above her head to block them both at the same time. As the hatchets embedded into the wood, Quinara hopped up and slammed both feet into Jerinne's chest. The oar was wrenched from Jerinne's hands as she went rolling down the hill to the water, stopping herself before she reached the bank.

"I'm going to carve poems on your bones, girl!" Quinara yelled, tossing the oar to the side. She twirled the hatchets and stalked down the hill.

"Get up, Initiate," said the voice in her head. "You need to breathe and get your feet under you and keep fighting."

Jerinne pulled herself up as the woman came down at her with the hatchets. She might be unarmed now, but she was a Tarian. And that meant she was never defenseless.

She dodged to one side as the next flurry of attacks came, Quinara now purely on the offensive.

"Stay in it," the voice told her. "Wait for the moment."

Quinara was a machine, relentless. Never giving an opening.

"Initiate!" Madam Tyrell shouted.

That wasn't in her head.

Jerinne heard a familiar whistling sound of metal

cutting through the air, and took her moment. She jumped backward to dodge the next swipe, going as high as she could as she reached out to catch the shield that was flying to her. She spun with the force of the throw, and used its momentum to hammer the shield right into the shocked expression on Quinara's face.

Quinara was laid out on the dirt, and Jerinne kicked both hatchets away as she stood over her. The woman didn't move as Madam Tyrell ran over.

"Satisfactory maneuver, Initiate," she said.

"I was certainly satisfied with it."

For once, Madam Tyrell smiled. "You're well enough?"

Jerinne handed over the shield. "I still have fight in me, if that's what you're asking, ma'am."

"Good," Madam Tyrell said. She had two swords, one in her hand and another on her belt, and handed one of them over. It was a bit heavier than Jerinne cared for, but she wasn't going to complain. "There's still quite a few goons out here, and we're probably about to get swarmed."

"Hemmit's over there, and he's not looking good," Jerinne said. "And there was a cloistress, she helped me, but . . . I don't know. She ran off, but . . . something was off with her."

"Lin went for sheriffs, and Dayne . . ." Madam Tyrell shook her head. "Dayne went in there to talk them down."

"That's all we have?" Jerinne asked as they approached Hemmit. He was sitting up, wiping filth and sewage off his face.

"I'm just going to stay at the Rabbit and write stories from now on," he said.

"What's going on?" Madam Tyrell asked. "Maresh is here somewhere?"

"He's in there," Hemmit said, looking like he could barely breathe. Given how he smelled, Jerinne couldn't blame him. "But they have the Scallic ballots and the election officials, and they're all covered in lamp oil. They'll burn everything—everyone—if—"

"Sweet saints," Jerinne said. She looked to Madam Tyrell. "We have to—"

"We will," Madam Tyrell said. "Let's move, Initiate."

They both turned toward the building just as two more goons came around the corner. Madam Tyrell launched herself at them with impossible speed and grace, and before either could properly react, she laid them both down. During Jerinne's whole Initiacy, she had heard whispers about Madam Tyrell, how she must have cheated somehow to advance to Adept after one year of Candidacy, but in those moments of brutal efficiency, she saw exactly how incredible Amaya Tyrell truly was.

"Rutting amazing," Jerinne muttered.

"Hemmit," Madam Tyrell said as she came back over. "Go up that road to the highway, look for Lin and any other help she's bringing. Jerinne, we need to move fast. Eyes on me, follow my lead. Lives are counting on us."

"I won't let you down," Jerinne said.

"I know you won't." Madam Tyrell turned away and stalked toward the building like a cat.

Jerinne wiped the tears from her eyes, grateful that Madam Tyrell wasn't looking.

Amaya peeked through a few dirty windows to get a bit of sense of how many people she was dealing with. Near as she could tell, there were about a dozen potential fighters in there, with Osharin and the half-naked fellow with the whips as the standouts. When she looked last, the whip guy had bound Dayne's arms, though she suspected that would only last as long as Dayne tolerated it.

And Dayne seemed to be tolerating things in there. Hemmit had mentioned the hostages—ten of them, bound and gagged—were doused in lamp oil. That was probably why Dayne was biding his time. Though the clocks would be ringing on them soon. Lin went for sheriffs, and once they came, these people would probably light up the place. So she had to defuse the situation before that happened.

"All right," she whispered to Jerinne. "We've got about a dozen folks in there. Most of them, I'd guess, are mercenaries. Former army or Constabulary. Trained, but not like you. The key thing is to neutralize them, fast and hard. As many as you can. Can you handle that?"

"Yes, ma'am," she said.

"All right. Don't engage Osharin if you can help it. Once things move, Dayne will hold him off," Amaya said, taking her shield off her arm. She handed it over to Jerinne. "If a fire starts, though, just get people out. Don't worry about anything else."

"Won't you need a shield?" Jerinne asked.

Amaya pointed to Dayne's lying on the ground. "I've got that covered. Be ready."

Jerinne stayed crouched next to the window, while Amaya dashed over to the shield. As soon as she was spotted, things would break out, so the most important thing here was speed. When she reached the shield, she stomped on it, sending it flying up to her hand. Without a second of hesitation, she pivoted and charged the window, breaking through shield first, and aiming herself at the first of the mercenaries in her path.

He went down in a heap.

She didn't slow down, landing on the shield and sliding across the floor to sweep the next one in her knees. A well-placed kick, a shift of her weight, and a hop later, she was standing on top of the mercenary, boot on her neck.

That was all the cue Dayne needed. With a yank of his arms, he ripped the whips away from the shirtless fellow. He put himself in front of Osharin, spinning the whips in a wide circle. Osharin dove into the fray with him.

Jerinne was in the room, sweeping through folks with skill and style, each block and takedown efficient and effective. The mercenaries tried to gang up on her, but she was too fluid, too fast; none of them could get around her.

The shirtless man dashed for a burning lamp, and Amaya kicked her last mercenary in the head for good measure before crossing the distance to him. She did a quick count of the room—there were four lamps in all. Once she dealt with this naked fellow, she'd douse the sources of fire.

She tackled him, but he was literally too slippery to get a hold of. This fool had actually greased up his body. He reached for the lamp, but she was able to get her shield in front of it, and then smacked him in the chest. With her free hand, she grabbed the lamp and threw it through the window.

While the slippery bastard was trying to wallop her, she noticed Dayne grappling with Osharin, keeping the man from drawing his sword, all the while still trying to convince the man to stop fighting. She had to admire him, even now wanting to talk Osharin down.

Jerinne blew out another lamp as she continued to clean her way through people, broad smile on her face. Saints, that girl was having fun. Amaya noticed two more players in the room. The old man behind Maresh was screaming and ranting at his people. He must be the leader of this outfit. Once she finished with grease boy, she'd deal with him.

Then she noticed the cloistress, standing out in her red habit. Jerinne had said something about a cloistress helping her. She wasn't fighting, but crawling over to each of the hostages and cutting them free. Good. One less thing to worry about. She had already gotten one out, and was working on freeing a second.

Amaya's opponent slipped away from her and made a break for another lamp. She spun around and hurled her shield at him, smacking him clean in the face, and closed the distance as he staggered, landing sharp punches in his sternum and tenders.

That was enough to take him out of the fight. She blew out the lamp while he moaned and crawled away. One lamp to go.

Dayne had Osharin in a lock, pinning his arms back. "Don't make me hurt you!"

Osharin dropped to a knee and flipped Dayne over his head, sending him flying into the group of hostages. Amaya reclaimed her shield and charged at him as he went for the last lamp. He grabbed it just before she hammered into him, and when she connected, he tossed the lamp away. The two of them collided into each other, falling over a table with their momentum. It took her a moment to recover and see where he had thrown it.

The old man, holding the lamp high over his head.

"You right bastards!" he shouted. "You've ruined everything, and this is what you all deserve!" He threw the lamp on the ground by Dayne.

Flames leaped up all around them.

# Chapter 27

FIRE BURST FROM the shattered lamp, and Dayne couldn't waste a moment. He had been grappling with Osharin, but solely to keep the man out of the fight while Amaya and Jerinne neutralized the other threats. But with the fire spreading, the threat had changed, and the only thing that mattered was saving the hostages before they were incinerated in a horrible, fiery death. He heaved Osharin away from him and went to the hostages.

Sister Frienne—how was she even here?—tackled the closest hostages to the flames and smothered them with her robes, tamping down any flames before they grew, letting herself burn instead.

"Amaya!" he shouted as her ran to the covered lumber equipment. "Tarps!"

She cued into his idea and met him at the closest giant saw. Together they grabbed the great muslin cloth and yanked it off. With a wide swoop of the tarp, they covered the next two hostages as the lamp oil on their bodies started burning. Amaya went to work cutting their bonds, and Dayne tried to beat down the fire before it reached any of the other victims.

"Dayne!" Jerinne shouted.

That warning gave him the chance to dodge a thrust of Osharin's sword. He was able to move away, pivot, and slam his shoulder in the man's chest, picking Osharin up off the ground and driving him away from the fire, the hostages, and Amaya. Keep the fight off of her, let her save lives.

Osharin slammed the pommel of his sword into Dayne's back, hammering it again and again until Dayne dropped him. He landed on his feet, sword at the ready, and Dayne jumped back to avoid getting skewered.

"This could have been a triumph for the people!" Osharin shouted as he made several attempts to run Dayne through.

"What people?" Dayne asked. "The ones you tried to silence?"

"We're serving the silenced voices!"

Another flurry of attacks pushed Dayne toward the fire. He scrambled to one side to avoid getting burned, but his foot slipped, sending him tumbling to the ground. Landing on his back, he couldn't move away in time to avoid Osharin's sword.

*Clang.*

Another sword blocked the blow.

"Mind if I dance?" Jerinne asked.

She parried Osharin's attacks, which were no longer angry and wild, but tight and focused. Jerinne's only advantage was having shield and sword together, while Osharin had only his sword, but her intervention gave Dayne the chance to get back on his feet.

"Think this is yours," Jerinne said, blocking one blow with her shield and tossing her sword to Dayne. She then rolled out of the way of Osharin's next blow, which Dayne parried.

"We need to get these people safe!" Dayne said, partly for Jerinne's benefit, but hoping he could talk some sense into Osharin. "You are a Tarian!"

"I am also Acoran!" Osharin shouted back.

Amaya and Sister Frienne had gotten most of the hostages out of the building, which was now starting to burn hotter and heavier. As Amaya pulled one hostage out, he pulled out his gag. "The ballots!"

The lockboxes were in the middle of the fire. Those were the Scallic votes, the will of those people. That had to be saved. Dayne blocked another blow from Osharin, and took the opportunity to grab the man's wrist. He had no choice but to disable the man now.

"I'm so sorry," he said, and twisted with all his strength.

"Ahh!" Osharin cried out as his arm made a definitive crack, and fell to his knees. Dayne left him on the ground and went to the lockboxes. But the fire was already too hot, impossible for him to grab the boxes.

"Help!"

Maresh. Still tied to a chair. Both he and Valclerk were trapped by the flames, and Valclerk was trying in vain to beat back the fire with his expensive coat.

"Jerinne!" Dayne called. "Shield!"

She nodded and tossed it to him, and then following his eye line, ran through the fire to Maresh. She would get Maresh out, he had to trust that.

Dayne focused on the lockboxes, and took a few deep breaths before diving in, shield first. He couldn't touch the boxes, hot as they were, but he could push them with the shield. It made a wrenching scraping sound as he slid the boxes across the ground, even as the flames licked at his arms and legs. Didn't matter. He needed to get them out. He could barely see anything, behind the shield, smoke filling the room, and he was hopeful he was heading toward the door.

Another few feet and his uniform was burning.

Above him he heard a groan and creak, and then great crack and tumult. The fire had reached some of the support beams and the roof was coming down. No more time. He needed to get out.

Then there was a whoosh as he was walloped with the heavy cloth.

"Let's go!" Amaya shouted, battering at the flames.

"The ballots!" he said. She threw the tarp over them, and helped him pull them out into the sunlight. Coughing, he looked about. Jerinne had dragged Maresh—chair and all—onto the grass. "Is that everyone?"

Amaya helped him to his feet. "All the hostages. Most of the mercenaries as well."

"Where's the Sister?" he asked. "And Osharin? And Valclerk?"

Amaya paused for a moment, and nodded. They went back in together.

"Osharin!" he called out, despite the smoke and haze. He could barely see a thing. "Where are you?"

"Here!"

They followed the voice to find Osharin, pinned under a fallen burning beam. "I can't move!" he cried, and then he saw who had come to him, and his face fell. "I guess you won."

Dayne pulled his sleeves over his hands. "Get ready to pull him out."

Osharin looked in surprise, then chuckled. "That girl wasn't kidding about you."

Dayne got his hands under the beam and pulled. Heavy and hot as all blazes, but he couldn't let that stop him. "Only . . . need . . . a . . . few . . . inches."

Amaya grabbed Osharin by the shoulders and dragged him out from under. As soon as he was clear, Dayne dropped the beam. He was about to ask Osharin if he could walk, but the answer was clearly no. The man's leg had been thoroughly crushed.

"Get him out, I'll find Valclerk."

Amaya said something back, but the roar of the flames had grown too loud. Dayne couldn't hear her. Nevertheless, she grabbed Osharin and pulled him out of sight. Dayne, half from memory, worked his way toward the part of the work floor where he had last seen Valclerk. Pushing his way through the heat and smoke, he saw two figures, one pinning the other to the floor, knife in her hand.

"I won't kill you!" Sister Frienne shouted. "I swore to God that I wouldn't kill again, but I can keep you here and let the fire take us both!"

Dayne couldn't get close; a wall of fire blocked him from them.

"Sister!" he shouted. "Sister, you need to let him up! You both need to get out of here!"

"She's crazy!" Valclerk shouted.

"It doesn't matter!" Sister Frienne said, looking to Dayne through the fire. "My soul is already lost, and his should be as well! We will be damned together!"

"You're not lost, Sister!" he said. "You both can still—" He looked about. There was a clear path from where they were to the far door. They still had a chance. "You need to run now!"

"Help!" Valclerk said.

"I can't—" she said. "He's evil and I can't let him live! I will suffer for it, but I will give my soul for Scaloi!"

"The ballots are safe!" Dayne said. "Everyone is safe except you two! You can get out now!"

"No!" she shouted.

What had Ret told him? "Sister! I need you to help me. Ret told me to tell you—"

She looked up at that.

"What did he say?" Her knife hand trembled.

"That helping me—that would be your penance."

She stood, dropping the knife, and stumbled backward. "My . . . my soul isn't lost?"

Valclerk grabbed the knife. "It is now!"

Dayne had to act, despite the fire and smoke. He dashed through the wall of flame, ignoring the pain for now. It didn't matter. He would bear it, he would survive. He managed to close the distance and grab Valclerk by the wrist as he tried to bring the knife down on Sister Frienne's back.

"None of that, sir," Dayne said, pulling the man up off the ground and plucking the knife out of his hand. Valclerk dangled in the air, kicking uselessly. This was no moment to gloat or dally, as the heat and smoke were oppressive. They only had moments. He slung Valclerk over his shoulder. "We need to—"

Another part of the ceiling came down, bringing with it a wave of smoke and ash. Dayne was engulfed in darkness, not seeing where to go or how to get out anymore.

A hand found his and pulled him forward. He let himself be guided, doing his best to keep his sleeve over his mouth and nose while still carrying Mister Valclerk, who had gone limp. Dayne couldn't breathe, couldn't see, and had only that hand as a point of reference, until suddenly there was light and a rush of cool fresh air. Dayne managed a few more steps before he dropped to his knees, gasping and wheezing, and deposited Valclerk on the ground.

He looked to the hand holding his.

Jerinne.

"You all right?" she asked. "It was a miracle I found you."

"You—you found—but where is Sister Frienne?"

"The cloistress?" Jerinne pointed to the woman on the grass. "She came out and collapsed. That's how I realized you were still in there. You even went back for this jerk."

"It's what we do. Stand be—" He coughed hard before he could say anything else.

"I know," she said. "I get it now." She dropped to the grass, and pointed to the moaning and wheezing mercenaries Amaya was pacing among. "But it was pretty satisfying to wallop those guys around."

Dayne started to laugh, which triggered another coughing fit.

"Easy," she said. "Just rest and—"

She was interrupted by the drum of horses thundering down the road: Lin with a half-dozen sheriffs, and a lockwagon trailing behind. Right now, that was a beautiful sight.

Dayne had to hand it to the sheriffs, they were very good at their jobs. With incredible efficiency, they assessed the situation and had more people come with horses, carriages, and supplies. Acting as constables, Fire Brigade, and Yellowshields all at once, they ironed up the Deep Roots members, put out the fire, and tended to the injured. They even brought a cask of beer and several loaves of bread, which Dayne deeply appreciated.

Within an hour they had lockwagons loaded with Valclerk, Quinara, Osharin, and the rest of the Deep Roots. Only Scanlin was unaccounted for, apparently having slunk off into the woods before the sheriffs arrived.

"Not surprised," Osharin muttered when he heard. "He was just hired muscle, not part of the cause."

Sister Frienne did not wake up, so they arranged to bring her to the nearest hospital ward on the edge of the city. As she was being loaded on a wagon, Dayne noticed that the scars on her arms had receded, no longer angry red welts. Was that part of Ret's power, or was it just that Sister Frienne believed she had served her penance? He wasn't sure what it meant, and also wasn't sure if he wanted to know.

More carriages, as well as blankets and clothing, were provided for the authenticators, who were mostly grateful and in good spirits.

"We owe you and yours more than we can say," Mister Beninaugh, the ranking member of the authenticators, told Dayne. He was holding one of the lockboxes stained with scorch marks. "We'll have to see how extensive the damage to these was, but I have faith that the most important records are intact. Thanks to all of you."

"Can't you open it and check?" Jerinne asked.

"Not until we get to the Parliament," he said. He held up one of the keys the sheriffs had found once they put out the fire. "Double lock, takes two sets of keys to open each box."

"Then we should get there in haste," Dayne said. He called out to the master sheriff, a stout man named Indlebrook. "We need to get to the city, get these people to the Parliament. And the marshals will probably claim jurisdiction over the arrests—"

"They're welcome to it," Indlebrook said, approaching. "Let's get you all loaded up and back home."

"Are we all going to the Parliament?" Maresh asked.

"I need the longest bath ever," Hemmit said. He had already jumped in the river and put on the clothes the sheriffs provided, but he still smelled decidedly rank. "But I will see this story to the end. We earned this, and we'll print the whole thing."

"I'm not letting you two out of my sight," Lin said.

"Blazes, yes," Jerinne said.

Amaya raised an eyebrow at that. "Are you forgetting something, Initiate?"

Jerinne bowed her head to Amaya. "I meant, may I see this mission to completion, Madam Tyrell?"

Amaya gave the barest of smirks, and said, "Blazes, yes."

By the time they reached the Parliament, the sun was hanging low in the sky, and Dayne was feeling every scrape and singe, every bang and bruise, over the whole of his body, and he was still wheezing with every breath. As they disembarked from the carriages, every step caused the discovery of some new source of pain. But that didn't matter right now, because he was here, safely delivering the Scallic ballots, with those responsible for abducting them in irons, and all his dear friends were safe.

And everyone lived.

This time, everyone lived.

That made this an incredible day.

When they reached the war room, he was limping so much, both Jerinne and Amaya had to support him. They entered to find much the same collection of angry faces from before, only angrier and wearier, including Donavan Samsell and Grandmaster Orren.

"Heldrin," Samsell said as they came in. "You all look like sewage. The blazes you been up to?"

"I see they rescued Miss Fendall," the Grandmaster said. "But I fail to see why they brought her here."

"Sir," Dayne said with a weak salute. He stepped aside for Beninaugh and the others to come in. "I'm here with the Scallic ballots and the authenticators. And those responsible are in lockwagons outside in the custody of archduchy sheriffs."

Samsell signaled for some of his men to go outside, then approached the authenticators with a salute. "Very glad to see you, sir," he said to Mister Beninaugh.

"I'm afraid some of our papers were lost, and some of the ballot documents may be damaged, so the verification process might be laborious."

Samsell chuckled. "I'm more than happy to go through it. This year's election results are quite well earned."

The Grandmaster approached, his face hard to read. "I assume the rescues of Miss Fendall and the ballots were convergent."

"One and the same," Amaya said. Dayne was content to let her speak. She was the ranking member, and it hurt his throat to talk. "Both were in the same place."

"And Mister Osharin?"

"Arrested with those responsible. The Deep Roots."

"He will need to be expelled, in addition to whatever consequences the law has. It is a shame that one of ours is so entangled in this scandal." He glanced at Hemmit and Maresh, standing in the hallway outside the door. "And I imagine that morsel will be dragged through the press."

"We'll also focus on the heroes who saved the ballots," Maresh said. "We'll report that the Tarian Order got the job done."

"Well, then," the Grandmaster said. "Miss Tyrell, I think we should get Miss Fendall back home. This excitement today has caused us to lose all the discipline of Initiate training. Routine should resume tomorrow. And Dayne, of course, your place is here."

"Yes, sir," Dayne said.

He went out, and Jerinne gave Dayne a tight squeeze on his arm before following. Amaya went to follow, but stopped and put her hand on his cheek, and in her eyes he saw warmth and affection. He hadn't seen that from her since before he and Master Denbar left for Lacanja. She gave him a tight smile, and then said, "Go see a doctor. You're a mess."

"I feel it," he said. "I will."

"Good," she said, patting his cheek just hard enough for it to sting. Probably from the burns.

Out in the hallway, the marshals were starting to bring the Deep Roots people down to the cells, with Quinara at the lead.

"Why did an Acoran group take the Scallic ballots?" Samsell asked.

Hemmit stepped into the room. "They had a plan to demand an alteration of the Acoran results, holding the Scallic results hostage until it was done. Their leader was, apparently, a Parliamentary functionary named Valclerk."

"Valclerk?" Samsell asked. He shook his head. "Parlin's chief of staff. Odd bloke, and I heard he took Parlin's death hard, but I never thought he'd . . ." He trailed off, shaking his head.

"Given all that," Dayne said. "It might be prudent to release Ret and the rest of the Open Hands with a profuse apology."

"Ret?" Mister Beninaugh asked. "As in Bishop Ret Issendel?"

Samsell raised an eyebrow. "Yes, that's right."

"You have him in custody?" Beninaugh bit his lip and looked at the other authenticators. "I shouldn't say anything out of turn before we've finalized the authentication of the ballots, but . . . it would be most advisable to release him. Quickly."

# Chapter 28

JERINNE KEPT QUIET ON the carriage ride back to the chapterhouse, while Madam Tyrell briefed the Grandmaster on the full events of the day, which he listened to with a slightly distracted air.

"Well," he said as they reached the house. "We should be pleased at the good outcome. Miss Fendall, report to the infirmary immediately. You have more than a few scrapes that could fester if untreated."

"Yes, sir," she said, more than happy to get out of the carriage. She assumed he was prickly because of Osharin's betrayal, but she felt his disapproval aimed at her. Possibly for the reasons Fredelle said. Perhaps she was just imagining it.

Her time in the infirmary was short, as most of her wounds were superficial. "Is it all right if I go to the baths?" she asked the sew-up.

"I'd recommend it," he said. "Do that, and then stop back here. I'll do fresh dressings when you're dry."

She went down to the baths, and for a brief moment

her heart raced as she approached the bathhouse. Which was absurd; there was no chance that she'd once again find a surprise traitor who would try to murder her. Two nights in a row of that would be astounding bad luck.

Instead, she found a good portion of the third-year Initiate cohort all engaged in collective soak, the water so hot the room had a steamy haze.

"I see you all were ready for me," she said. All attention turned to her, with a collective whoop of joy.

"What the blazes happened?"

"Did you escape?"

"Where did they take you?"

"Where's Osharin?"

"All right, calm down," she said, stripping out of her uniform and skivs. "I've been in quite a bit of business, no sleep, barely ate, and everything hurts. Let me get settled, and then I can tell you the whole story."

She slid into the water in the tub with the other girls, taking a spot next to Raila, a small thrill firing through her as their bare legs touched. The water was delicious, just at the point where it was almost too hot to bear, and was just what she needed.

"So, talk!" Enther said from the other tub. While everyone used the bathhouse at the same time, the informal rule was that comingling in the tubs was "poor form." She had remembered that in her first year, one of the third-year Initiates told her, "I mean, we all have to use them, so don't be gross."

Jerinne launched into the story, making sure to emphasize her more heroic moments without embellishing them.

"You really said 'or do we have to make this hard'?" Tander asked at one point.

"Wait, who was this cloistress again?" Iolana asked.

"How did you carry Heldrin out? The man is like a bull!" Haden asked.

"I didn't carry him," Jerinne said. "I just led him out. He could still walk."

"Sounds suspicious," Haden said.

"You look at the burns on her body," Raila said, taking Jerinne's arm and holding it up. "And you tell me she wasn't in the thick of things."

"She's puffing herself up to be the big hero," Dade said, big stupid grin on his face.

"Big heroes were Dayne and Madam Tyrell," Jerinne said. "I just followed their lead."

Raila turned to her. "Well, I think you're a big damn hero." And her eyes and smile took Jerinne's breath away.

The door of the bathhouse opened, and Madam Tyrell came in, wrapped in a drycloth. "All right, out," she said. "You all need to hit the barracks. Tomorrow may be a holiday, but we need to make up for lost time."

Everyone scrambled out of the tubs, grabbing drycloths and clothes before running across the lawn to the main house. Before they all left Dade stopped at the door. "Hey, Madam Tyrell, is it true Jerinne fought off three guys at once while you took on the guy with the whips?"

"Three?" Madam Tyrell raised her eyebrow as she got into the bath. "I counted five. Now scat."

They headed back in, and Raila waited while Jerinne stopped back at the infirmary to get fresh bandages. As they walked to their bunkroom, Raila asked, "Were you scared?"

"Terrified," Jerinne said. "But also, the fear didn't matter. I knew I still had to fight."

"Right," Raila said, outside the doorway. "The other day, on the ridge, I . . . I held my own in the moment, and then went and threw up right afterward. I still get . . ." She shook her head, and moved in closer. Dangerously close. "Does it get easier?"

"The fear never goes away," Jerinne said, and she was afraid of holding eye contact with Raila, and afraid to look away. "But you know what I remind myself?"

"What?"

"That I am rutting amazing."

Raila laughed, warm and full, but the spell of the moment was gone. Whatever courage Jerinne had in a fight, it did not apply to kissing Raila Gendon.

Not yet.

The marshals' doctor checked Dayne over, applying a salve on his various burns, and giving him a vile-tasting medicine. "Could have been worse," the doctor said.

The verification process of the Scallic votes went on, and while Dayne didn't supervise the whole affair this time around, he also didn't feel right just leaving until it was done. It was nearly nine bells at night when they finished, and the full results of the Parliamentary election were known. The results were mostly uneventful, with one notable exception.

"We'll make the announcement in the morning to the collective press," Samsell told Dayne. "Aren't you exhausted?"

"Utterly," Dayne said with a weary smile.

"Then go to bed," Samsell said. "Job well done and all."

"I should. But I'm famished. Is there any food?"

"Let me take you to the commissary," Samsell said.

The marshal commissary was simple fare—bread, cold meat, cheeses. And it was just what Dayne needed. Samsell opened two bottles of beer from the icebox and gave one to Dayne. "Well done for your first week."

"I hope it isn't indicative."

"Saints, no," Samsell said. "But you'll do fine, I think."

"I appreciate that."

There was a knock on the doorframe. Ret Issendel stood there, looking a bit out of sorts and disheveled. "Sorry, I didn't mean to disrupt, but—"

Samsell got to his feet. "No, sir, no disruption. I trust . . . I trust everything is well, sir. You and your compatriots were all released, yes?"

"Yes, yes," Ret said, looking a bit disconcerted by Samsell's overeager politeness. "But it seems that Sister Frienne isn't among our number. Someone said she was taken here."

Dayne stood up. "No, she wasn't. She—she was taken to a hospital. I'm afraid I don't know which one."

"Hospital?" Ret asked. "Oh, dear, how? Why?"

"She saved a lot of lives," Dayne said. "The ballot authenticators, she helped get them safe. But there was a fire, and she was in the smoke a bit too long—"

"She was with you all?" Ret asked. "How did that happen?"

"I was hoping you could answer that, sir. Somehow she was able to just find Jerinne. Did you have something to do with that?"

"Who is Jerinne?"

"She's the young Tarian girl you touched this morning. You told Sister Frienne to look to her, do you remember?"

Ret just shook his head. "That sounds like a miracle."

Dayne wasn't even sure what to say to that. Did Ret not know, not realize, what he had done in the stationhouse? Did that not come from him? Dayne was even more confused.

"I have to go to her," Ret said. "Where is she?"

"I'll find out right away, sir," Samsell said, and rushed out.

Ret watched him leave and turned back to Dayne. "Is he all right? This morning he seemed ready to claw my throat out and now . . . did he have a revelation?"

Dayne chuckled. "Of sorts. The official results won't

be released until tomorrow morning, but . . ." He extended his hand. "Congratulations, Good Mister Issendel, Tenth Chair of Scaloi."

Ret blinked several times, and then stumbled to one of the benches. "What?"

"You won the election."

"You're having me on."

"I would never joke about something like that, sir," Dayne said.

"No 'sir,' Dayne. I'm still just Ret."

"Well, get used to polite deference."

Ret chuckled drily as Samsell returned.

"She's at Eastpoint Ward. I can have a few men escort you over, sir."

"See what I mean?" Dayne asked.

"Indeed," Ret said, getting to his feet. "I have quite a few things to contemplate. But for now, I must see to Sister Frienne. So, yes, I would appreciate the help, Chief."

They left, and Dayne finished his beer and went to his chambers.

"I was wondering when you'd get back," a sleepy voice said as he came in to his suite. Lady Mirianne was lying on his couch, her boots left carelessly on the floor.

"I had no idea you'd be waiting," he said. "How long were you here?"

"I forget," she said. "I definitely dozed off. But it was quite pleasant to have a quiet, private place to hide away from the bustle of my household."

"How is the household?"

She sighed as she sat up. "Shambles. The repairs will be extensive. And a few of the staff were quite badly injured. But it could have been worse."

"And you?"

She gave a weak smile. "Also shambles. But happy to see you. All worked out well?"

"As well as we could hope," Dayne said. "The ballots and the authenticators were rescued."

"Modesty again. You probably did all that single-handedly."

"It was definitely a team effort."

"Well," she said. "I'm not going to reward the entire team the same way." She got to her feet and kissed him. He tried to respond in kind, but winced.

"A girl might take offense at that."

"Sorry," he said. "I am in quite a bit of pain."

"I understand," she said, leading him to his bed. She sat him down and started to remove his boots. "Then let me take care of you, for once."

"I won't object," he said.

"Good." As his boots came off, she said, "Tomorrow is a holiday, so they can't expect you to save the country again, right?"

"I sincerely hope the fate of the country will not be at stake tomorrow," he said. "Did you have plans?"

Caressing his feet, she said, "Well, I'm being a horrible person, because the store will be open. But I'm paying all my employees double wages for the holiday."

"That's far from horrible."

"And of course with that comes responsibilities. Meetings and the like. Hopefully I'll have my managers in shape to run things unsupervised in a few weeks."

"I understand," he said. "We are busy people."

"But I was thinking we could have a simple lunch together. Perhaps at The Nimble Rabbit?"

He looked up at her and grinned. "You would be seen at The Nimble Rabbit?"

"I am a humble businesswoman," she said. "I can't be bothered with society luncheons that drone on for hours."

"You never liked those."

"Hated them." She gave him a wicked grin and crawled onto his bed. "Now, where *doesn't* it hurt?"

# INTERLUDE: The Justice

HIGH JUSTICE FELLER PIN was a powerful man, an influential man, one of the five high justices of the Royal Bench of Druthal. A man whose legal decisions could only be countermanded by a Royal Decree, and in the one hundred ninety-seven years since the foundation of the Royal Bench of High Justices, no king of Druthal had ever given such a decree. A feckless weeper like Maradaine XVIII certainly wouldn't be the first to do it. He was a man with the position and authority to decide what exactly the law meant in Druthal.

He should *not* have to come to his office on a holiday.

"It's Reunification Day, Mister Gendorin," he said to his young clerk as he stalked down the back hallways to his chambers. "Why did your page say things were urgent? I shouldn't be called on urgent matters."

"I'm sorry, sir," Gendorin said. "I know that you have a lot of comings and goings and—" He stopped short, then coughed. "I mean you're terribly busy, and normally I wouldn't even, but—"

"But what, Gendorin?"

"It's Miss Mirrendum, sir. She's here and—"

"Damn all to blazes, Gendorin! Arthady Mirrendum is a minor functionary not worth the boil on a pig's backside! You're telling me *she* summoned me?"

"She is the representative for the Tharek Pell case—"

"I know whose lawyer she is, fool. That doesn't mean she gets the privilege of dictating times or schedules to me."

"He's in the building, sir."

That made Pin stop. "He's what?"

"She had him brought here from Quarrygate. He's in the Micarum Cell, with a full and thorough security protocol, of course, which I checked myself. But . . . he's here."

"Saint Marian, why?"

"She says there's relevant case work that cannot be done while he's locked up in Block Twelve, since she needs access to her client, and—"

"Stop babbling, man. I understand it all now. She had him delivered here, and since I have claimed full judicial authority over Tharek Pell and his case, receiving him here requires my signature. And since it's a holiday, he can't be brought back to Quarrygate until tomorrow at the earliest. She's a devious one, that Mirrendum, I'll give her that."

In his energetic youth he would have been envious of someone like Arthady Mirrendum. Perhaps even a bit smitten. She was a dogged legal fighter, ready to use every letter and line of the law on behalf of her clients, and she was definitely looking to make her name defending Tharek Pell. It was admirable, if it wasn't so damnably inconvenient.

He reached his office, where Miss Mirrendum and another man were waiting. "Where's whatever I have to sign?"

Miss Mirrendum held a sheaf of papers close to her

chest. "Why, your high honor, is that any way to say hello?"

"Hello, Miss Mirrendum. Give me the papers so I can sign them and get going."

"I've been trying to meet with you, sir—"

"Schedule a meeting with Mister Gendorin. But be aware that I will not be holding Mister Pell's trial until the autumn at the earliest."

This had been the challenge on his plate in these past few weeks. There was no true reason, in terms of law, to delay Tharek Pell's case. They could go to trial tomorrow, if Pin wished it. But Barton and the rest of the Grand Ten wanted any and all lurid details of trial and testimony out of the public eye until the new Parliament was convoked. As usual, they worried too much about irrelevant details.

"I've scheduled many appointments with Mister Gendorin, and you keep missing them."

"He's a very busy man," Gendorin said, almost reflexively. When Pin looked at him, the boy actually blushed and looked to the ground. Guilty.

What did he know, or at least thought he knew? It was true, Gendorin was privy to details of his schedule, his correspondence, his accounts of exchange. The boy annoyed him to blazes, but he wasn't an idiot. He might have sussed out more than Pin wanted him to.

"Yes, well, so is Mister Landorick, here," she said. "He's a former inspector second class with the Constabulary."

"Retired," Landorick said with a lift of his cap. "I do a bit of investigation for hire to pay the bills."

"For the Justice Advocate Office?" Pin asked. "Unusual for a former constable."

"Their money still spends, sir," he said.

She took a folder from Landorick and put it on Pin's desk. "He's uncovered some irregularities, namely with the finances of Regine Toscan."

"What does that matter?" Pin asked. He kept his face neutral, calm, but the mere mention of Toscan and money was nerve-wracking. Paper trails of account houses and goldsmith notes might lead to Barton, Millerson, the archduke, Lady Henson . . . all of the Grand Ten. That was no good, especially since his role, as the Justice of the Ten, was to protect them from these very things. "I mean, we suspected that Toscan and these Haltom's Patriots were part of a larger revolutionary organization, that's nothing new."

"Yes, but it is evidence that should be introduced—"

"In the case of Tharek Pell?" He couldn't have that, but he couldn't make it seem like he was impartial. Not in front of this woman. "I will review it and make a ruling. But you should remember that Pell is on trial alone. Toscan is not being tried posthumously."

"All I ask, sir," she said, handing over the file.

"Give me those papers," he said, signing the acceptance of Pell at the holding cells at The Bench. "How long are you having him stay here?"

"Until trial, preferably," she said. "His conditions at Quarrygate, given that he is not yet convicted of a crime, are unconscionable."

"He's a definitive danger, Miss Mirrendum," Pin said. "He killed a man with a coat button."

"Allegedly."

"Allegedly," Pin conceded. "I'll allow a provisional stay of five days so you and your client can confer, but we are not equipped here to hold anyone long term. That's what Quarrygate is for."

"It's for criminals," she said. "Which he is not yet."

"Yet, Miss Mirrendum. We are rightfully giving him his trial, but you cannot deny the evidence of his guilt."

"Don't presume to tell me what I can or cannot do, your high honor," she said.

Pin scowled, and gave the signal to Gendorin to usher them out.

"I'm afraid that's all for today," Gendorin said, taking them to the door. "Thank you and joyous Reunification."

With them gone, Pin sat down at his desk, glowering at Gendorin. "Keep an eye on them while they're in the building. Especially any meetings with Pell."

"I can't—"

"Without violating his rights of counsel, of course," Pin said. "Saints, the last thing we'd need is Mirrendum arguing a dispersal of trial." He waved Gendorin away, leaving him alone in the office.

Of course, he was a high justice, and no argument from Miss Mirrendum would change the fact that he would convict Tharek Pell on all charges and sentence him to life imprisonment at Fort Olesson. Once a man went there, he never saw the sun again.

He would still review Landorick's report, but mostly to see how much of a threat he was. Landorick might need to be dealt with. Perhaps a bribe to forget things, perhaps an unfortunate accident. The Grand Ten would take care of it.

And perhaps they would have to take care of Gendorin as well. Which would be a damned shame. He was a decent young man.

But decency was a vice Pin couldn't afford these days. The Ten certainly couldn't risk everything for its sake. Far too much was at stake. He understood that, better than anyone.

# Chapter 29

JERINNE WAS UP AND out of her bunk before Vien came for her wake-up call. She dressed and left the room with the rest of the third-years still sleeping, passing the ranking board without a glance. It wasn't going to tell her anything she didn't already know. It certainly wasn't telling her anything she needed to know.

She went to the training room, which was sparsely populated, and went through her stretches and calisthenics. Her body was still sore, but it felt good to work through the pain, push herself. She finished up as Vien came in, looking like she was forcing herself to move. Her face was still a mess of bruising.

"Morning," Vien said. "Sun is up and so are you."

"Couldn't really sleep," Jerinne said.

"I know the feeling," Vien said, heading over to the weapons on the wall. She stopped and turned back to Jerinne. "I let you down the other night. I should have done better."

Jerinne wasn't sure what to say to that, what comfort

she could give that wouldn't sound like condescension to Vien's ears. "Not as much as I let myself down. We got beat. But at least we're both still here to do better next time."

Vien grabbed a staff off the wall. "And I damned well will."

Jerinne took another staff. "Then let's work on that."

They sparred until Vien went to wake up the rest of the Initiates, and other Candidates and Adepts came in and out of the training room with a kind word or silent nod to Jerinne. Those little moments of quiet respect continued through breakfast and the morning run. When they returned from the run, Jerinne had someone waiting for her in the lobby.

"Miss Fendall," Arthady Mirrendum said as they came in. "We're ready for your appointment."

Her appointment. With Tharek Pell. "That's now?" Jerinne asked.

"We're prepared at The Bench."

She looked to Madam Tyrell. "I'm sorry, miss, but—"

"It's fine," Madam Tyrell said, her expression telling Jerinne that it absolutely was. "Take care of what you need to."

"Thank you," Jerinne said, and went to clean up. Her dress uniform was in shambles, but she didn't want to be wearing that for this. Instead her simple Tarian tunic, clean and crisp, was perfect.

Miss Mirrendum brought her to a carriage and quietly drove her to The Bench, the grand building of the High Court of Druthal in Justice Plaza, where the neighborhoods of Oscana Court, Welling, and Gelmin converged. The high walls of Fort Merrit, the army base in the middle of the northern city, cast long morning shadows over the plaza. Miss Mirrendum led her through a few hallways and down stairwells until reaching a heavy iron door with four uniformed marshals standing outside it.

"Wait here one moment," Miss Mirrendum said,

nodding to a marshal. The marshal released a series of latches before opening the door, and Miss Mirrendum slipped in. They shut the door behind her.

"That's elaborate," Jerinne said.

"Damned well right," the marshal said. "You know who's in there?"

"Yeah."

"I'm not taking any chances."

Jerinne waited for a few moments quietly, as none of the marshals looked like they were worth making conversation with. And she didn't need idle small talk right now. She wasn't sure what she needed, or even why Tharek Pell wanted to talk to her, why he felt she would be useful to his defense. She wasn't sure what she even felt.

Standing here, with him on the other side of that door, she should be terrified. Her stomach should be in knots right now. Tharek Pell beat her, snapped her leg. He killed people in front of her while she was powerless to stop him. He was a nightmare in human form.

But all she felt was calm. She got beat. But she lived, and that meant she would do better next time.

There was a tap on her shoulder. She turned to see a young man in a somber suit.

"Pardon me, but . . . you're Jerinne Fendall, yes?"

"That's right."

"You were—you helped stop . . ." He looked at the door nervously.

"I was there," Jerinne said. "I don't know how much I helped."

"But you were a part of it, yes?"

She shrugged. "I was there. What's this about?"

He glanced about, eyeing the marshals suspiciously, and then swallowed hard. "I should tell you about—"

The door opened, and he stopped suddenly. Miss Mirrendum came out and scowled at him.

"Mister Gendorin, why are you talking to my witness?"

He straightened his shoulders. "I was just saying

hello, congratulating her on her part in stopping Mister Pell here."

"Leave her be," Miss Mirrendum said. Looking at Jerinne, she added, "You can go in now. Don't touch the glass."

Jerinne went in the room, which was a high, wide chamber of solid stone. In the center of the room was a great glass cylinder that spanned from floor to ceiling, with small holes near the top. Inside the cylinder was a cot, the man himself lying on it. He stood up and walked close to the glass wall.

"Miss Fendall, pleasure to see you again."

She approached, keeping some distance from the glass. "Even for you, this seems . . . extreme." Glancing about, she noticed there were murder hole niches in the wall, and crossbows sticking out of them.

"I've made an impression, apparently."

"Did they make all this for you?"

"No," he said, pacing about a bit. "Apparently, during the Incursion, they imprisoned Oberon Micarum in here. That's illustrious company." He raised his voice. "They might have forgotten that Oberon escaped, though."

"He had an Imach mage and a few others helping with that," Jerinne said.

"You know your history."

"But I don't know why I'm here." She wanted to sit down, but there was no place for her to sit. "You wanted me to testify in your defense."

"I did," he said.

"I have no idea why you would want that. I saw you murder, six, seven men. Including Mister Seabrook."

"Yes, you did," he said. "You saw what I did, what I was trained to do. You saw me, as the perfect elite weapon, the ultimate expression of a Spathian warrior, with skill that is unparalleled. Can you deny that?"

"Yes, you're very good at killing."

"I am what I was trained to be. But I was denied my

destiny as a Spathian Adept by foolish men and their politics. Men who had no right to decide that fate for me. And I think you might know something about that."

"Why would you think that?"

"Am I wrong? Tell me, Initiate, are you being fairly judged for your skill? Do you have faith that your fate will be decided by anyone who has the right to?"

Jerinne, despite herself, burst out laughing. She laughed so hard, she couldn't even stand. She fell to one knee, taking a minute before she could get her breath again. When she looked up, he was right up to the glass, one hand pressed against it.

"What is so amusing?"

"That's your pitch, Tharek?" she asked, getting to her feet. "It's funny, because if I had heard that a week ago, even two days ago, I might have been shaken. Even confused. But today?" She came close to the glass, looking him right in the eye. "Today I know what I can do, and I know that I'm the only person who decides who I am."

"I let you live!" he shouted.

"Yeah," she said. "And I am back on my feet, stronger for it. So thank you for that lesson, Tharek." She walked away.

"You let a member of Parliament die!" he shouted as she approached the door. "They'll never let you be a Tarian!"

She pounded on the door to be let out, and turned back to him. "But they'll never stop me from being me."

"And from Scaloi, three chairs were up for election: the two held by Josiah Illington and Jebediah Porton, and the seat open due to the death of Jonas Cotton. Good Mister Illington, of the Traditionalist Party, has won his bid to retain his chair. The other two chairs, now the Ninth and Tenth Chairs of Scaloi, respectively, will be held by Good Mister Hasprick Ollist, of the

Traditionalist Party, and Good Mister Ret Issendel, formerly the Bishop of Iscala."

Once Dayne had read this, hands went up among the members of the press. They probably all had the same question, and Dayne considered selecting Hemmit, but instead picked a woman from the *High Maradaine Gazette*.

"Are we to assume that Good Mister Issendel is a member of the Ecclesial Party?"

"I don't have a statement one way or the other about that," Dayne said. "No party affiliation is noted for him, beyond his devotion to the organization known as the Open Hand. I don't think we can safely presume exactly how he will position himself. He may well declare membership in a new party of his own."

Hands went up again. Dayne pointed to Harns from *Throne and Chairs*.

"By my count, the former Ruling Coalition of the Minties, Frikes, and Crownies now has only forty-seven members. But the Opposing Coalition of the Books and Dishers also has forty-seven. With neither side holding a majority to form a government, what can we expect from the new Parliament?"

"I can only speculate, sir, same as you," Dayne said. "But I have a feeling the five members of the Populist Party, as well as Good Mister Issendel, might find their voices strongly sought after." Hands went up again. "I really can't comment on any of that. The marshals are handing out packets of all the results, including the local city elections. And one final result of note: in the Archduchy of Oblune, there was a motion on their ballots to approve the suffragette petitions, and that motion passed."

The room went quiet, and then the woman from the *Gazette* stood up. "Women will get the vote in Oblune?"

"Yes. Starting next year."

She sat back down—almost fell down, as if her legs

had given out on her—tears streaming down her cheeks. Hemmit started to applaud, and half of the members of the press joined in with him. Some of the other half, Dayne noted, looked more than a little put out.

"That's all," Dayne said. "We'll be resuming these briefings once the Parliament is in session. Thank you very much."

He left the podium and the press room, with Donavan Samsell walking out behind him.

"I think you enjoyed that last part," Samsell said.

"I rather did," Dayne said. They went down the stairs to the marshals' offices, where Samsell started shaking the hands of men as he passed them, most of them carrying boxes of papers. "What is going on?"

"This is it for us this year," Samsell said. "Election is done, another success. Thanks to you."

"And you," Dayne said.

"Well, we'll see what Marshal Command has to say when they assign election duty next year," he said. "But it's time for me to leave here." He pointed across the room to an older man in a marshal chief uniform, with tufts of graying red hair. "Let me introduce you to the new man."

They went over to the man, who was working off a clipboard and calling out orders to some of the other marshals. "Quoyell?" Samsell said as they came up. "You need to meet Heldrin, from the Tarian Order."

Chief Quoyell glanced up at them and grunted.

"Hi, I'm Dayne," Dayne said, offering his hand. "I'm liaising with the Tarian Order, working with you and the Parliament and—"

"Don't be underfoot," Quoyell said. "I've got enough on my plate right now." He brushed Dayne's hand away and stalked off.

"Don't take that personally," Samsell said. "He's like that with everyone."

"Charming," Dayne said. "So what's next for you?"

"We'll see," Samsell said. "But I have a suspicion that they're going to need an election expert in Oblune to help them organize a few things over the next year. So I've put in a request to transfer out there."

Dayne offered his hand. "Then good luck with that, Donavan."

"I appreciate that, Dayne," he said, taking Dayne's hand warmly. "Take care of this place. It's . . . it's your home now."

Morning exercises and training completed, Amaya let the Initiates off for lunch. She noticed that most of them had a bit of extra spark today, pushing just a bit further, trying a bit harder. Even the ones who had been spooked by the battle at Miniara Pass seemed more together. She was proud of them. The next year was going to be hard on each of them, but she was glad to see that pressure was steeling their resolve instead of breaking them.

"Miss Tyrell?" One of the servants approached her as she came out of the practice room. "The Grandmaster wants you in his study."

"Thank you," she said, and went up to see him. She found him at his desk, finishing writing up a list.

"Ah, Amaya, just in time." He blew gently on what he'd just written to dry the ink. "I'm afraid I do have a bit of sad news. It seems that Master Nedell is going to take some time to recover from his injuries. I have no idea how long he might be recuperating. In fact, given his age . . ." He let it hang there.

"I'm very sorry to hear that, sir," Amaya said.

"So, obviously, he won't be supervising the Initiate training any further this year. That will be more burden for you to bear."

"I can handle that, sir. I presume I will continue to preside over the third-years, and Kissel and Searl with the first and seconds?"

"Yes," the Grandmaster said, getting up from his desk, the paper he was writing still in his hand. "Given what we've gone through, no need for further disruption of the system, yes?"

"I agree, that's sensible," she said.

"Now, with Master Nedell unavailable, and with Osharin's unfortunate . . . choices, we are faced with a challenge."

"What might that be?"

He handed over the paper. "Here are today's rankings for the third-year Initiates, as well as their mentor assignments for the year." Amaya found it very interesting that he had developed new rankings for the third-years, with no observation on his own part, or input from her. She was beginning to wonder how much of it was sewage concocted to torture the Initiates with. In her year, she and Dayne kept pushing for the top spot, and on any given day it could be either one of them. Was that just a game? For all she knew, they flipped a coin each day to decide which of them to put on top.

No, Master Denbar wouldn't have done that. She knew him, she knew his heart. He would have treated it as something sacred.

But she wasn't sure about Grandmaster Orren.

"As you can see, since we are now short a Master and an Adept, not every third-year could be assigned a mentor. It is regrettable, but we do what we must."

She looked down at the list. The ranking was largely what it had been for the past two days, switching around a few of the people in the middle. Jerinne still at the bottom.

And, most notably, Jerinne was the only one not assigned a mentor.

Amaya pursed her lips and chose her next words wisely. "Are you certain this is how we want to proceed?"

"It is regrettable," he said, as if the situation was entirely out of his hands. "But I feel it is for the best. Have that posted outside their barracks, with instructions to meet with their mentors for the afternoon."

"This can't be right—"

"Amaya," he said. "Please believe me when I say that this is, indeed, regrettable. But trust me to know what's right for the Order."

She folded the paper, keeping her disgust buried in her gut. "As you say, sir."

She left his study and went to the barracks, writing the listing and the assignments on the slateboard herself. Normally, she'd have passed that on to Vien, but she didn't want to taint herself or Vien by discussing it further. She certainly couldn't bring herself to order someone else to write this sewage out.

That unpleasantness handled, she went down to get something to eat, if she could find the stomach for it. Before she reached the mess, she passed the lobby, where Jerinne was talking with Fredelle Pence.

"You're back?" she asked Jerinne. "Everything all right?"

"Everything is fine," Jerinne said, her face a sunbeam of joy. "And look who I ran into."

Fredelle looked just as happy. "I was feeling a bit nostalgic for this place. Silly, I know."

"You did spend three years here," Amaya said. Feeling a need to say something else, she added, "And you were very good."

Fredelle shrugged. "If only my rankings had reflected that."

"Rankings are meaningless," Amaya said. She looked to Jerinne, and made sure the girl understood what she was saying.

"Yeah, well I'm over it," Fredelle said. "But I wanted to say goodbye proper to this place. And to you."

"Are you going somewhere?"

Fredelle sighed. "We have a morale tour throughout northern Druthal. Thirty army forts in as many weeks."

"I—" Amaya grabbed the woman and embraced her. "I'm sorry I was always such a clod."

"Yeah," Fredelle said. "But I liked you anyway."

Amaya pulled away. "Good luck with the tour."

"Thanks," Fredelle said. "I'm going to wander about, maybe bug Clinan for a session with those hands of his. We don't have anything like him in the army."

"Now I see why you came."

Fredelle shrugged as she went up the stairs. "He really is a miracle; don't take him for granted." She pointed to Jerinne. "You keep your head up, girl. Remember what I told you." With a wink she added, "Everything I told you."

Amaya looked to Jerinne, who was blushing slightly at that. "What was that?"

"Nothing," Jerinne said quickly. "Just a joke we had at the party."

Amaya remembered something of Fredelle and her "jokes," and understood perfectly. "All right, then."

"Is training on a break for lunch?" Jerinne asked. "Should I head to the mess?"

Looking at Jerinne, an idea settled in Amaya's mind. "Actually, no."

"All right. What do you need me to do?"

Amaya took her by the arm. "We're going to go have lunch ourselves, away from everyone else. I have a few things to tell you."

Jerinne walked with her out the door, a look of concern on her face. "What's going on, Madam Tyrell?"

"First off, when it's just you and me, drop the madam. It's Amaya."

# Chapter 30

DAYNE FOUND LADY MIRIANNE waiting for him in front of her carriage at the bottom of the Parliament steps, looking dashing in her dark blue striped waistcoat, cravat, and trousers, with leather cap and boots.

"How is it you make a man's suit look like high fashion?" he asked as he approached.

"This is going to be high fashion for ladies," she said. "Mark me, this is the look young women of Maradaine will be sporting in the autumn. I'm seeing to it."

"I don't doubt it."

She laughed, sweet and infectious. "The hat is a Marikar suncap. It was *the* hat the suffragettes in Oblune wore this year, and by all the saints I will make it the thing to wear."

"Show that Oblune is leading the way."

"Exactly," she said. She opened the carriage door, but on the seat was a pile of newssheets. *Throne and Chairs, High Maradaine Gazette, First News*

*Maradaine*, and more, including *Veracity*. She fanned them out. "Would you look at that?"

All the papers, of course, had headlines about the election—though only the *Gazette* and *Veracity* prominently placed "Women Get the Vote in Oblune!"—but the main story in every newssheet was about the rescue of the Scallic ballots. Included in each story was a drawing, the same drawing in every one—a flattering depiction of Dayne holding a shield up to keep a plume of fire off the ballot boxes, while Jerinne and Amaya were in the background rescuing hostages and fighting mercenaries.

"This isn't right," he said. "I'm not the story here. Amaya and Jerinne deserve as much credit."

"So humble," she said. "But I can be proud of you. Now, I am famished, so let's go."

The Nimble Rabbit was quite busy, as would be expected on a holiday, and most of the outside tables were full. However, Hemmit, Maresh, and Lin were at their usual table, joined by Jerinne and Amaya. Mirianne took the lead approaching the table, clutching the newssheets to her chest.

"So he's apparently gone to ground," Hemmit was saying. "Not that I blame him, but—"

"Are we interrupting?" Lady Mirianne asked.

"Not at all," Hemmit said, getting to his feet. "Please, join us."

They sat down. "Who's gone to ground?" Dayne asked.

Hemmit took a sip of his wine. "One of the Patriots who was working with Tharek reached out, said he had—he had a story for us, but he got clobbered when the Deep Roots abducted us. So I can imagine he took it personally."

"Why were you even wanting to talk to such a disreputable man?" Lady Mirianne asked.

"We do somewhat specialize in the disreputable, my lady," Lin said.

"I suppose you do, and—" Before she finished the waiter approached.

"What can we get for you today?" he asked.

She looked at Dayne and gave an impish smile. "Lamb sausages with onions and duck-crisped potatoes, plenty of bread and . . . you do have Jaconvale mustard, yes?"

"Of course we do, ma'am," he said. "Is there any other kind?"

She beamed. "That is very much the right answer." She gave a wave to the whole table. "And the bill for all of this is going to me."

Amaya started, "We couldn't—"

"No argument," Lady Mirianne said. "It is the least I can do for all of you, who have done so much to save our country." She looked to the waiter again. "And wine all around, except for that one who should probably have cider."

"Hey now," Jerinne said.

"That I agree with," Amaya said.

"Settled," Mirianne said, and the waiter went off. "Now, where was I?"

Dayne recognized the look on her face. "You have a plan."

"Of course I do," she said. She took the pile of newssheets and passed them out. "Mister Niol, I believe that is your drawing sporting the front of all these papers?"

"It is," Maresh said, scowling as he looked at it.

"You drew this?" Amaya said, looking at the picture. "It's very good."

"Well, I did have a good view of the whole thing," he said. He shook his head angrily. "Can you believe they all swiped it? Those bastards."

"I'm not that shocked," Lin said.

"So I'm correct in assuming that you were not paid by any of these newssheets for your work?" Mirianne asked.

"Certainly not," Maresh said.

"Good," she said. "Because I've already had my law-yer write up actions against each of these on your behalf."

Hemmit almost spat out his wine. "You did what?"

"It's not right, and I want to make sure that you—all three of you—are credited for the great work you are doing, and properly compensated for it."

"That's very kind, my lady," Maresh said.

"Tish," she said. "And no more of that 'my lady' stuff from the three of you. You can call me Miri, as my clos-est friends do."

"Are we?" Hemmit asked.

"Of course," she said. "All of you, at my party, pro-tected people, stayed calm, and kept things from being much worse." She reached across the table and took Amaya's hand. "And I'm so glad to see you here. Yester-day I received so many notes from people who spoke so highly of you and your actions that night. Let alone how you saved the Acoran votes. Please say we can be friends."

Dayne saw a bit of discomfort on Amaya's face, but despite that she said, "Yes, of course, my l—Miri."

"Capital," Mirianne said. "Along those lines: Hem-mit, Maresh, and Lin, I think the work you are doing with *Veracity Press* is vital and critical to the health of this city. You are providing a viewpoint that more peo-ple need to be confronted with. So I want to start financ-ing the *Veracity*."

Dayne was a bit surprised by that, but perhaps this was more of Mirianne's "armchair subversive" attitude coming forth. She did like to appear shocking, and funding a small firebrand of a newssheet like *Veracity* would certainly do that.

"Are you sure, my lady?" Hemmit asked.

"Miri," she said firmly. Food and more wine arrived, and Mirianne filled Dayne's glass and her own.

"I am positive," she said. "I don't expect returns on my investment, and I don't want you to do anything different with what you're writing. I just want you to not worry about the money, and be able to get this out to more people." She tapped energetically on her copy of the *Veracity*. "I want you to be so big they won't dare steal from you."

The three of them looked at each other a bit confused, but none of them looked displeased at the idea. "Well, then, we'd welcome that," Lin finally said. "Saints know we were barely scraping by as is."

She raised her glass. "Then we are settled."

Hemmit raised his glass, and then everyone did, glasses clinking together. Everyone drank and then began eating, and Mirianne and Hemmit began discussing details.

Lin slid down the bench next to Dayne. "Jerinne told me about the sister finding her, the bishop at the stationhouse."

"I don't suppose you want to talk about it?"

"Magic, as I do it, is only part of the mystical world. What . . . what I think Bishop Issendel can do is called 'Faith' by scholars."

"Fitting."

"In that no one, as far as I know, truly understands it or its limits. Or can prove it's real."

Dayne shuddered, and took another sip of wine. "I think it's quite real."

"As do I. And it terrifies me. From what I've seen, what I've read, it's the . . ."

"Power?"

"For lack of a better word—that can actually *change* a person. Change who they are. That kind of power, in the hands of someone in the Parliament?"

"As you said, terrifying," Dayne said. "Or it would be, but I can't see Ret being terrifying with it."

She looked skeptical. "Maybe he's a gentle soul. But

imagine that power, wielded by someone without his moral code."

Dayne didn't want to think what that could mean. Before he could respond, Mirianne turned to them and gave them both a little scowl. "I don't know what you're talking about, but it's making your faces quite dour. I don't approve."

"Yes, my lady," Lin said, filling her plate again. "Drink up, Dayne. I fear we'll need to fortify ourselves in the coming months."

After they all had several plates of sausages and potatoes and more wine, Amaya leaned over to Dayne. "How are you doing?"

"I could sleep for another eight days or so," he said. "You?"

"About the same." She looked at Jerinne and back at him. "I'm worried about her, and things at the chapterhouse."

"How so?"

Amaya was about to answer when the bells of one in the afternoon rang out. Mirianne stood up.

"I'm so sorry, I didn't realize it was already one bell. I need to go meet with my managers." She kissed Dayne, just a little too long and hard for polite company. He was blushing when she released him, and then she put a goldsmith card of account in his hand. "Get that back to me tonight, my love." Then she was off.

Dayne composed himself and turned back to Amaya. "Sorry, you were saying?"

A few emotions played over her face, and Dayne wasn't sure how to read her. After a moment, she settled on something. "Jerinne, listen up."

"What is it?" Jerinne asked, moving closer.

Amaya looked at them both, lowering her voice, and turning away from the others, who were discussing logistics of the new phase of *The Veracity Press*. "I don't want to go into it all right now, but something is wrong at the chapterhouse, and . . . I'm not sure I trust the Grandmaster."

That was a shock. "Why?"

"For one, he keeps putting Jerinne at the bottom of the rankings, despite my insistence that she does not belong there."

"I knew it," Jerinne said.

"Ease down," Amaya said. "So that means she's stuck with no mentor. The only one without one."

"That isn't right at all," Dayne said.

"And you," Amaya said. "Are stuck at the Parliament, away from the chapterhouse. So whatever is going wrong there, wrong with the Grandmaster . . . and maybe I'm wrong . . . but whatever it is, you will be clear of it."

"That's one way to look at it."

"Well, this is what I nee—what I hope you can do. Both of you."

"Both of us?" Jerinne asked.

"You two, I trust," she said. "So, in as much as Jerinne is under my authority, I want her to work with you as her mentor. Informally."

"Because it can't be formal," Dayne said. He looked to Jerinne, who looked upset and angry, but she also looked full of purpose. She nodded at him. "That would be my honor."

"Good," Amaya said, drinking down her wine. "When I have more than just a feeling on the back of my neck, I will tell you. But right now, my gut is telling me to keep the two of you together, so that's what I'm going to do."

"Whatever you need," Dayne said. "I trust you, Amaya."

She patted his hand, taking an extra moment to hold it, and stood up. "I should get back to the chapterhouse. Jerinne, be back by five bells. And we'll—we'll figure out the rest."

"Will do," Jerinne said. Amaya left. Jerinne moved

closer to Dayne. Hemmit, Maresh, and Lin were engrossed in their discussion, clearly excited at the prospect of what they could do with proper funding.

"Was that all strange?" Jerinne asked him.

"It's been strange for a few days," Dayne said.

She nodded. "So I guess you're my mentor now?"

He shook his head. "Given that we both seem to have precarious standing in the Order, that doesn't seem quite right. How about partner?"

She offered her hand. "Partner."

And that felt right.

# CODA: The Lady

LADY MIRIANNE HENSON KNEW quite a few things, but the thing she understood the most was how to keep a secret. And the easiest place to hide one was buried in an innocuous truth. She had known that Duchess Leighton's threats were going to come, so she was prepared. The Grand Ten needed a new place to meet and it would be placed on her shoulders to provide one. These were the sorts of tasks that were expected of her, and she performed them with grace.

Everything was done with grace.

If she was going to host the Grand Ten, it would damned well be convenient for her, so she placed this new meeting hall in the basements of the new store, with a special secret staircase leading from her office to it. She had made sure to use different builders for each element: one to make the staircase, one to make the secret door, one to build the meeting room with its apparently normal entrance, and so on.

But the important thing was to hide the meeting

room in plain sight, so no one would think it odd for nobility, members of Parliament, and other power brokers to be slipping into a back alley behind Henson's Majestic. So she had commissioned an elite clubhouse—drinks, food, music, and exclusive membership. Access gained with a special knock and password. All legally done, properly filed with city regulations. The Majestic Underground would give the gadflies and hangers-on of the Maradaine social scene the vicarious thrill of subversion, and provide the perfect excuse for any of the Grand Ten to come in at any time.

She had even planted the rumor that there was a second level of membership, deeper and even more exclusive, so no one would question why, for example, they saw the Duchess of Fencal go into the Underground, but then not see her inside. She would never confirm the rumors about such a thing, but she knew these people and how they thought. They would all speculate, but not one of them would publicly admit they were not part of that inner circle.

So easy to manipulate.

She told her secretary to not let her be disturbed, locked her office door, and opened the panel to the stairway down to the meeting room. The rest were all there, wearing their masks for their prescribed iconic roles. While she knew the masks themselves were an absurdity, Mirianne felt it was important to take the names, the iconography of the Grand Ten, as when the time came, it was crucial to have a narrative in place. They were going to have to craft a story for the people, and a simple one, easily understood, was best.

That's what the original Grand Ten were, after all. A simplified story of the messy foundation of the current Druth nation. The narrative that was sold to people who did not want to learn the full truth. The people wanted something easy to swallow spoon-fed to them.

The real power came from holding the spoon.

She donned her mask and sat down. "I see we are all assembled."

"That's because you're late, Lady," Barton said.

"My apologies." Barton believed he was in charge of these things. Of course, so did Millerson, so did Archduke Windall, so did . . . most of them. And she let them believe that. She had made preparations to destroy each and every one of them if the situation called for it. She had already crafted a paper trail that would implicate Baroness Kitranna as "The Lady" of the Grand Ten, and arrangements for her to tragically leave a confession next to her beautiful suicide. No matter how the wind blew, Lady Mirianne was ready to take hold of the story, paint herself as the brave hero or tragic victim. Whatever was needed to save the nation.

"I do appreciate the new surroundings," High Justice Pin said.

"The opera house had a certain mystique," Millerson said.

"And now it will be a proper opera house," Duchess Leighton said testily. "Can we continue? Some of us have other places to be."

Bishop Onell scoffed. "Where do you have to be?"

Archduke Windall answered that one. "It is a holiday, your grace, and some of us are expected to make appearances."

"Fortunately, the barbarity visited upon my home means nothing is expected of me," Mirianne said. She looked to Altarn. "Your man inside the Deep Roots did excellent work steering them at my affair."

"I still feel that went too far," Colonel Neills said. "I know we need to use these subversives to push the city into unease about the current government, but this was too much. One of the First Irregulars was injured, and any number of Orren's Tarians could have been hurt as well."

Altarn sighed. "While a couple of well-placed infiltrators can accomplish near miracles, there are limits. But our man in the Open Hand made it very easy to lead the marshals to the wrong side of town."

"And me," Grandmaster Orren said. "My chapterhouse was in crisis yesterday, but I was stuck playing the fool for this charade."

"And that kept your hand on the tiller," Colonel Neills said.

"I shouldn't have been personally involved at all." Orren turned on Altarn. "I would have appreciated the warning about Mister Osharin."

"We didn't know, and I apologize about that. But didn't it give her man the impetus he needed to hunt the Deep Roots down?"

Grandmaster Orren growled. Once again, Lady Mirianne had to spell out their aims for him. The man was decidedly impossible.

"Look at what we have now. A sense of things in chaos, and that the King's Marshals are incapable or incompetent. We now have an incoming Parliament that is certain to be impotent."

"Well now," Barton said, a bit offended. "Our coalition might—"

"But it shouldn't," Pin said sharply. "And you two need to see to it."

"And we have a hero for the people, lauded and praised, in a Tarian uniform. Exactly what you crave, Grandmaster."

"Dayne Heldrin is going to be a problem," Duchess Leighton said. "I think you're blind to that."

Grandmaster Orren sighed. "I can only isolate him so much from the Order. Amaya is definitely suspicious."

"Let her be," Lady Mirianne said. "Dayne is where we need him now, isolated from everything else Tarian, and at the center of our plan. I'll handle him."

She smiled under her mask. Dayne was perfect. Who

better to be the face of the people, of a strong Druthal, than this common champion? He played the part naturally, the perfect actor in the play she was writing. She loved him for that, for being everything she needed right now.

And if he proved too problematic, she had already planted the seeds for his downfall.

They were just waiting to be watered.

# Appendix

## The Archduchies of Druthal

Druthal, as the nation stands in 1215, is comprised primarily of ten archduchies, which had been separate kingdoms until the reunification of 1009.

### *The Archduchy of Maradaine*
The terrain of this archduchy consists of mostly wide, rolling tracts of fertile land. Sheep ranching and wheat faming are the two biggest parts of country life in this archduchy, and are framed as being central to the national character of Druthal as a whole. Wool from Maradaine sheep is a greatly valued commodity, as it is of the highest quality. The people of the archduchy of Maradaine are, for the most part, friendly and open, but somewhat conservative in their concern for propriety.

The city of Maradaine is officially in this archduchy, but the city is actually split in two by the river. The north side is the newer, wealthier, and more opulent part of the city, which has the Royal Palace, the Parliament, and most aspects of local and national government. The south half is more densely populated, with the middle class, working class, and impoverished citizens, as well as the foreign-born districts. The south side is considered to be part of Sauriya in terms of elections and archducal authority. As it is the capital of Druthal, Maradaine is a city of tremendous activity, being the last major city on the Maradaine River before it reaches the ocean. It is a very cosmopolitan city, with at least ten percent of the population of either foreign birth or descent. Other cities: Delikan, Itasiana, Ressinar, Solindell.

### The Archduchy of Sauriya

Similar to Maradaine in both climate and temperament of people, Sauriya consists of farming plains and woodlands. Wheat farming is most common, as well as a wide range of all sorts of other agriculture, including potatoes, oats, and vegetables. While shepherding is still very typical, it is more commonplace to raise animals that don't demand as much land use, such as chickens, pigs, and rabbits.

Kyst is the most major city in Sauriya, with a seaport (the closest one to Corvia) and one of Druthal's five major naval shipyards. Sauriyan goods, including perishable foods, run daily from Kyst to Corvia. Other cities: Abernar, Telin, Maskill.

### The Archduchy of Patyma

These cool grasslands and forests are dedicated mostly to ranching sheep and cattle. It is also known for dairy and the finest cheeses in all of Druthal. The people are friendly, although somewhat less concerned with proper manners and propriety as their Maradinic neighbors. In Patyma, the rudest behavior is trying to hurry or rush someone. Patymics respect work ethic, and look down on someone who isn't willing to get their hands dirty. Fishing along the northern coast is a major industry, especially in Hechard, which is the key seaport in the Gulf of Waisholm. Other cities: Erien, Drosa, Plenin, Midista.

### The Archduchy of Acora

The cool, rainy woodlands of Acora are the most sparsely populated part of Druthal, with only a handful of cities making up most of the Acoran populace. The primary crop grown in Acora is potatoes, but lumberyards and forestry are the most important aspects of Acoran industry. The Acorans are known to be reserved, often keeping to themselves and speaking to strangers in as few words as possible. Raising animals is uncommon in Acora, as they prefer hunting game, mostly deer and boar.

Porvence is the largest city in Acora. It is the usual destination of most trading caravans coming from Waisholm, Kieran, and Kellirac. It is also a city that has been, at times, controlled by the Waish and the Kelliracs, so its people are often of a mixed heritage. Other cities: Astonic, Lonyll, Borrun, Talite, Vaytinwood, Gorivow.

### The Archduchy of Oblune

This interior archduchy is, in many ways, the most militaristic. In the Druth Army, twenty-five percent of the soldiers are from Oblune, as are forty percent of the officers. Also, the art of Druthalian Pike Fighting originates here. Militarism pervades the Oblunic mindset, and that can be seen in how they run their farms and mining camps. Oblune also has a wide variety of goods that are produced, possibly the widest variety in Druthal. Many of these goods travel downstream to the rest of Druthal from Marikar, the city that is the center of Oblune trade. Other cities: Torest, Wenikar, Irlion, Yassin.

### The Archduchy of Kesta

Kesta is the true breadbasket of Druthal, with wide fields of flatlands used to grow wheat, oats, and many other crops. With the exception of the Kestan salt flats in the east, almost the entire archduchy is usable farm or ranchland. Kestans are typically warm, friendly, and intensely proud of being from Kesta. The city of Fencal, located on the Maradaine River right after the Waish and Oblune rivers merge, Fencal is a major center of trade, as well as being one of the oldest cities in all of Druthal. Ocean vessels from Maradaine rarely travel farther upstream and most traders from farther inland often unload here. Merchants have a saying: "If it can't be found in Fencal, it probably can't be found." Other cities: Kessin, Pillinflat, Greilmar, Opiska, Wrennit.

## The Archduchy of Yinara

On Druthal's west coast, Yinara is noted for its warm, sunny climate, as well as the warm, sunny disposition of the Yinarans. Some in the capital even consider the Yinarans to be frivolous, not taking matters seriously. Yinarans tend to be more interested in fashion, ships, and the water than propriety or work ethic. Sailing, fishing, and shipbuilding are the primary economic sources for Yinarans. Most of the population is along the coast, except for those in Yin Mara (a city known for being the artistic and intellectual center of the archduchy). Lacanja, a coastal city with a naturally protected bay, is the heart of the Druth naval industry. The largest shipyards are there, both military and commercial. Other cities: Birmin, Posam, Oriem.

## The Archduchy of Monim

Monim is, perhaps, the archduchy with the greatest dichotomy. At one time it was broken into two separate nations, a division that it never fully recovered from. The northern areas are very urban and educated, with art, philosophy, and intellectualism thriving there. The south is more stagnant, with more conservative (and often highly religious) opinions. Monim has three main industries: cattle ranching, mining, and cotton growing. The foothills of Monim are rich with a wide variety of metals. Vargox, across the river from Marikar, is Druthal's intellectual center, as it has seven colleges and universities, as well as several libraries and museums. Artists, scholars, and especially mystics flock there, since it is a city in which they are greatly appreciated. Other cities: Sirrencar, Molkane, Voreen, Donnil.

### *The Archduchy of Linjar*

Considered by many to be the most "foreign" of the Druth archduchies, Linjar is noted for being mostly swamps and wetlands. The Linjari congregate almost exclusively in the cities, but there are a few pockets of small, reclusive (and some would say "backwater") communities (where even the language is corrupted to incomprehensibility). The Linjari are a friendly people, in an aggressive sort of way, and are tolerant of just about anything, except restraint. The general sentiment of the Linjari is that the pleasures of life are meant to be enjoyed. This means that many people in the rest of the nation find the Linjari scandalous and immoral. The Linjari tolerance means, however, that almost anyone can find refuge there, and so in the cities one can find people of very mixed parentage, from Waish or Kellirac to Fuergan or Turjin. The city of Yoleanne, another major Druth port city, is noted for its cuisine, as it is considered in all the Trade Nations as the capital of gastronomy. Cooks from Yoleanne are highly prized, and the chefs have their own particular hierarchy of ranks. Other cities: Solier, Cason Tinar, Jiet, Ganimoux.

### *The Archduchy of Scaloi*

Scaloi is the archduchy that borders with Acseria, and is the one most influenced by Acserian thought. Scallics consider themselves to be of the highest moral caliber, and morality and propriety are of paramount importance to their mindset. They are a deeply religious people, and the priests of the Church of Druthal hold much sway in Scallic politics, as does the Acserian Church. The warm climate makes the major farming industry fruit, especially citrus fruit. Scaloi also is rich in minerals, especially copper and other more uncommon metals and gems. Scallic cities are widely spread out, and sparsely populated, so even the largest city, Iscala, is considered a minor city compared to the rest of Druthal. Other cities: Matixa, Calimar, Treelsan, Nerifon, Polinan, Korifina.

## Other Parts of Druthal

- *Monitel:* Monitel is a city with a unique situation, since it is not officially in any archduchy. High up in the Briyonic Mountains, Monitel was all but abandoned in the ninth and tenth centuries, and is now again a growing community surrounded by mines and quarries, which ships its goods down the Oblune to Marikar and Vargox. Monitel has no representation in the Parliament (since it is not in an archduchy), and its highest-ranking noble is the Earl of Monitel. As it is a rich source of metals (both precious and practical) and stone, it is a factor in the Druth economy that cannot be ignored.
- *Corvia:* A large island off the Sauriyan coast, Corvia is another part of Druthal with a contentious status. Corvia has been many things over the centuries: a penal colony, a refuge for those escaping from cruel kings during the Shattered Kingdoms, an independent kingdom, a source of insurrection, and a target of Poasian invasion. Corvia is currently a part of Druthal, but it is not recognized as either its own archduchy or part of Sauriya.
- *The Napolic Colonies:* Three islands in the Napolic island chains are under Druth rule: Falsham, Halitar, and Fendrick. These are considered to be Holdings of the Crown, and while the residents are Druth citizens (save the Napolic natives, though legal precedent exists for them to claim Druth citizenship), they have no voting rights for national matters, and no

representation in the Parliament. It should be noted that the city-state of New Acoria, on the largest Napolic Island, is *not* part of Druthal, despite much of the population being of Druth descent.

7460

# Jim Hines

## The Legend of Jig Dragonslayer

"Clever satire… Reminiscent of Terry Pratchett and
Robert Asprin at their best."
—*RT Book Reviews*

"If you've always kinda rooted for the little guy, even
maybe had a bit of a place in your heart for Gollum,
rather than the Boromirs and Gandalfs of the world,
pick up *Goblin Quest.*"
—*The SF Site*

"A rollicking ride, enjoyable from beginning to end…
Jim Hines has just become one of my must-read
authors." —Julie E. Czerneda

The complete Jig the Goblin trilogy is
now available in one omnibus edition!

978-0-7564-0756-8

DAW 100